HODD

HODD

ADAM THORPE

JONATHAN CAPE

LONDON

Published by Jonathan Cape 2009

2 4 6 8 10 9 7 5 3 1

Copyright © Adam Thorpe 2009

Adam Thorpe has asserted his right under the Copyright, Designs
and Patents Act 1988 to be identified as the author of this work

First published in Great Britain in 2009 by
Jonathan Cape
Random House, 20 Vauxhall Bridge Road,
London SW1V 2SA

www.rbooks.co.uk

Addresses for companies within The Random House Group Limited can be found at:
www.randomhouse.co.uk/offices.htm

The Random House Group Limited Reg. No. 954009

A CIP catalogue record for this book
is available from the British Library

ISBN 9780224079433

The Random House Group Limited supports The Forest Stewardship
Council (FSC), the leading international forest certification organisation.
All our titles that are printed on Greenpeace approved FSC certified paper carry the
FSC logo. Our paper procurement policy can be
found at www.rbooks.co.uk/environment

Mixed Sources
Product group from well-managed
forests and other controlled sources
www.fsc.org Cert no. TT-COC-2139
© 1996 Forest Stewardship Council

Typeset by Palimpsest Book Production Limited
Grangemouth, Stirlingshire

Printed and bound in Great Britain by
Clays Ltd, St Ives plc

in memory of my father

John smote of the munkis hed,
No longer wolde he dwell;
So did Moch the litull page,
For ferd lest he wolde tell.

John struck off the monk's head,
No longer would he stay;
The like did Much to the little page,
For fear of what he'd say.

Robin Hood and the Monk

And now all the wood-ways live with familiar faces . . .

David Jones, *In Parenthesis*

Introduction

Robin Hood is a mystery. Apart from the thinnest of evidential shreds in judicial documents, there has been no proof (up to now) that he was ever anything more than a popular literary creation. He is first mentioned rather caustically by William Langland's personification of a priestly Sloth in *Piers Plowman*, around 1377:

> *I can noughte perfitly my pater-noster as the prest it syngeth,*
> *But I can rymes of Robyn Hood and Randolf erle of Chestre.*[1]

Of the very rare 'rymes' of Robin Hood that survive in written form, the earliest is the poorly copied *Robin Hood and the Monk*, from a badly stained mid-fifteenth-century manuscript of miscellaneous texts. The poem was likely to have been recited by a minstrel rather than sung. As the following 'Preface' points out, it is to this so-called 'ballad' that the *Hodd* text bears an uncanny relation.

This scarcity of evidence has not prevented a wealth of conjecture, of course: J. C. Holt, in his definitive work on the subject,[2] does not quite rule out the 'Robert Hod, fugitive' of the Yorkshire Pipe Roll of 1225 [*de catallis Roberti Hood fugitivi*], whose chattels are valued at 32s 6d by the royal justices, and who appears again as 'Hobbehod' in 1226. 'Hobbehod' may be familiar or derisory: 'Hob' being the

---

[1] *The Vision of William concerning Piers the Plowman in three parallel texts*, ed. W. W. Skeat (Oxford, 1886), I, 166 (B-text, Passus V, l. 401–2).
[2] *Robin Hood* (London 1982, revised 1989). See also R. H. Hilton's essay *The Origins of Robin Hood* in *Past and Present*, No. 14, November 1958.

Middle English diminutive for Robert, as well as a generic name for the common man, with a shadowy suggestion of 'hobgoblin'. There is only one appearance of this diminutive in our text, which is hardly definitive, as 'Hob the Robber' is a stock term (see, for instance, 'John Ball's Letter to the Peasants of Essex', a poem of 1381: 'chastise wel hobbe the robber'). However, that obscure legal mention of a 'Robert Hod' is of crucial importance to the present book, as the reader will see; Professor L. V. D. Owen came across the name in 1936, the very year in which the translator of our (missing) document died, presumably unaware of the discovery.

It seems that as early as the mid thirteenth century – when the ballad as a literary form was already emerging in England – our hero was in full circulation as a legend; someone, perhaps a clerk, changed the name of William son of Robert le Fevere (a Berkshire robber) to William Robehod, on the King's Remembrancer's Memoranda roll of 1262.

There are numerous subsequent instances of criminals adopting or being given 'Robinhood' as a nickname or alias, as well as those of his companions (including Little John), in much the same way that, in our own day, Jack the Ripper's grisly appellation resurfaces from time to time, granting a special gleam to the homicidal maniac. The underworld likes its myths: whether you are a small-time crook or a big-time gangster (or, for that matter, a terrorist), perhaps it helps to play a role bigger than yourself, to part-fictionalise your unpleasant acts, to fill out a flamboyant costume. Thus the Robin Hood legend spread, until by the mid fifteenth century it appears in written form, as lively ballad or crude play; echoed by the odd, terse (and mostly disapproving) chronicle entry, recording Hodd's activities some two centuries too late.

These early ballads, and most especially *Robin Hood and the Monk*, are bloody, amoral, fast-moving, tough. There is no Maid Marian or Friar Tuck, and certainly no Allin-a-Dale, plucking his little harp. Will Scarlett and Little John do appear – the latter usually at odds with the outlaw chief – as does Much the miller's son. The Sheriff of Nottingham is already fair game, along with Guy of Gisborne and various despised members of the landowning

Church, while the setting shifts erratically between Yorkshire and Nottinghamshire.

It has to be stressed that the Robin Hood of these early ballads cares not a nail for the poor. His attraction for the audience comes from his dash, bravery and wit, his anger against the landowning class, and his forest-dwelling difference from the mainstream. At heart, however, he is a homicidal gangster, although that is somewhat anachronistic when put into the context of a quasi-lawless, casually violent age.

The softer, cuddlier, more socially aware and romantic Robin Hood had to wait a while. His leap to mass popularity was probably via the springtide festivals during the fifteenth century, when he became Robin, King of the May Games – his queen deriving from a character called Marion in a thirteenth-century French pastoral play. Associated with the unruliness and disorder of the festivals, he also took on courteous, gentlemanly qualities, until by the time of Shakespeare it could be said that to live in the forest 'like the old Robin Hood of England' was to 'fleet the time carelessly, as they did in the golden world' (*As You Like It*, 1.1).

Despite that immortalising appearance, the outlaw was only to reach his literary apogee in the nineteenth century, with the bestselling novels of Sir Walter Scott (*Ivanhoe*) and Alexandre Dumas (*Robin des Bois*), before the medium of film turned him into his current incarnation as an international celebrity, symbolic of an anti-establishment justice, and as far from the Middle Ages as you or I.

Hodd is not the medieval thing itself, but a translation from the Latin of a lost original. This startling document came into my hands by complex chance some years ago, in the form of a printer's foxed and dusty proof. The translator's name is Francis Belloes.

A wealthy, amateur scholar, Belloes was born in Wiltshire in 1890; read history at Trinity College, Cambridge (overlapping with a student by the name of Ludwig Wittgenstein); fought in the Great War with the 2nd Hampshires until repatriated with a serious head wound in early 1918; returned to Trinity, where he sporadically tutored medieval history (having already contributed to various learned journals); lost his ancestral home in a fire on the night of 5 April 1922; and remained a bachelor to the day he died, poverty-stricken, in Paris in 1936, having dribbled away his hefty inheritance to cards.

We know from his textual commentary that, among other things, he had a red beard; that Ash Dunhay was in those days extremely 'rustic' (it is now a dormitory village); that his experience of the First World War was as nasty as any other combatant's, leaving him not only with a head wound and probable shell shock, but also an anguished grief for at least one close friend. The odd, occasionally vehement, pencilled note in the margins of the proof (included and identified in bold as by 'FB' wherever of interest), add a tantalising human presence to the picture, but nothing more. Both the printers and the publishers have vanished without trace – along, perhaps, with the Latin transcription of *Hodd*, awaiting its scholarly edition.

Surprisingly, despite numerous searches in archives and on the web, I have identified only one photograph of Francis Belloes: it consists of a small, grainy newspaper image, showing a clean-shaven [*sic*] face accompanying the report of the fire in Ash Dunhay, which describes 'the entire destruction of the Georgian manor house. Although modest in size it was of considerable elegance, and incorporated an Elizabethan wing with some original and finely-carved cherrywood panelling'.

The shadowy, phantom-like face could be anyone's, I'm afraid.

A.T.

Translator's Preface

The translator of the following document must confess to being something of a felon himself.

The manuscript was rescued by him from the ruins of a bombarded church in what had lately been an isolated hamlet on the Somme, in the form of a leather-wrapped bundle tied with string, fallen open into the eviscerated crypt and looking as unprepossessing to the layman as all such documents do. The exigencies of warfare meant that no close examination was possible, and the hamlet along with the church having being wiped from the face of the earth by dint of being strategically vital, it was not clear to whom, or to what ecclesiastical authority, I should return this find. My superior officer, despite being the direct descendant of a twelfth-century baron, remained impervious to the delights of medieval scholarship, and was no help in the matter, finding it all a bit of a joke. He was killed by a sniper soon after.

Thus I found myself in sole possession of a bulky, stained and occasionally illegible manuscript, stitched crudely together with gut, on whose parchment pages the damp of many centuries had joined forces with worm (a particularly learned specimen had bored through the first thirty-five leaves), while the end of time itself seemed to be raging around me in the guise of a very modern doomsday.

I first unwrapped the find in a cellar, to the shivering light of a candle welling in its stub, while brick-dust powdered the air or fell upon the pages in sudden gasps, released by the pounding overhead. I lit a cigarette in preparation and then, through a faint pungency of chlorine gas (our position having been well soused the night before), found my weariness vanishing to a febrile excitement as I skimmed the ancient text.

The hand was a neat cursive in the customary two columns to a page, with errors of haste in the Latin that made it clear that this was a hired scrivener's copy – probably mid-fifteenth-century – of an even earlier manuscript. There was little marginalia. My eyes repeatedly fell upon a name, in all its variant spellings, that echoed one far better known: *Hod.* I seemed to be in the possession of a text of quite extraordinary significance to the deep culture of England.

I was, indeed, somewhat surprised to discover that the author and his subject were so thoroughly English – even though, as a medievalist, I know how much more genuinely 'international' those times were than our own secularised and violently nationalistic present. Even in the so-called hundred years of peace that are now (1921) to replace many hundreds of years of European warfare, I doubt we shall return to the common culture of those times. Like Gerald the Welshman and many similar before him, our provincial author (who is aged about fourteen or fifteen in 1225, thus making him an astonishing ninety-four in 1305, one of the stated years of composition) was able to converse in the scholar's lingua franca of Latin.

It seems, from the sparse indications in the text, that he spent the bulk of his adult life in the abbey of Whitby; this does not preclude him having had contact with, or even visiting, the place where I discovered the manuscript, in the rolling hills of Picardy: local historians declare the (now-obliterated) church and its grounds to have contained vestiges of abbatial origins. But why or how this copy ended up there remains a mystery; unless it was thought too inflammatory for its country of origin, and was hid as a result – the original being destroyed.

My own subsequent collision with the rock-hard god of war, and the many months of convalescence required, allowed me a period in which to sink deeply, as it were, into this strange and resonant text, and attempt a first tilt at translation. Despite a lack in him of that extraordinary generosity, compassion and tolerance one finds in that later teller of tales, Geoffrey Chaucer, my fondness for the author grew: and it must be remembered that he is not a raconteur or fabulator (although not without literary skills and sensitivities), but a devout old man confessing of a dramatic and rather terrible past.

Tireless research on my part has uncovered no trace of the ur-manuscript, nor a single clue as to the identity of the author. I have risked my health, my nerves and my eyes in scouring countless manuscripts, and have been misled many times – even so far as to be standing on Billingsgate Wharf at 5 a.m., having been informed that a particular fish-porter under one of those curious leathern hats was the possessor of a single sheet of 'antique' writing, upon which the name 'Hod' could be clearly delineated. The poor man, somewhat bewildered, pointed me to nothing more ancient than last week's newspapers on a hook, 'to wrap abaht cod', and while the term 'Billingsgate' as a synonym for coarse language has long since passed into the domain of pointless slander, its aspersion on the homonymous market was briefly justified on my realisation that a hoax had been perpetrated upon me by a mischievous colleague.

There is no fishy smell, however, about the text's clear parallels with the earliest of the Robin Hood ballads, *Robin Hood and the Monk* (Cambridge University MS Ff.5.48). This is a version dated to about 1450 – a century and a half after ours was penned – and written (as all the outlaw's ballads are) in English, but based on much earlier sources. There are many startling similitudes of narrative and detail between this ballad and our own manuscript, going far beyond the generic or the conventional (the monk's 'wide head', for instance), as well as an atmosphere of savagery, crazed beliefs and revenge not usually associated with the romanticised figure of the greenwood Robin we are accustomed to from later times; an atmosphere most clearly delineated in *Robin Hood and Guy of Gisborne* (British Museum Library Add MSS 27879), whose antique, peculiarly pagan or 'folkloric' details also seem to be anticipated by our text. The geographical coincidences need no comment, and I have myself (in a motor bus and on foot) visited and sketched the relevant areas to the point of exhaustion, from

Nottingham's busy heart to obscure brown woods – although the struggle to conjure the thirteenth century through a mind cluttered by petrol stations, hosiery, toasted scones, coke smells and the Player's factory took considerable effort of imagination, and most succeeded in the emptier, muddier stretches of the Midlands landscape. Yet still it was as in the British Museum picture galleries on so-called 'student's days', when the easels of the copyists interfere with the free view of the paintings: for all their fidelity, my own conjurings obtruded upon the real thing, which is forever lost, and merely (and rather tantalisingly) haunts.

Speaking of which, there is a single incident in the former ballad that has long cast its shadow upon the outlaw's later manifestations, or at least threatened to cast its shadow, if it were not locked up in the secure vaults of academe; this being the murder – by Robin's companion, 'Much the miller's son' – of the monk's little page, 'for fear he should betray them' ('*for ferd lest he wolde tell*').

This incident is the centrepiece of the ensuing document, whereas it is only a passing morsel of action in the ballad, and uncoloured by any kind of moral comment or regret.

It is, to my mind, this ballad of Robin and the monk in some much earlier form to which the author of the present manuscript refers several times as his own 'infant', cursing it as 'disgusting' or 'crippled': an emotional approach that may startle our modern sensibilities, for whom literature in whatever form has become a mere fireside pastime rather than the symbolic expression of our deepest souls and intents. In this regard, it may be of interest to note that in an early-sixteenth-century play quoted in Bishop Percy's notes (*Northumberland Houshold Book*, 1770), it is none other than 'Ygnoraunce' who speaks the lines:

> But yf thou wylt have a song that is gode,
> I have one of Robin Hode
> The best that ever was made.

As implied above, bits of our manuscript, apart from being error-strewn, are missing or made illegible through time's vicissitudes, and I have left certain specimens of rhetoric, more suited to the taste of the Middle Ages than our own, for a forthcoming complete edition with scholarly footnotes. I have, it might be noted, mostly avoided modernising or 'standardising' the spelling of names (mostly kept in their English garb, with ecclesiastical or regal exceptions – *Henricus* etc. – they are islands of familiarity in the sea of Latin); sometimes left an English word *in situ*, and here and there used a word or a grammatical form that, although utterly dead or obsolete at the present time, may yet give the sharp, true note of medieval speech without falling into quaint or 'Gothic' floweriness.

Much of the paragraphing, as well as the modern division into 'parts' and 'chapters', is my own, to make the unbroken blocks of text easier on the reader's eye; I have introduced inverted commas wherever speech is distinguished, merely for clarification. I have echoed the medieval habit of using coordinate clauses linked by *and* or *then*, only because the Latin is similarly constructed, but endeavoured to modernise with more complex sentence patterns wherever the sense is not disturbed. Words left in italics are as they appear in the manuscript.

As the author at several junctures claims the text to be a written confession, if primarily intended for the eyes of God, it is perhaps worth emphasising, in the light of the narrative's content, that medieval adulthood began at the age of fourteen, which in the eyes of the Church meant that children younger than that age could not sin (in the conventional sense), and were therefore exempted from confession. However, this did not excuse even unbaptised infants from being shut out of Heaven, though most contemporary theologians agreed they would not suffer Hell's agonies.

Having a shard of plain medieval window-glass here on my desk before me, that I rescued from the shattered church mentioned above, and which, when brought to the eye, remains thoroughly opaque in that misty manner of its Roman equivalent, keeps me in mind of the truth of translation: that it is never (and should not ever suggest itself to be) entirely transparent.

While we cannot be sure if this pious, ex-minstrel brother has always confined himself strictly to literal fact, what remains, with its picturesque incident and passionate narrative manner, I hope is sufficiently of interest (not only to those seeking enlightenment in the thickets of the Robin Hood legend, but also to anyone searching in our more distant past) to have justified my labours in a college room a few degrees warmer than the open cloister's 'outer bench' complained of so frequently by the author in his extreme and (even for our time) astonishing old age.

F. J. Belloes
Ash Dunhay
Dec. 3, 1921

Publisher's note: Since the above Preface was penned, a disastrous fire in Mr Belloes's country home has spelt the complete destruction of the original manuscript. The planned scholarly edition will, therefore, not be forthcoming.

Part One

I

The seas are folded over us, above our heads, the lower sea becoming the upper sea and yet still blue when not girt with sea mist, which is grey and melancholy. Some men when they look up see birds, but I see only a kind of fish, sometimes in great shoals. These fish are beaked and feathered, as we all know, and return to dry land to nest in trees, shrubs, meadow grass or crops, rocks or walls, or even under our own thatch, where the nestlings make a great beseeching noise that might keep us from sleep.

Only birds pass from the sky's air to its water without harm, for they have the property, like the fish of the lower sea, of breathing underwater. And I have seen with my own eyes a cormorant swimming under the water of the lower sea, and a myriad of gannets plunging into its waves at a good distance from its cliffs. Likewise do birds plunge into and out of the blue of the upper sea without harm.

If men sail far enough, namely a sufficient number of leagues beyond the horizon, they unwittingly pass over our heads, yet too high up to discern us or the dark of our forests through the blue of the waters of the upper sea.

It has been recounted to me that mariners have lost knives overboard and that these same knives have been found caught in trees, or that they plunge through a [thatched] roof to stand upright and trembling in a table, to the surprise of those eating. And fish sometimes fall (as we know) from the sky, like arrow-struck birds, but with no visible wound.

I myself once found a piece of cork ballast in the middle of a field, very far from the sea. I looked up and saw a dark cloud in the shape of a ship, as if I was perceiving it from underneath. In former ages perhaps men knew of such things, having greater clarity and knowledge, since it is well known that we have declined in wisdom, and are running further and further into ignorance as the world approaches its end in the manner that St Paul foretold. I myself have heard the faint echo of infernal torments discernible on the wind, as these come closer and closer towards us, heralded by the blast of trumpets.

If I had happened not to have met with the outlaw called Robert Hod, so many years ago that none are still living from that time but myself, I would be less tormented in my spirit; for quite apart from the other matters it was Hodde[3] who put strange ideas and questionings into my head.

Alas, the autumn day I first saw him long ago was indeed grown so wet, that the upper seas must have spilt much of their waters in their seething. My master [brother Thomas] and I were travelling the main highway between Yorke and Dancaster: this being a journey of some ten hours,[4] for we had set off at dawn. There was no thick, wild forest, as foolish men now tell when they sing of 'Robyn'[5] or cavort like buffoons in his plays, but only small woods or copses, though albeit dark and tangled, between uncultivated heathland [*locis incultis*].

The chief vice of my master brother Thomas being that he loved wine immoderately, like a lecher loves women, he would pass easily from cheer of heart into sin, uttering gross words. And these sins of the tongue were worsened by his shrill voice, that despite his fatness was almost like a sparrow's. He was the cellarer of his house,

[3] It is interesting that our manuscript never uses the variant spelling 'Hood' or 'Hoode', which suggests a difference in pronunciation similar to modern usage; although 'hode' is used to mean a hood in, for instance, the fourteenth-century *Brut* (EETS, 1906, p. 249): 'the Englisshe-men were clothede alle in cotes and hodes'.

[4] This seems optimistic for a wet day, especially in winter and with a pack pony; although York and Doncaster are only some twenty-five miles apart, horses have to feed, and no one travelled out of daylight hours. Watling Street, now the Great North Road, had long lost any serviceable Roman paving.

[5] Robin is, of course, a diminutive of Robert.

St Edmund's of Dancaster; and he would say, when drunken, that the cellar was his *stewe*,[6] full of smooth-limbed maidens besporting for his pleasure.

My master having conducted his business at the Order's house in Yorke (following the sudden migration to the Lord of brother Bernard, their own cellarer), we were returning thence to Danncaster. I accompanied my master everywhere, because he had a love of ballads and music, as much as he did of wine and fishing and roasted meat, and we had lessons together in writing and reading that the glory of books might be opened to me yet wider, for his great desire was that I might become a master scrivener [*scriptor*] – if not to take the cowl myself one day. It was well known that I was not merely a kitchen servant but brother Thomas's page, and might have been an oblate[7] were I the possessor of a parent with a fat purse.

Brother Thomas was not a monk by choice, but by fate; he would ne'er call it God's will. He had fled after scandal into the silence of the high walls of the monastery, from a family he claimed was noble and of Norman stock. Despite his reckless nature, he had a great fear of Hell, and of its heat and its cold, and when one day a fire consumed one of the abbey's barns, the stink of charred wood that lingered afterwards made him very melancholy, at the thought of what might await him. He was very kind at times: when it was once extremely cold and I was feeble with a chill, I turned blue and seemed as if dead, and there being no heating except in the calefactory where I was not permitted, he and the other monks pressed me in a circle to their bosom (as a sow might warm its litter), and I was revived.

We were returning to St Edmund's after an absence of six days. Although we had a pack pony, aside from my master's mount, I was on foot. We knew it was a perilous journey, even by day, for that way crossed the high heathland; but in those times all journeyings had

[6] As in MS, meaning a bawdy-house. The whole of this rather startling simile is vindicated later on in the manuscript.
[7] A child offered by his or her parents to be a monk or nun for life: a cruel custom already dying out by the fourteenth century – and clearly (from this mention) already somewhat corrupted by the thirteenth.

their perils where robbers and murtherers lurked behind trees or thickets – and we must trust ourselves to God e'en now, for nothing has changed for the better except that the Day of Judgement is closer, and perhaps very close, maybe but an hour or two off!

Unlike our going northward, where there was a continual clatter of carts, pilgrims, pedlars and so forth, the way was emptier on our return. Because it was a Sunday, and the clouds most thick and dark to the west, and there being a witless rumour that a group of some twenty singing lepers were on the road, measling all in their path including pigs and cattle, there was no one else in view either way upon that wild stretch, which caused us much alarm.[8]

The black clouds coming over our heads and their heavy load beginning to fall, our progress was slowed: my master's horse slid about in the clay and my own tread was hampered by the sucking of the slippery earth. I might have been mounted with the baggage, but our pack pony [*equus parvus clitellarius*] breathed as though with small bellows,[9] and my master having been given much weight of gifts (including a barrel of ale and a mantle furred with miniver), he said I must not overload the midriff.

There being several steep declivities, the way became perilous, and the river where we must ford it was already swollen, so that the great crossing-stones were scarce visible.[10] From thence we climbed the road with some difficulty onto Beornsdale Heath,[11] past the three gibbets that let their miserable occupants look out from their bony sockets upon a great distance of hills.

My master drank much from his leathern flask, for gladness and to keep himself warm; his tongue corrupted, he began to curse, the

---

[8] A rare circumstance, evidently: medieval roads (such as they were) were relatively crowded. The speed with which the traffic of hooves and cart-wheels can chop an unmetalled road into a quagmire is, of course, well known even in our own day.
[9] What is now called 'broken wind'.
[10] Likely to have been Roman stones, since (as previously noted) the route in the early thirteenth century faithfully followed Watling Street, half a mile west of where a bridge was built soon after. The Great North Road is now finely surfaced but still dangerously steep for motor cars at the eponymous Wentbridge.
[11] Now Barnsdale Moor.

whiles I was struggling in silence with the pony, my precious *harpe*[12] safe wrapped in leather upon mine own back. My master might have been very close to the Doom of Judgement (for we do not know what His Will bringeth after death), but not only was his tongue darting out and stinging me with words, he also began to blaspheme horribly, for there were neither people nor houses nearby: it was a wild, heathy part with many gorse bushes and heather, and not even fit for grazing. 'By the Lord's blood,' he cried, and much that was most noyful to my ears; 'I reck not the crust of a pie for your efforts, or for these windy horses, and would this Devil of a rainstorm be blown to Hell, where it belongs!' Yet his horse was a handsome palfrey, for my master liked to hunt: how it gnawed at its snaffle!

'Tis true that the business matters at Yorke had tired him, and he had scarce slept for the scrabblings of rodents in the damp hospitium, before a servant stirred him at two o'clock for Matins – this poor servant receiving a night shoe on his head for his pains. How could I have comforted him? For then I was sitting with the kitchen servants before the fire, and slept there upon the straw. So my master took the name of the Lord in vain, and the Lord punished us swiftly.

'Ey, Christ's foe,' he cried, 'if thou dost not tread faster, and stop slipping at every step, we shall be caught on the road as night descendeth, and forced to stay in an inn, and innkeepers are oft in the pockets of the outlaws!' He also had a great fear of those wrinkled goblins that, after nightfall, travel unseen on the saddle and, at a certain moment, take hold of the reins and bring you sideways into the ditch.

He shouted down at me again, saying, 'By God's *corpus*, thou miserable hireling, I shall leave you behind to be dined on by the

---

[12] As in MS (the instrument familiar to us being of northern European origin); from henceforth I will transcribe it in modern spelling. Much loved by medieval painters from whom our only knowledge of it derives, this would have been a small, portable harp for the lap: 'A simple diatonic instrument with charm of tone ... with but one scale ... To obtain an accidental semi-tone the only resource was to shorten the string as much as was needed by firmly pressing it with the finger, robbing the harpist for the time of the use of one hand.' (*Dictionary of Music and Musicians*, 1889, Vol. 2, p. 699.)

felons like a rib of pork!' For truly I was thin, as be many boys of fourteen or fifteen. I moved faster, slipping and floundering, yet my mounted master began to draw ahead of me in the mistiness, and I began to curse the wet myself with a blasphemous muttering that ought to have blistered and scabbed my lips, setting them about with pustules of the kind that had already sprouted upon my cheeks and forehead, as they do upon many boys of that age, ruining their beauty. And raising my sodden head, I perceived through the thickened atmosphere that my master was falling off his saddle, but in a slow manner, and that dark shadows were clustered about his grey horse – that was soon joining him on the ground like a newborn foal.

In great fear I turned in order to run away, but a felon stepped from the gorse with a knife. I was too frightened to move even my lips, and prayed in silence. The man was hooded [*capite velato*] so that I could not see his face clearly, just as Death hides his bony features in deep shadow under his cloak. He held the knife towards my throat; flight would have been but a helpless wallowing in the mire. Snatching the rope of the pack pony, he asked me what our business was – 'So urgent seemeth it, that it bid you take to the road on such a foul day, with naught but a pair of worthless nags for company.' And I answered him without thought: 'Nay, God of truth, my master's mount is no nag!'

He laughed mightily, revealing a face as battered as his cudgel. 'What is it then?' he said. 'A trick horse? A heifer?' I replied that it was my master's horse of excellent breeding and daintiness, adding: 'He is a good and holy brother of the monastic house of St Edmund's at Dancasster, which has a fine stables.'

He struck me across the face so that I fell into the liquid suck, my harp uttering a complaint through the leathern bag. 'No monk is good nor holy,' he cried. 'They are but a plague of lechers and devourers.' Another hooded felon came over from where my master was shouting for mercy, and pulled the harp off my back, but with such violence that my right shoulder felt pulled like a candle from its stick: my heart was as a bridge sounds when a messenger crosses it, bearing urgent letters.

I smelt ale on this other cut-throat's skin, and I could see there were lines dug in the skin around his mouth, and a large well-pitted nose, but naught more. A third villain, of great lankiness, took the harp and the pack pony with all our baggage away into the bushes. I wept to see my harp disappear.

Having a knife under my tunic, yet was I helpless to use it, being so outnumbered. They dragged me over to where my master was on his knees, his fleeced robes caked in filth, as was his mount all on one side, so that it was as Enyde's horse in the tale.[13] 'My boy,' he cried, as if I were present only to save him, 'vouchsafe us a song! Quick, sound thy sweet voice, I beseech thee!'

He was driven almost mad with fear, with a blade pressed to his throat by a giant felon with shoulders like a blacksmith's, addressed by the others as John. Yet before I could e'en ope my mouth, my trembling master brought out the heavy purse from his black habit, in which a hundred pounds nestled – this being the amount due to our abbey, after the aforesaid business dealings with the brother house at Yorke.

The one who took it had fingerless leather gloves with fine stitching, his features hidden under a grey hood [*mitra*][14], very like the wolf-cowls of Fountaynes or Byeland[15] (though he was as truly close to them as be a swine to a saint). He untied the strings of the purse and bit upon a gold coin withdrawn from the jingling of its companions, and the outlaws were silent before its lustrous surface. My master was pleading for his life, while his palfrey's flanks shivered likewise.

---

[13] A reference to the first work by Chrétien de Troyes, *Erec et Enide*, in which Enide's horse is black on one side and white on the other: our monk appears to be familiar with French romances.

[14] *Mitra* is a general term for headdress (in the Greek and Roman world usually female or at least effeminate), the Latin not allowing for medieval distinctions between the ubiquitous 'capuchon' – a cape the upper half of which was drawn over the head, or allowed to hang down at the back as a liripipe – and the monkish and more volumin-ous 'hood'. Hod clearly wears a type of the latter form, whose term I henceforth mainly use whoever the bearer, for simplicity's sake.

[15] The grey Cistercian monks in monasteries near to the author's Benedictine house at Whitby.

Then it was that the hood of this felon fell back and I saw him clearly. He was above twenty-five, by my reckoning, and his face was clean-shaven and handsome enough until he spoke: then his mouth moving in a curious way over uneven teeth, it seemed as though its lips were sucking on a plum or a sloe, not forming words. His eyebrows were thick and dark, meeting in the middle beneath a blemish of the skin, and the balls in his sockets were as if swollen, lending him an exalted look.

'Harken to me, monk, lest your blood ooze [with?] the mud,' he said. 'The loss of your hundred pounds is due to the calamitous conditions of the highway; yet if you were to speak of it otherwise, and inform against us, then the lord of the outlaws – meaning myself – will descend upon you worse than twenty famished wolves.' My master nodded fiercely, glad to be spared. And so was I glad, although the loss of my harp sore grieved me.

Then the felons took my master's palfrey, pack and saddle and all, and vanished into the bushes, remaining only as the phantasms of dreams sometimes do, to trouble us.

Because they had robbed us of all our possessions, our backs at least felt not the loss of our horses, and proceeding on foot, and avoiding a flooded pit in the road by passing on a little way patched with stones for two miles, we reached by happy chance the first dwellings of a village straggled upon it. We knocked upon doors, until kindly received by a woman in a cot whose fresh thatch nigh touched the ground.[16]

She did not say, like the others, 'Let God provide for you,' for we had no money; instead, being of devout faith, she was glad to give a holy monk and his page a meal of bread, gruel and ale by the fire;

---

[16] The present translator of this MS lives similarly in a cottage some six hundred years old, whose thatched roof inclines to a level only two feet from the ground at the rear, and is exceedingly warm and cosy. It may be that we have exaggerated, along with the poor state of most medieval people's teeth (probably superior to our own), the flimsiness and draughtiness of the average of their dwellings superior to the hovel, even in the town – but certainly not the crowdedness, for their homes generally consisted of two rooms divided by a thin partition, with a palliasse (straw-filled sacking) for a bed.

my master recounting to her the false tale that the chief outlaw had instructed him to tell. Shivering still, despite the heat from the flames, he blamed the weather for our plight, that made his horse to slip, and drown in the ditch. 'This ditch flowed with water like a stream,' he said; and added, 'nay, more like a filthy sewer.'

And the woman, who was stooped and (though she was young) had hands that were gnarled – for to sweat and swink [*laborare*] was all her life – asked, 'Where are your belongings, good brother?' 'The water took them!' my master cried, and then wept so that I could not tell whether this was part of the fraudulent tale or a true sorrow. He agreed, as payment for our meal, to lay his hand upon the head of the woman's husband (who lay sick abed from a witch's curse), and to say prayers for him, that the demon within might flee, who gazed out from his eyen.

My master's mind being distracted over the foulness of the farmer's palliasse, I heard 'one hundred pounds!' muttered between the sacred words. While the serfs in the lord's fields plodded outside, as if through pottage (the slough splashed upwards e'en onto their chins),[17] the homely flames beat on my face, and I was grateful to God for being alive.

Yet was I intent already on retrieving my harp, as precious to me as one of my own limbs – though the source of my foulest sin so far, at that time; one of the many stains, indeed, that the angel-sentries at the gates will smell upon my risen soul, though the sweet savour of the trees of Paradise (such as aloes) be all about in the sacred air.

[17] Cf. the wretched ploughman in Langland's *Piers Plowman* (c.1394), with the graphic picture of his wife staining the ice with the blood from her bare feet, that so haunted me when I first read it (or rather, extrapolated its sense) as a boy, in Mr Skeat's great edition – unhappily tucked (this being my father's library) between Sir G. Cornewall Lewis's *An Essay on the Government of Dependencies* and Mr C. P. Lucas's *Historical Geography of the British Colonies*.

2

My harp's strings are broken. Damp has long ago buckled the wood.[18] Age has buckled my fingers. I am already Death's head, but I cannot die, perched on the outermost bench of life's cloister, blearily twitching my goosefeather – e'en by candlelight! And so we are all old, for our time itself is old, our world being in the sixth and last age, a mere cloth stretched over worms and fire . . .

Following some convoluted reflections on the diligence of the Saints and the Holy Virgin versus the faithlessness of the present times, the author proceeds with the pith of his narrative in a characteristically abrupt manner.

. . . It was the year of Our Lord 1225 when we were robbed on the road to Dancaster: King Henry of England was a youth.[19] I still hear in my waking hours (some eighty years later) the voice of Robbert Hodd saying to me, in my pinched ear, so close that his breath seems to stifle me again: 'You are one of the chosen. I choose you. Rise, and be blessed as one of us.'

I must shake my head to banish him, for this is really a fiend of the size of a flea, assuming in my suffering ear the voice of the outlaw; just as minstrels, who are really buffoons, take on his voice when

[18] This is metaphoric, given the eventual fate of his last harp, revealed towards the end of the narrative.
[19] King Henry III, responsible for the rebuilding of Westminster Abbey: a minority council ruled in his name until 1232.

singing of his merry exploits, that are all lies – or when wrestling in the disgusting plays of the outlaw Robbin, that are now become the delight of fools all over the kingdom.

And this wantonness, this false message, was put about by my own hand; and as fathers of crippled infants or disgustingly wanton youths can scarcely sever that blood-tie, then how can I disclaim responsibility for what I engendered so long ago? For the all-seeing Lord and Judge of mankind doth not miss a single lie, as a brother secretly slipping into the back door of a bawdy-house cannot but be reconnoitred by Him.

Wearily I set this down, alone on my bench against the cloister's outer wall, that future ages may understand the gravity of my sin, as a leper claps the lid of his dish, alerting all of his approach.

Then God's voice comes unto me and is untarnished silver, every word, with the breath of forgiveness in it, and takes my hand and moves it over the page . . .

Here follow several passages of pious tendentiousness, which I again omit. The narrative resumes with the olfactory likening of Hell-mouth to a tannery pit.

. . . This [stench] I well know, because my master's house of St Edmund's was afflicted with the stink of a great tannery that lay downwind with its several foul pits of excrement, and caused much trouble to the brothers when the wind was disfavourable. And also, being hard by the river, the house was much affected by smoke from the boatyard when they were tarring therein, and e'en within the cloister the blasphemous curses and obscene ribaldry of the boatmen in the vicinity of the wharf could sometimes be heard, as peasants in the fields about us here similarly shout, their women squealing in turn like sucking-pigs.[20]

[20] This passage reminds me of our Padre who, upset by the obscenities issuing from our Company canteen during Church Parade, suggested our language could do with a dose of 'God's chlorine'.

It was hoped by the prior and other brothers that more land might be purchased along with its close-cropped serfs and their progeny,[21] that high stone walls around this additional acreage might be built to shut off such nuisances. But the grievous loss of the hundred pounds made this harder to justify to our abbot, Father Gerald, who was a careful[22] man and did not seem to notice the wintry blasts whipping through the cloister and the dorter,[23] cruelly exposed on the north side; for the abbey church, owing to the uncertain nature of the river-ground, had been built some thirty-five years before on the eastern side.[24] Within it was the reliquary in which exceedingly valuable items were to be found in a glass tube, including among others the hairs of St Mary, a fragment of the bush that burned before Moses, and a piece of the Lord's winding-sheet stained with his sweat, that had healed a man whose side had so rotted away that his liver was open to the air.

The abbot decided in the chapter-house that flogging of my master by birch-rod might assuage his shame [at losing the money]; for father Gerald considered that brother Thomas had been foolish in passing through that dangerous section without escort, and that the loss was a reckoning by God for his well-known negligence of the Rule.

As my master could not appeal, he suffered the punishment with dignity. The brother charged with the punishment was a lean man of great strength and holy zeal, whose forehead sprouted beads of sweat as his instrument smote with a slapping noise such as one hears in the bakehouse when paste is being prepared for bread [in the kneading-trough], my master being exceedingly fleshy behind.

I had secretly peeped upon the punishment from [a slit in] the wall of the dorter's day stairs, that looked down upon the chapter, yet said nothing of the shadows about my master's mouth, as of fluttering

[21] *Sequela*, literally 'litter'.
[22] *Accuratus*, presumably when *avarus* might have been preferred.
[23] The monks' dormitory.
[24] The cloister is similarly exposed to the north (instead of the sunnier south) at Chester, Gloucester and Canterbury, although in the above case the church would at least have blocked easterly winds. Vestiges of an abbey outside Doncaster were discovered by chance a few years before the late war, but they amounted to no more than a few tiles, paving stones and fragments of stained glass.

black flies – which were no doubt devils fleeing the pain; 'tis well known that the evil spirits who take up residence within us feel the pain of righteous punishment when it is administered to the body, as much as they feel the grate and itch of the hair-shirt, or the pinch of cold, or e'en the pangs of hunger during holy fast, when only a crust of bread and water is allowed and their discomfort turns one's breath foul. And they also experience our pleasures, for by doing so they enhance and encourage their host bodies to steep themselves further into sin, whether the sweetness be found in the arms of a comely woman, or the ale pot, or the laden dish.

In truth, these devilish little guests had not so much opportunity for pleasure since brother Gerald was made abbot. Before his appointment some two years before, the refectory had been witness to the brothers' gross appetites; five courses of meats and fish disguised in rich sauces, swallowed down with wine and other intoxicating liquors, in a hymn to the sin of gluttony. But the new abbot reminded them of the Rule and of the need for parsimony, and month by month withdrew their dishes, which would have given rise to complaint were it not for the severity of his demeanour, and the lustiness of the birch-rod, and the recognition among the brethren that a brief temperance or moderation in this earthly life is better than an eternity of torment and griping pangs – with the possible reward of heavenly bliss in the after-life, wherein our useless dust may be transformed into the body of spiritual delight.

Although after [the beating], my master complainingly showed me the marks left by the wealing instrument on his buttocks, which were bruised and cut on their white flesh, and into which I had to rub ointment of honeysuckle, it was from this time that his fatherly ardour towards me and my education and general advancement in the world grew lukewarm [*tepidus*], for in his heart he blamed me for his disaster. Furthermore, I was no longer a musical balm to him, since I was lacking my harp.

His coolness grieved me, and I feared being cast from the house, for I had no family left nor roof to go to, and I felt a great hunger for learning; this hunger having been started, years before, in a sea-cave: the wet sand before it being all my slate, with nothing but a stick for my pen, and my teacher a hermit of exceeding holiness and humility. And I had fled him as a serpent flees the leaves of the ash tree e'en into the hot fire, so virtuous is that tree, and utterly unworthy the serpent!

Without my precious instrument, so abruptly stolen, I was no better than a beggar, and yet I looked upon the oblates with no envy; for the abbot believed that boys were naturally perverse and ordered them to be given many stripes – sometimes so severely that their ribs were blackened and came up swollen in red weals. Many were the times I had secretly spied upon them being stripped of their frock and cowl and beaten in only their shirt, with smooth osier-rods, or having their hair (already cropped about the neck) plucked like chickens, for they oft slept during the Hours instead of singing, so weary were they and poorly fed – though some were of noble families.

Neither were they permitted to address one another without permission, not even in the dormitory, where a brother always lay between two children that they might not converse at night. Sometimes in the cloister I did whisper to them through a *chine*[25] in the kitchen wall, despite the Master [of the Boys] standing close by, and would pass them choice cakes still warm from the oven, for I felt pity for them and was foolhardy and reckless.

Even my master pitied them, and especially the youngest who was of very tender years and an outwardly angelic countenance, called Henry; and [my master] did often say (after St Anselm) that caresses were more fruitful than stripes. Having fled my home some years earlier, an orphan with naught but a harp upon his back, and been discovered lying on the wayside grass, half starved, by brother Thomas, I was glad of caresses, yet stripes were all I deserved.

For though he believed, on so discovering me in the wayside ditch, that the harp was stolen (as it indeed was), and that I was a houseless vagabond, his astonishment that I already knew my letters, and could pluck the harp gallantly, fitted him to treat me kindly. Being well taught by one with no name – my earliest master the hermit

[25] As in MS: chink or cleft.

considering even names to be a possession, shielding him from God and His Creation – I yet had this grievous fault: a foolish pride, that should have been scourged from me there and then.

And as I lay my first night in the hospitium of St Edmund's on the imperial luxury of a palliasse, in brother Thomas's care, at the tender age of nine or ten, I was forever darting and swooping across the sea-cave's cliff-face as doth a gull, watching myself trace letters upon the sand of the marge, knowing e'en in my fever that the tide would come to erase my efforts: as might this very strigil on this parchment, that wipes away the efforts of my weary pen when the point is careless or splits.

And if my good saviour, the portly monk, had regarded the harp closely, he might have espied salt in its grain, and e'en smelt the sea – for we know that smell is a vapour of particles, and that these adhere to objects that are long remaining within that odour, to be drawn inside the nose where the brain might capture it with its moist teats. Yet I invented another lying tale, after I was saved: that of a feud between wealthy merchant families that had led to our ruin, and thus to my wandering life – heir to no riches but the road's, and this one treasured possession of my relatives, who were all lost to poverty, disease and grief. And scarce had these lies left my mouth, when the good, gullible brother embraced me as though I were his own – and so I remained until that fateful robbery upon the road.

By dint of questioning those passing through the abbey, including pedlars and even those miserable or afflicted creatures begging for alms at the infirmary kitchen, or hovering by the bakehouse and the malthouse, I was furnished with information concerning the felons and their leader, whose name was given as Robert Hode, and about whom many knew tales of sufficient terror to chill the blood, but which others regarded as of no more worth than a bundle of straw.

This Hodde was certainly a fugitive, and was reputed to have magical powers equal to any witch, as well as axes, [cross]bows, swords and staves, and was skilled with the use of the longbow, that pierceth a man through more easily than a white bear of the land of glass might break ice with its claws, to draw out fish through the holes it has made[26] as doth an arrow draw out a man's sinews, veins and many inner substances, if pulled from the wound.

An apprentice glazier of some eighteen years, who had come to our house to estimate and measure for the lancets in our freshly built chancel, informed me that Hod's felons wore steel caps beneath their hoods and a coat of leather under their cloaks, like yeomen fighting for the king. 'He is a brazen-faced villain,' I said, 'and no yeoman.' This apprentice, whose name was Rycherd, gathered ferns upon the wastes (near where we were robbed) to burn for the ash.[27] He had hair the colour of straw, but his skin was dark from the burning of fern and of wood, and he smelt as the lower devils must smell as they pitch sinners into the eternal bonfire. Richerd, laughing at my answer, said that I must have been robbed myself to speak in such a wise.

I told him of my grievous loss at supper,[28] while he dipped his bread into the ale pot; then he offered that I should return with him to the glassworks on the morrow, and to accompany him after to where he must burn [more fern], this being the autumn season when the plant begins to wither and is dry: 'For that brackeny spot upon the heath is but half a league away from the thick wood where the outlaws are said to have their lair.' And Ricchard laughed again, for he no doubt thought he was making a fine jest.

I straightway seized his arm and said, 'I will accompany you, for I mean to take back what they stole from me; namely, my harp.' He drank and wiped his mouth, saying that I was a fool. 'But you are not afraid,' I said, 'to burn the fern nearby.' 'That is because I am poor and have nothing to steal,' he replied. 'I will work with you by

[26] This somewhat digressive simile bears a striking similarity to the entry on Iceland from Bartholomew Anglicus's *De Proprietatibus Rerum* (1250s), the first of many such borrowings in the text. The earliest known surviving MS of 'The Properties of Things', which was the standard encyclopedia of the Middle Ages, dates from 1296 (Ashmole Collection), with a French MS dated the following year – thus easily within the period of our author's composition. Bartholomew was an English Franciscan, the encyclopedia written for those with little, if any, learning.

[27] Fern being often used as a cheap source of potash in traditional glass manufacture.

[28] Usually taken soon after 5 p.m., for both monks and laity.

day,' I declared, 'then crawl on my belly into the wood and they shall not see me though they have ten sharp-eyed sentries, for I hunt pigeon and other fleet creatures in the same way, seizing them with my hands.' 'You are lucky they have no hounds,' he said, 'not even the mangiest, to warn of your approach.'

His master bidding him to come into the abbey church, where a ladder was set to measure the new lancets, and to draw their shapes like a mason traces his mould, through which the naked light at present fell unpainted, I followed and helped them by holding the ladder, which rose exceedingly high into the chancel like Jesse's tree.

At the very moment that Rycharde set himself before the unglassed window, the late sun came from behind cloud and shone upon his face and fair hair, making them resplendent against the gloom of the church. I thought of the angelic messengers, the Light of Lights, and felt a flame rise within me as I gazed, knowing that I must go forth and seize back my treasure that was the harp; as if the unfinished cherubim painted on the wall, still only shaped by the workmen in the sombrest hue of green,[29] had settled in my heart and stretched forth their golden wings.

Alas, that I heeded such a false vision, and failed to think rather of the same place a few months previously, when the leads of the new windows in the nave had been liquid, melted in a hearth near the door that poured forth its ugly fumes, thus causing the brothers to cough without cease during Terce; for the abbot had ordained that no Hours were to be lost on account of the works – and it was, he maintained, a fitting reminder of what awaiteth those who sin. For in the lead's grey vapours the tortured souls' lamentations were plainly to be heard, though in truth it was the cries of the lead-makers to each other, who are e'er coarse and dull-witted. Mayhap then I would

---

[29] This pigment being the first coat, that formed the subsequent areas of shadow: the medieval painter had no notion of green deriving from blue and yellow, thus this green was a primary hue. Cherubim were generally painted with red skin, as devils would have red hair, beards and wings.

have quelled my pride, that thoughteth naught of puffing me up like a bladder; for in this state I saw myself as gilded in fame.

Let me say that, though I was a boy minstrel, I was never a play-actor grossly contorting his body behind a loathsome mask, cavorting upon a wooden stage and making horrible noises as loud as Pilate for the pleasure of fools and simpletons gathered in the market place; nor was I a buffoon, the type that wanders from court to court and jests wickedly, biting men behind their backs to make lords and ladies laugh; nor was I the type of actor who sings to his instrument only to drive men and women to wantonness, lechery and lewd gestures, and that urges them to dance upon the tables in taverns or inns, enchanting them ever more deeply with his music until sometimes they see phantasms and are transfixed among the broken pots of ale as if by a wicked spell.

Instead I was of that calling approved by the Pope himself, that is called *joculatores* or, in the base tongue, *jongleur* or *jougleur*.[30] I sang only of princes, saints and other great men and their deeds, that men might find solace from their sufferings and their anguish.

In truth, I was no *jougleur* but merely an orphan kitchen boy of fourteen or fifteen, dreaming that he might one day entertain great lords and even the king himself. I am on the very rim or marge of this life and must not lie, for lying is to invite fiends to your table, whose red leathery wings, bloodshot eyes and frisky, busy claws are hid beneath fine cloaks and manners and smiles, and only their stink – as of an old hound pulled out by a rope from the dunghill to be drowned – might give their presence away. I was a vain child, not seeing the traps laid all about me. And now I am a mere bag of bones with the gout in every joint, and half deaf, and no teeth to speak of, and my few hairs white as lint; and yet my sight suffices to write these pages e'en by candlelight, until weariness snuffs it a mere two or three hours before the bells of Matins and Lauds and [Prime?] . . .

---

[30] The line was dangerously fine between the approved minstrel and his non-approved colleagues – whose skills placed them on the lowest rung of society, along with prostitutes, and among the advance guard for Hell.

A page severely stained to the point of illegibility. It appears that the author has been inspired to take the apprentice glazier's offer seriously, in order to retrieve his musical instrument from the outlaw's camp.

. . . The weak morning sunlight had already vanished, like all vain hopes in this fallen world, including those of rich men whose garments furred with vair are eaten by moths as their cadavers are chewed by the worm, when we set out on two nags, myself mounted behind Rycchet on a threadbare pack saddle, as eager as a gallant knight.

We rode in the company of some teachers from Cambryge with doctors' hoods;[31] a thin leech [*medicus*] who carried a leathern bag in which he kept dried nettles and powder of myrrh (for female maladies that he described to us with much lechery); a stout yet sick-looking friar who snorted with a rheum, though wearing no socks and shod only in sandals;[32] a buffoon with a broken fiddle on his back who rode a one-eared donkey; and a very fat goodwife sitting sideways upon a broad-flanked sumpter carrying fish that smelt evilly.

My master had received permission from the abbot that I should depart for four days, even knowing that my enterprise was exceedingly dangerous. But my life to them was no more than a bundle of straw, for my master cared more for the hundred pounds and his reputation than myself. He said that if I spied his light-grey palfrey in the outlaw's wood, I should snatch it and escape upon it. And that if I should be caught and murther be done and my body left for carrion, then he and the brothers would pray for me many days following, that my soul rise heavenward on their breath from this corrupted earth.

He seemed distracted, and scarce looked at me, only caressing the new down upon my chin outside the infirmary (whence I was carrying a bowl of water for a dying brother of great age, though twenty years less than mine own is now), while saying that the smell of my skin had the flavour of pond-fish, smirking at this because I was no longer

---

[31] Cambridge's university had only recently begun to rival Oxford's at this time.
[32] *Sandalii* – a very rare instance of this word.

smooth and effeminate [*vulsus*], as was the aforementioned Henrie, the newest of the aforesaid oblates. This Hen[r]i had a great skill in singing that surpassed his tender years (these being eight or nine), and was the son of a merchant of Taddcaister.[33] This merchant, ill from grieving of his late and beautiful wife, had taken to tavern-haunting like the lowest sort, and thus his family gave his youngest son to the monastery that God might look more mercifully upon the father. My master appeared to revere Henrie for his sweet voice and angelic countenance, yet I saw beneath to one who was spoilt fruit before he was ripe.

Alack, that I should have succumbed to the serpent of jealousy, and not crushed it underfoot with prayer, when it was ever a small worm!

One day (let me relate), I had come from the kitchens with a pitcher of wine for the infirmary, and crossing the cloister had seen the oblates gathered in a corner by the closed end, for it was blowing cold through the arches; and Henry (not knowing of my kindness to them with cakes and suchlike) sent a stone craftily flying that caught me upon the ear, and turning round with a cry, I spilt the wine upon the flags – spying the catapult in Henrie's hand before it was hid again inside his robes.

The master of the boys noticed nothing: I believed then that this boy was an angel only in appearance, as fair ladies are often no more than subtleties of needlework and plaited tresses. And on hearing him singing and chanting in the Vespers, I was again ravished not by the Lord's mercy but by the venomous worm of jealousy.

The Devil oft appears in the guise of the Blessed Virgin in her finest cloak, or counterfeited as a lewd bawd with painted face, that he might tempt men to sin with him; or e'en as a pink-cheeked cherub! And thus I thought of Henri, so much so that anger and suspicion clotted inside me, and the very next week I spat a pellet through a hollow pipe so that it struck him on the nose in the garden, when the oblates were walking there and reading their prayers.

Stopping, he held his hand to his nose with a sharp cry, and red

[33] Tadcaster, some thirty miles from Doncaster.

blood ran, not black — yet was I so heartily a-feared of the Devil's powers, that I well nigh tumbled from the wall from where I had aimed. I was not descried, however, and the master of the boys gave that poor, doomed imp a great clout for breaking the silence.

3

For my foolhardy expedition to the camp, my master [had] offered me a black hooded cloak [*amiculum*] worn by him before he became a brother, that I might creep up to the outlaws at night, as well as a little ampulla of lead, containing holy water from the shrine of St Cuthbert in North[umber]land, to shield me from harm, which I placed in the purse upon my belt. Thus he still cared for me as a father for his son, though unneth showing any grief or worry, saying I was no longer a child.

Though indeed no longer a child in [terms of] age, and having long put away any toys,[34] yet I was still too young and foolish-brained to think of the danger; or rather, I could not think that the danger of the enterprise might prove mortal and swallow me entire, for I also had an undoubting faith in the guidance and shield of Almighty Christ Jesus and the heavenly divine, that down through all its heavenly hierarchies was concentrated, like a beam of sunlight, upon my modest head of fourteen or fifteen years.

One Wiliem, a wielder of rake and hoe on the abbey farm, parted from his right ear by the action of a bailiff's blunt saw for cutting a rich man's purse, and cast from that town [of Nottingham?] – until the true culprit was caught by chance later with the said purse – was an outlaw for a month with the band [of Robert Hod], and furnished me privately with information, for he hated them every one. He said

[34] The absence of toys from the medieval records is only owing to their disposability, and the stuff they were made from: wood, cloth, moulded pottery and so forth. There is no doubt that little girls loved dolls then as now, and boys likewise played as keenly with spinning tops, whips, soldiers and toy horses as do the youngsters of today.

they were cut-throats and villainous and put him in a deep pit for refusing to slay a merchant on the road. He informed me that the felons had their camp on a wooded hill not three miles from the glass-works, with high rocks where one or two men stood on watch. The rough country thereabouts having been laid waste in our great-great-grandfathers' time,[35] the camp's sentries could see far. There was a cave in the rocks where the villains kept haunches of venison, man-traps, flitches, plunder and firewood.

He said that the wood was small and dark, yet broad enough for a man to stand in the middle and not see the light from the edge, but you could reach the edge in the tenth part of an hour.[36] Quoth he: "Tis no higher than a pastie to look at, but fathoms deep if you fall into it:' following this with a lecherous remark that I privily asked God to forgive, though in my shamefaced colour was read my discomfort, and Williem laughed the more heartily to see it; for his mind was ever on women, and his spleen and liver close conjoined.[37]

The weather was dry and calm at our departure, although cold enough that we oft rubbed our noses, while certain of the puddles were still fast with ice. Many were the carts that came creaking towards us, their drivers hailing us, sometimes with unseemly words if they were tipsy, that the teachers from Cambrygge answered most wittily. After a while our party ceased talking, and we were soon startled by a flock of crows making a pestilent noise above our heads, that did drown out the clatter of our mounts upon the firm way. There being no thieves' gibbet full with carrions at that spot, nor a crossways where suicides or hanged criminals be too lightly buried, it seemed we ourselves must be the miscreants. Yet I heeded not the warning!

The friar muttered prayers until this ill omen was gone; but I was affrighted suddenly, and even the soft wind blowing either side to the

---

[35] Presumably by William the Conqueror in his harrying of the north during the winter of 1069–70.

[36] i.e. six minutes.

[37] The liver being regarded as the seat of love and voluptuousness, and the spleen the seat of laughter, as Shakespeare well knew.

far horizon methought full of dread whisperings, until Rycherd before me on the saddle began to sing.

A short distance before the wilder heath, and none of us having breakfasted, we stopped at an alehouse with a bush placed so low that the buffoon plucked a sprig from it.[38] The teachers from Cambrydge quipped and jested, oft breaking into Latin that I craved to understand fully, for my progress in the aforesaid tongue had been slowed by the imperfect grasp of my master, brother Thomas, following the excellence of my first and most learned teacher in his humble sea-cave. The goodwife was so coarse of word and ill-smelling with sweat corrupted by her scaled and glimy produce, that she was expelled from the room by the alehouse-keeper, her distended limbs being not those of a female's but each like the trunk of a pig; though she protested exceedingly, we were scarce in agreement with her.

The teachers playing dice like any group of fools, they bid me join them, because they knew from the apprentice Richerd that I was a minstrel, but I denied this, saying I was a monk's page and performed only for his pleasure, and that dice were the makers of poverty. And they said that I was indeed no minstrel if I did not play dice, and I felt aggrieved. Meanwhile, the leech continued to regale us with his unclean tales, for his fingers had touched uncounted women in every place on their flesh; being forbidden to play with us for this very reason, he sat apart and filled the room with his words, as if breaking wind from his mouth.

We ate there before the fire, but the food was greasy and thin. The buffoon sought redress, saying, 'You have baked garbage in these pasties, very like rabbit, and not hen, and it is a stinking pottage.' We agreed that it smelt, and was more like rabbit than pullet, but the alehouse-keeper called out the cook to show us his pullets and woodcocks and teal. Then the buffoon was joined by the fellows from Cambrygge, for there was no doubt the pasties were stinking, though

[38] Alehouses, best thought of as types of estaminet where only drink and simple food might be procured, were generally indicated by a bush or corn sheaf on a pole. The average medieval consumption of ale (made from barley, or more cheaply from oats) has been estimated at a gallon per man per day.

the keeper said it was the air of the goodwife remaining like a vapour. Methought rather it was the leech's unclean tales that had contaminated the food, as father Gerald had described in a sermon not long before, when he talked of vile gossips, and I secretly called on God and His Spotless Son to remedy the pasties, but the corruption remained.

Then the culprit[39] stopped up his left nostril with his finger, saying that it was the side that inhaled air and must be closed lest his brain turn into a fish. And the assembled party struck the tables with its fists, roaring merrily so that our ears were near to bursting after the quiet of the journey; and lifting the jub of ale, one scholar claimed its emptied contents were also sour, for it had been brewed not from malt but the wits of a clerk of Oxenforde – and other tiresome jests that such learned minds do love. A fight ensued in which one of the scholars was struck upon the head by a bag full of parsnips and fell insensible as if dead, and the quack doctor's bag was cut open by a cooking knife and his myrrh-and-nettle powder did dust the whole room to his great grief, though to my mind the myrrh was only ground brick – for there was no fragrance in it, save that of cinnamon.

Yet no one dared set a finger upon the leech, not even to pull his goat's beard, for he had handled women on every part and even beneath in the secret places where the stink and scorch of Hellmouth lies. And he had boasted that no matter how much the patient weepeth and howleth, he must cut and burn the rotted part, or grope among the entrails for the sickness, e'en on the opposite side to the pain; and this he had done many times, he said, showing us his long fingers with their filthy nails, so we felt afeared of suffering and sickness and death; although (unbeknownst to us) it was to him that lean and hooded Death was already crooking a finger!

The master glass-maker and his apprentice had slipped away [*aufugerunt*]; I ran out from the melee to join them on their slow

[39] i.e. the leech or quack doctor.

nags, protesting that they had abandoned me, at which they snorted;[40] and the goodwife also [snorted] with them, saying it was no wonder, for I had less flesh on me than a *heysoge*.[41]

We left the highway and took a little way over the heath without the goodwife, leaving her stench and coarse talk to the [main] route north; our humble track having broad views either side, we feared robbery less, and after two hours reached the glassworks, that stood some three miles short of the spot where the waste of bracken was, which in turn was no more than a mile and a half from the enemy position.

The glassworks had watchmen posted, numbering some ten men armed with pikes; around it spread a vast stretch of land owned by our monastic house, which included even the robbers' wood. All the glass of our abbey church had been made within this simple structure for some thirty years: it being a large tile-roofed building puddled over in clay, standing below the edge of a wood, whose oaken trees lay darkly beyond. A monstrous heap of felled and hewn timbers were spread nearby, recalling to me the pale corpses piled up by Hell's mouth, waiting for the furnace, painted on the walls of our chancel. And truly, it was indeed like Satan's kingdom, with incessant dark smoke billowing through and smarting my eyes as mustard doth.[42] The oak wood was pollarded [*amputatus*], giving a dismal air, and before us lay a huge trench full of clean river-sand, stirred by men with long spades.

Richerd told me that the men with spades were mixing the ashes [of fern and oakwood] into the sand, this mixture being then carried in great pans to the building, within which stood something like a monstrous beehive, that was really a set of ovens glowing with a heat and light I had never witnessed before; and I was aghast at the sight. Cast into the oven, the mixture[43] cooked for a day and a night. The oven's raging was fed constantly by a man whose horrible grimace was like a Turk's, for his skin was dark with soot and blistered all over.

---

[40] *Fremere*: possibly 'snarled', though unlikely.

[41] A hedge-sparrow.

[42] Possibly in the form of a medicinal mustard bath rather than as a condiment.

[43] Now named (from the sixteenth century onwards) as 'frit': a calcined mixture that fuses without melting.

'Each unnumbered grain of sand is truly a soul,' I said, 'and we might hear them screaming together as they do in Hell.' But Richard only laughed, for he was jovial of temperament and his love of God had waxed cool.

I felt faint with the heat and the clamour, and hardly listened as Rycherd shouted and joked with the men, so that sometimes they sounded like the fiends that cackle and hiss over the unhappy wretches continually consumed and tormented e'en as I write – the same wretches still, and merely added to, tipped out from the monstrous pans that scoop them from the mercy of the Lord, for these torments are for eternity, countless leagues from the majesty divine of Christ Jesus . . .

Here follows a page of dismal reflections irrelevant to the main theme, and which I have unapologetically lopped.

. . . The worst fires, however, were to come, for upon the far side of the beehive structure, half-stripped men placed clay crucibles in a covered furnace within it, whose unearthly light might have blinded the basilisk. These crucibles held the aforesaid mixture; the unceasing, extreme temperatures of the furnace, that glowed horribly around the edges of the oven door, and belched forth a most reeking heat when opened, melted that mixture to a pliant liquor. The glaziers then let their breaths blast into this liquid, that glowed like a monstrous firefly, thereafter swelling it to a bubble and spinning it about until it flattened; whereupon I saw, as in a miracle, the flatness of a window's glass.

There, on trays against the wall, lay the glass that had cooled, in hues of green and blue and yellow, that would soon be gracing our chancel and the churches of other houses of the Order. I thought of these pieces colouring the winter light and the summer light of days unnumbered; or the moonlight that sometimes fell upon the brothers between the sparse candle-glow during Matins, Lauds and Prime. I also pictured these shapes of glass with the fresh glory of spring light upon their smoothness, or feeling the spatter of autumn rain or the soft showers of April, or being rubbed by the warm shoulder of the sun at harvest time – and e'en smitten by the violence of hail that would trouble the brothers' chanting, yet lie about the garden like jewels.

I felt my soul lift in humble rejoicing at this miracle, that had been torn from the very furnace of the abyss, just as I should tear my treasure from the felons' camp, and perhaps from the very hands of Satan himself: who was otherwise named Robert Hod.

I slept in the place where the other glassworkers lay, while the fire in the ovens burned all night, casting a glow over the adjoining woods and up unto the heavens. Forthwith at dawn, Ricchet and I set out on foot with mules for the bracken, carrying well-whetted knives. We crossed several miles[44] of wild, heathy country before we arrived at the spot, which was a gentle rise cloaked in dried fern, as though mantled in copper, wherein sheep oft love to rest with their lambs; there we set to [cutting], crawling as flies do upon a great rug. Richet told me that I must not mount the crest, for there were always the felons' eyes upon it.

He said that e'en now they might be watching us from an un-expected quarter, and I looked about me in some fear, seeing only the brackeny slopes spreading afar, naked of habitation, and swept over by many a peeping *plovver*[45] and other chattering fowl, including the haughty hawk who might have taken us for a pair of mice, so high did he soar. And wherever there was a clump of bush or a twisted tree, I imagined a felon's face fixed upon us with beady eye: and my flesh tingled as if with ants, imagining an iron point pricking it at any moment.

Our agreed plan [*ratio rei compositae*] was to tether the mules and to spend the night in that spot, covering ourselves in the bracken for warmth, as was customary [for the fern-cutters]. Soon after I must set off for the wood in my borrowed cloak, to enter it only when the

---

[44] The distance appears to have grown from Richard's original description.
[45] Presumably the green plover, otherwise known as a lapwing or 'peewit'.

night has ebbed but the light not yet grown beyond a greenness to the east. First, however, I must see where I was to go in the darkness. My impatience knew no bounds. I worked harder on the bracken with my knife until I had left Rycherd behind, and soon arrived at the crest, from where I engaged my sight furtively to the south, cutting all the while.

Upon a low hill at the furthest horizon lay a menacing form that was the wood, its darkness falsely clad in autumn gold, with a lumpen shape of rock at one end, that was the hill's peak; the ground sloped away from there full bare and gently curved, smooth as a maiden's limbs, that made any approach as hard as if it was the den of the cockatrice, which slays with its sight alone.

That night we bedded down under our heaps of bracken, and yet I shivered. Our labour had made us weary and Riccherd, after wishing me the courage of the weasel, for only the weasel might slay the cockatrice, soon fell into slumber. Indeed, he himself showed little sign of courage, for he had said again that he would not accompany me to the hideous wood were I to offer him good silver, and then made much jest with a false penny, pretending he was a priest and that this coin was my howsel, to absolve me of all sins, putting it into my mouth like the holy bread.

The night sky was clear, for there was a northerly wind. Ricchet snored, and his large feet against my skin were cold as frost – that I e'en feel now, as I shiver on this bench in our seaward cloister, where the cold gnaws at my toes as I scratch these very words.

Lo, how wonderingly I looked upon the great and unfathomable depths of the upper sea, its waters sprinkled with the lights of sea-monsters, and the moon floating as doth a wooden painted platter upon a lake. These monsters are yet so afar that their great lamps appear to us like pin-pricks in a black drape (as some men foolishly insist they truly be); and probable it is that they resemble the whale that swallowed Jonah, with glowing eyes. We do not know on what they feed, nor why they swim in the same direction, so that sometimes a shoal is clustered close into a constellation, while another is sparse and lonely-seeming. If one stays gazing long enough, the shoals increase, and one begins to descry in the thickening glitter ever fainter stars, that are really monsters of the same great bulk but deeper in the upper sea and thus further from us; and one is overcome by a giddying sense of what is wondermost, which replaces the quizzical searchings of the mind and is much to be preferred, for it is less dangerous.

It is not for man to question too closely mere natural occurrences that are God's creation and not marvels to Him, let alone miracles, but only 'a finite power working its own proper effect', as St Thomas Aquinas termed it. Yet soon I could see huge fins and tails and mouths full of teeth, and looked at Ricchet for comfort, and then at our mules, who were nothing but shadows. Alas, I did not want to go to the felons' wood for my harp, for I feared being torn limb from limb by those who had been made *wolfeshede*.[46]

But then a voice came into my ear and spoke in Latin, the words appearing before my eyes as if the voice bore an inkhorn at its side, writing them out. It ordained me to go and fetch my harp, for by so doing I would set myself upon a path by which I would attain a great name and gain wide renown in the land. If I did not do so, I would die a miserable death in years to come, all ambition quenched. And foolishly I took this to be the voice of God, and not the Arch-fiend's honeyed hiss.

I rose immediately, setting off for the wood in brother Thomas's hooded mantle [*paenula*].[47] It being too large, I gathered it up about my legs, stumbling here and there into hidden holes and ditches, the rising of a thin moon and the starlight yielding me a brightness of air sufficient to glimpse my way along that dark-wrapt nomansland. In spite of my hide [*pellem*][48] that was black as pitch, I started hares into trembling haste, and recked not my rashness, that was the heat of any younghead.

[46] Once the law had termed someone a 'wolfshead', anyone could hunt him down and kill him, as they could a wolf.
[47] Previously described as the (vaguer) *amiculum*. Cicero cites the *paenula* as a sleeveless garment, to be worn on journeys or against wet, cold weather.
[48] In a metaphoric sense, as the cloak is not presumably of leather.

And thus like a weasel I crawled the last distance uphill through short herbiage, and came to the edge of the wood that was like the wall of darkness about the Devil's abode, and my blood was very fervent and I could feel every vein pulsing, most especially the one that runs up from the heart to the brain; fearing it might burst I prayed silently and felt God the king of glory walking beside me as I slipped through a fringe of birch towards the interior thicket.

Great was my horror when I struck my head against a dangling object, this being the head of a deer hung from a great bough. The sight and stench cast disgust and terror into my heart, for I knew then that this wood was given over to pagans, whose practices and superstitions still lie about the country in embers, ready to blaze at the slightest relaxation of our efforts; believing as they do that demons are gods worthy to make sacrifices to, when they are in truth once-angels too cowardly to take either side in the war between the Lord Our God and Lucifer, and who were thus righteously cast out to skulk in seas, rivers, forests and rocks; taking upon themselves the colours of their various abodes, forever dissimulating in their wild places and lying in wait for the unwary, who know not that one sign of the Cross is sufficient!

I took my knife and, climbing to the bough, sliced through the rope, that the offering fell with a thump, yet no thunder shook the wood, nor furious demi-god assailed me; but only I felt, on that night air, a sudden heat as of a demon's nostrils close to my face. If I had owned an axe, I might have felled the tree itself, as St Amateur felled the pine long ago.[49]

Beyond the afflicted oak, stretched a thick-planked hurdle no higher than my chest, for a deep pit or trench lay behind it, that gave vantage to the defenders of the wood, when stood upon an earthen firestep. Yet no one lay on night-watch, and soon the true wood enveloped me as if there were no horizon but forest, and I was astonished by this. I could make little more perceptible to my eyes but a

[49] St Amateur, bishop of Auxerre (died 418), uprooted the pine in whose branches the future St Germain had hung the heads of wild animals.

baffling tangle of branches and cold-hued leaves;[50] I was like a blind man left in peril by the child that leads him. Yet I struggled on through the desolate thickness of boles and branches and creeper-weft, where no righteous man should be found, for all was waste. And it felt to me that I was making a great noise of rustling and panting, and that the felons should find me soon and draw out my tongue with a hook, to keep me silent after my great impudence.

Tripping over tree-sprigs and lurking roots, the blindness that of a crypt, I more than once found myself stopped by a denseness of hazel brush or thorny matter, such is the pitiable state of nature when it is fallen and not tended by God, as it be tended in the sweet-scented garden of Paradise where all is virtuous and chaste and where, below the low murmur of prayer, through birdsong and the trickle of the fountains, only the laughter of innocent maidens is heard when the angelic choirs' harmonies draw their breath.

An owl hooted close and I was startled. Then another, further off, its call seeming to echo. I waited a short while, gripping in my left hand the purse containing the lead ampulla and trembling with fear, for owls are portents of death and stare you into submission. And in places I thought I saw more dangling heads of wild beasts or game, but the shadows were shifting and the low moonlight playing its customary tricks that sorcerers and witches do love, so I could not be sure if it were not my eyes feigning. Then a peacock screeched, very horrible as it always sounded to me, for there were peacocks (bearing heads like serpents, yet puffed up with pride in their tails' extravagant beauty) kept by the lord of the manor, whose lands abutted St Edmmund's at that time.

O foolish boy! If I had known more about fowls I would have fled from that place, for peacocks do not inhabit wild woods. Yet I continued in my ignorance, thinking to come nearer to the camp, and saw a fitful red glow through the boles and branches amongst which I besought my way as stumblingly as a beetle, well scratched

---

[50] i.e. the autumn colours of yellow or russet, caused by the changing balance of the elements.

upon my hands and face; this illumination was not dawn, for the sky above was still brilliant with stars. And I hoped it was not Hell's glow.

Many diverse woodland creatures who live night-wrapt were fearful of my presence, and rustled away unseen in the sodden undergrowth and through fresh-fallen leaves; it seemed wondrous to me that they could make their home in the same wood as the felons. And there were natural hollows and dips into which I stumbled: for the wood, though cloaking a hillock, was like a little country of uneven relief, with its own vales and crags and mountain ranges.

Then an unnatural silence fell upon the place; but it was I who had stopped, in truth, for chancing upon a meagre sylvan trail, I saw it led straight to a clearing, dimly visible in the glow of a banked fire (this being the source of the illumination), as once I spied a *myracle*[51] in a grove, performed by buffoons with much dancing and shrieking.

Then as I crept forward the peacock made its screech again, driving into me as a nail into a board . . .

Alas, a crucial scene seems to be missing, the scrivener either omitting a section or following the damaged source; at any rate, we jump abruptly in the narrative to a scene in which the protagonist has been seized, and it is already dawn. I take the opportunity of this hiatus to begin a new chapter.

[51] A miracle play.

4

The fire was in the middle of the clearing, that had a great oak on its edge, with boughs thicker than a serpent. They kept that fire burning, or at least covered, night and day. Here and there in the trees stood huts of woven branches and bracken,[52] as hunters and so forth build for hiding-places: it is said that goblins live in similar dwellings, only of a tinier size to suit their stature of half an inch.

A felon called Ives, whose breath smelt as foully of garlic as a demon's, shoved me into one of these huts: he had a lip cleft at one side, no doubt from a wound, that resembled a straw pressed upon wet clay. I said yet again that I was a famished lad hunting for rabbits: 'Well!' cried he, with a foul oath, 'now thou art a rabbit in its burrow, and when the pot is simmering, we will come for thee.'

There were no windows in the hut and it truly seemed dark as a burrow, the door being a woven plate of reeds like the lid of a basket, just short of the height of a man. A curious feigning of the eye is that small dwellings oft expand when entered, as woods do, or as foundations of houses seem very mean, until roofed: tiny as it was, the hut took five men easily. There were six other men within, and I fell among them, making seven.

The hut stank of sweat, urine and flatulency [*ventus*], and also most sourly of vomit.[53] I knew from the same stench in the alleys of Dancaster, where bodily matter of both dog and man is left to rot in

---

[52] Presumably more similar to the charcoal-burner's huts that still survive in our thicker beech woods, than to the flimsy hides of hunters.

[53] The medieval writer was altogether more frank about elements which, to us, seem too repulsive to be mentioned in polite (or at least 'civvy') society.

46

the gutter, or is cast on the foul heaps that swell e'en hard by the kitchen doors,[54] that it would diminish as I became accustomed to it. Yet I also knew, because father Gerald himself had told me, that Satan's realm smells disgustingly of new-spouted vomit in the day and of freshly dropped *toordis*[55] at night: though you be there for all eternity, your nostrils suck in the vapour anew each moment. [It is as if] they are smelling it anew at each moment.[56]

Lying there in the hut's gloom among silent strangers whose breathing I could hear whistling through their noses, I remembered that this day was the holy day of St Narcissus,[57] and drew comfort therein, for we were but two days from All Hallows' Eve and the triumph of the saints. Men have long memories: the comfort and joy you feel from a nightingale's song does not last longer than the song, but the hatred you feel from someone doing you wrong can last until death; a grudge may last longer e'en than grief.[58]

The prisoners were recovering from drink and its noxious fumes, yet told how they had been stopped on the road and invited to dine with Robert Hod and his men, whereby forced (for the felons' merriment) to drink great quantities of the strong brew [they had been transporting?] to the priory at Blythe. The men were sick with the effects of the ale, and wished they were dead. It was an evil place to be a prisoner, which was why I had been cast into it like a bone into *cannel donge*.[59] My eyes growing accustomed to the poor light, I saw the leech and next to him the rheumy friar – the same that had accompanied us on the northward road. I was extremely glad that Ricchet

---

[54] Archaeological evidence is scanty at present, but if this seems alarming in terms of hygiene, given what we now know of the fly as a carrier of disease, I found its counterpart in farm billets on the Continent, where one generally stepped out of the house into the midden. Cess-pits and drainage systems only began to be introduced in the century of our narrative; during wet periods the smell of the streets' sludge must have been scarcely endurable. Dwellings no doubt swarmed with louse and rat.

[55] Pieces of human dung.

[56] This repetition is possibly the copyist's error.

[57] 29 October.

[58] This eloquent interpolation seems misplaced; possibly a textual mutilation copied by the scrivener.

[59] Gutter-dung.

had not come with me, for mayhap he would raise the alarm, were I not to return: what great dearth of experience there was in my youthful brain, to hope thus.

Much astonied was I to see them, since it was the practice of felons in those parts only to rob those travelling south. The leech's surcoat under his mantle was patched in coloured squares that were skilfully sewn, and the fur hat upon his head was like a mangy cat asleep. Being very near to him, I was afraid that I might touch his flesh, polluted with the feebler kind, for he had very long legs. And he had touched all over e'en the bodies of women no longer maidens, for virginity is a tender thing and soon deceived by the serpent, that draws open the treasure and plunders it with his horrible claws, and spares not even the handmaidens of Our Lord, though they be walled about by convent stone: for the shameful members of man, swollen and bulging in their stockings [*bracis*], are full of wicked intent.[60]

Then of a sudden I saw that the quack's eyes were on me, even in the gloom of the hide, and he grinned and showed sharp teeth. Meanwhile one of the carters, snoring in his slumber, was woken by his own foul waters, soaking his stockings so that the ground was as sodden and stinking as a garderobe's in an inn. He had a broken nose, dinted as deep as a loaf. 'Benedicamus domino,' said the friar, but the others cursed. I shifted away from him, thinking only of my harp, as a mother thinks of her infant missing from her lap. A minstrel had once offered me eighty pennies; which being the price in those days of a healthy ox, I had told him, 'This harp be worth fifty oxen to me.'

I reflected, not on how it had led me into this danger – as the sweet odour of a rose, though needful to our hot brains in its coldness, might lead us to stray into carnal desire – but on how I might escape with it.

[60] Cf. Chaucer's '*The Parson's Tale*' [ll. 423–31], without the colourful detail of 'the horrible swollen members, that semeth lik the maladie of hirnia': the similarity suggests a common source – probably Guilielmus Peraldus's *Summa seu Tractatus de Viciis* (before 1261). 'Stockings' or *chausses*, rather than breeches or trousers, were worn at this time: the term 'hose' belongs to the later fourteenth century.

As the hours passed the men began to talk softly, recovering from their surfeit. The friar rubbed his paunch and said he would perish of cold and hunger: and his feet in their sandals were indeed blue, and his nose glimy. To which the others, holding their heads as if they were bowls of hot oats, said all his holy brethren should be cursed for brewing ale (though he was only a mendicant).

'Rumm ram rufe,'[61] said the quack, and he performed the trick [*praestigias*] with three cups, that some call an enchantment [*fascinationem*]; making three pebbles move from one cup to another, with a tap of his finger and a magic instruction. The others laughed and laid bets: but the *tregetour*[62] – for so he was, [a fairground conjuror] as well as a quack – refused to gain from their present misery.

He was the best at this trick of any of the devilish tregetours I had seen already. At the end he put the pebbles back in his mouth and swallowed them, taking them out of his ear; swallowing them again, he produced them from his buttocks. He offered the pebbles to my broken-nosed companion – who would not touch them, but squealed like a woman, for they had travelled smoothly through the pipes in the quack's body and into the heat of the stomach, emerging uncleanly from his buttocks! Whereupon the felon Ives burst in angrily, saying we would soon find ourselves laughing at crows from a high rope.

To the clearing then he led us, where the fire was smoke more than flame, for rain had fallen. I could see a mass of blackness through the trees, this being a rocky bluff with deep caves within. We thought we might be murdered by the men gathered about, whose appearance was at first sight savage: they were dressed, many of them, in rough-stitched goatskin, bearskin and suchlike, and their faces were dark and worn from their wild, forest ways, and mossed with hair, their nails filthy as a peasant's.

I trembled, for whoever these outlaws were – whether of noble stock or serfs, or mere cut-throats – I knew that they would show no mercy if they were so inclined. A life following the way of a beast, that skulks in the forest without a decent roof, makes the man beastly. Also, the

---

[61] Popular nonsense words of the period, like our 'fee fi fo'.
[62] Juggler or trick magician, familiar on market days.

magnificence of certain great oaks about that clearing, that towered above the forest sward, struck terror into me more than wonder, for they made e'en the horses tied below them look like kittens. Among these horses, it must be said, I recognised my master's mount, stood beside another grey that dimmed even the former's splendour. It seemed that none so far had perceived me as the page of the monk they had robbed.

[There were?] some twenty men in all, including several with each a crossbow [*arcum*][63] resting in his arms, fixed upon us. And that weapon's sound, like a great crow snapping its beak against the thread of life, still wakes me from sleep, that I think I am struck by its point; thus memories grow more robust with old age, as the vital fires of the body gather in older rooms of the brain.

A man appeared from one of the bigger huts, beyond the smoke of the central fire. A certain movement among the assembled men scattered about, leaning against trees or squatting on their haunches, gave sign that he was the chief. His tightly woven mantle kept off rain most nimbly, for I could see that it was greasy and the drops that fell from the branches were disperpled by it. It might once have been a fine red, but was now the colour of dried blood, and had a great hood behind, in which several faces might have been concealed, and beneath the cloak was a thick pellice [of wool].

He came towards us, stopping at some three yards' distance. The smoke thickened and, hiding all behind him as the sea-fog doth our present coast, made it look as the underworld must appear beyond the Prince of Hell.

I recognised him as the very villain (calling himself the chief) who had taken my master's purse and examined the coins most lustily; his eyes were still somewhat swollen in their sockets, as one sees in drowned

[63] I am assuming a crossbow rather than a longbow, as the latter is not cradled in the arms. It was a vicious, highly effective weapon dating back to at least second century BC China, firing short, thick bolts released from a catch by a trigger, and so popular that it was banned by the Pope from use against fellow Christians in 1139. Alas, no such ban has at present been made against other mechanical weapons of far crueller disposition.

men, and the blemish on his brow most like a splash of molten wax. I did not realise that drunkenness was so deep in him that it did not show upon the surface, until he was angered. I guessed his age at twenty-six or -seven, although he was at that time over thirty.

'This must indeed be Robert Hode,' I said to myself, with a pang of fear.

He sat down upon a hewn log, staring about him as if weary. Having talked softly to a felon beside him, his gaze falling once more upon us, he made a gesture, and a rope was thrown over a smooth branch that grew from the most towering of the oak trees.

Thereupon the tregetour was pushed under the branch, his mangy hat falling off, to reveal a head quite bald. His eyes grew wild with fear, but also with the cunning that all such tricksters show, for they draw upon the powers of the Devil e'en when they do naught but juggle and feign. And we saw that the rope was a noose and that execution was to be carried out, and the tregetour asked what was to happen to him in a most trembling voice. The outlaw chief stood up and told him that if he had magic powers – nay, any powers at all – he should show them now to save himself; for he had heard he was both a lecherous meddler in women's flesh and also a magician: which observation made all the felons in the clearing laugh.

And the tregetour replied, trembling in his limbs, 'I would rather pray to God, being a devout man who wishes no harm to others.'

Hodde then shouted, as if he had been touched on a wound, that there was no God, and no Heaven, and not even a Hell (in which, of course, such hideous blasphemies might meet their just punishment). Then he declared: 'There is less than nothing, not even an eternal darkness, for darkness is a thing in itself, whereas nothing comes out of nothing!'[64] And he was screaming his words now, as if suddenly choleric. The words echoed between the trees, e'en on that

---

[64] *De nihilo nihil fit.* A phrase from Boethius which indicates Hod's learning: in medieval garb, as actually uttered by him, we can imagine it as approximate to this celebrated later rendition: 'Nothing ne hath his beynge of naught' (Chaucer, *Boece*, 5. pr.1. 54); this being echoed two centuries later in Lear's infamous retort to Cordelia: 'Nothing will come of nothing: speak again.'

sodden, dismal day full of the smoke of the smouldering fire, the whiles the rope swung above with its ghastful noose. And the felons gathered there cheered at this terrible blasphemy, like fiends; and I felt I should faint, for it seemed we were in the court of Satan himself. And I saw again how strangely over his crooked teeth his speaking mouth moved, as though sucking upon a plum.

Then the poor juggler of wits hurriedly took out a tiny leathern pouch and opened it, and poked his finger within, that he began to lick. Whereupon Hod backed away a step, as if the conjuror might turn into a scaly serpent, and asked him [what he was doing]. The quack babbled of a powder that was the most precious in his possession, for it gave the man who drank it the power to grow wings and fly. He had great conviction in his eyes, under his bald head, and his goatee beard quivered as doth smoke when blown. Hodd, stepping forward boldly, forthwith snatched away the bag, opening it to sniff the savour. The other men laughed, but he silenced them with one look. It is known that certain cut-throats have the sway of kings, e'en o'er their burliest followers.

Then Hod said, 'Where are your wings?' The quack replied that sometimes they take many hours to grow. Robert Hode asked if they grew on a dead man, and the tregetour laughed and said, 'Nay, for the body's spirits are extinguished and cannot carry the powder to the bones of the shoulderblades, where the wings flourish like plants in rich soil.' The outlaw asking what the concoction consisted of, the magician said that it was mostly the berries of *pettie morel*[65] ground up with a feather of the rare phoenix, for morel climbs without fingers or hooks, but by its upward force alone. And that in return for his release, he might give the pouch and all its powder to the outlaw.

This last rubbed his face as if in reflection, then said, 'Climb the tree, to see if thou canst fly from it when the wings are grown.' And the tregetour, after much complaining, climbed from branch to branch like a boy, until our necks hurt from watching; the outlaws urging

[65] The very familiar woody nightshade of our hedgerows, which can reach four or five feet by leaning against a stouter growth.

him on with great cheer and forcing him yet higher with the judicious use of their bows:[66] the slender arrows swooping skyward and splitting the bark under his feet here and there with great accuracy, until he stopped.

Whereupon a point striking between his legs, seemingly an inch from his privy members, persuaded him to climb yet further up, so that we feared he might plunge to his end at any moment. He had shrunk to [the size of] an acorn high in the bare branches, and his white face peered down, but I thought that he had at least escaped hanging – having no idea then of Hodd's peculiar ways.

When it was my turn [to be interrogated], my courage failed me and I confessed all. Those then chuckled greatly, by whom brother Thomas and I had been robbed – including Hode. The harp was sent for, and I was mightily relieved to see my treasure unharmed. The chief villain bid me play, saying: 'Sing a song to Robertt Hode, king of the outlaws and of the realm of the *othair*.'[67]

By '*othar*' [*sic*] I assumed he meant the realm that was beyond the law of the forest justices and of the sacred Church of Our Lord that leaves the darkness to its devils, while emblazoning the righteous through her vitreous glory. I was used to contriving[68] songs: it is not difficult to weave a new colour onto the loom of melody and words, if the original weave be strong enough. Seated upon a log, finding strength in holding the harp on my lap and tuning its strings of strong wolf-gut, I was less faint from fear and hunger.

I began to pluck a tune from the harp that was both plangent and

---

[66] From the description of the arrows as 'slender', and their accuracy, this must be the deadly longbow, made of yew, that the later 'Robin' legend would fuse to the outlaws with the heat of romance, and which makes such a contrast to our present armoury of stick-bombs, rifles, machine guns and so forth, and the unimaginable din and violence of the greater calibre weapons.

[67] This simply means 'other', but in medieval clothing. True, there is no precise equivalent in Latin, except perhaps – but rather too feebly – *reliquus*. The variations in the spelling of what, for this text, is such a key, ambiguous and resonant word may not be the copyist's responsibility.

[68] An interesting use of *comminisci*, customarily negative.

lovely, as thinking of spring in autumn might be both forlorn and hopeful – thinking of what has gone and what is to come. I danced the words upon the tune, the known words that I would always sing with that melody, turning the huntsman into Robbert Hodde, king of the outlaws.

Whether an effect of the rocky bluff that, as I have said, made up one limit of the wood, or my state of giddiness, I do not know, but my song seemed to come back to me on the instant, louder than I meant it. I heard my own words, and in their clarity and in the brilliance of the strings of my harp, I heard my own treachery – for what else was I doing, but praising a horrible blasphemer, for whom men's throats existed only to be cut? And yet I sang on, as if each step forward [in the song], each ripple [of my fingers] over the strings, was delighting me as [doth?] sin.[69]

I had a high boy's warble, sometimes cracking to manhood, yet rarely at this time. Once I had a conversation with one of the brothers, a learned man only in his middle twenties, yet known for his brilliance of thought that darted about as a hare doth, jinking in a field. This was brother Edward, our expert in canon law. He asked me, 'Dost thou think the singing voice lies within you, or without?' I could not say, so he continued: 'Doth it begin in the body, to be carried intact onto the air, thence to transport the spirits of the listeners by entering their own ears and stirring their humours? Or doth it materialise in the air itself, beyond the singer's lips, mysteriously conjoining with the notes of the instrument, then to be taken in portions by the ears of each listener – as a bowl of soup or pottage is emptied by several persons at table, yet containing all the taste within each part?'

Again, I could not give him an answer, never having considered it, nor aught else of that quizzing nature. Brother Edward also considered the workings of the echoes in church, when the brothers were singing together: believing these echoes to be fragments of the divine or angelic Voice accompanying us, but that Heaven being situated

[69] The original Latin is very obscure here, and may well be corrupted.

so far from Earth, the angelic accompaniment (a verification of the brothers' holiness) took a little morsel of time to be transported to us on the intervening ether, though travelling swifter than an arrow. This did not satisfy me, as the echo existed even when a mason or a carpenter shouted a command or – as had indeed happened many times – swore loudly upon dropping a hammer on his foot, or some-such. But brother Edward did not hear the same sort of echo, in these cases: that, he claimed, was the Devil's mockery; yet I doubted whether the Devil's mocking voice could pass into the sacred space of any church.

We shared many such discussions, thenceforth: he had great hopes for me, and he said, one time: 'Thou shouldst enter the monastery as a brother, when you reach maturity.' But my ambition was to sing at court, not (as I thought to myself) to shave my head and be hated by the common people for feasting while they went hungry, and then taxing their hard-won harvest. What I saw of the brothers' behaviour at that time did not endear me to the monastic way, though it did not occlude feelings of affection. The house was a roof and food and warmth and companionship: those elements of human sustenance that bring us close to the lesser beasts, who need no more, whereas we also need – if we are not the simpler type of peasant – learning and intelligence and love.

I scarce knew what I meant by love, for even as a *jocatores* I was praising in songs a higher type of carnal love, that is connected by a pipe from the brain to the shameful parts, and thus to the lower form of carnal love – which, as St Augustine writes:[70] 'upon reaching its apogee, causes an almost complete extinction of mental alertness;' and such songs are therefore an encourager of lust in the expectation of such indecent pleasure, and might overthrow a man's reason.

By 'love' I meant to myself at that time, foolish youth that I was, parroting my elders, the highest possible love for a woman: that prick of love that bleeds the heart and will not be staunched until her fair

---

[70] In *City of God*, Book XIV, cap. 16.

body's warmth is felt softly against your own.[71] My songs claimed this to be the very joy of life, of which I sang most often in my boyish warble. And often, too, I sang of the pain that will not be assuaged: the love towards which you run but that forever runs away from you, and faster than you; the love which you dreameth of whilst waking and sleeping, but that remaineth a dream. And sometimes I sang (though no higher than usual) in the voice of the girl, who is also sorrowing for her true love; a type of song taught to me by a Galician with a black tuft under his lip, and which is called *cantiga de amigo*.

When my song was finished, there was a silence, as if the whole wood and all its myriad creatures had stopped to listen. Then the chief felon approached and lifted me to my feet by the left ear, as a schoolmaster might, and as painfully. He said, in my pinched ear, so close that his breath seemed to embrace me in [the fug of] a tavern: 'You are one of the chosen. I choose you. Rise, and be blessed as one of us.'

Since I was already risen, I could ascend no further unless I stepped onto the hewn log. He walked away, having spoken to me in a hoarse whisper, so that no one else could have heard; yet three of his men took me respectfully to one side, by the fire, and thrust a bowl of soup into my hands.

The other captives were delivered to the mercy of Hod's men, and made to strip naked and dance horribly to a great drum struck by one of the outlaws as if it were corn being flailed; then they had to mime lewd and filthy acts together, resembling the devils that masked players [*larvati*] act. Outlaws with thorny whips shouted out instructions, and encouraged them when they were flagging; the felons laughed uproariously, as if at a tournament,[72] when the waggoner fell off his

[71] Again, the sense of the original is somewhat tortured by curious syntax.

[72] Neither class nor position makes much difference to the Middle Ages' widespread acceptance of physical violence, that we have curiously retained in the sordid arena of modern warfare. See, for example, the *Roll of the Justices in Eyre at Bedford, 1227* (recently printed in *The Publications of the Bedfordshire Historical Record Society*, Vol. III, 1916), which, as the editor points out, catalogues 'an amazing amount of violent death, considering the small population'.

stout donkey whose knees had buckled: this donkey being the friar. I looked up and saw the tregetour looking down from his great height of oak, and feared lest he might fall.

All this resembling very greatly the scenes of Hell freshly painted in our abbey church, showing the damned souls' shivering nakedness and the devils with their whips, howling their delight, I wondered if, after all, the fiends' true kingdom was not elsewhere, but secretly here on this earth. Yet my harp was beside me, and I had little doubt that I would soon be on my way back to the monastery, for I had taken no heed of Robert Hodde's last words. While these devilish antics were going on, a great spit was erected over the fire, on which a wild pig was turned, beside a brace of thin rabbits and a plump goose; and from another part of the contraption hung bags like giant purses, in which meat of other beasts was seethed, for the bags were their own skins – the outlaws having no cauldrons.

It seemed, from the banter of the felons near me, that this meat was venison and mutton, being the flesh of sheep and deer snatched from one of our lord king's estates – and the goose likewise, from a farm five miles away. I had never before seen beasts boiled in their own skins.[73] And I did not refrain, hungry as I was, from swallowing all of my soup; yet feeling myself in a giddiness, being as though taken from the real world into dream.

[73] A culinary technique familiar to the Scots on their campaigns: 'They nother care for pottis, nor pannis, for they seeth[e] beastis in their own skynnes . . .' (Berners's *Froissart*, ed. Ellis, 1812, chap. XVII, pp. 18ff.)

5

While the drum was still beating for the hostages' mortification, I was led into the largest hut, that displayed either side [of its entrance?] a deer's skull upon a short pole; and therein sat Robert Hodd, looking down at the ground, who did not stir a limb when I entered, so he resembled a graven image.

The hut was dry, and given comfort by fine woven carpets spread upon the straw of the floor. The dimness was relieved by two candles in silver prickets either side of the chief outlaw, and I said within myself: 'He looks most horribly like a god, that heathens worship.' He bade me sit down, amidst a sweetness of incense that was no solace, for it was a false sacredness. The white bark of birch trees, stitched together so that they resembled the scaly skin of a snake, glimmered upon all four walls. Upon this white skin were scribbled words and phrases in a language I did not recognise, along with lewd diagrams and drawings that sorcerers oft use: this had been done with charcoal, or a burned stick.

When the felon began to speak, he fixed his head very still throughout, but little looked at me – his eyes darting about as if seeing presences invisible to others. This frightened me more than his words; and as long as I am in this corruptible body, I shall feel that fear still. He knew that I was from the monastery of St Edmund's of Dancaster, which owned this very land and thus the wood itself, and he furiously cursed the abbey and its monks, for they wished to cut down the wood to the last tree, to feed the fiery furnace of their glass-making: 'Felled will be this forest, for thus they fatten upon every living creature, yet give naught back, for covetousness is their only badge.'

I was sore amazed that the holy brothers wished to fell the wood, and he perceived that my ignorance was true. Upon asking me many details, he enquired about my parentage; being most puzzled that, as the orphan child of a cottar,[74] I could read and write and play the harp. He asked me how this was possible, and I told a great lie which was to dog me ever after: 'I woke up with the skills complete in my head, one day, having been very near death with a fever.'

'You have been summoned by the *hother*,'[75] he said, which I took to mean Satan, because he had said he was an unbeliever. He had returned from travelling upon the Continent to put all to rights in this benighted country. He then told me an extraordinary thing, pouring its potion into my eyes with his sudden gaze. I have no doubt, now, that he had this power latent in all of us, but that is rarely used except by players [*mimis*] in a shallow way, or when a woman wishes to cleave your heart to hers and thus torture you with her beauty: that is, the power to influence you [through the eyes] by means of an invisible pair of slippery darts, each of which is continuous to its full length, which is about three feet; and that would, if materialised, be of the substance of meat jelly, and warm.

He told me, not that he was God, but that he was more than God.

By way of explanation of this profound blasphemy (that I had only ever heard before from the mouths of mad beggars sitting in their own dung), he said that everything in Nature is inhabited by the Spirit [*spiritus*], and that when it dies this Spirit within us, which is called *anima*, becomes the *othwre* [*sic*], that is not anywhere but in this world and merely invisible, like many floating veils, until it is required to inhabit another material being, whether a tree or an infant rabbit or a rock or e'en a person. 'God is merely an invention, as is the after-life. At first I believed God to be the Spirit, but now I see deeper into the truth and know that God does not exist, that there was only Spirit, and Spirit was not God.'

---

[74] The term does not exist in Middle English, but has only recently been derived by historians from the medieval Latin, '*cotarius*' – as used here. The cottar was not a serf but the lowest of the unfree tenants, holding no land on tenure outside his cottage garden and paddock (unlike a villein), and doing day or piece work for others. For a discussion of the worsening of villeins' rights and freedoms from the late twelfth century in particular, see P. Vinogradoff's magisterial *Villainage in England* (Oxford, 1892).
[75] Again, 'other'. The arbitrary spelling of this word seems particularly exaggerated.

Then the youth that I was, forgetting the danger my tender soul was in, asked him how he could think he was more than God, if there was no God (brother Edward having taught me the rudiments of logic). He laughed, as if he liked the question, the which [laughter] seemed to wrestle with the stitched walls of pale birch, upon which floated many colours; and I found myself transported by the laughter into a delightful foolishness of mood, where nothing could disturb me. Yet I was indeed more present in my body, that felt the softness of the fine carpet, and smelt the sweet aroma of the incense, than I had ever been before.

'My good friend,' he said, 'for a time we need God, so we create Him that we name God, and worship Him and fear Him; as did the dwellers of Canaan dread Him, and e'en the strong men of Edom and of Moab. When we achieve perfection and dwell in our original being, which is the divine essence, we can throw God away as the snake discards its skin. Then we fear nothing, because there is no sin. The only sin is not to recognise that we are more than God.'

'"Thou shalt not slay,"' I cited, marvelling at the way my words came out of my mouth as if writ there by a pen. 'Nothing is a sin,' he replied, 'when you are pure essence and the source of all Creation.' Then said I: 'This that you say being the sin of presumption,' accepting with equanimity the manner in which the walls were covered now in shifting shapes as brilliantly hued as the freshly painted walls and columns of a church.

'There is no sin,' he repeated, his words blurring deliciously [*suaviter*] inside my head. 'The one who is perfect, who has attained perfection, cannot sin even if he wished to, for everything he does is necessarily perfect.'[76]

---

[76] The notion of a mortal as 'perfect' might remind the reader of the Cathari, in the process of being suppressed with the utmost brutality by the French Church at this time: there is, however, little relation between this heresy and Hod's. The latter is, in fact, far closer to the beliefs of the 'adepts of the Free Spirit', whose neo-Platonic, pantheistic, mystical anarchism – possibly inspired by Arabic Sufism – first appears to historians in northern France in about 1200, and spreads throughout Europe, to become (despite intense persecution) the cradle of peasant revolt in the fourteenth century: see A. Jundt, *Histoire du panthéisme populaire au Moyen Age et au 16ème siecle* (Paris, 1875), and my own *Self-Deification: the Doctrine of the Brethren of the Free Spirit* (London, 1920).

I blinked and his face became fifty eyes, all gazing upon me with great solicitude. I opened my mouth and again the words came out in a strip, as if painted on a cloth: 'If, however, he decides he is no longer perfect, then he would be sinning, you said. Thus a perfect man can sin by thinking he is no longer perfect.' I was delighted by my chopping logic, and wished . . . [*hiatus in the MS*].

That wicked heretic (for so he was) then leaned forward and struck me across the face as a schoolmaster might, yet so hard that I fell to one side; but my pain floated above me and not on my cheek. It was even more of a marvel, to be lying on my side, and I fingered the carpet's weave, now as vast as a wild wood seen from a cliff, and more wonderful and precious than damask silk from China. And my nether lip began to stretch exceedingly in order to cool my face from the sudden heat, and I had a plain face without nostrils, and found myself likewise tongueless and with only one great foot, beshadowing myself with the foot, as the satyrs that go about and stare in the desert of Libya.[77]

And he said to me, that I had been summoned, but was not yet innocent. This was a strange phrase, which the effects of my intoxication did not fail to repeat in my head, over and over, as softly sounding as the chants of Terce heard through slumber. Little did I know that my mind had been polluted by a soup of mushrooms,[78] of the kind that sorcerers oft use, and that fill certain chambers of the brain with a fumosity of pictures, every one of them false.

I lay all night in the villain's hut, having visions. It would be tedious to relate them all, or all those I could remember afterwards; but in one I dreamed that Hode was the Antichrist, and that in order to test the truth of this, I arose from the straw where I was lying and cut his cheek with my knife, so that the blood flowed over the carpet of the hide. It was black, which is the colour of the blood of the

[77] Cf. the entry on satyrs in Bartholomew.
[78] Probably the common toadstool *Psilocybe semilanceata*, known for its intoxicating properties.

Antichrist. I wanted to tell my father, but my father (being long dead) was nowhere to be found. I ran through the wood at great speed, and the white trunks of birch trees in a grove at the wood's marge [*limes*] flashed either side, as the sea's foam doth under moonlight.

Then I found myself in a great palace, drinking from the crystal waters of a fountain in one of the courtyards of the palace. I knew I was in the Holy Land, but the palace was deserted except for the cadavers of Crusaders, bloated and blackened, lying about in a drone of flies. Eventually I came across a wizened old man, squatting against one of the walls of the shattered temple of Jerusalem. He told me that he was doing penance for a lifetime of dissolution as a travelling minstrel. I asked him his name and he replied with my own: he was myself, in many years to come.

I fled, coming to somewhere I had never been to before [in reality], although I seemed to know it well: this was a farm, with a midden before its tumbledown house, set in a valley of poplars and a stream that flooded into marsh either side. Silvery rushes waved in the breeze, the flooded stream sparkled, and I felt a great happiness.

It was in this state of profound contentment that I woke up in the hide. Robert Hode was snoring in the far corner, on a palliasse of straw thicker than mine own. There being no one else in the hut, I might have slit his throat, as all men have the right to slay one who is outside the law; yet any escape would have been thwarted by the watchmen outside. As I lay there, very sick in my belly, I could hear these sentries murmuring and chuckling.

The bright, deceiving pictures and the dark hut with its vicious, blaspheming occupant became great adversaries in my mind. I closed my eyes again and swiftly entered a garden with high stone walls and well-tended flower- and herb-beds, therein coming across the loveliest woman I had ever beheld, dressed in the most delicate apparel. I glided over to her [like] a ghost, but [it was] not as a ghost[79] that I stole my arm about her, so that my fingers appeared from under her arm,

[79] The sentence is hard to translate, the Latin unusually corrupt: possibly an interpolation.

reaching e'en [further] to lie on her breast. She had delicate, pliant breasts set high under a chemise of silk edged with an intricate brocade, from which emerged a smooth, flowing expanse of neck, as perfectly white as the inside of an apple.[80] I kissed her mouth and began to fondle her woman's parts as if I were her husband in the privates of my chamber; she was naked under her chemise, as most women of any refinement be, and her perfume was musk like that of Eve the temptress, and I tasted violets from a *muscadin*[81] in her mouth.

She broke away from me, suddenly, and told me that she was already betrothed to another man – a great count called Mars, who was away fighting in the Holy Land. I found the harp in my hands and began to play and sing the most passionate of the love songs I knew, but I had no voice and the harp was woven from spiders' webs and wrapped my hand in its sticky [*tenacibus*] threads. I woke up in great shame and confusion to the girl's shriek of laughter, which was (in truth) the outlaws' horn blowing outside: a very strange and frightening sound, for as I later learned it was the horn of a ram that had belonged to a Jew, robbed and slain on the same road as we had been – a horn made to be blown in the Jews' synagogues, not in a wood, and which is called a *shofar* in their tongue, and is the only instrument permitted [by us] in their places of worship.

Thus it was that I was doubly bewitched, both by the devilish mushrooms and by the Jews' horn that creeps into the ear like a goblin and howls with delight.

Hod stirred, swearing lustily, and shouted for a bowl of water; he was truly like a king. An outlaw entered with the water and Hod cleared his nose into it, a nostril [at a time], and then offered the bowl to me and ordered me to wash. I shook my head, my brain lying atop my hair.[82] Hod stared at me with protuberant eyes, holding the

---

[80] It may be no coincidence that a smooth white neck was traditionally an indication of a lecherous appetite.

[81] A mouth pastille to freshen the breath.

[82] Compare *The Tale of Gamelyn*, ll. 593–4: "'Nay, by God!' seide thei, 'thi drink is not goode, / It wolde make a mannys brayn to lyen on his hode.'" [Harley MS 7334]. Skeat dates this ballad *circa* 1340.

bowl in his hand, his expression that of a clawed beast judging the prey, that is unneth worth the effort to pounce on and tear.

He drank the water himself, gulping it down as if he was suffering from a great thirst. The man who had brought the bowl eyed me as if to say: 'You must be favoured. Normally you would have been slain.' The man's cheeks were bursten-veined [*sanguine suffusos*], and his nose was pitted and swollen: it was the same felon who had snatched my harp from my shoulders the time we were robbed, and I instantly felt an iron dart of hateful choler.[83]

I was made to follow Hod out of the hut, leaving my harp within. The hour was yet early and it was very chill, although the ground was not frozen. The fire was smoking fitfully, thickening the mist that hung about us and that crept under my clothing, for it was the twilight that forerunneth the sun's rising.[84] The morning air and the freshness of the autumn wood eased my sickness and the heaviness in my head. I looked about for my fellow prisoners, and saw no one but the watch. Then I stared upwards into the greatest oak where the tregetour still perched like a tiny hawk, for I could see his long legs either side of the tree-limb, and was glad he had not fallen from that height in his sleep. And Hod said to me, 'We shall see if he can fly,' and laughed for a long time as do gentlemen in a dicing house when one cries *ffissh ffissh*,[85] or like an infidel acted in the false merriment of masked players [*larvati*].

As in the camp of an army besieging a town or a castle, there was great idleness among the men, from want of tasks. This was worsened by their leader's manner of conducting affairs, guided by his belief in the divine rightness of whatever he thought to do, so that his orders were erratic and even fruitless [*vani*]. At times, no orders were given at all, because nothing came into his head: as I imagined it, he was waiting for a messenger to arrive from the realm of *thother*. The outlaws would grow restless and impatient, arguing with each

[83] Iron being associated astrologically with Mars (the count in the author's dream was called thus), one of whose effects is anger.
[84] Dawn.
[85] Repetition as in MS: 'fish fish'. A lost reference.

64

other and coming to blows. They might only indulge in bow practice or contests of archery on Hod's orders, and yet like bees one
travail was common to them all, one common working and one
common meat and one habitation which was the wood; and if a
woman was taken into the wood, she was common to them all until
thrown out like a goshawk that is old or no longer living, yet which
before was formerly beloved of its lord, and borne on his hand and
stroked on the breast and tail and is now thrown out on a dunghill.[86]

There was a great metal plate on the fire, and on it they cast a
paste of oatmeal to harden it for biscuits [*panibus*], which was my
whole fare that morning, yet afterwards my stomach was filled.
Knowing where the harp now lay, I was planning my escape [with
it]. I had slender legs and was swift in running, but the wood contained
many armed men: I risked certain death, even if the horses tethered
among the trees would not be used to harry me, as they had harried
the deer on the lord's estate.

Then I saw the friar and the carters being led towards the clearing,
tied together with a single rope knotted around each of their waists,
as official prisoners have when led to the market-square for execution.
They were filthy with mud, and were naked as Adam before the Fall,
without even stockings. I imagined they had not eaten, as they gazed
with longing upon the little biscuits tempered by the fire, that was
now well ablaze; yet when I offered them some, the sturdy felon
guarding the naked captives rebuked me sharply. This man's face was
so cut and scarred, like a veteran soldier's (as if by the sharp steel of
a lance in many affrays), that it made me think of great battles and
of knights in armour, and of the strokes of lance or mace on head-
pieces that might be heard from a distance of a mile or more, such
was my boyish greenness and the lingering effects of the [mushroom]
soup – when my poor head should only have been filled with prayers
to the Lord Our God, Creator of all things visible and invisible.

But in this lack I was only as our clerks and country priests are

[86] A simile drawn once more from an entry in Bartholomew. The entire passage antici-
pates the author's months with the outlaws, rather than obeying the strict narrative
progression we would now expect.

at this very time in Yngelond, who understand so little of what they service that they are no better than ignorant boys themselves, and preach insufficiently, keeping their mortal sins hid as deeply as their chaplains do their filthy concubines; who store their barley, wheat, peas and so forth in the church, which is oft in poor repair or even ruined entirely. And even when a witch resides in their parish, they cannot root her out by asking her to repeat the Creed or the Lord's Prayer, for they barely know anything themselves – though they maintain on [episcopal] visitations[87] that they are good and faithful Christians . . .

I have somewhat abbreviated and truncated the above diatribe (familiar in the Middle Ages), for being detrimental to the flow of the narrative.

. . . Hode then appeared out of the morning mist, his breath thickening it with clouds that hung in the damp woodland air like the smoke of a dragon [*serpentis*]. I took it as a further sign of his devilish [powers?]. He stared at the men and I [remembered what he had said?] about the impossibility of sinning. Whatever he decided to do would be right, because he was [in his own eyes?] perfect.[88]

He ordered the guards to undo the ropes. Then he signalled to one with an outgrowth of red beard, and told him in his ear to fetch a thing. The prisoners covered their [privy] parts and shivered, dipping their heads like seed-fowl, certain from the look on their faces that they were doomed to be miserably and horribly slain. The friar held his great paunch and wept, no doubt also from cold, by which he was all over blue; I felt pity, but then he gazed upon me with a look of such exceeding venom that I knew he believed me to be behind his plight, for why else was I free? And there are indeed boys who lead innocent travellers to traps on the road, or to wild places where

[87] When *synods-men* (sidesmen) were required to testify.
[88] The text is badly browned from an inserted wheat-stalk pressed between the leaves, no doubt left as a bookmark long ago.

the same [travellers] are robbed or murdered; but I could say nothing, for the battle-scarred outlaw was standing by, holding a stout cudgel.

Hode was stirring the fire with a long stick as the pox-marked felon returned with a large sackcloth parcel in his arms; this he untied, pulling out a glistening [*lucidam*] robe. At first I did not see it was a lady's silken gown, but thought it a lordly vestment: other gowns followed and rustled in the felon's hands like the leaves at our feet. Hod indicated which captive should receive which vestment, for they were of bright and tempting hues: yellow, citrine, red, blue and green. The prisoners being forced to don these garments, I saw they were ladies' gowns of the finest Byzantine silk. One of the carters, in his fear, caught his foot on the hem and tore it. He began to weep, thinking his last hour had come, as the poor wretches pulled each bodice about the chest, doing up the clasps with some difficulty, for the fastenings were fine and their fingers chapped and cumbersome. The friar, being tall and stout, could but squeeze into a green gown, looking as doth a bean swollen in its pod, the hem of the full skirt coming only to his lower calves from his belly.

Even in the mistiness, it was plain that all the dresses they wore were women's garb and not cloaks or tunics or robes or men's skirts or gowns,[89] for they all had a bodice wherein the greater breasts of females customarily sit and remain hidden, lest they infect others with lechery, though pale as whale bone. And in place of a maiden's swan-white throat was only stubbled and ill-coloured flesh.[90]

The victims made no effort, as travelling players or buffoons [*scurrae*] might, to imitate a lady's mincing, pliant comportment, but stood about as men, wondering, 'Ey, what might next befall us?' Two of the gowns were long, and their wearers short with hefty shoulders, so they must hold the folds to keep them free from the ground. The faces were mostly like those of ugly women or female serfs of the rougher sort, and stubbled or bearded on the jaw so they might have

[89] *Cappa*, a gown worn by priests and university students.
[90] What we are told of this odious parade reminds us of the moralist's tendency, at any period, to indulge in gruesome, detailed descriptions of the very vices he most disapproves of, thus unconsciously touching on the indecorous or even the obscene.

been crones or witches (whom all righteous men fear), yet robed in splendour. And the fearful name *Lucifer* spread in my mind like a banner, and all his glittering host following like summer fireflies from ear to ear.

Hodd did not laugh, and so the felons under the trees kept silent likewise: this I found remarkable, for they were cruel men, and delighted in others' misery and humiliation. He gazed upon the shivering captives, nodding slowly, as if he was discovering something afresh. When he looked about him, any smile was extinguished like a taper, and the entire band of felons was now gathered in anticipation: I counted above forty. Watching R[ober]t Hodd, I understood then what it was to fear a man, not for his strength but for his diabolical influence, as sorcerers and witches are feared; and e'en the scar upon his head, like drops of molten wax, seemed invested with malign powers.

The captives were made to dance hand in hand, which to my mind was a mingling of two evils, for the dancing of women is horribly wicked, and men dressing in women's attire is also an unnatural vice, and thus Hod mixed a brew that was corrupt and stinking and which the outlaws might drink from with their eyes, as the fiends of Hell sup upon pitch and sulphur, to strengthen their evil.

And when, after this buffoonery, the prisoners were driven from the encampment by the outlaw guards – being permitted to scramble away in their finery through bramble-weft and thicket, their costly silken stuff grievously torn, as was their flesh, the five of them resembled a horrible dream in the mist, a dream of disorder and the end of days, when gentlefolk become muddy serfs, and men become women, and lepers and beggars feast in noble halls and filthy concubines wield swords and lances, throwing groaning men to the ground and treading them underfoot, that the very substance of the world is sodden away and immoderate mirth becomes the wailing of unceasing plague.

Then Hod turned to me, as I watched (secretly plotting how to escape with my instrument), and told me that I was favoured to be his servant: 'For verily I am in need of music, and you have been chosen by the *othar*, to reside here in our New Jerusalem!' This name he delivered with much mockery, looking about him at the wood-ways on every hand that were not true ways at all but utterly wild and traced only by beasts: for the felons, too, were no more than beasts. And then he added, for I had said nothing, that if I were caught escaping, I should suffer the punishment of a poacher caught with a bow or an archer caught by the enemy in battle: 'That is, to lose three of the fingers of your right hand, that you might no longer pluck your instrument for me, or for anyone.'

Then we heard a shout, and looking up, we saw the quack or tregetour still perched high among the remaining golden foliage of the oak tree, clutching the great branch like a squirrel doth, and pleading for release now that his companions had been set free. Hod took up his bow, that was of his own size and exceedingly well made of the *ewe*,[91] with fletchings[92] bound with red silk and a barbed head of bluish-grey [*glauci*] steel, and drew it back bodily;[93] shooting with a sharp hiss [*sibilo*] its arrow upwards towards the poor man.

And so skilled was the villain in archery, that the missile pinned the quack to the branch by the very hand that clutched, leaving no more showing of the arrow than a few inches above the fletching, as it seemed to us below, so deeply did the point drive into the wood through the flesh. A great shriek sounded, that shook the birds from the trees – these mostly crows and suchlike – and then a sobbing that was grievous to hear, though faint to our ears below, and obscured by the cheerings of the other felons who had seen the action. What pity did I then feeleth, for the man shuddering upon his high perch!

'Now he can boast and brag of flying all he wishes,' cried Hodde, 'for only a surgeon can unpin him, e'en after every leaf hath fallen to the ground.' And I marvelled at his cruelty as much as his bowman's skill, for the leech had done little to deserve such a fate: if he fell he would not die promptly, but dangle by his pinned hand as though from a gibbet.

[91] Yew: the favoured wood for the longbow, before ash.
[92] The feathers of an arrow.
[93] Presumably with the English technique, wherein the body rather than the arm alone is behind the strength of the pulling action.

Alas, I now well believed Hodd, concerning the punishment to my own hand if I were to attempt to escape; and I cursed the day I had ever set out to retrieve my beloved harp, a mere bauble (it seems to me now) that had replaced a finer love in my mind – of that eternal Light that will never dim, even after the promised End of Days[94] have brought darkness over this wretched earth, and which Light that horrible play-acting and buffoonery had recalled to me: for (strange to relate!) that scene took me back to the sandy marge of the sea, and my first and most holy master, the aforementioned hermit, who yet had no name.

[94] I have pointed out in my little monograph *The Early Church* (1919) – partly composed during the absolute wet tedium of the trenches – that Christianity was founded on patience, for the imminent end of time promised by Jesus failed to come. As the excommunicated M. Alfred Loisy has famously commented: 'Jesus preached the Kingdom, and what arrived was the Church.'

Part Two

The manuscript is here separated by a superfluity of prayers and pious thoughts from the previous section, creating the equivalent of our modern blank leaf – which in the medieval period would have been regarded as shockingly wasteful. It is impossible to know whether this was a later interpolation or the author's original indication of a division in the narrative, which I nevertheless acknowledge, although the transition seems to be otherwise smooth.

I

Now I must tell you something of my early childhood, and how I came to learn in this wise.

My mother told me how, when I was not yet born, he [the hermit] had come to our northern village from afar, and knocked on our humble door. He received kind welcome from my father and mother, though he was a stranger to them and they were ever-hungry, being mere cottars [*rustici*] dressed in hodden grey, and their bread coarse, and the land all abouts very wild, windy and desolate, with little habitation. My parents respected holy men who were not false beggars or thieves, and he ate with them at their meagre table and laid a hand on their careworn heads and blessed them. Which, when my mother felt it, was like a wing of goosedown (as she told me much later), or as if the Saviour had brushed her face with his chestnut[95] hair. 'The poor shall inherit the earth,' he told them, 'for they are Christ's treasure.'

There was yet frost on the ground, though he was barefoot and ragged and very thin, having eaten nothing at times but wild grasses, tubers, acorns, beechmast, *eldre*[96] and e'en nettles from the woods, and drunk [the juice of] birch. In those earliest days the hermit still had long hair and a crisp beard like flax, above which his cheekbones stuck out like plough-shares. He did not care a clove of garlic for coins and wealth, supping on my parents' thin gruel of beans as if at a feast. 'You surpass the rich as gold surpasses silver,'

[95] The tradition that Jesus (rather than Satan or Judas) had red hair is still alive in our rustic village, where the presently bearded translator is known as 'Walking Jesus' by the local children.
[96] Elderberry.

[he went on]. 'Being in material want, you are held in grace by Our Lord.'

He told them that men fighting in the Holy Land had seen crosses appear miraculously between the shoulderblades of the Christian slain – but only on those of the poor. My parents, who were hungry and short of fuel in that fierce winter, felt his words warm their souls with hope, and my mother would say that she did feel, at that very moment, a hot finger trace the Holy Sign on her back, that caused her almost to cry out.

As a young child, I would examine her back, under her clothes, as she sat on the stool – but there was no trace of red and no scar, as sometimes the divine touch leaves on even ordinary mortals, so that the flesh blisters or erupts with the force of holiness, yet without pain or dolour. My mother was always disappointed and [would maintain that] she felt a tingling on her spine as of a saint's anointing finger. (*And I also suffer from a tingling in my spine, but it be in no wise a saint's finger, rather that of this labour and travail, that pricks like a dagger.*)[97]

Our simple cot having two rooms, the holy beggar was lodged alone for several nights where e'en the hens and our two pigs were shut out. When he left, he followed the guidance of a voice, walking until he came to the sea. Our village was but five or so miles from a wild, rocky part of the northern coast, uninhabited and seldom visited even by fishermen, though lying but two or three hours [on foot] from the holy abbey of Whittby.[98] There he found a cave in a great crag or cliff and lived on seaweed and fish and gulls' eggs, his whereabouts unknown to anyone else.

I asked once the whereabouts of my father, in my childish way, whom I had no memory of, and my mother told me (as she was to do many times), how one day the army of King John passed by and put

[97] The matter within the parentheses is to be found crammed into the margins of the leaf, in a similar if rougher hand: a rare example in this document of an insertion, which suggests an oversight by the copyist, or the weary copyist's own heartfelt intrusion.
[98] Founded in 656, an early seat of great learning. It might not be too fanciful to associate the present-day Robin Hood's Bay, lying between Whitby and Scarborough, with the locale of the hermitage, for reasons the denouement of this narrative will make clear. The cliffs are backed by moorland remarkable for its exposure and lack of habitations.

the village to the torch, for it lay in the area controlled by one of the rebel barons;[99] the inhabitants who had not fled were pitlessly slaughtered. 'Alas,' quoth she, 'your father was among them!' Chased over the baron's ploughland, whose thick acres he had been tilling with oxen,[100] he was shot down like a hart, and lay unburied. 'I carried thee upon my back into the wood beside the village, but some servants in the king's retinue spied us and harried us between the trees, shouting and hallooing as though we were hares. Yet of a sudden our pursuers thereupon disappeared as if swallowed by the ground, and a silence fell upon the winter wood.

'A man then appeared, walking slowly, and I was led to the sea-cave you know, some few miles' walk from there, for the man was none other than the good hermit. After a few days in that dismal sanctuary, I returned with you to the village, where those who had fled were beginning already to rebuild their homes.' And enquiring after my slaughtered father, I would receive an answer thus: 'Alas, his body vanished, I know not where.'

We were very poor and there was oft a murrain of sheep and too much moistness in our meagre valley. Yet was I nesh[101] of flesh and quick to learn, and suffered little from fever or rheum (that had took all my siblings),[102] and was as careless and evil-mannered and vain as most children are.

At the insistence of the holy man, he became all my school, and thus I learned my education from him, else I would have remained an unlettered peasant. I was taught by him to read and write, to sing and to play music. And soon I could say which city lies where the sun goeth to rest ('tis clept Sarica); how long Adam was in Paradise

[99] About 1215; the northern barons were well represented at the meeting at Runnymede in 1216, that led to Magna Carta.

[100] At an estimated rate (for oxen) of less than an acre a day, theoretically measured in strips 22 yards wide and 220 yards long (viz. a furlong). Medieval farming was crude and exhausting, lacking any incentive to improve itself, though fundamentally the same as that of the present day.

[101] Meaning either 'soft' or 'moist', this is a word that seems to me in need of rehabilitation.

[102] The death rate among children was, of course, very high: it has been estimated that well over a third did not survive beyond the age of nine.

(seven years, before his trespass with the apple on a Friday); of what height is Our Lady (six foot and eight inches, which is five inches more than her Beloved Son); and which herbs God loveth best (the rose and the lily): and many another answer vital to us.

At first my mother went with me to the hermit's cell, and I would stay one night each week in the cave, and then she would fetch me the following noon with bread for the holy man; later I walked the few bare and windy miles alone, e'en with unshod feet.

The sand of the beach was my tablet, and a pebble or stick my pen. At first I approached my letters as I might have approached the coast of Fennonia,[103] with mute ignorance and awe. I would draw them on the nesh sand, [copying] what he had written, until the beach was covered in words. My ears would be full of the sea-surge – and even now when I read, with my failing sight, the sound I hear is not that faint roar of the present sea upon our cliffs, but that of the past, louder still: for all my letters were learned in the rude voice of the waves, the wind flailing our cloaks like sails – making my blood strong and more boisterous still, as I think it now, in my extreme old age that is the strongest proof [*firmissimum hoc afferri videtur*].[104]

In the early days I would write, not words, but only letters, the same letter over and over until I could form it naturally and almost as beautifully as my master could, my hand scuttling sideways like a crab. My delight in the forming of these letters over and over was so complete that today I feel a shiver of it, e'en down in my shame-fast loins, when I recall those times. Yet I inwardly curse my writing [hand], for it is so stiff with hard use and age that the crack of its fingers [*digitorum crepitus*] stirs me from my old man's slumber; and my eyes and all my senses, e'en that of speech, are weary; and even when the *swealewe*[105] swoops above the cloister, I cannot hear its screams.

*　　*　　*

[103] Finland.
[104] The Latin is very corrupt, but the sense clear.
[105] The swift (not formerly distinguished, at least linguistically, from the swallow).

None of this did I tell a hair of, to Robert Hode. Instead, I was already bound fast like a boat to its painter, for his admiration of me was my own doing, and built upon a lie; thus the Devil had twisted the rope. Indeed, there was also profit in't for me, for Hod blew upon the embers of my poor pride, that the hermit had last stoked; I cannot say that my second master, brother Thomas, puffed up that sin, for he would strike me before praising me, which I now see as being a surer way to God, for no man walks upon rose petals to the Lord.

Why did the Heavenly Maker grant us bodily pain, if it was not to strip us of the luxury of self-pride costumed by the Arch-fiend and return us, in our sufferings, to recognising the blinding effulgency of His pure Light instead of the miserable taper of our turpitude, or the false glitter that gold radiates from its substance, unless it be leaved upon the sacred walls of Heaven . . . ?[106]

Hodde had a wild way of talking that at first I could not understand, for his phrases seemed to lack meaning, though I knew all the words. He was fond of sermonising to the assembled felons, and the first I ever heard was on the evening – e'en after dark – of that very same day my five companions fled through the bramble-thicket.

He began under a rising moon, after the camp had glutted itself upon roasting meat; talking loud enough for the whole clearing to hear, yet he did not quite shout. The felons sat upon the ground, or upon logs or the lower branches of the great trees, like a flock of the Arch-fiend's angels. Their master talked in a grimly voice of treachery and injustice and the foulness and greed of the lords, merchants and bishops, and of the blood on the head of the sheryffs of the kingdom, and that a golden age was to come when all evil customs would be ended and all land would be free.[107] Not intently did these wild men listen to him, though pretending to, like schoolboys fearful of a beating. Yet the outlaw clept *lyte John*,[108] who had held the knife to brother Thomas's throat on

---

[106] I have considerably abbreviated these reflections.

[107] This rant is not to be confused with the latent 'Internationalism' of a Wat Tyler, or of the later and thoroughly romanticised figure of Robin Hood.

[108] As in MS: 'lyte' meaning little. The earliest known reference to Robin's most famous companion.

the road, and was of great stature with a blacksmith's shoulders, called out, 'No man be so free that he may not plough and carry [*qui non debeat arare et ferre*];' which Hodd answered by saying, 'Thou speak'st like a charter, John!' – making all present laugh.

As for myself, I felt that as long as I sat mute at his right hand, as bidden, I was safe and would soon be released unharmed, or find a means to escape with my harp without detection, for the latter would be fatal to me. Meanwhile, upon the heights of the tree above, the quack or tregetour was making sounds something like a pigeon of the woods, that was horrible to hear; for it was evident that not only was the arrow in his hand piercing his mind with the agony of the battle-field, enticing a host of ants and suchlike in its wound, but thirst and hunger were needly working in him, and all he could do was whimper, yet not fall. And once or twice a terrible screech was let out, e'en during the sermon, but all Hode said was, in a great voice: 'Let us see if the leech can grow wings, as he maintained to us, and tear himself away as 'tis said men shall travel to the after-life!'

And all the assembled felons howled like dogs before a chase, as no one there had a peck of Christian beliefs, nor even pagan or infidel, but something that denied e'en the son of darkness; for Hodde believed neither in the Maker, nor in the Antichrist, but only that he himself was more than the Maker, for the Maker existed not – as a flea is perforce greater than something that does not exist. And because he was but one of very few who knew this awful truth, he was of great power, and might follow his will without fear.

Yet at other times he did talk of himself as greater than God, for God did not intend to give him so much power; this was because he needed a plinth to his power, for as I said e'en a flea can be great compared to nothing, or to a mote of dust that is almost nothing. And Hodd most feared being of small weight, or weighing of naught as a dead leaf does (that makes no report when it strikes the ground); so that he used God as a necessary comparison, as be a coin in the scales.[109]

Yet already, despite the vile nature of these idolatries and heresies,

---

[109] The text is somewhat corrupt here, or at least confused, but the general sense is plain.

the Arch-fiend was hurling his long javelins over my tender walls, for there was something in Hodd's vicious talk that drew me. I was a youth, and knew nothing, forgetting the lessons of both my previous masters as if they were so many straws in a gust. The fiends that slumbered in me awoke, and outside the holy influence of the brothers' house, they felt at ease to creep up in my veins and mine my heart and mind with their secret workings, as if every syllable of Hodde's was their steel-forged pickaxe [*dolabra*]. For Hod talked now of a great truth that would come with full understanding, and banish the clouds of ignorance, wherewith the dreadful fear of both God and the Devil would vanish within the twinkling of an eye, and all men be free, and not tethered to that which 'tis said be most proper to man, but not to the animals – that being sin.

And he went on: 'Lo, that world in which it is not possible to sin – for sin is like a property made of paste, as a shield or sword is in a *myracle* [play] – shall blind us with its glory, and we shall be as naked as the beasts!' And he cried out, as doth an emperor before a battle: 'All spirits shall be free in a state of nameless wildness, as I alone already am! And all things created shall be the property of the free spirit, whether living or inanimate; and so the poor shall be made rich, and the present and horribly covetous rich be slain and cast into ditches, and every great house or abbey or palace burned, and no man's wife or daughter be any more his and his alone, for lechery and adultery are vices only in the fallen world, and the world of the free spirit is unfallen!'[110]

After this there fell a great silence, as if the last words of the sermon that still hurried through the depths on the backs of fiends had silenced e'en the creatures of the yellow-hued wood. A great roar then went up, and I saw how all Hod's men had been lit and made merry [by this speech], as if pitchers of wine had flowed instead, and some of them danced. For it is well known that heretics and idolaters

---

[110] As noted above, Hod's rantings are so similar to the beliefs of the Brethren of the Free Spirit, first identifiable in France and along the Rhine at around the time of our present narrative (1220s), that one wonders whether his late travels upon the Continent had not infected him with what are strikingly 'foreign' heresies. Alternatively, it is possible that our author has sought to fit Hod's somewhat contradictory beliefs into that particular hole – rounded them off, as it were – in order the better to condemn a movement that, by the date of our document (*c*.1305), had become alarmingly active again.

dance, which is why the Church looks severely upon it, and in dancing they give off a stench like that of a hog-stye, and grunt like swine, as any man who has entered an ale-house during a dance must know well: and so they become loosened further from God.

One felon struck a great drum of stretched ox-hide, and another blew upon a hunter's horn, and yet another a pipe, and a cask of the carters' ale flowed into every throat. I also was made to drink, though of tender years. Meanwhile the fire blazed ferociously into the night, illuminating those savage faces and twisting the trees about into horrible shapes. And thus have I seen Hell many times repeated on this earth.

But the worst was to come; for having sieved the sins of pride and gluttony, lust yet remained to be plucked. There stood a large hut, like a hall, with a thatch of bracken and crude walls of oaken planks laid vertically, down a thorny but well-trodden way from the clearing, in which those women either fleeing justice or cruel husbands, or taken by force from the road in their beggars' rags, were kept as in a *stewe*, though without the freedom to leave when they wished.

A wicker fence surrounded the whole, of the height of a man, thus both hiding its filthy activities and rendering some chance of air and exercise to the unfortunates within.[III] The rough place was made more civilised by thick pelts of bear and sheep and a window that opened on a wooden hinge; there were raised areas either side on which lay pallets of straw, hidden behind fine, hung cloths robbed from merchants' carts. The hearth in the middle was kept alight always. The hut was called many filthy names such as *Cockepallisse* and *Prikksdelite* but mostly (and most blasphemously) 'The Nonnerye', and was guarded by two bowmen.

The women numbered four or five, and did not ever stay longer than two or three months. None were diseased, for if they were seen to scratch themselves or bore red pustules or other unclean matter, they were cast out of the camp; and likewise if they were seen to be heavy with child. If they were maidens and comely enough, then

---

[III] During the late world deluge, in a well-known Belgian city, a wooden fence was built around three streets given over to military brothels, in order to hide the long queues of waiting servicemen from passers-by.

Hodde had his will with them first, for he was greater than God and all was of his own essence.

I told him I had never e'en touched a woman. He laughed and told me that this bawdy-house was to prevent vice among his followers, for if a man lie with a man, then that is unnatural and damaging to the free spirit as blight is to a tree, and he did hate catamites as he hated monks, and thereby made loathsome accusations against the holy [brothers], such as . . . [*matter erased*]. In this I understood that he was no different to St Augustine or other great Christians, and not like a heretic.[112]

And he showed me the great hole dug out long before for marl at the edge of the wood, that they called the *dragouns pitte* or sometimes *deork pitte*; here were felons cast (as sinners be into the infernal regions), for this or that transgression, until Hodd saw fit to release them. And the sinner being tied at the wrists, and the crater being the depth of three men and of a sucking mud at the bottom, it was truly a horrible punishment e'en for a day, let alone a week – and thus would I fare if I were to touch any of the women, or steal, or otherwise displease my new master.

All this I discovered in the first days of my captivity; indeed, I had been led to the Nonerrye by Robert Hod himself, although no fornication took place. The fire glowed hotly on its stone cushion [*pulvino?*],[113] and the women were half naked on pelts around it, and there was perfume mixed with the smoky air. Their round breasts did not surprise me, for while the Lord Our Maker had permitted me to see mothers suckling, and the withered dugs of a madwoman dancing naked before a church door, the Devil had also enticed me to watch, through a chink in a certain wall, the practice of foul lechery.

Permit me to explain! Our abbey at that time made great profit

---

[112] The insistence on this peculiar contradiction in Hod's character seems to weaken the argument for a worked-up, authorial charge of heresy, since heretics were frequently associated with such carnal and 'unnatural' impulses – and specifically the type delineated here, resulting in several lines being piously erased. This particular impulse was, however, a familiar one to medieval commentators on monastic discipline, including Augustine.

[113] The text has the nonsensical *fulmino* ('to thunder and lighten'), probably the distracted copyist's misreading.

from two [bath-houses] that it owned in Dancaster, of great size and comfort, to which it was said that certain wives, married to elderly and respectable burghers, did repair to satisfy their lusts among the clients of the proper bawds, who were regularly inspected in their secret places on the body since the day one was found to be a leper, caught from an unclean customer.[114] And right up to the time of good Abbot Gerald, sad to tell, I would accompany my master [brother Thomas] to that lewd place, waiting outside with his horse whilst his thirst was satisfied within.

My curiosity inflamed by a whispering fiend, I did not resist through prayer but crept up a stinking back alley, slippery with gutter-dung filling the ruts as deep as my shins, that ran behind the *stewe*.[115]

There I pressed my eye to the hole and saw my master in a tub, his tonsured pate gleaming . . . and the girls about him comely and pliant and white as whale-bone, and one of them [in the water?] also, its steam moistening [*contingens*][116] the flesh . . . so that I was driven to the solitary [vice] and felt the hot breath of the aforesaid fiends upon my neck, drowning my reason. Miserable youth! For that one lone [self-]fornication, shall I soon pay with a thousand thousand suitable torments . . . [when] the long catalogue of my sins is over, and only this single one [remains]? And thus be parted longer from the true eternal bliss, of which lust's momentary pleasure is but a glint in the sewer?

[114] A modern theory that 'lepra' was a form of syphilis might be noted here (though syphilis in its current form is said to be unknown before the New World discoveries of the fifteenth century). More relevant is the generalised aura of sexual guilt that surrounded the medieval leper, who was thought to be the result of parental incontinency.

[115] Such houses of pleasure were a most common appurtenance in medieval towns and cities, especially following the Gregorian reforms concerning marriage. Again, a pious successor to the copyist has seen fit to erase this extraordinary passage, but not sufficiently, the ink still being dimly visible on the vellum in most parts: consequent elisions are indicated.

[116] Or possibly 'touching', or 'defiling', or 'sprinkling', among other less likely meanings.

2

I shall tell you yet more of my very earliest years, for this be a necessary part of my full confession set down on this date of [*blank in MS*].

So much of what was written by my first master the hermit upon the sand, or shown to me in the one book of his library (this being the Holy Gospels, stained and swollen with straws), I could not comprehend in the early days; and even the simplest of phrases I skipped over or dragged in my reading, as so many priests now do with the sacred psalms. And we were not always alone, for though it was an isolated place and even the gatherers of *glaseworte*[117] and such like rarely ventured there, yet my saintly master's reputation had spread, and many came to give him food; and some of these being the type of pilgrim who sings and dances foolishly and even lecherously instead of praising God, he was eventually forced to leave instructions upon the cliff that the victuals be placed in a basket, and lowered down, that he be left in peace – though the pilgrims were still blessed by the act, and by touching the basket that the hermit touched. And soon a simple, low chapel was built with a roof of reeds, that three or four [at a time] might sleep therein and pray, though it was barely distinguishable from the rough grass and rocks upon the top of the cliff.

My earliest lesson was the setting down of an abc, as it is to be found on a board in any school: three rows of letters ending in *est amen*. My master wrote that for me, then bade me copy it. My efforts

---

[117] Glasswort (marsh samphire).

were painfully poor, each row entangled with the next, for at that time these letters that now sound their shape in my head and on my lips were mere marks scratched on sand, no more than the worm scribbles that lay between the weed's wrack. Yet during the scratching of it on my humble parchment, I felt a great excitement and pride, though pride opens the portal to the Devil. So when, after that good hour's work, my master swept all into oblivion with his naked foot, my portal was also shut with a *clac*.

'And again,' was all he said. Then after many a further hour of work the tide took it all, as time has taken both my masters and my mother and my foster-mother, and the accursed felons and their villainous leader and all those I knew then, and all my friends and brothers of mine own age, or even younger, so that I am stranded as on a spit, and have understood one lesson: that the good are good, and the evil are evil, and the evil are now greater in number among us, for the final Judgement approacheth like a storm felt at first only with a sudden gust, that claps the door in the room wherein we slumber from our vain ignorance, but does not wake us. For to fill his bags is all man's aim in these covetous days, while the poor drop in the fields, dead of hunger; and five thousand, one hundred and seventy-nine years after the first [murder] was committed, Cain's brethren are faithful to his memory, and do multiply his example, though he himself be tormented for eternity in Hell's heat, and they shall follow him down beyond the pit of slime forthwith.

By translating with my master from the Gospels and so forth,[118] I mastered a simple Latin in two years, so that I could both read and write. The salt wind that at times beat on my child's face as I worked hardened my resolve, and I would feel like a seafarer, bound for unknown shores. And my love of letters and the making of them over and over, e'en before I had fashioned words, was deeper than I can describe: I was as a hungry man who cometh upon a feast of dainty

---

[118] This was the standard method in schools, which from about this period became far more numerous, though still affordable only by a minority. It was not unknown, however, for ambitious peasants to send their sons to school in the local town. The picture is very unclear due to scanty records, and requires far more research.

fare, or a poor man entering a castle, who is told that all its possessions and rooms are his.

At other times I grew restless and angry, feeling I was not advancing,
for children think only on things that be and reck not of things that
shall be; and my master would bring his harp from the cave and work
my nimble fingers on the strings, and teach me songs, rather than
serve me with stripes as any other schoolmaster would have done, for
this is the only danger children dread.

In this he was strange, and not like other men, who believe that
learning must be driven in deep by bruises, as leather is hammered
for a shoe, or fall away unshod from our brains. And his face, though
lined before his years and especially about the mouth, and yet with
a smooth beetling brow and a large, well-shaped nose, was kindly
upon its slender neck; although the rest of him was also slender, he
had great strength, and his skin was hardened and chapped on the
elbows and knees and such like where it did rub against the world,
and even the whole of him was salted by the sea wind and dark as a
sailor who reaches the limit of the lower sea and travels into the upper
above the clouds; and sometimes upon his bare head he did wear a
tattered cap[119] like a labourer's, made of woven reeds, to keep off the
spray.

How oft did that sandy marge of the illimitable sea show itself to me
in my brain, when I stood in the sodden wood of the outlaws – and
more vivid to me was it than e'en the dry straw of the abbey, or its
aisled choirs! For the wind would blow in that tree-roof, making a
sound like the waves smiting the shore, that always broke asunder the
wood before me, and drowned it in a memory of my first and holiest
master's simple habitation, as captives dream of sunlight e'en in the
utter darkness of a dungeon. For, of my three masters, one was a
villain, one was weak and foolish, and only the hermit bereaveth me
in his loss e'en now, as a bird be pained by the cutting down of a fair

[119] Probably not very different in style from the broad-brimmed, felt type we still see in
use in our modern fields.

apple-tree in which is lodged the nest. And this I shall explain forth-with.

Yet was I not dungeon'd in my own captivity, having a small hut to myself, near to Robertt Hod's – this being my privilege as the chosen one. My hut's floor was boarded and dry over a sunken pit in which straw had been packed, and its wattlework walls had been smeared with cow dung, so that it was little inferior to the cottar's dwelling I had been born to, except that it was of one room only and had not a stick of furniture around the [central] hearth, save a heap of bracken for a bed and a ragged blanket, and was dark as a kennel when the woodland sunlight did not penetrate its many chinks.[120]

Its previous occupant had perished some weeks before in a skirmish with the bailiff's men, who had also been waiting on the high road for a rich convoy of merchants, there to rob them secretly (and lay the blame upon outlaws), and were pounced upon by Hod's men from behind; and this late fellow being of large girth and exceedingly sweaty, the hut and its bed still bore a lingering stink over the smokiness.

Yet its privacy [*solitudo*] was welcome, for the other huts, numbering some nine or ten among the trees and mostly of the same low-curved fashion and thatched in bracken (so that a stranger might think himself among charcoal-burners or woodsmen, and not felons), had two or three men in each. I was able to keep my harp by me in the hut and play upon it, to grow more nimble still.

Alas, my pride swelled e'en more fatally one day when H[o]dde told his men that I was granted my skills in a dream, and how this was the doing of an enlightened spirit of the same level as himself: 'For the brave youth knoweth he is to be part of the subtle in spirit, and serve that vast soul until he achieveth union with the divine and be set entirely free!'[121]

---

[120] The outlaws' huts seem more sophisticated than in the romanticised legend where damp and chill winds do not exist; and furthermore provide interesting textual clues to the construction of simple medieval dwellings of the sort that have left no trace, bar their 'post-holes'.

[121] See my note above on the Free Spirit heresy, which this passage almost too smoothly echoes.

And when he looked upon them each in turn as they sat before the fire, his gaze protuberant beneath his eyebrows – these last met together, just as Satan's be – they nodded and lowered their heads as if fearful of what his serpent glance might do once entered into their bodies; all except for Lytle Johnne, closing his lower lip over his upper lip in a scowl, seeming defiant.

I felt anger with this felon – infected as I was by Hodd's words. Everything the bandit leader said was a revelation to me, as though I were some hideous heretic who yet believes God has more to reveal – when every last morsel was revealed in the divine person of Christ Jesus until the end of the world, at which time He shall come again. For as St Judas says in his epistle, such false and unfaithful teachers are 'waves of the mad sea, foaming out her confusions; erring stars, to which the tempest of darkness is kept without end'.

Yet I was fertile ground for this corrupted seed: many the times before when I felt that it had been better had I not been born, that I was nothing more than a miserable worm and deserved the stripes and blows given me by my master [brother] Thomas and the others and even the cook, for although I could read and write and play the harp, the holy brothers soon discovered I was from a ploughman's litter, and that my stories of merchant feuds had been a lie. Now I was being seated at a veritable banquet of false blessings, when I should have been chastised with rods on the hinder parts, as a man may beat his wife for correction or pay the price. Yet many times had I been told [*sentence unfinished*].

And bloated I so became with presumption, that I did not feel the wood's moistness, nor the roughness of our dwellings that were no better in truth than vile hovels, nor the frosty bite of the wind, nor even the bites of my pallet's fleas, but reckoned myself to be under spring's blossom, gorged with sunlight and joy. And I was blinded to the low banditry around me, merely by the contamination of words, whose venomous hiss I did not hear but took for the sweet drone of the honeybee.

Yea, nothing is sweeter and holier than silence, for which each day I thank the Lord, and praise its blessings, the greatest being that no fiend can carry its poison from lips to ear between e'en the best of men![122]

That first night in my own hut I had a nightmare, dreaming that the poor steel-pinned quack fell down yet was halted in his descent by the arrow [in his hand], and hung there by his arm, and was Christ the son of God, and I myself a Jew or a Mahumetan who laughed to see Him thus; and danced about an idol made of a donkey's skin stuffed with straw, that had three heads, being fashioned out of the lewd will of man.

So, for all that my head was filled up with evil, I still quickened to an impulse of mercy. The following morning I pleaded with Hod to release the leech, whose moanings were grievous to hear high above us; the crows were gathering in the branches about him, for at times he fell silent and did not move, as if dead; yet when they alighted upon him to try to peck out his sight as though no more than a dying rabbit's, the poor leech did fright them away with his shouts.

Hod straightway summoned a slender-faced fellow with short crisp hair and a pale, ravelled growth on each of his fingertips that was horrible to see, as if he had touched burning coals delicately in the ordeal.[123] Hode told me that this man was a master forger who, for feigning papal documents, had his fingertips cut away to the bone with a shard of glass (for they had touched many sacred words), and how this punishment of the Church was carried out by a master-leech.[124] 'And is that the leech who did this?' I asked, sorely disturbed by the sight of the scars, and pointing to the sufferer in the tree. 'No,' quoth Hod, 'but all leeches are liars, and this one most especially. For did he not say how he would grow wings with the powder? Yet he hath not,' he added, like a child that is lightly wroth.

And I saw that many types of men were hated by Hod, and that lying made him hate a man most of all; though he did not believe in

[122] This suggests, not that the author has moved to a Carthusian monastery – where a strict vow of silence prevails – but that age has rendered him deaf.
[123] The ordeal by fire, officially abolished as a test of guilt or innocence in 1218.
[124] I have proposed the Middle English term for *chirurgus* (a surgeon).

88

sin, the sin of lying made him choleric. And because I too had lied, I felt more fearful that he would discover me. And I had great fear of being cast into the great pit, for at the bottom its filth was now flooded, made for water-fowls not men.

The forger touched my face with his awful fingers, that had no heat in them, for the ends were grey bone (as I now saw). Wherefore methought I heard again the sea-surge that sounded in the air about the hermit's cave, for I remember that holy man recounting how the Saracens obeyed their own sacred book, in smiting off both the heads and the fingertips of unbelievers – these being (to them) any follower of Christ the Redeemer, for my first master had e'en read the holy book of Mahumet.[125]

And then Hod said, after perverting both the Old and New Testament with many citations (for he knew them better than most priests do, as heretics are wont to): 'So this lying be frequent with all Christians, for they are full of foul thoughts and yet are displeased, and are tormented greatly and dream of cutting [these thoughts] out with the knife of faith, when in truth they are heard only by our inward ears and are not the product of Satan; for neither he nor God exist, no more than two drops be distinguishable in the one boundless sea of spirit. And I am that sea,' he went on, looking at me so intently that I felt I was bathing (no bigger than a shrimp) in that illimitable ocean; and that truly Hod's power was greater than any pounding wave, and might put out the very consuming flames of the stake he so deserved.

I thought with pain, that night in my earthen hut, of the storm that had broken ships anigh the very edge of the world, where the upper sea beginneth. For that was when I first knew he who, being my chief rival and cause of my first-ever temptation, led me to this sorry pass.

*　*　*

[125] This being either the Latin version of the Qur'an by Robert of Ketton (1143), *Lex Mahumet pseudoprophete*, or the more literal translation of Mark of Toledo. The relevant passage is probably the following: 'I will cast terror into the hearts of those who disbelieve; smite ye above their necks and strike off all their fingertips.' (chap. viii, 12).

It was like this. There burst such a great storm in that part of the sea that ended where the hermit lived, that a ship's broken remains were left upon our beach. The local populace, poor and part-famished at this time, came as was their right to recover its cargo, rumoured to be Arabian gold bound for Yorke. The ship was in truth carrying only sacks of grain to Caledonia.[126] There were some thirty or forty people on the hermit's strand when I arrived that day; slitting open the sacks of sodden grain or kicking aside the shattered timbers, they made a low tumult on the shore as do gulls over bread. Several of the ship's drowned crew lay about or wallowed in the shallows, but these were ignored by those careless of the fate of souls.

Among the people was a boy of twelve or thirteen, brown as a nut and restless and loud, that I noticed without hailing him, for I was eight or even nine by now,[127] and of a timid disposition. It was hateful to me to see our strand invaded thus by loud and ignorant strangers, the news of the wreck having travelled far.

I perceived my first master standing by his cave, among the great rocks. It surprised me that he was showing himself, and I scrambled up to him; laying his arm upon my shoulder, he drew me to him, as if to ward off an impending evil. It came soon enough: two of the men, pointing at him from the beach, clambered up to us and asked, in harsh tones, where we had hidden the gold.

'The ship was carrying grain,' said my master the hermit. And one of the rascals said, 'Liar! Yea, I know you holy men too well!' Ten or more of the others joined the men in searching our cave, including a scraggy woman with a foul-mouthed tongue. They had no tapers, as it was day, and the darkness of the cave defeated them. 'Give us a tallow,' they demanded; and my master did so.

Its light throwing wicked-seeming shapes over the stone walls while they searched, cursing and shouting, it was as if their bodies were secretly inhabited by demons. My master sat on a rock by the

---

[126] Scotland.

[127] At no point is he ever certain of his age, and (typically for a medieval author) tends to telescope narrative incident.

cave-mouth and together we gazed upon the wreckage: shredded canvas and timbers and the foremast entire, along with broken casks and several more drowned men in the shallows whose souls he bid me pray for.

Having no beard, as do most such holy men, and shaving his chin and cheeks with a sharp-edged seashell and likewise his scalp unto the smooth brow, he did look strangely to others, and the restless boy I had already noted approached us with trepidation. My teacher asked him his name, and the boy answered that it was Edwinn, and asked, 'Are you mad [*insanus*], as certain men say?' And my master replied: 'It may or may not be so, for if I was truly mad, no answer of mine would be trustworthy.' At which reply the boy called Edwyn spat upon the ground[128] between the holy man's feet; but I was too small and timid to strike him for his insolence.

The men and women's shouts echoed in the cave like cries from Hell-mouth in the [miracle] play, that is also like the brawling of a tavern. When they emerged from the cave, they looked at my master with anger and one said, 'Box his ears!' And another with the hands of a butcher took out a long knife and threatened the holy man as if he were a mere huxter cheating them at dice. And my master looked up at them unflinchingly from his seat on the rock, saying, 'Who told thee there was Arabian gold on board?'

'Everybody,' said the one with the knife, whereupon my master stood: 'Yea, everybody,' he said, 'and thus nobody.' A man shouted again, 'Liar!' Then the scraggy woman, who now doth forever kiss the fiery flinders served to her by fiends in their leathern *barm-fells*,[129] pointed at my master and shouted: 'You holy men and monks and priests alike are robbers and thieves, and take goods on pawn from the poor, and e'en sons from their mothers, and stink like five-day-old fish, and your souls are like wine that smacks of pitch from the cask!' And it was certain that she spake thus because she

---

[128] Spitting on the ground was so common in the Middle Ages as to be not necessarily insulting, and our own awareness of pulmonary or tubercular infection is modern.

[129] A blacksmith's apron (lit. 'bosom-skin'). See the contemporary Arundel MS, 292, f. 72.

was a witch and the servant of the Devil, who spoke eloquent wickedness through her, with interjected oaths I cannot repeat. The gulls were screaming over the wreckage on the sand, some of them alighting on the sacks and stabbing at them, and in all this tumult of voices I felt afraid, and certain the mob would make us suffer a great hurt.

Then the boy called Edwyn shouted jestingly: 'He was a monk, and then he was found with a woman, and she sprouted a beard, and he lost all his hairs!'

Whereupon the hermit, in his wisdom, stretched out his arms and cried, 'Hic genuflectitur!' – as if he was a priest with the whole parish assembled before him, telling them to kneel. And the assembled mob laughing as one, it seemed as some stupidity had broken in them, for they descended onto the beach forthwith. Edwinn alone remained, and I believed my master was going to berate him, but instead he said to him, 'I thank you, for you saved me from injury or worse.'

I could not help scoff at this, and asked how was this, that the boy saved him so; and my master looked down at the men picking their way over the wreckage. Some were carrying off the drowned for burial, in case of hauntings, and the dead men's hands swung as if they were living. 'By making me a kindred spirit,' my master replied, rubbing his hairless skull with the flat of his hand, as he oft would. 'That I, being no longer set above them, was not a mystery and a terror to their simple-mindedness.'

I much marvelled at this, thinking it over-tender, for I did not believe the lad worthy to be thanked: he had not intended this outcome, but something fatal to us both. And then it was that the fiend flew into my mouth like an owl, bruising my heart with the claws of jealousy [*livore*]; for the boy called Edwyne said, 'I watch thee write words.' And when my master asked how this might be, the boy pointed to the cliff-top and my master nodded, for we had seen figures appear and disappear on the cliff's rim as we worked at our lessons. And Edwyn said that he, too, wished to understand words, and stepped closer to my teacher as if to hang off his tattered raiment, as the sons of the prophets clung around Elisha,[130] but instead said, 'I see words in the church, but understand them not one jot.'

I groaned inwardly with jealous thoughts, for it turned out that he hailed from a village nearby, and could come regularly to be taught in the same manner [as me]; for the only disciples the hermit of the cliff adopted were those he might easily fashion, as a young vine against the wall of a house might be trained in a certain way.

And now I understand that much of my joy in my learning up to that moment was on account of it not being shared; for each time I saw, in my own village, the unlettered folk all about me in the fields and houses, my joy increased; just as we know that the joy of the blessed shall be further sweetened upon seeing the damned, squirming below in fiery torment, deprived of blessings, even when they be our own parents and friends. For this is written in the Psalms; though simple folk wonder at this, conceiving not how a parent can watch its child writhe in the flames and iciness of Hell, or the child its own parent, without suffering sorrow – forgetting that this is a matter of divine justice, to which no earthly grief, once blended with this divine liquid, can possibly remain material.

My master went inside the cave and we followed him. The men had kicked over the plank that was his table and befouled the cave wall with their bowels' matter, so that the gloom was already stinking.[131] Being a man of prudence, he had concealed the harp in a cleft in the cave floor, hidden under a slab: it was where he himself would hide if in danger, and be buried within after his migration to the Lord.

My master finding his pen on the cave floor, he showed it to Edwin; and now I felt the fiend within squirm in my belly. Edwyn said the feather was that of a goose, and twirled it in the dim sealight as if it were of no matter, for he had never seen the like in use as a pen. And my master explained to him as he had explained once to me: 'With this men may write letters of treason or love, or Bibles

[130] This somewhat peculiar simile is, in fact, borrowed directly from Abelard's famous account of his own life (he died in 1142).

[131] This being a peculiar habit of Fritz's early in the war, who left even schools and furnished houses similarly smeared with excrement.

entire, or orders that assign thousands to a hideous death in war, or learned works from the ancients, or revelations, or terrible prophecies, or lives like that of St Gerald's,[132] or chronicles, or cruel laws and statutes, or fiery sermons. And I do not use the ink of squid, but write on smooth, nesh sand, that no harm be done for the sea cometh and wipeth away all.' And he told Edwynn to return on the morrow, or the day after.

And at that very moment (which I did think the work of God) came a harsh shriek from below and it was the scraggy, foul-mouthed woman, who then called out the boy's name, crying, 'My laggard son, where the Devil be ye, get thee down here to aid us or I shall beat thee senseless, so help me God!' And Edwin blushed, and ran out from shame, to my infinite delight – for I was but a child of eight or nine, that kens not right from wrong.

And later, when the raucous flock [of salvagers] had gone, my master wondered why I looked so forlorn. 'What do you think,' he rebuked me; 'that I am a school of but one pupil?' I shook my head, blushing in shame.

What sodden timbers, shredded sail-canvas or hempen rope were left by the scavengers, we stacked together. I would fain have helped greatly, but my efforts were tiny crumbs, being still too small of limb to match what e'en Edwyne might have done. My master was strangely distracted, and saw me not as I toiled with him; afterwards he stood ankle-deep in the ceaseless surge, as he oft did, staring upon the waste of waters. And thus sometimes did Hodd also stand, in the thick leaf-mould of our earthen home; and of a sudden then would I be cast back years in time, to the sound of the sea, and feel naught but woe and grief.

---

[132] Presumably St Odo of Cluny's *De vita sancti Gerardi*. St Gerald of Aurillac died in 909.

3

For that first week in the wood was not without its afflictions, besides my homesickness and the strangeness of the woodland life, in which I still secretly said my accustomed prayers at the times when the brothers would be seated for Matins and the [canonical] Hours. One morning, on emerging from my hut, I saw through a dawn mistiness what I perceived as a dangling branch high in the oak; swiftly realising that it was none other than the quack or tregetour, who had slipped and now hung by the arrow through his hand, the bolt so placed in the bones that the flesh had failed to tear.

He did not move through the falling of leaves, so we judged him perished. He hung like a felon on a roadside gibbet, soon concealed under a busy cloud of black crows, and there was great power in the sight; for Hod told us that by such an end, then all lies would end, for only through steel-hard mercilessness would the greater lies be vanquished – that of the Church and all those who served and obeyed it, whether serf or baron. Thus did he talk, that e'en when only crumbs of sense were caught, we still felt satisfied as after a feast: he was the Spirit of All Error himself, to have such powers, blaspheming the symbol of the True Cross.

All this time I was both plotting within me to flee, with or without my instrument, while also sinking into an unwholesome attraction for this forest life, for (at fourteen or fifteen) I was trembling on the sill between a boy and a young man [*homo adulescens*], and this existence did seem to me very free and brave [*virilis*],[133] despite its cruelty.

---

[133] Possibly 'manly' or 'virile'.

95

Above all, it must be said, I was the favourite of Hod, for he had such fickleness about him, that he was attracted to novelties and believed them to be brought to him by spiritual hands or on the sea of his own divine essence. He addressed me privately in his hut, and even made me sup again on that enchanted soup of sorcerers, that changed the spirit in my eyes and made it as though of green pond water when the sun shafts through – so that I thought I saw bejewelled angels playing on the cythera and other such tricks, when it was all the work of demons who are skilled play-actors. He would say to me: 'You are not just as a son to me, but *homousios*,'[134] as though he were spouting the Creed, twisting it into a horrible blasphemy.

Yet how swiftly we become accustomed to the greatest of horrors! For high above my head swung the cadaver of the quack on the end of his arm, his entire form picked clean by the crows and soon ragged and grey, stuck fast by Hod's point; and upon whose hanging jaw, open like a semblant of a cry, still clung his goatee hairs. The wind brought down his stench, but not his bones, that failed to be loosened out of the socket of his shoulder; though three white pebbles eventually falling from him like seeds, I foolishly kept these, yet I could not emulate his trick.

Oft a felon would look up and maketh the sign of the Cross in mirth, never hearing in his mind the hiss, as of hot fat in water, when his soul would be cast into the pot for this one terrible blasphemy alone. Then after a certain time, as upon wayside gibbets, certain bones would indeed loosen and fall, as though thrown by the leech's phantom; and one shin-bone e'en struck the head of one among us with three lips,[135] hurting him so sorely that he cursed filthily through his defect – yet the quack's touch had cured him not

[134] As in MS: 'of one essence', 'consubstantial'. The Creed was established at the Council of Nicaea in 325, which wrestled with the relationship between Father and Son, and with the question of Christ's divinity; finally incorporating the Greek word *homousios*, thus allowing the Son to be both human and divine – a crucial doctrinal development, nevertheless disputed by those who said that the word, not appearing in the fonts of revelation, was illegitimate.

[135] i.e. a harelip, sometimes surgically dealt with even then, though at huge risk to the patient.

of this disfigurement (japed the others with much laughter), but only added another on his pate.

That Hode made me play and sing often, e'en in a single day between dawn and the hour of sleep . . . [*sentence unfinished*]. He was as great a lover of ballads as my previous master, brother Thomas. And oft do mirths of song and moods of music accompany the most wicked actions, such as dancing with harlots or the brawling of drunkards in a tavern, or the ceremonies of witches under the changeable moon. And he called me not by my real name,[136] but by another.

This is how it came about.

There was an outlaw of tall stature, very slender, with a darkness under the eyes as of illness, yet ruddy-cheeked and hale, by the name of Phylip. He had a jacket upon him of rough donkey-skin sewn on the inside with rings of iron, that was his hand-hewn coat of mail. He was ordered to teach the proper skills of bowmanship to one who had only played with a crude bow as any spirited boy might, with the indifference of a pastime. Phyllip set me to shatter an oyster shell in the middle of a round target of leather stuffed with straw, some four-score [yards] off, which he performed easily. He gave me his bow, taller than myself (though I was already near to a manly height) and which I could not bend more than an inch, at which the other felons scoffed, even in Hod's hearing: pricking me to greater efforts.

A bow was found of my own size and weakness, with softer sapwood, though still strong to draw, and after rapping my nose with the string so hard that I bled, standing as I was like an old bent man and with a hideous grimace on my visage, my second shot missed the target [*scopum*] entirely and vanished into the briars before the shielding clump of rocks: for this was where the *buttes*[137] lay, that no one be striped or killed accidentally, and that the arrow points might be cleaned and sharpened upon the stone. I continued for many hours until my three fingers were blistered and my palm raw where I held the bow, and my shoulders and arms were pulled like yarn; yet the

---

[136] Which interestingly remains concealed throughout the narrative.
[137] Butts: being a range for archery practice.

oyster shell remained whole, with a few of my piercings about it in the leathern-bound straw.

At first I felt the arrow striking the side of the bow, yet soon I could make it slip past freely. Philipp made a noise like many tiny bells when he moved (sporting his jacket always); he was of a frigid disposition and of fewer words than a monk, able with his bow to snuff out a candle's flame from ten-score yards. He wished to be one of the elect, but although he earnestly believed in the *othair* he had not yet felt it, albeit as infected with filthy heresies as the rest. He said that the strength and dark powers of a yew were in the bow, and the guile of a wolf in the gut, and the far sight of a goose in the fletching, and the virtue of the ash in the shaft; that I must welcome the first into my arms when I drew and the second into my fingers when I released, that they might both enter the arrow[138] the moment it flit, and make a greater hurt on piercing.

Pricks [*virgae*][139] were also set there in the ground for us to shoot at, so thin that to clove them or come e'en within an inch demanded great skill. Soon I cleaved one, and then another within days, and Phyllipe said my shooting was good enough for me to be called a true brother of the temple of the free spirit – that was in truth a feckless band of cut-throats!

A look-out stood upon the height of the rocks, the other side of which lay open ground falling away from our wooded rise in shallow heathland – the same coarse ground I had traversed on first coming here, if by a more westerly approach. One cold morning, when left alone by Phylip, I shot my arrow deliberately wide, so that it flit past the rock's cliff and I must needs retrieve it in the area beyond. No cry came from the look-out, though I felt his eyes upon me. I could by now distinguish well between the thirty-seven felons; this man was

---

[138] The usual medieval colouring aside, this is quite a reasonable description of what happens scientifically, in terms of the translation of kinetic energy, when an arrow is shot.

[139] *Virga* meaning a 'thin green twig', I have assumed the Middle English 'prikke': a thin branch cut from shrubs and set vertically as a target (cf. *Robin Hood and Guy of Gisborne*, stanza 28).

called William Scerelack[140] and [had worked] in a slaughterhouse before stealing and murdering; he was of very moist humours, with a face the [yellow] colour of saffron and exceedingly melancholy, drawn down like melting wax or a drowned dog, and always weeping in one eye.

I made to look for the arrow, or rather its white fletching of goose-feathers – treading upon the rough grass between the low thickets and glancing outwards now and again. It was a dry day of clean wind, yet I could not identify the crest belonging to the hill upon which Richerd and I had worked, cutting the bracken: there were many low hills rolling right unto the horizon, and all empty in that waste, and I conjectured that the place was visible only from the far side of the wood.

I proposed casting aside my bow and running for freedom, yet knew that a single shot from Will Scearlacke atop would have pierced me through, for e'en in high wind when the arrow yaws from its true course, Hodd's men could shatter the oyster [shell] as if it were a barn door; and there was no cover upon the slopes, only shallow trenches carven by water in the soft ground, and a few great pits or holes wherein they would tip their rubbish and bad meat and gnawed bones (for there were no dogs), with a stench when the wind blew towards us worse than the great cess-pit beyond the stables. And even perished felons they buried behind the rocks – with a strange and blasphemous ceremony that was of no more use than a Jew's or a Mahumettan's or a heathen's, and less than a man saying *cokkow*[141] a thousand times: what use could it have had, never once mentioning God or His Only-Begotten Son?

Will Scarelock called down from the rock, wherefrom he had spied the arrow sticking up from the heath at some distance, and was pointing. I went down the slope towards the shaft and, upon pulling it out of the heather, looked back whence I had come: the wood seemed as the high wall of a great castle doth, and was very dark

---

[140] As in MS: readers may recognise the 'Will Scarlock' of *A Gest of Robyn Hode*, which Mr W. H. Clawson has lately dated to *c.*1400.
[141] Cuckoo.

either side of the rocks – though the low sun shone upon its boughs, now leafless, and struck the camp's smoke that it looked most like the loosening of a thousand pale spirits into the air.

Indeed, the wood was no doubt smaller than the area of a kingly castle, though always feeling vaster within. And Will Scarelock hailed me again from the rocks, for I believe he did fear me running away and himself being forced to pierce me, though it was of no matter to him in truth, for he regarded a hare and a man with the same indifference [*aequitate*].

Then I raised an arm to him, my heart receiving my thoughts and beating very loud and fast; and I knew of a sudden that I did not wish to run away! For in the holy house of St Edmund's, what was I but a boy minstrel from the kitchens, whose voice was now cracking and thus less pleasing to his master? And I saw as in a vision the angelic face of young Henry grinning upon me in triumph. Here in the wood, yet full of robbers and murderers and blasphemers and idolaters, I was the one who was chosen: for thus did the chief lord of the wood saith, and he had the power of all demons to change the serpent's hiss into the sweet hum of a honeybee.

What is more, the boyish part of my spirit had awakened to this forest existence, that seemed (despite the exceeding roughness of many of the felons) easier than the discipline of father Gerald's rule. I considered that were I to become a novice monk, I would be bound to a hard life of chastity and devotion, and maybe suffer the same stripes as the oblates, who must not even talk together lest they receive a blow with an open hand upon the cheek, or a book broken upon the head.[142]

Then the ampulla that brother Thomas had given me, with drops of holy water from the shrine of St Cuthbert, leapt suddenly inside my shirt as a mouse might; being as I was in great peril of instant

---

[142] No doubt this was not a precious book, but the product of an ordinary scrivener: the invaluable Mr G. G. Coulton calculates the average copyist's rate later in this century to be about 3,300 words a day, paid at an artisan's rate of 6d a week with board and lodging (*Social Life in Britain from the Conquest to the Reformation*, Cambridge 1918, p. 102).

damnation, the sacred fluid was eager to be far from me, as sheep are from wolves. And it was as if I had died at that moment, and the Devil being my lord of the manor, had took from me my most valuable possession – this being my soul.

And it appeared to be taken in a flash of light, for such did I see on the horizon, to my great surprise! Indeed I saw another, flashing more; and when I turned my eyes back towards the bluff, I saw Will Scarlack holding a great fragment of glass, that by means of its great lustre and transparency, did bend and rebound the lines of light from the sun, to cause the glass to flash itself, as snow or ice doth, or as the sunlight doth off our abbey's windows. And the two flashings far and near, appeared as it were to be speaking, as armies send signals by means of smoke or fire when no messenger can pass.[143]

In this way, I later understood, Hodde learned of ripe fruit to be plucked upon the highway, of what fruit it was, and of what number; though no one would tell me what secret accomplice held the glass afar off, upon the crest.

When I was again at the foot of the rock, Will Scarelock leaned over and cried, as if I were a stranger: 'Whence cometh this young devil?' (which was in mirth, though he never smiled). I replied, calling up: '*Fro moche aventure!*'[144] for already the demons were working my lips. And he answered, as if disdaining me, which was his habit: '*Moche? Nay, litel, for this [felawe] be smal to seyen.*'[145] And I shook my arrow and said in childish defiance, though it were half in jest, '*Moch!*'

When Hod and the other felons heard of this, they laughed and

---

[143] Such signalling could be very useful: after an impromptu night raid on the German trenches had left me the sole survivor in a party of five, I was guided back to our lines by the flashing of three orilux lamps, despite the enemy flashing theirs to confuse me, and keeping up a lively fire.

[144] 'From great adventures.'

[145] 'Great? No, little, for this fellow (rascal?) be small to look at.' It is possible that the copyist is French-speaking and, unfamiliar with the English, has written the nonsensical '*fefalwe*'.

called me *Moche, the litel mynstrel sein.*[146] And so Muche became my name among them, as if my previous name was a skin sloughed away.

This Muche (that was my myself) took part in many robberies; he awaited on the road, skulking behind trees and bushes with his skilled sword and bow, and terrorised innocent wayfarers, yet he housed my own soul. I was as a stone falling from the dizzy heights of a cliff, bound for Hell-fire, or a loathly dragon covered all over in that first health and beauty of young men. Muche was a loathsome thief and murderer, a succubus of Satan, yet was my soul saved; for though the spirit be suffering the greatest thirst in the desert, as long as there is a single drop of water that remaineth, so there is hope of forgiveness and salvation. The Lord loves each soul that gives itself up to Him, but those that are stubborn like the Jewes or Mahummetans, He despises.

In my woodland dreams at this time, and then again later (during the week of Our Lord's Passion, this being ignored entirely by the outlaws), I was oft visited by the dream-shape of my smooth-browed master and teacher [the hermit], cleaning the filth from me in a great sea wind that flapped his tattered robes; but my disease was too insidious, for though the Devil was in me, Satan was nothing but satisfied by the booty and gain of that evil purpose. Only grievous chastisement can hurt the cloven-hoofed beast, only when the rods break the skin with red welts can they reach the furry back of the Arch-demon crouched within, and expel him squealing in pain. Or if a holy man of great sanctity press him out by prayer or the scattering of holy water, then he departs swifter than a bolt.

But no holy man came near the outlaws' wood in corporeal form, as if the many heads of wild beasts suspended from trees at the marge

---

[146] The bewildering variants in the spelling of *much* as both adjective and name are faithful to the text, and equally present over a century and a half later in the written Hood ballads, where 'Much the little minstrel seen' has become, through what seems to be a natural distortion of eye or ear, 'Much the miller's son' ('*Moche the mylner sun*'). In the same way, the here-mentioned Will Scarlack, Scathelock, etc., eventually became Will Scarlett: these two being among the very few named outlaws (along with Little John and Robin) at that 'primitive' stage of the legend (c. 1450).

did make a powerful throng of frenzied monsters thick enough to baulk even a saint. Thus it [evil] was left to seethe and corrupt beneath the boughs. And after the chill suffering of winter, sheathed in frost and snow, where icicles hung upon the rocky bluff, spring soon clothed the wood in lovely greenness, hiding its pollution the better, so that every demon hidden in the rocks and trunks and soft, mossy hummocks rejoiced in their dance with the felons – and most especially with our emperor, Robert Hodd, whom John did call *The Robbynge Hoode*:[147] for he always wore such a guise, like Death's great cowl, to conceal his wickedness when he did rob and slay; this hood pulled down lower than his waxen brow-scar.

Methinketh now I must return (in my telling) to the sacred sea-place: dwelling too much on those times when I was a felon hath made me weep and [turn] weak, that I desire God to take me at last in my present great age from this cloister-bench of cold stone, upon which a glimmer of sun yet danceth, warm upon my hand, though my tale be unfinished.

In truth, I should never have departed from his [the hermit's] influence, but I was a spirited young boy; and my mother having passed to the Lord in the year 1219, when I was eight or nine, of a sudden *cancre*[148] that tettered her skin like drops of black lead, I was tended to by a neighbour in the village who received as her reward a despising by me.

This neighbour was unmarried, for she was crooked in the body, and as hairy and rough on her arms as an ass; yet she was of a kind disposition and kept a clean house and many hens. In my grief and surprise, that I locked away (for I shed not a tear after the funeral), I became bitter at heart and my liver swelled – the seat of love being the liver, that loss maketh swell with absence.

At about this time, the hermit spent more and more time in

---

[147] The earliest known reference to, as well as explanation of, the outlaw's more famous appellation.
[148] Cancer.

prayer, wishing to know God more deeply while still on this mortal earth, and scarce ate or drank. He became more like a length of [drift]wood, that is twisted like water from imitation of the sea in which it is tossed, and was salted the same, and much bleached under his shaven skull. So thin did he become, living on morsels of fish, coarse bread and wild sea herbs, that his *throte-bolle*[149] did become very prominent, like a heron when it swallows a fish. He was scarce of this world, so exceedingly pure and unpolluted was his fleshly body.

He was not to be disturbed at prayer, even if he sat upon the sand and the tide lapped about him, or a storm broke upon his head with spray from the lower sea and falls of water spilt over from the upper [sea]; and when strong winds coming into the clouds like water into a bladder, burst them open for lack of egress with a flash of fire that lit his stilled visage, the ensuing thunderclap (that our ears – duller organs than our eyes – hear moments later) shivered him not a whisker.

I sometimes had to wait an hour or more before greeting him in my high voice, but that was no matter; I could work my letters without him as oblates continue their study of the Bible in private, and also I ran errands for him and even laboured at tasks, just as they [the oblates] till the vegetable garden, or shake the dust out of their palliasses, without supervision.[150] Striving to be away from the pain of this fallen world, of which the beat of the sea and harsh screaming of the gulls did remind him, he could shut these out by meditating upon the angels, entering sometimes into a marvellous trance.

I saw that around his chest he wore a knotted cord tightly drawn, that rubbed his flesh and caused sores in which worms would breed and wriggle unplucked, for he said that not only are all God's creatures of His kingdom, but that his father was a frivolous and careless man, and as it says in the Bible: 'I am thy Lord God, a strong jealous

---

[149] Adam's apple.
[150] The clarity of the Latin suffers here from several verbal contractions (e.g. *ex* for *exitus* and *effr* for *effringere*), but the general sense is plain.

lover, and I visit the wickedness of fathers into the third and the fourth generation of them that hateth me.'[151]

The people, as is their wont, soon heard about his holiness and flocked in greater numbers to the simple chapel atop the cliff, though few came down: in those days they lived in awe of such hermits, and some said that the greedy sea-ravens [*corvi marini*][152] that nested in the cliffs were jealous demons in disguise, awaiting sinners, for they always stood upon the ledge with their black wings spread wide.

Edwyn sometimes accompanied me (by happenstance), or I would find him already present in the cave, and the monster jealousy would work within my entrails; though I said nothing, not wishing to come to blows with an older boy. Our holy master would not allow us to use slates, as in a proper school, but only the fine sand where it was moist. We were working upon the clove curl, a letter which gave me much difficulty, and Edwinn mastered it faster than I, and earned much praise.

I was not an idiot, nor even slow as most peasants be, yet Edwinne merrily called me such, clapping me on the shoulder – whereby my jealousy and resentment grew luxuriant in my small body, for such remarks were manure to their soil, though meant in jest. He was two or three years older than me, and no different from other boys, who jape and jangle and pretend to bite like colts in a meadow; yet was I gnawed and rent.

Furthermore, Edwin did play the harp as if born to it, for not only were his fingers nimble, but he was merry, dry and airy of element, soon waxed to hot anger but also as swiftly cooled: and this is good nurture for minstrelsy. He had a great love for it and gladded with his playing whoever listened, though his voice was not as pretty as mine, and was less steadfast with the notes. I was earthern and moist; lacking both my parents, I would at times draw up the waters from the well of melancholy in my thirst for comfort. I discovered in the playing [of the harp] a door by which I might enter a walled garden

---

[151] Exodus 20.5: I have adapted the translation from the Wycliffite Bible (Bod. 959), c.1382.
[152] The cormorant.

enamelled with many brilliant hues, whose motley lustre was further polished by my fingers upon the strings and my singing voice, as a breeze shakes the aspen to silver.

My holy master preferred Edwyn's playing, for it gladded him more than mine. I redoubled my efforts, but was as the tortoise to the hare. I found grease upon the gut and even spotted upon the sounding board, for Edwynn would sup on fish we had netted and then play without washing his fingers; I told my master but he scolded me, saying I was not the father that chastiseth, and (laughing the while) said that I was as the strings of wolf-gut put into an harp with strings of sheep-gut, that then fret and corrupt and destroy the strings of sheep-gut, as wolves do destroy the flock.[153] And I threw down the harp and ran away over the sands, scrambling up the cliff like a goat, but heard no call or rebuke over the ceaseless surge.

Envy is a grievous sin, and corrupteth all: now I know that this truth is what my master meant: not that Edwine was the sheep and I the wolf, but that I was both sheep and wolf, the mild lamb of my soul slowly devoured by the wolf (or rather, the demon within) limb by limb, whose meaty breath is enough to sicken a man, as surely as a mouse is already paralysed by the stare of the owl. I became yet more sullen with my foster-mother, whose crooked spine and hairy arms did make me think she was beastly, though she was kind and seldom gave me blows; when she did so, blood always ran down from my nose, for her arms were like a blacksmith's. The slender arms of my departed mother, though strong also from field work, were like a scented lady's in comparison, and I would dream they were taking me in like a lamb to the fold.

[153] A further borrowing from Bartholomew, though the original observation is Pliny's.

4

In that other time, which then lay in the unknown future and now lies in the dim past, I was Muche the mortal sinner on the road to absolute perdition: though but a few years parted him from my innocence, yet might they have been a bottomless trench, so far and strange seemed my childhood!

I made but one attempt (of a kind) to escape, after the Lord had filled my mind with sudden contrition: this being the night before the holy day of [the Purification of] the Blessed Virgin.[154] In a dream I saw Richerd the glassworker in the form of an angel with goose-down wings and mantled all over in gold; his eyes were clear glass through which I peered (for this angel was very great) as into a window, or as the horse[155] in the buffoon's play. There I looked down upon a tumultuous feast partaken by heathen idolaters whose meat was the flesh of babes, and the blood even spattered the windows of the angel's eyes. One of those feasting there raised his look towards me, and beckoned me down: it was Hodd himself, with great leathern wings and black claws, his mouth smeared with the offal of innocents.

I woke in a sweat, vowing to leave instantly, as if my months of outlawry had been but a night in a dangerous inn. I had learned much about the felons' watch, and the ways of the wood, although I had not penetrated certain corners shielded by thickets or undergrowth: one lay not far behind my hut, and I crept out in the darkness with my harp and could hear the outlaws snoring or muttering in sleep,

---

[154] 2 February.
[155] In other words, as the man playing the front half of the hobby horse.

as if they were an army. Three of them remained awake about the glowing fire, with their bows at hand, as was the custom, murmuring to each other and jesting softly. My heart's spirit was being drawn out to nourish my fearful, weak brain with such a thudding that it might have turned their heads.

I waited, knowing that eyes are cumbered less with darkness as they catch more lines coming to them through its black vapour, though the beams of the moon (which was but a half) confused and were contrary through the bare branches, as though the Devil were directing its white form.

I flitted to the undergrowth without the crack of a twig, for the angel was with me and rendering me more light and fleet; but on finding the bramble-thicket impassable, and scrutinising a way about it, I heard the familiar peacock shriek – that was no peacock – and the answering by an owl, and knew that I had been descried! Foolishly I plunged away upon a near trail, clutching my harp close betwixt the weft of tree-limbs and gaining much ground in my nimbleness – until of a sudden a dark shape reared before me, arm upraised. Scarce did I know whether this being was human or demonic; and I should have turned to flee, but already I descried a cudgel descending, and raised my precious instrument as if it were a targe, without thinking, for we had practised much swordplay and staveplay – and thereupon the weapon struck the harp's sounding board a fearsome blow, splintering the very wood that had thus, along with an angel's wing, protected me from further hurt.

I was seized and taken back to my hut by the creature, who was in truth an ogre, but of a human type, being Littel John. He had destroyed my most precious device, but showed no remorse: he and Hod were rivals, and oft John found disagreement with the leader. Yet Hode allowed him to disagree, I knew not why!

For example, there was a pond or water-hole at the marge of the wood, that one day Litl[e] John looked into in his shagginess (as a great wild boar might while drinking), and said, with a gravity of voice: 'Ah, I see the divine essence face to face, that is greater than God.' And Hod burst out laughing, for in truth it was a mere childish [*ineptus*] echo of his own words. And Little John glared at him in hatred, and cast a stone to shatter the reflection like glass, but said nothing.

For several days I was confined to the hut, chained like a dog, yet not one word of rebuke, nor any word at all, was conveyed to me – neither was I cast into the dragon's pit. I knew not what Hode felt about his unworthy disciple, and feared meeting the same fate (or worse) as the tregetour or quack, whose bones I fancied I heard creaking in the long nights.

More likely was this the creaking of leather boots, for when I awoke I would find, each morning, the cadavers of woodland creatures laid inside the door, that served as a warning of what night-wrapt perils I might face, if I ventured out alone in such a wild place: these being adders and like venomous snakes; black spiders; a bag of beetles with mouth claws;[156] a giant tusked boar; a mangy wolf; and parts of other fearsome beasts such as I had never before seen: a griffin's head with a great, bloodied beak beside its claws like a lion's;[157] or the face of a savage animal much like a cat yet with sharpened teeth and worms in its eyes. There were also [left]: a bat with leathern wings; the head of a great, staring owl that caused me to cry out in terror and hide myself under my ragged blanket; and rats bigger even than those in the monastery's barn. I feared rats greatly, as others fear spiders or bears or imps.[158]

To think I might have been crawling among all these night terrors in that tangled waste, while the demons and spirits of the wood would likewise have [thronged?] . . . [*hiatus in the MS*]. A twisted branch was left, like an arm with a bony wrist and four fingers like boiled leather; and also a piece of birch bark in which the visage of a fiend could be discerned over a beard of ivy, waiting for the unwary to pass below.

---

[156] i.e. mandibles.

[157] This was no doubt an ordinary eagle's head or other bird of prey; the claws unlikely to have been a lion's. The medieval bestiary included many 'marvels' (*mirabilia*), that were a vestige of the folk or mythical tradition and reluctantly tolerated by the Church – whereas anything designated 'magical' was thoroughly condemned.

[158] The medieval fondness for both lists and minute detail is here perfectly illustrated. [**Additional note in margin in FB's hand: 'Inherited by the military'.**]

No more would I consider escaping, not even in the day! Thus, without a word spoken, was my courage and resolve vanquished.

I wept in the hut for my harp, though in truth I wept for my soul, knowing that the harp was stolen, and I the thief, and no repentance was now possible: for ever since I had stole the harp from my holy master the hermit (the which act I shall describe forthwith), keeping it with me over the years in the monastic house [of St Edmund's], I had thought it a mere borrowing, as money is borrowed, and one day I would return it secretly. This being as false an illusion as believing the sun doth not travel under the earth at night as under a rock, to conceal itself, but is swallowed by a great tortoise, or put out in the waters as a torch might be, to be rekindled each morning by God in His mercy! And now I knew also that the angel had deserted me, after shielding my head with his wing (for though the harp was shattered, it would not have saved me on its own); and I was alone with my contrition and shame.

Then on the fifth or sixth day, Hode entered my hut as if drunken, and began to beat me soundly with a stick as I lay, saying all the while that I was a traitor, and less to him than a snail that is crushed underfoot. And when I wailed in my terror, and admitted I had been tempted by my own miswandering desires away from the true path of Hodd, and pleaded forgiveness, he left off; and weeping from his protuberant eyes, he embraced me as his closest disciple, bidding me play to him as of old. 'I cannot,' I cried, my face swollen with bruises. And on asking why not, his lie-hating ears heard me say, 'My dear harp was broken when I was caught in my foolish escape.'

I said no more, wiping away the blood and tears painted upon my face by that false and horrible tyrant, just as the scar upon his brow was painted by a white-hot iron: for then and there did he describe to me, as to no other disciple, what was done to him for preaching (in the market-squares) of the freedom of the spirit of every man and woman: 'For this one truth among the world's innumerable falsities, I was punished as a heretic, by public branding. Alas, I smelt the burning of my own flesh under the pressed iron, little Moche. From thenceforth I vowed destruction upon the Church and its ministers, and that naught should remain of this letter [H], I burnt it anew with a stick from the fire.'

And he bid me touch it, which methinks sent further infection into me: for it felt as hot as a coal from Hell, and yet fatty and slippery as a leper's flesh.

On learning from others, the next day, of how the instrument had come to grief, Hode called John a rebel and a fool and other cursed names, upon which the giant took up his stave and threatened his leader in the clearing, which caused great consternation among the men, and that I spied on through the chinks in my hut's wall. 'Nay,' Johnne cried, 'thou art the fool, and being greater than God, thou art a greater fool than any!'

'Slay me then, for by doing so you might become an even greater fool than myself,' replied Hod; 'for without me nothing exists.' This was a most mysterious thing to say, and even silenced the others, who did believe Hodd in all things. Yet he raised a hand to stop them coming forward and restraining Lyttyl John as he stood warlike and threatening, like a champion in single combat, and so none laid a finger upon him. Then Hod, though without arms of any kind nor further words of rebuke, did cause the felon to cast away his stave, by gazing upon him from a head so fixed it might have been carved, in which his eyes sat prominently under the joined eyebrows.

As the basilisk slays by sight alone, so Hodd made men obey – though whether through fear or evil influence too subtle to detect, I do not know to this day. For strength is not only in muscle or arms or cruelness, but subtle influence. Methinks now that J[o]hn did not fear being torn limb from limb by the other felons (as would have happened), but was weakened by a beam like a moon's beam travelling from the gaze of the Arch-Devil, striking the crystal within his [John's] eye,[159] and thus causing grief also to the spirit.

[159] Cf. the following: 'In the middle of the eye . . . is a certain humour most pure and clear. The philosophers call it crystalloid, for it taketh suddenly divers forms and shapes as crystal doth.' (Trevisa's *Bartholomew*, Libra III, cap. xvii.)

For the rebel slunk away like a great wolf into his hut, where he sulked for several days, emerging only when the other outlaws implored him to join in a felony upon the high road, of which I also was ordered to be a part. As the man who kills another on board ship, is bound to the corpse and thrown into the deep, so my soul was bound to Robertt Hodd's by evil deed.

Nor could the few drops of holy water in my lead amulet save me, since I did not seek to be saved. Only by a great lesson could I be shaken out of my peril. The destruction of my instrument ought to have plunged me into a misery that was nigh to despair, and likewise the understanding that I was a prisoner of Hode's will; but instead – puffed up by his devilish words concerning my great worth and future distinction – I became a lover of transgressions, and a despiser of all things holy and good.

As a spirited boy entering into manhood, without a father or mother to guide me, I was easy prey to such flattery and guile, like a vagabond youth [*juvenis*][160] eager to be dubbed a knight, afore tasting battle.

Yet e'en my very first master, seethed in holiness and fasting, had been such a youth, thrown upon the world like myself, and prey to all temptations. For one day, when seated in the sea-cave (I was seven or eight), I asked the hermit about his former life. And it was this account that came to me most hauntingly, after Hod had revealed himself a branded heretic.

'I was the son of a disinherited knight of pure Norman lineage, but dissolute temperament. Being orphaned at ten after a calamity in which a fire destroyed my home and only I, of the entire household, fled alive, I became a vagabond.' I was much surprised, being innocent of the world, but the hermit went on: 'I was adopted by a drunken innkeeper and his malicious wife. After much misery and many blows from the pair's fists, a morning came when I heard from the yard a great noise outside like the hissing of steel in a blacksmith's trough,

[160] Although *juvenis* in classical times referred to men or women between twenty and forty.

and saw thousands approaching the town in a tumult of songs and shouts, calling on the people to liberate the Holy Lands: the mob was of all ages, but reunited in poverty.

'I ran after them, determined to go over the sea,[161] and on the way through Francia and through the great mountains to the sweltering deserts of Spaigne, the pilgrims hanged or put many Jews to the sword who refused the divinity [of Christ], stubbornly remaining the soldiers of Antichrist, as be their wont; I, however, took no part in these killings, for the Jews erred in ignorance when they brought Jesus to the Cross, and even now they are blind, not knowing what they do.'

He told me that only a handful [of the crusaders] survived, for when those that had not succumbed on the way from fevers came to the sea,[162] they believed they would walk upon it fully clad, and instead did summarily drown in the waves. And I asked him, in my ignorance (looking out upon our northerly waves), if he had seen Noah's Ark upon the mountain, not knowing then that it is to be found in the mountains of [Ar]menia, far beyond the Spaynish sea; and he caressed my hair and said: 'Not only did I see it, but I heard the first stroke of Noah's axe, for it is said that all the world heard it.' And I was amazed, for I was but an ignorant child.

'I returned home the next year,' he said, 'and was lodged with a wealthy relative in Wyndesore, who had somehow learned of my plight. These were happy years, even when I was tortured with headaches and deathly visions, for in my bedroom I had a feather bed and a fine *shewer*,[163] and upon my trenchers lay choice meat, even grapes. And here it was that I discovered by chance this harp, lying in a room unplucked. And mending its broken wolf-gut, and bidding a local minstrel tune it and teach me his skills, I became very adept.

'At the age of eighteen I went to Oxenford and studied law. I lived with three other clerks down a damp, ramshackle alleyway near the river, noisome with the loading and unloading of boats, for my wealthy

---

[161] i.e. to Palestine.
[162] Presumably at the Straits of Gibraltar.
[163] A looking glass (for it 'shews'; a 'mirror' is so called only when curved).

foster-father had died, and his widow was grasping and cared not a fig for her adopted son.'

The saintly hermit my teacher, shame yet colouring his face, then related how his heart had been stirred by a certain young woman (married to a goldsmith of mature years), and how she tore his flesh with goads of lust by promising that she should remain in his power for ever (though she was already married), for his young body pleased her greatly;[164] and hers likewise pleased him, for she was the comeliest in the city, if not the whole realm.

Once or twice he came to her in the guise of an intimate lady friend, dressed in a lady's gown and a shirt sewn with two fine sleeves that he had stolen from his foster-mother; and he sported upon his head a pair of long fair tresses, braided and worn in a net, and covered his face with a veil, that no one might know him save the true lady, whose red mouth he had already pressed as a man, and now pressed as a woman, though he was none such; and he enjoyed the pleasure of her body under her carmine mantle and had his will of her pointed breasts, mistaking a lover's bliss upon the mattress for the eternal bliss of the Lord's mercy.[165]

Then one day amidst all this carnality and youthful foolishness the future hermit heard voices, and was visited by the Virgin Mary, Mother of Mercy and Shamefastness, who stretched forth her arm and bid him seek out a wild, isolated place and tend to the mystery of the Word. And so terrified was he by this vision, that he left Oxenforde there and then, taking only his harp, and after the careless life of a ragged minstrel, came to a monastic house near Yve,[166] where he told the brothers of his vision, and thereupon they persuaded him to take the cowl. After some years, he became conscious that a zeal for God was lacking among the brothers, who wished to build a lofty stone tower to their church, venally wringing money from the

---

[164] This familiar situation was later to be addressed by Chaucer in 'The Merchant's Tale'.
[165] It seems odd (at least to our modern sensibilities) that this frank account should have been related to a young boy, who when he finally left the hermit was still only nine or ten.
[166] St Ives in Cornwall.

rich and the poor alike that their tower might come nearer to God, when as my master thought it: 'Its weathercock might more likely touch the black hairs of the Devil's left hoof, than the soles of Our Eternal Father.'

Then began a wandering, mendicant [*mendicam*]¹⁶⁷ life through many sweltering summers and many bitter winters that led at last to our village, where he came *forwandred.*¹⁶⁸

I believed his story – why should I not have done? – and would often imagine him in these earlier years before he cropped his head and became a hermit. Yet so differing were his two lives, that it was hard for me to see them as belonging to one man, for children seldom care for the past, that is swiftly decayed to them, though it be but a month ago.

Indeed, the two lives were as different as mine own, for I had once been in the midst of God's influence, whether in the sea-arrayed hermitage or the quiet-aisled abbey; and was now cast into the wastes of wickedness, as if cloven from mine own past. For this small wood had become my complete world, and the Lord seeing fit to send us a season of sunlight and soft showers that spring, our wild place was much beautied, and its great trees and lees of grass and fragrant herbs beguiled me further and deeper into its rough ways, wherein many tiny demons and imps lurked and winked as poisonous as toadstools in clefts of boles and under stones, and in the movement of the verdure.

And much pleasure I had in swordplay, staveplay and archery, e'en when bloodied, for I was a quick learner; and soon the two-handed sword was swift in my grasp, though it be weighted like a blacksmith's hammer. The frequent climbing of trees made me nimble, and so skilled is the Devil that he can stir our vital spirits and animate our blood with such exercise, neglecting our reason, and make us think we are content. Furthermore, like any proud knight, I had my own

---

¹⁶⁷ Literally begging rather than as a friar seeking alms, as the Dominicans only came to England in 1221.
¹⁶⁸ Spent with wandering.

horse from the outlaws' stable, a dappled rouncy granted to me on Hodde's orders – upon which I soon learned to ride as well as any man, though being thrown twice for the beast was restless.

Without a saddle or harness but only on the rough hair did I ride, and always accompanied by a pair of felons on their swifter mounts lest I attempt to flee over the heathland, though such a hot thought never entered my heart. And out of some forty horses in the wood, that were stabled in simple shelters on the easterly edge and well provendered with stolen oats and hay, making a stink through the trees as of a wealthy town, was added an unbroken colt of great promise, snatched from a meadow belonging to my former abbey. And one of the outlaws by the name of John Cardinall broke it skil-fully over many days, that it became tame as a lamb.[169]

So familiar to me did the leech's poor dangling bones become, I ceased to see them as horrible, and e'en when innocent wayfarers were slain on the road (for putting up foolish resistance or hallooing too loud), I felt it only as a soldier might feel the loss of an enemy in battle or siege. How weak my defences were, to crumble so fast! How inconstant our loyalty and faith to the spotless, all-powerful Lord! Yet He lets us sin, for we are free in our will – not being dumb beasts of the field, but as frisky in our hearts as a neighing colt.

Many times in the preceding winter months, before the cuckoo or the turtle-dove were calling for their mates, and only the jay's scorn [*contemptus*] sounded[170] in the lifeless cold, Hodde had bid me play to him in his hut. He would preach to me between songs in his usual manner, that I found sweeter than before, as poison is oft disguised by honey; though his import was preposterous. And filled with wonder at his impenetrable wisdom, I had allowed my ears to become the corrupter of my soul. Now my harp was broken, he called me less, yet still I knew by certain words that I was especially chosen, and his most resplendent and gifted disciple: thus giving my morsel of a life, of no more worth than a scrap of crust thrown to the ground, some bountiful reason to be.

[169] It is unclear whether this is the same 'rouncy' that has just been referred to.
[170] Cf. Chaucer's 'the scornynge jay' in *The Parliament of Fowls*, l. 346.

And though we ate salted meat from the bluff's caves – for scores of stolen bucks, harts, cattle and sheep had been salted and stored there before the winter – it seemed to me of the freshest and choicest kind; and so also did I indulge in the evil of intoxicants of the type that sometimes led to drunken blows between my companions, and foul oaths under the trees, for most revelous were the outlaws; yet fornication of the flesh was not yet permitted me, on pain of mutilation, though I was oft set to guard the palace of the women.

Polluted as I was, I had not yet seen a robbery, save the one of which I was the victim. We set off for the highway, that lay some four miles to the east, on a morning of blustery wind that had pushed away the clouds, and the night's rain lay all a-glitter upon the herbiage and on the blear wastes of heath: riding on my steed to the rear of the fifteen or so felons, speaking merrily with them, a sword at my side and a bow on my back, a clutch of barbed arrows in my belt and a cloth wrapped about my neck that I might draw it up to hide my face, I was truly 'Muche' the outlaw, and not mine old and better self.

The wily and cunning Arch-Satan rode in front on his fine black Spanish destrier[171] worth above £40, with its large nostrils and good wind that permitted him swiftly to depart the scenes of his crimes. He had promised me that one day soon I would have not only as fine a mount but also a resplendent harp, to be taken from a baron's castle by his own hand. Thus we are beguiled on the road to Hell by satiating visions and golden promises, by a feast laid out upon a table draped by samite and brocade of Bagdad, assailing our nostrils with scents of cardamum, honey and cloves – but which banquet (when bitten into) crumbles to dust, to the very last muscat-nut or morsel of jellied quince. For what was Robbert Hod but a simple horse thief, worthy only of the rope, or to hang in chains at a crossway?

We passed Salise and lurked in the bushes along the highway called Watlinge Strete, the same that brother Thomas and I had been taken

---

[171] A war horse, the highest class of mount. £40 sterling is the equivalent of about £700 in our own day (1921).

upon, and near that very spot where it comes up onto the heath at Barnesdayle[172] towards Dancaster. The melancholy felon called Will Scarelacke, of very moist humours and yellow skin, and always weeping in one eye, lay in wait beside me. He made a fitting companion for the balance of humours: I was exceeding dry and airy and excited, for my melancholy had been thinned, as if sieved by this manly, woodland life.

We knew there to be a convoy ripe for picking: three rumbling waggons laden with silk stuffs for the milliners of the town, a fourth carrying choice French wine, a mule with a full barrel of salt strapped to its back, and a small cart loaded with well-stitched leather harness for the [coming] tournament; while accompanying the carts (though not of them) was the Bishop [of York]'s man with a payment of gold about him from the palace at Yorke. How Hode knew these things to the last detail was through the speaking flashes of glass, that also told him of the travellers' progress; for we did not wait upwards of an hour before the waggons appeared on the brow, after the carriers' whistles to the horses upon the steep hill were carried to us first by the blusters of wind.

At the last [moment], it seemed, there had been added a guard, for the convoy was flanked by six or seven men indistinguishable in their countenance from ruffians, on bony chestnut cobs, and armed with long swords. Each of these was grappled easily off his mount by two felons who leapt out of the bushes – a skilled manoeuvre much rehearsed in the trees. One corpulent guard made the error of resisting – wounding the horse breaker, John Cardinall – and was soon guzzling upon an arrow piercing his throat almost to the fletchings, that had flitted from the bushes; the others (save one) were dragged into these bushes and stripped, and made to flee for their lives over the bare heath in nothing but their shirts. The one guard remaining, whom I recognised as a felon recently absent, was laughing

[172] See my previous note on the local topography. Both 'Salise' (Sayles) and Watling Street are mentioned in *A Gest of Robyn Hode* (as, of course, are Much and 'Will Scarlock').

at his ruse: he had greased the company's stirrups in the town stables with mutton fat, that the men's feet kept slipping, giving rise to many choice oaths.[173]

A frightened young cob had struck out behind and felled an outlaw, whose companion thereupon pierced the poor beast with his sword. Will Scarlack and myself had seized the mule with the barrel of salt, while the others had done likewise with the silks and the wine. The carters and drivers offered no resistance, nor did two well-dressed citizens – a fair-haired damsel and her elderly male companion, who were travelling without encumbrance of baggage among the carts. John Cardin[al] was pouring blood from his thigh as from a jug, and blaspheming at it; while the hoof-struck felon was insensible, his skull nigh cloven.

All this taking place among a great medley of shouts and cries and whinnyings, I yet heard no distinguishable words, for my ears were buzzing with excitement, and my heart pounding. The Devil had filled me with a sweet sense of glorious adventure that was yet heedless of caution; failing to pull my cloth mask over my face, my features were seen in full, though spattered horribly by the road's mud.

The pack saddles [*clitellae*] of our pack horses and sumpter-mules were loaded with the captured goods and departed for the camp, the whiles our prisoners were led away until out of sight and earshot of the bloodied roadway; and I accompanied them as their guard, with other felons. There our captives were tied one to the other and sat upon the heath grass between the furze that grew thick around, pleading for their lives; while the Bishop of Yorke's man was struck many times with one of the driver's whips, until his head was sorely cut and the blood soaked his tunic: for the outlaws did especially detest bishops. He whimpered like a hound, the gold spilling from his purse as Philyp stabbed it with his dagger, that their contents might fatten a bag held proudly by myself.

[173] This would also, presumably, have made their unseating easier, and rendered them less in control of their mounts.

I had eyes not for this lustrous hoard, that to the Lord Our God is always but filthy excrement when compared to the gold of His eternal glory, but for the fair sample of young womanhood on her bay palfrey, of no more than sixteen or seventeen years; her tender white skin was flushed with fear, as her eyes of a startling bluish-grey [*glaucitatis*][174] looked about in bewilderment under her smooth brow, yet ever turning away from the bloodied victim of our ire. Love stole into my young heart and pushed out all other senses, and I became its loyal simpleton. As the wasteland's thorns and wild roses were in flower, and the morning sun alighted upon us at that very moment between high clouds, the pitiful spectacle was transformed into one of a delicious sweetness. For God of truth she was fair!

The man I took to be her father or uncle, whose mild and scholarly appearance had not deterred the outlaws from unseating him from his saddle, had not been further injured and was permitted to remain on foot beside the damsel. Hodde rode hard towards us from the road, eyes alight after the devilish work, and spoke in his usual preaching manner to the terrified prisoners; these understanding no more of what he was saying about the divine essence and the *othaire* than they might a Frenchman or a German. As Robeytt Hodde's reputation was exceeding broad, and included unspeakable acts of cruelty such as the gouging out of eyes, or the cutting off of feet (though these might have been exaggerated),[175] and no other man so dominated the area as he did (not even the abbot or the sh[e]rif), they were eager to show compliance: thus tyrants rule by fear alone.

[174] Recognised by Roger Bacon in the thirteenth century as one of the five essential colours.

[175] Such horrors were vouchsafed by the general violence of the age, when even the law in most countries practised torture and prolonged execution; two of the acts cited occur in the Old French thirteenth-century romance *Eustace the Monk* (*Wistasse li Moine*, Bibl. Nat., 1553, fols 325v–338v.). The whole passage is an interesting indication of the impunity with which powerful bandits acted in a period with no proper police force, and in which the law itself was swayed by vested local interests.

Hod then turned in his saddle to the fair maiden, and I saw his eyes gluttonously feasting upon her beauty beneath the wimple[176] of fine linen; his lips moving with soft, private words to her, his fingers were laid lasciviously upon her wrist below the buttons,[177] and I witnessed them prodding under her glove. Her guardian stepped between the two in protest, only to be swept aside like a ragged curtain by the outlaw's hand, sheathed in its fine fingerless leather that seemed stitched to the skin. Whereupon the old fellow lost his footing and lay prostrate upon the heath's meagre grass.

We roared with laughter, for the man was a venerable fool, with white stubble and lean neck, and his smell was of fish three days old. See how pitiless I had become! In truth my heart was filled with jealousy, that my master had touched that beauteous flesh. I had seen her flinch, and pull her member away and tremble all over, though this sight failed to dint the fattening demon of jealousy within. Tears moistened her flushed cheeks as she regarded the poor old man upon the ground, nursing his face with its bloodied nose; yet never (at this time) did I question the vileness of my master's actions, not even the meanest, for I was flush with pride at being a member of the elect.[178]

A peacock's shrill cry sounded, which being a warning that unwanted company had been spotted on the highway a good mile off (even though these may have been simple wayfarers and not the sheriff's men), Hod bid us through clenched teeth to take the maiden prisoner. We all sped away with our prize, leaving the old man tied up weeping among the carters in that blear wasteland, till some passing shepherd or pedlar take mercy upon them, hearing their cries; or mayhap one among them contrive to gnaw away the tough rope. For

[176] 'A band usually of linen which covered the neck, and was drawn up over the chin, strained up each side of the face, and generally fastened across the forehead.' (W. W. Skeat, *The Student's Chaucer*, 1897, p. 125.)
[177] Thirteenth-century sleeves were usually buttoned tight from elbow to wrist.
[178] I witnessed the same strange phenomenon, whereby perfectly decent men can become cruel or even savage in their obedience to higher authority, in the miserable conditions of the late war.

there being nothing tilled there, they could not hope for a Jack the peasant to untie them.

And thus was I dubbed this day a worthy outlaw, merry as could be.

5

A few days after the robbery, walking with him alone one morning on the marge of the wood, in the company only of crows cawing above us, I enquired of R[o]b[e]rt Hod what was to become of the grey-eyed maiden. 'We shall offer a mass for the Blessed Virgin,' he said; this being oft his manner, that a blasphemous wit might deflect enquiry. And so might a fox be seen to be grinning while leaving the hen coop, his mouth well bloodied (a sight witnessed by me only a week ago, snow fresh upon the ground, while I limped in my drear old age about our abbey's outer court).

And then seizing my hair, he drew me close to him and said that were he to couple with the damsel in the manner of a dog,[179] and then drown her after in the foul swamp of filth that was our camp's cess-pit beyond the stables, that would perforce be no sin, for the only sin is to believe that the elect of the sea of the divine essence can indeed sin.

I paled, sickened by the thought, and began to weep while uttering no sound. Yet it was not the pain of his grip, that tore a clutch of hair from my scalp, that caused my tears, but the crazed love I felt for the girl, whose look alone had dragged my heart through its portals, and conquered my reason. Thus do women madden us with their beauty, a beauty that is relished by the serpent Satan.

---

[179] An abuse punishable, according to canon law (even within marriage), by ten days fasting on bread and water (see, for example, the eleventh-century *Decretum* of Burchard of Worms).

Then Hodd released my hair and laughed, saying that the girl had not been touched in any wise, for she was to be his virgin bride. Astonied, I said, 'How is this to be?' And he replied (speaking like a quack),[180] that a message had come from the *othur* on the night air, carried by the goddess that is the Mother Earth, though in the form of a bat. This bat entering his temple (meaning by this, his simple hut lined by birch bark), addressed the one who continually spins all of Creation from his bowels (namely, the 'free spirit' of himself), that he must conjoin with her of the grey eyes; for this damsel, and not Mary Mother of God in her heavenly spotlessness, was the true Virgin.

Setting his hood over his scalp, lest (as I secretly thought it) a crow stab at his heretic's brow-sign, he added: 'She was sent for this very purpose on the sea of the divine essence, like the loveliest of ships.' I asked, feigning delight, though my heart was a plumbstone in a well: 'Prithee, master, when shall the nuptials be?' To my surprise, for I had not thought him serious, he answered, 'Upon the next solstice.'

Alas, such obsolete dates do heathens and heretics ignorantly take as significant, while ignoring saints' days such as the Feast of St Valentine or St John's Eve, or even Pentecost or Good Friday, and other hallowed marks upon the calendar that guide our gaze upward and not down into the trodden mire.

'Thereupon the cup's measure will be full,' he continued, with eyes very prominent and shining under his false cowl, 'and the end of days be accomplished, for we are near to the very rim. Paradise, separated from us by the upper sea, and too long a journey for the span of a man's life – the last stretch being all frozen ice – shall be conjoined likewise with Mother Earth, after all those who are not free in spirit have been burned by a great fire. All this shall happen at one hour after midnight on the day of our marriage. Believe me, little Moche, for nothing is but what is ordained, and I ordaineth all

---

[180] An obscure reference to the common use by medieval doctors of startlingly pagan incantations when administering medicines. See my entry 'Leechcraft and the Great Mother', in *A History of Medicine*, 1913, vol. I, p. 217.

things even when my right hand knoweth it not; and the world shall be full consumed in the time of *halve a milewey*.'[181]

And so fierce and powerful was his look, aided by a sudden gust that smacked against the wood's edge, flinging the crows upwards like blown ash, that I shuddered from fear of the purifying fire but a few months off: for the hermit and even brother Thomas would also say that our measure was full to the brim, and our age was the last, as senescence be in a single life.

In truth, I had not seen the grey-eyed maiden since she had been taken to the Nonnerie, lamenting her fate in weeping, after the robbery on the highway some days before. It was told me by the wounded John Cardynel, rank with a stink of verdegris[182] and his leg very swollen, that he had been tended by one of the women, who had (though a rough bawd) strong skills in healing: 'The damsel being held for ransom, is an exceeding annoyance to them; for she ever complains, bewailing her fate or falling into a sulk. And since she has arrived – no felon being allowed into the Noneryye for fear she might be misused, but authorised only to know a woman in the trees without, well guarded by a companion – 'tis very vexing to the bawds among them, for the rough woodland floor doth prick their posterior flesh!' He recounted other tales, of a more indecent than amatory nature, that I feigned enjoyment of.

I was appointed to guard the hut on the fifth or sixth day; and during my watch I heard the murmuring of women within, most like turtle-doves, and their shadows flitting beyond the wattle fence when they came out of their prison, and my mind was moaning, 'Ey, therein lies my love!' No watchman was permitted to enter the gate, for not only was any visit by a felon to be authorised by our leader, but no guard must risk being tempted or overpowered by female wiles. This glimpse goaded me further, as the sweet smell of apples or plums, more than the full sight of them, must tempt a boy to scale a wall.

---

[181] As in MS: a standard medieval measurement of time, in which time and space are mingled. A 'mileway' is twenty minutes – the time it takes to walk a mile. 'Half a mileway' is therefore ten minutes.
[182] A common, strong-smelling salve for wounds.

And it is well known how lascivious knights crave to break down the door of a true nunnery, when the open bawdy-house is but two streets away! Thus are we the honeycomb for the demons' busy offices, diligent as wasps in our cells.

I understood by Hodde's awful reply that I must conceal my ardour from him, and henceforth e'en took to ignoring the filthy offal that frequently spewed from my companions' mouths, lest they think me eager for carnal relations. Being fourteen or fifteen, the sap of manhood was yet rising in me, with all its temptations to stray even further from the righteous path: though I was already lost in the thickets and drear wastes of evil ways.

At night, when I lay sleepless, the damsel appeared to me as the Virgin Mary would appear before I fell into heresy: yet the present lady was in a less decent form, and tempted me to sin, leaving foul traces. As many a novice monk doth grow to wakefulness and weakness from such indiscretion, putting into peril his body and soul until saved by the succour and counsel of his companions, so was I engulfed in solitary vice: yet none there was to save me, nor any confession to be made.[183]

Tormented by the damsel, who was locked up as in a tower until the solstice of warm June, when she was to become my master's bride, I took part in robberies upon the highway, as though engaged on tremendous exploits in distant lands or faerie realms – like those I had once sung of, singing to my previous masters most sweetly over my nimble fingers that were now softened, alack, no longer calloused by the wolf-gut – for the harp was so [broken as to be unmendable?],[184] even by the most skilful carpenter among us. Truly, I sorrowed that I was without my instrument at the very time I became lovelorn, and might have poured the honey of song over the vile prison in which those bluish-grey eyes were shut fast amongst defilement.

---

[183] So similar is this in word and content to an anecdote in the thirteenth-century Preacher's Manual of Etienne de Bourbon (*Anecdotes Historiques*, etc., d'Etienne de Bourbon, ed. A. Lecoy de la Marche, 1877, p. 198), that one assumes the book was familiar to the author.
[184] The words judiciously obscured by a stain.

And if my new master was speaking true? Satan whispered thus in my ear, even as I rode out to rob and ambush (though not yet kill), or practised my bowmanship, or clattered my stave against another's.

Breaking my nose during the last pastime, and fearful of being blemished (for it is the fairest member), I set it straight again with great suffering that my visage be not defouled. Yet deeper fouling was doing its mischief. Loading hay for the stables, or cutting wood, or increasing my skills in horsemanship, I was much invigorated [*corroboratus*] in body, but this drew vital spirits from my head and my mind weakened; thus I began to consider whether Hod might indeed be following in truth's footsteps, just as the Lord Jesus Christ did.

Mayhap his powers are indeed very great, I thought (or rather, the Devil slipped into my enfeebled mind and caused me to think); and if they say that those thousands who scorned Christ for a false prophet do now burn eternally in liquid fire, then who is to say that those who scorn Robertt Hodd, calling him a wretched felon and thief and murderer, be not equally mistook?

Then it was but a small leap to considering, with brother Edward's type of chopping logic, that if Hode be true, Christ be false, and thereby not a single heathen, Jew or heretic be burning at all; for if the Church and its teachings be but a great palace of pasteboard, and even Hell-fire a painting upon a board, to strike terror to dumb peasants and children [with their mouths] agape in the square . . . [*matter erased*].

And so I reckoned that if Hode's voice was a jug of bronze, pouring out wisdom from its lip,[185] I was indeed a great fellow bound (as his disciple) for vast powers, thrust into the world for a reason so far hidden, as St Peter was, or St Luke. Pride is the worst sin, and tooketh me by the throat in the heart of the outlaws' wood. And it is my contention now, at the extreme marge of my life (so long unwinding its thread), that there is great peril in living amongst natural growing

[185] Only the finer houses used metal vessels, which were otherwise of wood or pottery; the wooden bowls (judging from the extremely rare survivals) most beautifully fashioned.

things, instead of staying within that which is built by man in praise of God: for nature is fallen and the very leaves measled with Adam's sin, her ground infected with snakes and crawling beasts of disgusting appearance, feasting on the rottenness that Heaven itself knoweth not – for nothing there [in Heaven] falleth with the cold but is eternally ripe and green in the balmy air, and without night. Yea, 'tis better to seek the very rim of the land, where all is naught but rock, sand and endless-seeming ocean, as did the founding fathers of this our great abbey, and also my first saintly master the hermit, to live as though upon the very portal of everlasting life, in utmost purity, far from the leaf-sodden mire of the forest, or the town's stench.

Many hundreds of feckless young men, I hear, do now find solace in the woods of this or that baron or lord, fleeing the evils of the city or their own misdeeds; and some spurred – alas! – by the wretched progeny of my minstrelsy, do e'en dress in green and call themselves '*Roberdesmen*' or '*Robbinsmen*'! Though that be play-acting compared to our true outlaw life, which was as cruel and hard and wretched, in truth, as any hovel-dweller burning charcoal, and scarce redeemed by our plunder: many were the outlaws with gout in their limbs from dampness, that sometimes slew them with its frosted sword. The times are dangerous, therefore, if the fashion be for forest-dwelling, or sleeping in waste places thick with imps and demons, or e'en travelling to the sinister haunts of witches and sorcerers and pagans (and similar human servants of the Devil), such as giant rings or circles of stones – wherein the common folk go to be cured of their maladies, hideously mistaking that cold rock for the warm mercy of the Lord.[186]

I wondered further, that if (in Hode's reckoning) no lost souls be burning or suffering torments and pinchings as though their flesh be ever warm, then where do the dead resideth? Remembering what he had told me – that the dead join the sea of the divine essence, losing their bodies and scattering e'en the atoms of their souls; and

---

[186] This suggests, rather remarkably, that stone circles such as Avebury or Stonehenge were regarded as having the same kind of healing properties as saints' relics, and may even have been the object of secret 'pilgrimage' in an age when folk magic jostled persistently and no doubt dangerously with orthodox beliefs.

that there is no torment, nor fear of the after-life, and therefore no sin save awareness of sin – I found comfort in this, just as I had found comfort in my two previous masters, taking off and putting on their dress and colours as though I was but a child playing at tournaments or joustings.

In my manifold ignorance, however, I was all but the worst of heretics, applauded by Satan and his fiends. *Terrible confession!*[187]

Then the idea passed through me, with a great shudder, that I might slay Hod and see if all Creation dissolveth; although he once told me that were he indeed to die, he would become a shadow within all created matter, ever more powerfully subtle, and that he cared not a clove of garlic for his life. But horribly I pleased myself to think that if he were dead, he would not marry, in his flesh, the grey-eyed damsel! And so tormented was I, that I ground my teeth and suffered sleeplessness, and my face went unwashed like the most servile beggar. 'You look indeed like one of us,' said Phylip, though my face was not yet scarred and bludgeoned by accident or violence, and my tongue was not yet so foul with oaths as theirs.

One morning when again guarding the Noneryye, and seized by desire, I scribbled foolish words of love with a burnt stick upon white birch bark, [addressing it] to: 'The damsel with the bluish-grey eyes', and slipped the morsel under the wattle fence, believing she could read simple letters. Soon I heard high laughter, of a mocking sort, and regretted my action. One of the women, of a most vicious appearance from her forbidden trade [*negotia illicita*] beyond the camp, and smelling like a dunghill as do all bawds beneath their perfumes and decay,[188] then came to the fence where I was posted and bid me lower my ear to a chink [in the fence], for she bore a word from my sweetheart.

Foolishly, I did as instructed and received the word directly, alack-a-day! – for she thrust her hole [against the wattle] and let off a noise like thunder from her hinder parts, filling the air with a foul stench

[187] This last is a marginal interpolation in an approximately sixteenth-century hand, Hand A.

[188] This is a common exaggeration of medieval misogyny and not to be understood literally.

and saying after, 'Thus doth thy sweetheart love thee, my goodly knight! Daf thou art, to tilt at such a targe!'[189]

Then a message came, on the following week, that a great sum of gold was to be paid by the father, in return for the damsel's release. It must be set down here that our retinue did include several wastrel sons of the nobility, though not of the highest barons, but of the middling sort; and that these retained links with certain important members of the towns thereabout (even unto Yorke), that were of a corrupt nature.[190]

One felon of this sort named Ralph, while of handsome appearance, possessed a withered hand of great ugliness; he, being an ungovernable boy, had thrust [this hand] into the heat of the hearth when aged five, for a childish wager, half consuming it in the flames. It looked very like a peacock's rivelled foot; and like a peacock, that sees the foulness of its feet and lets fall its wondrous feathers in shame,[191] Raph was very ashamed of it, and covered it with his sleeve. He it was who brought the news of the ransom, and swiftly bruiting it abroad among us (for our leader was shut away in his temple-hut like a soothsayer, receiving visions), we grew excited. Verily, this gold was but small change for the father, an exceeding rich merchant of Notyngham, who wished to grant[192] his lovely daughter to an elderly baron of great influence at court – whose name I dare not even now divulge, for they say his offspring are as cruel and cunning and lecherous as he was, being of the same corrupt blood.

The deadline being but three hours, before this aforesaid baron had sworn by God to send a mighty force as great as his had been against the infidel, to wipe us out amidst horrible tortures and executions (this baron having the king's ear), Litel John went straight away to his general; only to find him snoring and nigh insensible, plunged

---

[189] Cf. Chaucer's 'The Miller's Tale'.

[190] Traditionally, Robin Hood's 'merry men' were of yeomen stock; the presence of disaffected minor nobility (apart from 'bad eggs', this might include younger sons unwilling to join the Church) does not, however, conflict with the documentary evidence.

[191] Cf. Bartholomew.

[192] Not necessarily in marriage, alas. King John, for instance, was a notorious borrower of his nobles' womenfolk. By such means men still think to gain influence and power.

into a deep sleep by the effects of the [intoxicant] soup, of which he had took many draughts, mingled with the fine Rhenish wine captured on the highway, by which he was oft diseased with the headache after.

Littel John took command then, saying, 'Ay, let her be given back in the presence of twenty of us, fully armed, upon the point known as *Hoddes Stone*,'[193] as was oft done with lesser ransoms paid.

So, like a turtle-dove let out of its cage, and without Hodde's knowledge or approval, the damsel was led away between the strongest felons, while the remaining number guarded the wood carefully all abouts, lest this be a trap to lure the main force away.

And thus I watched my *amorette* depart from the trees upon her bay palfrey, that I was sore envious of – e'en for the touch of her pretty feet on either flank.[194] She was surrounded by felons like a pearl within the roughest of shells, and I did crave my harp. Her face was indeed the colour of pearl, and her locks as yellow as a blackbird's beak, and her small mouth likewise lustrous, moistened by her free-flowing tears, that made her eyes to shine like crystal as they looked about; yet she espied not her young adorer sitting in a fresh-greening tree with his bow, though I waved my hand at her, for either the air did not bring the likeness of me to her, or her sight was cumbered by the tears' moisture, or her wit was too destroubled. And all about us the primerole was a-flower in such great abundance, seeming as though covering the greenwood floor in gold for her departure, that they minded not if her horse's step crushed them.

My heart was heavy, but also I was in great fear, for when Hode waketh from his drunken slumber, he must be furious to find his Virgin gone, that was his future spouse. Only I knew, as his principal confidant, of this matter of sacred marriage, yet said nothing to Litt[le] John, whom I feared as much as I feared Hode. What must he do, when he findeth her flown, that was to be his own blasphemous substitute for the spotless Virgin we are all betrothed to in spirit? He must tear me from limb to limb, as the one too cowardly to explain.

[193] There is mention of 'a stone of Robin Hood' in a 1422 Chartulary of Monkbretton Priory (erroneously dated 1322), to the east of the Great North Road some four miles south of Wentbridge, probably identical to the present-day 'Robin Hood's Well'.
[194] Strange as it may seem, women rode astride until the late fourteenth century.

Thus I approached Litylle Joh[n], on his return with a great amount of ransom in a purse of gold coins, worth some £400,[195] and told him directly what our leader had planned. The giant felon, closing his lower lip over his upper lip in deep and effortful thought (for Hode said his rival's brain seemed lacking in vital spirits that were drawn on overmuch by the demands of his huge shoulders and limbs), said to me that a flash of lightning had struck the Nonnerye, and changed the damsel into a bag of gold, leaving a circle of burnt earth: and certainly then I understood, for I had seen a felon go to the Nonerrye with a lit torch.

When Hodde awoke as though from death, with a face all red like a harlot's painted with lead and vinegar, he emerged from the temple-hut of birch with fresh visions: one being that his head had been cleaved in two and his brain replaced with one of silver, pearls and gold by a comely maiden in a meadow of flowers, that now his brain was exceeding brilliant and precious, of the value of £400. And this striking the men as extraordinary, for it seemed to reflect what had truly occurred (in the way supernatural dreaming doth), they fell to a murmuring like bees.

And Littl John, much astonished, took Hodde aside and said unto him: 'You have dreamed aright, and as things must be.' Hod did not understand, and looked at him blearily; then John recounted to him, not in the way we had agreed upon, though the earth had been burned with a circle, but only the truth: for he was much a-frighted by this reported dream, and did not care for lying and dissembling.

And Hode nodded calmly at this news, saying, 'You have swapped her for filthy lucre's sake, Johnne. She will return at the solstice, for it is written in my dream; I did see, after she had replaced my brain, the phoenix above my head. After it is burned to ashes, it becometh a worm in three days, that soon waxeth to a bird of the same great beauty. This meaning that in three months, when day burns equal with the night [on the solstice], she will appear again, for we are one and have no mate; for how can we have a mate, being one in essence, as indistinguishable as two drops gendered in the same sea?'

[195] Worth, at present-day prices (1921), about £7,000.

Lityle John muttered, and bit his lip that it ran blood; so Hodde said: 'You close like the oyster against me, but I am the crab, that awaits patiently for the oyster to open [its shell] and then puts a stone to hinder the closing of it, that he may devour and gnaw the oyster's flesh.'

For H[o]dde was truly in a great rage and sorrow, but hid all of it like a monk concealing apples in his great sleeves during Tierce, to nibble upon, that do in truth hold wasps inside their flesh.[196] And Litl John kept his silence, as if his mouth was indeed the hard shell of an oyster, and he was afraid of the stone that might keep it open.

Then, at that very instant, the skeleton of the quack did laugh, and all of us looked up in terror; but it was in truth the babbling of a *pye*[197] perched high upon the skull, that with the ribs, one arm and half a leg out of the hips, was all that remained of the whole man, as they say certain men appear after battle – albeit still fleshed and bleeding, and e'en alive in their groaning.

Hode was glad of the gold, despite his pain and sorrow, for he might therewith corrupt further the wits of important men, and buy their agreement as he saw fit, as great lords do even unto the judge and the jury, should any of us be taken.

Whereupon some days later, receiving reports that the lovely maid was returned to Notyngam and devoutly giving thanks thrice daily to her lady the Mother of God in the great church therein that is called St Mary, he did sit upon a fallen trunk in the clearing, gnashing his teeth and devouring his own lip, and said that he had not seen his own lady for a week, and must see her now;[198] and that if he did not, 10,000 crossbow-bolts would pierce his heart, for his heart was a castle

---

[196] This brilliant simile seems to draw upon experience, and certainly gives our prosaic narrator the flash of a great poet.

[197] Magpie: compare Chaucer's 'janglynge pye' (*The Parliament of Fowls*, l. 345).

[198] A remarkable anticipation of stanza 7 (out of 90) in the earliest surviving 'Robin Hood' ballad, *Robin Hood and the Monk*, wherein Robin expresses the same heedless desperation, but from an orthodox Christian desire to see his Saviour: '"Hit is a fourtnet and more," seid h[e], / "Syn I my savyour see; / To day I to Notyngham," seid Robyn, / "With the myght of mylde Marye."' (All citations from F. J. Child's masterly edition: *The English and Scottish Popular Ballads*, 1888.)

under siege. And I was thus so eager to espy her myself that I declared myself (in a loud voice) willing to accompany him with his guard, that must number twelve like the disciples.[199]

Then there was disturbance among the men gathered in the clearing, as of a hive when it is kicked and sets forth a humming, for to go to Notyngham would be to invite their own doom, though they be armed to the teeth. The gates of the city would be closed behind them, and though they might resist with much bloodletting, their pains could only be rewarded with death or arrest, and no amount of gold might spare them: for the baron's coffers were full, and he himself almost mightier than the king (who indeed feared him); and being betrothed to the damsel, this baron would utterly destroy any man who had ever done mischief to her, with the most horrible tortures.

Then Hodd rose, and shouted very loud, that all were put into a hush as a cloth over a hive doth to the bees within. 'Why, thinkest thou to announce my arrival with trumpets and such great clatter as might wake the dead, e'en those we ourselves have put into the earth with our murtherings? Fools! I will go in disguise, alone but for one, and that be [Little] John, for I needs must have a page to carry my bow.' And here much mirth burst forth, for the felons were quick and fiery of temper and ever-changing.

But Lytl John, as furious as a boar smitten by the spear of a hunter, did roar piteously that he would do no such thing – when it might have been better to have laughed also, and not frot his tusks upon the insult, whetting them for battle with his leader. Hod was nimbler sure, in wits and body, and instilled great awe amongst the men,

---

[199] Compare stanza 8 of the same ballad, in which 'Moche, the mylner sun' (the miller's son), makes the identical suggestion: 'Take twelve of thi wyght yemen, / Well weppynd, be thi side.' To which comes the reply: '"Off all my mery men," seid Robyn, / "Be my feith I wil none have, / But Litull John shall beyre my bow . . ."' It would be henceforth tedious to indicate the parallels, there are so many. Effectively, this part of the action of our present document is more or less replayed, in a conventional and popular form less displeasing to the Church, in the later ballad. We can thus make the extremely probable hypothesis that our narrator is also the minstrel-author of *Robin Hood and the Monk* in its original lost version, as is suggested later in the manuscript.

whereas [Little] John was perceived as being more brawn than brain, and all his merits housed in a boarish courage that broke heedlessly upon the enemy, and put them to flight in sheer terror. Yet, as we all know, the boar hath a shrewdness in him too, though more forthright than that of a fox.

And he cried thus: 'Never shall I bear thy bow, nor thy arrows, but only mine own, as thou shalt bear thine. Though it be for a mere wench, as be comely and nothing more, and for a mere lovesickness like a lily-livered boy's, yet shall I accompany thee, for thou hadst need of protection in thy weakness.' And this so angered Hodde, that he struck John across the face with his hand, and all present did gasp and cry out.[200] Then Lityl John drew his sword, as if to smite off his master's head, and all our lives – even the lives of the full green trees and the loud or muttering creatures within, and the daylight itself, and the grass that sparkled with dew at our feet (for it was morning) – did seem very brittle, as of glass.

But our leader stood firm, as he was wont to, only his hand resting upon the pommel of his sword, that was of very fine ironwork, and its blade of the sharpest steel. Mayhap if the birds were not singing so merrily in the verdure, as it was springtime, we might have heard a growling. Then John's choler, spread from his gall into every extremity, did begin to retreat, and his face grew less red. 'Thou art no better than a lovesick *gnof*,'[201] he declared; 'and if thou were not my master, thy head would now be rolling on the turf. Find another man to go with thee, for I will have none of it, nor this wench-folly.'

And he walked the length of the clearing towards his great sorrel courser, and mounted it in one leap, and spurred it blindly so that the hooves well nigh spilled us as though [playing] hoddmen's blinde,[202] and galloped away beyond the rocks and out onto the moorland – as

---

[200] A colourful episode of competitive archery is inserted here in the ballad, ending in a banal quarrel over the wager of a few shillings.
[201] Lout.
[202] i.e. 'Hoodman's Blind', a kind of blind man's bluff where the blindfolded player was hit by knotted capuchons instead of touched – clearly a much rougher game than its modern counterpart.

I guessed, for I could hear only his hoof-beats growing dim, the trees being thick with new leaves.

We were cast into a despondency, although the bitter quarrel had not ended in blood, for Hode wished to go to Notyng[h]am alone, to the astonishment of all; and not even donning a disguise, save his cloak and hood. Thereupon, after much protest from the felons, he showed me a great favour, by bidding me hold his bow and arrows and be his page on this foolhardy adventure; then indeed I swelled with pride, as (in my idiocy) I thought myself the equal of Litell John.

This caused much rancour among the others, and some e'en called me obscene names in a whisper, for these men were violent and most especially one called Flawnes,[203] whose face was so thin and pointed it was (as men say) made only of each side pasted together, and looked as sharp as the blade he carried, that had been a butcher's for parting sinews. He took delight in others' pain, and cut with his knife even the travellers we had no business with (who were poor or vagrants), that they might remember us, and have tales to tell in the taverns; for he left them with rips on their cheeks or their foreheads, their tunics soaking with blood and e'en their footprints [filling] as they fled.

And this Flawnnes, taken with a great jealousy, did call me under his breath, when I was saddling my mount alone, 'Hode's geld [*castratus*],'[204] twisting my arm painfully behind my back and saying he would one day do to me as the law did to sodomites[205] – and there was much noxious drink carried on the vapours from his mouth, that had less lips than a tear in a leaf. 'Verily,' he went on, 'I shall be helping thee into Heaven, brother, for the time is short that remaineth, and only eunuchs might pass into eternal bliss.'

'There is no Heaven to pass into,' I cried, as if the devils were moving my tongue, while other fiends were removing my shoulder-bone,

---

[203] Possibly a nickname given for its comic inappropriateness: 'flawnes' being a medieval baked dish of eggs, cheese, sugar and saffron.

[204] In the sense, clearly, of his 'catamite' – a boy kept for unnatural purposes. See also Chaucer's description of the effeminate Pardoner as a 'geldying'.

[205] The official punishment for this offence – mutilation or removal of the privy members before being hung in chains – was seldom carried out, however.

as a candle from its socket. 'Only the sea of essence awaits those who are free spirits.' At this he laughed, and methought my arm was being dismembered as traitors' limbs be in the square, the pain making the forest dusken to my eyes, and I fell to the earth by my horse like an iron tool when he released me [. . .] (at sight of?) his boon companions.[206] Yet he did not cut me, and for this I was much relieved, thinking almost to show my gratitude; as poorer wayfarers on the road would thank us for not slaying them, or taking all their chattels down to their underclothes, but only half – as would oft happen if we were of a sweet temper.

---

[206] There is corruption of the text here: I have taken *terramentum* as a clerical error for *ferramentum*, and assumed the loss of two or three words before *convivae*.

6

For he who has no money or worldly goods, as we say, sings in the presence of a robber. Only gluttons fear a lack of capons, or a dearth of pepper.[207] My first and best master, the hermit, spoke often of these things in my earliest years, for he had so retired from the temporal pleasures of this world, which he regarded as harmful, that this world was to him a kind of captivity, all save the sound of the sea and the simplest and most humble things, such as the shine of a pebble, or the scuttling of a crab, or e'en the sway of a thin reed on the marge. On these did he dine, that the utmost bliss was discovered in his life's cell, as the desert fathers found contentment in the wastes of desolation.

And he said that Heaven was not a luxurious garden of palaces and fountains, spread to the bejewelled walls of the New Jerusalem set upon a high hill cloaked in verdant fruit [trees], but surely a place wherein the natural simplicities of Christ's presence make of a petal something fabulous, and a grain of sand a dazzling sight, and the scent of a sea breeze nothing less than a thousand pillows filled with nectar. 'Then it is not a garden,' I would say, 'as it says in the Bible,' (for my Latin was then advancing every day), 'but a wild country.' 'Nay,' he would reply, 'nothing is wild or savage in Heaven, for the Lord God makes all tame, even the roaring lion; yet He fashions nothing falsely, and a garden be false.'

Thinner and thinner the hermit became, for he ate little but grey bread and *glasewort*,[208] drinking only sips of water or weak ale as

---

[207] Pepper being a costly luxury at this period.
[208] Marsh samphire.

befitted his thirst. Yet because he spent most of the day in prayer and meditation, he was like those creatures that sleep during the winter, and do not need to sup or sustain themselves in any way – as we see with swallows, who rest secretly under the earth till spring be returned, and then emerge to fly as swiftly as before, so that men say God hath loosed His barbed points [of arrows].

Edwyn was his best pupil, for I had something in me that was dull, like a plumbstone of lead, that one day or another would appear without warning and make me sorrowful and heavy, and slow my wits that the words would blur or fade, and nothing could be joined in the threads of grammar. On other days I sped forth, and even Edwyne would marvel, while our master exhorted me to even greater efforts. And so pure and clean became the spirit of our master, that oftimes I wondered why God did not take him there and then, to face the light immortal and not be blinded by its effulgence, and dwelleth therein. His face was become an old man's, with many wrinkles, but also smooth as pure things be, and of the colour of a bronze coin. His eyes were each a pool of water set under a cloudless sky; as of the type left upon our sandy littoral by the tide, that the hermit called 'holy bowls', as though they were unlocked fonts of consecrated water, safe from sorcerers.[209]

Edwin would be bolder than myself in all ways, while his work in the smithy made him strong of arm, though he was short of stature. When our master was on his knees in meditation, eyes turned upwards and hands clasped, in a circle of stones beyond the tide's reach, Edwyn would wrestle me to the ground and pin me there, causing me hurt; yet I dared not cry out for fear of disturbing our master. Eager would I be to pretend to have swooned, or give the bullyboy some simple fare from my foster-mother intended for myself, rather than cry out.

Neither did I dare tell on his antics, for he had a bousy, violent father of great strength; and our master was as close to Edwin as an uncle, yet with none of the disadvantages of a true family's carnal

---

[209] Pre-Reformation church fonts would be closed with a heavy lid, to prevent witches and sorcerers stealing drops of the holy water within, for use in spells.

[*libidinosorum*] relations, that hinder true devoutness.²¹⁰ Never did I feel the same closeness, though fain was I ever to receive it: I yet remained the pupil, and he the schoolmaster, and in my dogged, earnest way I thus gained my education. Among sea winds and grains of sand, with reeds or slivers of driftwood to mark the pages, and the surge for ever in my ears, did I become literate: nay, more than literate – learned, and well broken in to all matter of sacred words and forms.

The demon that feeds on pride had much sport with me, however, as a mouse does in a barrel of cheese; for every slight, no matter how trivial, became a deep stripe. For example, my master said once, 'This is slow work!' – meaning the perfection of penmanship, for we were scribing the letters of Carmentis²¹¹ before enduring [Latin] declension, with Edwyn ever ahead though his tongue protruded like an incontinent peasant's – and I heard it as: 'Thou art slow!' Bursting into tears, I ran from the cave. Foolish boy! I deserved twenty or thirty stripes from the sharpest rod, but instead the hermit, whose kindness cannot be exaggerated,²¹² told me afterwards that he had meant such work itself must be tackled carefully, and not hurried as Psalms and suchlike are hurried through by ignorant priests and deprived thereby of all sense. And that true learning must be drunk in deeply and slowly, as must true humility.

Someone in the village, covetous of my guardian's fine hens and cock, did start a rumour that she was a witch, and I her succubus, mainly on account of my sullenness; and this risked reaching the ears of the law and its full might.²¹³ We were only saved from arrest and probable burning by my master, whose great holiness and reputation had spread. Ten or twenty a day pressed into the chapel on the cliff, some

²¹⁰ 'Carnal' here is in the sense of 'worldly' or 'unsanctified', as opposed to the spiritual relations between the devout, united in the service of God. A view common to the age, if somewhat naive (or even hypocritical).
²¹¹ Carmenta Nicostrata, reputed to have brought the alphabet to Italy.
²¹² This contradicts what was said in an earlier episode and what is then recounted, although a softness can indeed coexist happily in the same person with a harshness; I'm thinking particularly of certain schoolmasters and army officers known to me. A solitary man on a near-starvation diet will, if not listless, be likely to show an instability of temperament.
²¹³ This last sentence is in Anglo-Norman, the language of judicial authority.

advancing to the beach below, despite the superstition of the sea-ravens, and even knowing he was a solitary and would not be disturbed. They sought to be his follower and pupil, or to touch him if they were sick, or cripples.

And this became so much of a trouble to him that one day he talked thus to both of us: 'I will not have any more of the common folk; though I feel compassion for them in my bowels, yet my head is turned to the Kingdom of Heaven, and the two elements war in me, that I begin to unstitch all the advances I have made. I will not preach, for they have plenty of preachers, and if they wish to be healed, they can touch that wretched garment of mine I have left in the chapel. I must find a more hidden spot in the far north, on the coast of Caledonia, though it grieves me to leave here, for even the sea-otters come and dry my feet[214] each morning, and I love this simple cave more than any.'

Edwyn and I complained bitterly, and besought ourselves to find a way that he might stay. Our master had bid us continue our studies while he betook himself to the [circle of] stones, when Edwyne said to me, 'We must start a false tale, for folk are easily fooled.'

Then we plotted together how to feign, not knowing the danger that lies in all untruths. We said nothing to the hermit our master, and set about during the following days to describe a sea-serpent we had seen from the shore by the hermitage, when we had in truth seen no more than whales and sea-pigs[215] [*porculos marinos*] and seals. So easy was it to spy this creature in my mind's eye, with its glossy scales, foul-stinking jaws and head like a peacock's on the end of a long and slender neck, that reached even unto the cliff's top as we cowered there at eventide, that I did not feel I was lying and thus committing a sin. I added that we were so close we might have picked its teeth of the rotting carrion lodged between them, and put our fingers into the moist and dripping crusts like cancres upon its tail, and other such trifles; and did marvel at how astonied my listeners were before our humble cot, and how readily I invented!

[214] As they did St Cuthbert's on Farne Isle.
[215] I have translated the Latin for 'porpoise' literally. It was much prized for its fat.

Edwinn feigned likewise in his village, adding that the serpent had four whelps, covered in tender white scales and of shorter necks, yet their heads alone were as big as dolphins. And the sea-serpent and her litter made such a fearsome grunting and roaring (said he), and so savage a sight were they, that even the holy man cowered in his cave, and only the Holy Book protected us from being dragged away by those jaws, that had already munched upon a whale.

By rubbing our childish bodies under our shirts with the foulness of *see wrek*[216] beforehand, we each feigned the stink and heat of the serpent's nostrils, that gave off a fumosity worse than a sea fog. We said that we could not delineate one another for an hour – nor the cliff, nor any of the coast, nor the sea itself save a glimmer like a steel blade, and we each thought it the End of Days. And all believed us, for we gave off a stench of slime. And my foster-mother, with the urging of our ignorant local priest, forbad me to return to the hermitage; but I told her that the holy man had given me a secret phrase in Latin that would protect me, and I spoke a line of Livy I had learned. Thus simple feigning turned into diabolical untruth, for such empty charms are forbidden, so dangerous are they when ill-used.

The hermit soon wondered that so few came to him any more, and not even to the chapel, yet he was not displeased. All pilgrims seeking him had to pass through either village on the way, where they were told of the visitation, that struck terror into most of these folk – man being naturally faint-hearted, and dreading most especially the monsters of the deep. Only those who approached from the coast itself, along the sand, were unawares – but these were very small in number, for the way was oft concealed by tides or storm. We did not tell our master why, save that there were rumours of sea-beasts here on account of a great crocodile that had been washed up some miles south. He laughed at that, and said he was glad, for he had worried that it might be the result of evil gossip: 'One day I might look up and see a mob come to try me for heresy,' he said.

We expressed amazement at this, but he continued thus: 'The Devil

---

[216] Sea wrack (most likely the beached seaweeds of bladderwrack or kelp).

finds slippery ways to defeat a Christian, and many times he does this through a woman's loose tongue, for it is in the nature of women to be gossips.' He added that at the time of the gossip this did not appear grave, as there was little passion behind the tongue, and little thought, so that the soul was hardly connected to the mouth; but afterwards the Devil worked on the feigning tales like a potter with clay, to shape it to an evil form. He said this with great feeling, so much so that tears started to his eyes and ran down his sea-fretted cheeks, hollowed by hunger.

Edwin agreed, and said that a woman must have in her mouth a short bridle like a horse, to rein in her wayward will. I was silent with worry, however, for I saw how our feigning might grow, like the serpent itself, and bring destruction upon our master, and e'en upon our little school (for we were scholars, in truth). I conjectured that our master had powers of prophecy, as do many holy hermits in imitation of the desert fathers, and that was why he was shedding tears.

I did not know then that he was being galled by a painful memory, of the type that ne'er dislodges from its throne in the brain until the day of death, or the rebellion of madness.

Alas, how many times did he appear to me in memory, as I lay in my hut in the felons' dark wood half my then lifetime [some seven years] later, or when aiding them in their sundry tasks – with the poor quack's bones swinging above us night and day, ghastly in my sight! Once, chopping at timber with the chip-axe to kindle their fires, alone under the great new-leaved boughs and my hand blistered from the helve, the sound of my task seemed to utter a line of the Lord's prayer over and over: *et dimitte nobis debita nostra.* And the hermit's figure stood over me suddenly, with the white surf behind pouring through the trees, as if I were in two times and [two] places at once. The holy man was scolding me for ill-writ letters, as I had inscribed in the sand thus: *et domitte nobis debita nostra.*[217] 'Only one letter is wrong,' I said: and this was indeed a true memory.

Seizing my hair, he answered that I might kill a thousand men

[217] 'And forgive us our sins' [lit. 'debts']: *domitte* should be *dimitte*, of course, but in this form could be heard or misread as *domito* (to tame), presumably.

143

with one letter, or corrupt their souls, for that is sufficient to change a word, and words guide men, for the first word was God's and the last word will also be God's, and no doubt arriving upon a blazing chariot too bright to behold. 'How did Christ heal? With his word.'

I replied, 'I am not God, nor Christ.' And dragging me by the hair, he threw me upon the shallows of the ebb-tide, furious at my ignorance, crying, 'Adam was created by God and given speech to name the animals, and all men, even a miserable wretch like you, be descended from Adam! It is better for you to remain dumb and ignorant, wordless as the sea's surge, than try to follow in Edwyn's path.' And he turned to wipe away my words with his feet; but the sea had already done so, leaving only soft welts like scars; and thereupon in the wood did the sovereignty of the present return, and wipe that holy man away, along with the sea. Alas, that I had never left its sound!

By this scolding, in truth, he had meant to instil in me the importance and the danger of words, but it merely increased my jealousy of Edwine. I said to myself: 'Meseemeth that the life of a holy man is chafing at his good spirits; I should seek another master. Seeing as how I can now read and write, I can join a holy house and rise to become abbot.' Indeed, I was in awe of such people, and consumed with ambition, wishing to divest myself of my humble origins with a great effort; though my Latin was but a half-worked bow, scarcely out of the yew, and my written letters still stumbling, and my reading so halting that it oft left a greasy trail upon the parchment.[218]

What is the greatest sin? Pride.[219]

A further full year passed at that foam-belaboured school, during which time I suffered many indignities from my faster rival, and further strokes of humiliation, while the hermit grew leaner and more like a half-starved beggar, as salted as a corpse that he did (with his shaved skull) resemble. Edwynn was the son of a blacksmith, thus he

---

[218] He has the schoolchild's timeless habit of tracing progress with a dirty finger pressed to the page.

[219] A marginal interpolation in Hand A.

oft brought back worked trinkets in iron, that he had fashioned when red-hot and pliant into resemblances of letters each the size of a horse shoe [*soleae ferreae*], that made finally an entire abc. Our master was amused by this, for never had such a thing been seen, save to make patterns[220] for the stonemasons and carpenters and painters. I scoffed, saying that to smite letters from iron instead of gold or silver or copper is an insult to the precious gift of the scholar. The hermit put me to shame by saying, 'Why, are you telling us that nothing beautiful can come from something so rough and hard?'

And I, ignorant of his deeper meaning in my pride and envy, agreed. And he said, 'Then go, and never come back, for methought I could break your barbarous iron into the gold of learning.' I did break, verily, but only into floods of tears, at which even Edwiyn did marvel, while my master put his thin arm about my trembling form and said, in a kindlier tone, 'Iron be nothing until made nesh and beaten; then with it we can till and shod and build and chastise and protect and bring dread into men's hearts, and so it be with written words. Something good of you we shall yet make, though you have come straight out of the earth as doth a turnip.' Being an orphan, I loved him greatly at that moment, and (ashamed though I was of it, after) seized him about the waist as a drowning child doth hug a floating branch; though affection is an earthly tie, and his mind was more and more heavenward.

He then laid out all the iron letters upon the marge of the tide, that they appeared and disappeared over the ensuing weeks and months, moved and concealed and restored to sight by the surf when it was stirred by wind; and the salts of the sea soon made the dryness of the metal, and the brimstone within it, rise outwardly into red rust like cancres; and this, he said, is all that happens to words.

---

[220] Stencils (the general comment is less startling than it appears – medieval shop signs, for example, were usually pictorial).

Part Three

I

How different from this holy man was my new master, whom
I was yet still eager to serve – for like all young men I was
fickle, as mortals are before the Lord God, until the immi-
nence of Hell-fire be licking at their flesh, when they wish themselves
to have been as obdurate in faith as the stone that suffereth not pain.
And it is said that, on the plummet towards the slimy pit and cauldrons of liquid flame, we shall feel the balmy breeze of Heaven upon
us, tinted with blossom and all manner of verdant sweetness, that is
[Heaven's] eternal Maytime, and shall grab with our hands in exceeding
grief, yet clutch nothing but air as we scream and shriek like children
plunging down a well. *Horrible fate!*[221]

Yet as I rode out with Robert Hode to Notyngham upon such
a fair day as maytime alone bringeth, with the sky blue-bright as
glass and the air delectable, and the wayside full fair with flowers,
drawing innumerable butterflies upon them – such day that lifts
and gladdens the heart and turns even the waste moor into a portion
of that eternal bliss that awaits the goodly, so lovely lies the heather
and the turf, and fragrant as incense, and mantled by the songs of
birds – I did feel myself a rival to him in love, and a worm turned
in my brain.

Many there were upon the road, including some twenty singing
pilgrims with great staffs and leaden medals on their caps, so that
there was a continual hum hither and thither, and a creaking of carts
whose drivers oft cast into our way many detestable oaths, that I was

[221] Marginal interpolation in the same sixteenth-century hand (Hand A).

well used to by now. My master's only disguise was a blue pelisse,[222] with a large capuchon attached, larger even than his usual hood, for it had belonged to a fat merchant; for my part, I wore the surcoat of a page, of a light-green hue. My thoughts were not upon the danger of our mission, but upon a pair of bluish-grey eyes and the moistness of vermeil lips, holier to kiss than the Book to my inflamed mind . . .

A missing leaf, likely to have been torn out purposely, brings us to the central market-square of thirteenth-century Nottingham, presumably on the morning of the next day.

. . . green cheeses and three cart mares beside a stall selling opium, rhubarb and precious camphor from Venice, guarded by two burly ruffians with great snarling dogs. My master and myself went unremarked, for there were all manner of folk, sometimes mere shadows within the smoke from the roasting capons, geese and suchlike, and the steam from the oxen dung (for it was a sharp morning); and few anyway had seen Robertt Hod's face in full, so low did he wear his hood when robbing.

I was so much afraid we would be taken, that I could scarce hold the great bow, and the din was very great and horrible after the forest, whose wood-ways were so calm, in spite of the forty or fifty felons within, that the quietest birdsong might be enjoyed. On passing the surgeon-barber's chair, where a fat wretch was being deprived of his tooth, and Hodde stopping there in the crowd for the entertainment, the tooth being stuck fast and resisting the pincers (though three among them held the man down), I had espied the Bishop [of Yorke's] man among the folk watching and laughing, and hid myself behind a stall of tethered hens that pecked my toes, till the tooth was plucked free on a great huzzah.

I drew my capuchon well over my head, yet so large was Hode's [capuchon], that he more resembled a mendicant or the figure of Death in the myracles, than any outlaw. The principal entrance to the church

---

[222] A long outdoor garment with a slit in the hanging sleeves for the arms; it became fashionable at about this time.

was by the north, on the market side, on account of the masons enlarging the south porch.[223] Hodd gave to each of the cripples in the [church] porch a generous amount of pennies; one there was, so horribly deformed in the legs, dragging himself o'er the filth of the square on two low crooks, that all who saw him expressed wonder; one woman was shouting shrilly without cease that his legs imitated a holy cross and that it was a miracle, but she was mad, and milk-white in one eye. Another beggar's visage was measled over with whelks and botches (though not a leper's, for there was no stench) that hid it quite, so that none knew whether the unfortunate beneath was male or female, even when the creature uttered its plaint; unlike the last, who was a comely young woman, but frouncen like beech bark on her brow, for she had lost her only daughter down a well – yet said not a single 'Gramercy' when we cast her a penny.

Within the church, where it was dark after the sunlight, and so full of straw-dust that many coughed over the priest's hurried words, expelling thus a thick vapour of garlic that e'en the sacred air could not dilute, Hodde's face in its cloth cavern was but a glint of moistness now and again, that was one or other of his lustrous eyeballs.

The church was noisy, it being market day, for the carousal that always attends such, had part entered the sacred building, and there . . . [*hiatus in the MS*].

. . . She was dressed in a rich cotte[224] brocaded with dancing lions in silver, fastened above the glistening folds with a jewelled belt, and a plain cap and wimple not fretted with any decoration. She walked upon the arm of her father, whose cotte reached only to his calf,[225] with a servant beating back with a knobbed club those persons thronging the nave, and so stoutly he might have broken their bones.

[223] The south door being the usual main entrance to a church, via the graveyard. Little remains of the original building, as it was entirely rebuilt in the late fourteenth century, 'classicised' in the eighteenth, and heavily restored to 'Gothic' some sixty years ago by Sir G. G. Scott.

[224] As in MS: a common type of dress in the period, for both men and women, with a low belt for the latter to make a fullish skirt, and very graceful in its simplicity.

[225] Therefore he was not of the nobility, who wore their cotte to the ankle. Any higher than the calf risked denoting a peasant (whose skirt reached no lower than the knee).

How strange it was, to see her there among the rabble! How wide did we all gape, not harkening any of the sacred words, that rang to me then (with Satan's persuasion) as a tin coin doth on stone!

She and her father had chairs reserved for them to one side, near the pulpit, with other notable persons of the town that their legs might not grow weary, though the finest and greatest chair next to hers was unoccupied; that portion being raised upon a dais, we could watch her clearly, though Hode pressed forward through the throng to be nearer, while I mounted upon the base of a thick pillar a fair way up the nave, to see above the myriad heads. Then waxen tapers being lit for the mass, and the bishop's cope of most costly workmanship, with a morse[226] of silver and gems, glittering among the other precious choir-copes as [the clerics] processed to the chantry, a lustre was sent forth upon her face: she was like an image of our spotless Lady herself.

Verily, I believed then in my master's horrible words, that he was to make a sacred union with her, that would bring about the end of days. For in the unholy tumult of the church, like a sheephouse full of bleating beneath where I pillar-perched, I was struck by a twofold certainty: first, of the imminent end of this world's decay and pustulence, whose clamour and stink did strike me like a mailed fist after the forest; and second, of the cause of this doomsday, that was the union of Hod on the solstice with the fair and shapely Isabell (for so her name was). And this certainty of knowledge was like a sorcerer's potion, that being secret is the more powerful – when in truth it be no more than ashes and bran in boiling water, with diverse herbs, and maketh men think themselves greater than other men, and even invulnerable to points and blades (though they wear no armour beneath their coat), until the day they are pierced like any poor flesh, as soft as a baked fish.

And in the same wise did I wish myself as hard as the cold stone I clutched, freshly hewn and most brightly painted[227] (yet already with grease marks upon it from the multitude), that I might not feel the

---

[226] A clasp.

[227] Churches then were not only lively places compared to their forlorn modern state, but brightly painted, for the age loved colour. Churchyards even held host to markets until forbidden to in 1285.

torment her face and eyes and shapeliness had newly cast me into, knowing she was my master's eternal spouse-to-be, and not mine own. Only once did she seem to look upon me across the nave, over the heads of the multitude, following a great burst of laughter and imprecations from the choir, so serious that the officiant was hindered in his divine service and had to stop.

I craned my neck to see through the [rood] screen, and descried those in the lower stalls rubbing their heads and shaking their fists at the ministers in the upper stalls, and straightway knew that the latter had dripped hot wax from the candles onto the aforesaid heads below, as oft occurred in St Edmund's before the arrival of father Gerald. At which the bishop himself bellowed (in the vulgar tongue) at the officiating vicar to make haste; I grinned like a clown, and then it was I saw her looking across at me, her glove upon her lips to stifle her giggling, and I seemed as it were to plunge into the greyish-blue eyes, so that I near tumbled from my perch like a foolish pigeon.

Hodd's hood was easily distinguished from the crowd in the nave, for his pelisse was the deep blue of the hour before dusk. He was but a few yards from the damsel Isabbel, and turned slightly as if ignoring her, yet I knew full well that he would be peering out from the cave of his capuchon as might a basilisk from its den. He was close enough that he might drink in the honeyed air about her, e'en through the sour odours of the market and of the congregation, that battled mightily with the sweet fumigation [of the censers?].

A commotion was then felt in the throng, as a surge is felt in a lake, and a short, broad-shouldered man did enter, dressed in a fine red surcoat to his ankles. Having five or six armed men about him, each clad from head to foot in banded mail sewn on red velvet and armed with sword or crossbow, he parted the congregation easily and with many oaths on both sides, though it was the Lord's house; and in a loud voice the newcomer berated the ministers for failing to delay the mass, that he would fain have heard. And the poor vicar was caught between the bishop and the lord, and stammered out the *Domine* as though condemned to the stake.

Then the nobleman – for such he was – clattered up onto the

dais on his pointed shoes, that seemed moulded to his feet, seating himself beside the damsel Isabel in the carved chair that was like a throne, his armed oafs throwing aside a youthful member of the clergy who had been eagerly nattering to her (though this be forbidden during divine service), so that the unfortunate cleric fell sprawling with a crack upon the flagstones, and lay insensible, as was his just punishment, for he was drunk; and neither she nor her father seemed a whit surprised, but rather amused.

From the quiet that descended upon the throng, I knew this must be the baron, whom even the king feared; his cruelties were well known, for he did administer the harshest justice for petty wrongs by means of the sheryff[228] in this town, with many a peasant and poacher hung in chains, and even his own surgeon being disembowelled alive for operating upon the [baron's] wife and failing (for she had perished under the knife). And it was said that as a young man he did seem to forgive another who had insulted him, by embracing and kissing him, but instead bit away those lips that had uttered the profanity, so completely that the fellow never again uttered an understandable word![229]

On seeing this gallant knight take Is[a]bel's hand in his own, with many a smile on his shaven, flabby face, that yet showed his swinish white bristles (for he was long past his fiftieth year), I wondered if they were already wedded,[230] for she did give him a wink.

Wretched sight! My liver, from whence love swells as anger does from the gall, and wisdom from the heart, and feeling from the brain, and laughter from the spleen, did then flood my body entire with fire, that sweat broke out upon my brow and I near swooned.

---

[228] The very sheriff, it seems, who was to play such an important part in later versions of the outlaw legend. The sadistic baron's identity remains unknown, although future scholars may narrow down the many possible contenders from the assortment of powerful northern nobles who had been responsible for the Magna Carta ten years earlier (see later note) – of whom some were little more than gangsters.

[229] Compare the medieval Spanish poem, *Tyran le Blanc*, where the victim is the hero's own mother.

[230] Marriage vows at this time could be exchanged anywhere, without witnesses or ceremony or the consent of relatives, and still be valid in canon law.

Meanwhile my master had approached the chairs, right anigh the armed guards, and I was sore afraid he would attack them, and in so doing lose his life: all he had upon him was his cutting knife. I had his bow slung on my back, and steel-tipped arrows in my belt, whose smooth horn nocks I craved to fit to the bow string; but little use they would be in all the confusion his action might produce.

I could hear the drum of the acrobats and jugglers begin to sound outside, for it was a great bull-hide drum, and it became mingled with my heart's thumping. So feeble be the faith of the common people, that the crowd in the church thinned, eager for such base contortions and bawdy foolery; and a face was thereby revealed, towards the rear of the nave, that froze me as though I was plunged of a sudden into Purgatory's icy, salty lake: it was the oblate Henry's visage, pale as ivory beneath his golden curls!

Beside him stood – I would fain have suffered a tooth pulled, than to have been espied by him – my old master, brother Thomas. Irked by the fickle folk pressing about him for the north door, his big head cloven across by his wide mouth like a hog's (that might have swallowed an apple entire), he was just as I had left him on that [October] morning, many months before, when setting out with Ricchet for the glassworks: yet I myself was utterly changed. 'S'death!' the good monk cried over the hubbub, so deep and loud I could catch it, yet not the rebukes that flowed from his lips as he was jostled.

E'en as I set this down with my crabbed and aged hand, do I feel the horror! I was but a targe set upon a tree, so clear was the space of air between us – and in my shock I had not noticed the capuchon had dropped, revealing my face. What should I see above the bruit of the plainchant, but that creature clept Henrie, that false boy-angel, tugging at my old master's sleeve, whispering in my old master's bent ear (as gossips and fiends do), then pointing towards my pillar, so that their eyes converged upon me like steel points!

I leapt from the pillar and bounded down the south aisle, weaving in and out of the lay folk gathered there, and thereby out into the churchyard through the scaffolding [of the unfinished south porch], where the great new wall, not yet capped, enclosed only the melancholy scrape of a spade: the one spade that must do us the most service when we can hear it not. Apart from the gravedigger above the fresh pit, there was a fellow with a pilgrim's rough beard and hat, easing his bladder against the stones left by the masons for the morrow, and a ragged beggar-woman chattering to the sky, wherein no doubt she saw many angels that were truly swifts, screaming about the spire. All this stands fresh in my memory as though planted yesterday, while whole years of my long life have become vapour, and less than wood-ash. Is this not strange?

Foolish youth! If I had kept my senses, I might have greeted my old master the monk, and spun tales to conceal the truth of my outlaw life, and e'en led him out of the church (for he was never devout), and not come to any harm at all, nor brought everyone else to their final doom. Yet in the storm of my alarm, that muddied my reason as it doth the clear waters of a river, I did not think of warning Hodd. Instead, I brought suspicion upon me by fleeing, for sometimes false-hood is the better course.

The gravedigger's hound, excited by my appearance, barked at me so fiercely that I ran up [the side of] the church, beyond the south transept, instead of crossing to the churchyard's gate, whereby I might have found the safety and tumult of the street. Yet finding that the transept's great bulk hid me from the yard, and the dog being quieted by a blow from its master, I pressed myself against the chancel wall, by the [leper's] squint[231] [*fenestra*], and opened its shutter to peer in, seeing straightway how the officiating ministers seemed undisturbed; then climbing upon a pile of half-hewn stones to one of the greater windows, I found all was set to costly coloured glass, which the gloom within rendered opaque.

I considered waiting for Hodd by the north door, to dissemble like a wretched play-actor if brother Thomas were to find me again:

[231] Low-set and narrow, enabling lepers to watch the service while hygienically removed from their fellows. There is currently, however, a fierce scrimmage among specialists over this issue, some believing that the open shutter enabled the sound of the 'sacring' bell to be heard outside on the raising of the Host, and that lepers never squinted through them at all.

telling him how I was hired to a builder of houses, as a carrier of bricks, that *Hod* might be turned into *hod*![232] To explain my great bow, of the best *ewe*,[233] with horn tips, and in the leather quiver these twenty fine arrows of ash whose fletchings were bound with red silk (Hode being very proud in this matter of arms), I devised a story, that I was on my way to the butts, carrying a bow and quiver for a wealthy merchant, upon whose house we were building an extension, and who assiduously practised his bowmanship.[234] And I falsely saw in my mind, as in a fever, brother Thomas clapping his eyes upon me, hurrying forth towards me (followed by his pretty page) and clipping me to him with great affection, saying he did think I was dead, murthered by the horrible felon Robbert Hod!

Thus garnered with the fret of lies and invention, I made my way to the other [principal] door, from which (as in a dream that cometh true) brother Thomas immediately issued in haste, his great hood lowered – not followed by Henry, but seeming so much perturbed that he was as if blinded, with a face pale and shiny as a spring onion, and saw me not. Fearing the worst, I watched him scurry away through the market's tumult, with great purpose in his stride, and I entered the church again to see if my present master was safe, and to bid him flee the town straightway.

By accident I encountered Henri in the rear of the nave, fair making him fall in my haste, and I caught him up, greeting him robustly and saying, 'Whither goeth my kind old master, brother Thomas? I wish to speak to him of old times, and tell my news, of my life in Notyngham as a builder's apprentice!' And the arrogant boy replied, 'Nowhere you would wish to follow, for I see you have become a wild boy, a little green man or a hairy goblin, and amazing it is you can still speak our civilised tongue.'

I was astonished, for I had forgot in what wise my skin was

---

[232] As in MS: perhaps no other passage illuminates better the stealthy wit and verve of the writer, somehow surviving the prejudices of his recaptured faith. Brick (moulded narrower than our own day) was coming back into 'fashion' in the thirteenth century.
[233] Yew wood (the finest being imported; lesser bows used willow or elm).
[234] Most Englishmen, including peasants, owned a bow and arrows.

browned by the forest air, and hardened like a serf's, and my eyes reddened by wind and smoke, and my boots chapped, and my nails filthy as my hair (still with hay in it from the barn),[235] and my youth's soft beard begun recently to sprout upon my chin. Alas! that he ever said such a thing, for it fed my anger and spite as doth a dry log in a fire.

I seized him by the throat and he squealed, although the congregation was repeating in unison the sacred words of the priest, and most raggedly, that it boomed among the stone pillars and vaults and drowned his complaint. Being a girlish coward and younger than myself, he was vanquished easily by my single hand on his scrawny gullet, and such fights and squabbles being common in those vicious days, we were not separated by others, but ignored by all but a small dog yapping lustily as I dragged the golden boy into [the area under] the great tower.

Thus vanquished in the corner, he told me in a whisper against my ear (his breath and skin sweet and honeyed, like a girl's), that brother Thomas was here on cellarer business; and had approached the chairs whereon the elect of the city sat, ever keen [to do business] on behalf of the abbey, as I knew well. And hoping also there might be occasion for Henry to play his harp before the baron, and thereby soften the wealthy lord's obdurate heart, and kindle his good humour, he did suggest this: yet the baron waved him away.

'Thus, by the dais,' said Henery to me (keeping his voice ever low), 'my master turned, and was startled to see a pair of hands in fingerless gloves of fine-stitched leather. Recognising these, and lifting his gaze, my good master likewise recognised their owner: this being none other than that horrible villain who robbed him of a hundred pounds on the road last year. And was this not the same devil who robbed thee of thine harp?'

I frowned, yet trembling within, and said, 'I do not know, for I have never gone to the outlaw's lair, not wishing to be murthered. And pray tell me, where hath my sweet old master now gone?' 'To alert

[235] Where he and Hod had slept, evidently, on their journey to Nottingham.

158

the *shryff,*[236] Henry replied, in a hiss like a serpent, 'and to bid him bar the gates of the city. For this devil of a felon is a cut-throat, and a very great criminal and nuisance, and we might render great service by catching him like a rat in this way. Beware! For he is in this very church! I know not why, as we heard he was a heretic!'

Then I ground my teeth with a noise like a mouse gnawing a nutshell, and said, 'Verily, the greatest service will be to brother Thomas, when he hath his reward.' 'Ay,' said Hennrie, 'my master wisheth to be rewarded more than his hundred pounds.' And I thought: 'He was ever eager to cloak his avarice;' saying nothing more, but bethinking a way of warning Hodde without Henry's sharp eyes pursuing me.

Then Satan, worming into that sacred place like a spider, filled me with e'en thicker hate of the boy, who was but three or four years younger than myself; for he was ever the one who had replaced me in the worthy monk's affection, and now (so he boasted) he was the owner of a fine harp, paid for by the brothers. And long before (as it seemed to me then, though it was but a matter of five or so years), I had similarly lost another master: this being the hermit. Truly, methought, life was but a betrayal, that is doom to all green and growing things, as ice and strong cold be, caused by fiends and making the soul's brief journey barren as Yslonde.[237]

I leapt upon the lip of the pillar beside us, and spied Hode's dusky-blue hood, ever near the armed guard of the brute baron, just as the Host was raised high and the [hand]bells rang out their happy news. Yet the baron himself was leaning towards the damsel and talking and laughing, as ignorant of the divine as any Jew or heathen: and so fierce I felt, I might have drawn my bow and run him through with a shaft, save a strange noise was heard through the open door, and a subtle quietening of the market roar without.

Dost thou know, dear reader, what it is to hearken the gates of

---

[236] As in MS: 'sheriff' – this being the High Sheriff of Nottinghamshire, Derbyshire and the Royal Forests, the city only being given its own sheriff in 1449. However, it appears the sheriff's HQ is Nottingham at the time of our account.
[237] Iceland.

eternal bliss closing with a distant boom like thunder, that hushes the naked hordes and tells you that you are trapped for ever in the desolation of pain and suffering? Sufficient 'tis to know it, and not even to be thrown into liquid fire or cold slime, or squeezed by weights, or pinched by iron pincers, or blinded with quicklime, or stretched upon the rack until your limbs burst from their sockets; for to have knowledge of the loss of eternal bliss is agony enough, when the cause of loss be, *exempli gratia*, a few fleet moments of carnal lust in a soiled bed, that passeth like a shadow on the wall.

Such did I feel, on hearing the gates of Noty[n]gham close, one after the other on their great iron hinges, so that the ground itself trembled.[238]

Henry cast a wicked, gleeful glance at me, and I knew not what action to take, for I was paralysed. Were I to warn my master of the hue and cry raised against him, he might doom us both by his impetuosity, inches from the armed guard: for Hode had upon him a two-handed sword in its scabbard, longer than his thigh, that was so sharp it might cleft through a man's brainpan all the way to the chin; yet in no wise could he defeat the baron's and the sherif's guard together, for already I could hear the faint cries of many men summoned by the sceryf, as if the assault of a castle was underway, and from both north and south.

Yet now I think it the good Lord's doing, this aforementioned freezing of my limbs, as the Host was raised and the choir sang sweetly enough, ignorant as my master of the closing of the gates, and of the many armed men pressing towards us through the streets and the market, like a flood, armed with staves, axes and swords: only He knew, in His infinite wisdom, that I still bore a speck of salvation within me, not yet found by the fingers of the Arch-fiend and his seven daughters,[239] and that I might one day return to the righteous path e'er all hope was lost . . .

The ensuing meditations do not warrant insertion here.

---

[238] Although the passage is exaggerated, the walled and gated part of the average medieval city would have surprised us by its small surface area.
[239] The seven deadly sins were commonly referred to as 'the daughters of the Devil'.

2

Once before had I been thus paralysed, and in like manner; I have long considered it my own feebleness, that stinted my advance in the world, for it took place before the young king [Henry III] himself. Yet e'en that was no doubt also the thumb of the Lord God Himself, pressing me to His secret will as a potter doth his clay upon the wheel, for He alone is our true master and eternal Father.

And now I think that I must explain what I mean by 'stinting my advance', for in truth life is made up of a myriad ways that connect one with another, for oft we leave the allotted path for a false one, yet find our way back.

My former life as a pupil of the hermit's proceeded quietly enough, summer upon winter, winter upon summer: happy state, no doubt descried by a messenger of the Scribe of All Errors! For early in the month of June, when I was eight or nine, there came a sea fog so thick that it blew inly and lay in white vapours upon the moor. I was reading by the cave, and our master praying fervently in his [circle of] stones, when, hearing distant calls of strange birds very like peals of trumpets, I saw Edwynn clambering down the cliff in great haste.

The youth rushed up shouting and, without reflecting upon his terrible action, seized the kneeling devout by his wasted shoulders and shook him as if to wake him, saying that the king's court,[240] being lost in the vapours on its way to Whittbey, was halted in the village where he lived, and had taken all provender for the courtiers and

---

[240] That of the minority of Henry III, who (as every schoolboy knows) forty years later was to face the rebellious barons headed by Simon de Montfort. In fact, Henry visited the north very seldom during his long subsequent reign.

sumpter-mules, and trampled the crops like a hail storm, for the followers numbered many hundreds and included dicers, tumblers, washerwomen, prostitutes and play-actors; and that his father, turned out of his own house by the royal stewards and becoming very drunk and sorrowful, had knocked a mincing courtier to the ground, by whom he had been called 'an oaf, with a brain no bigger than an oak-apple'; and that his father was now seized, and at the king's mercy (accused of grievous assault), and the smithy smashed to smithereens.[241]

Thereupon, instead of sympathy, Edwin received blows (from a piece of driftwood) as harsh as those his own father had delivered to the courtier – though the boy was hardened to blows, whereas the courtier was not, save perhaps from the lance in a tournament. When this assault was over, and the blood wiped from his brow, the victim sat dazed and weeping on the sand, saying that he wished to die, for he knew not why God had thus treated him on this day.

And the holy hermit, trembling from head to foot in his ragged cloth, explained that he had been, in his prayers, on the very sill of the light ineffable, wherein the sound of the sea-surge had become silenced, and the screaming gulls no more than whispers, and that the grace of the Sevenfold Spirit was stretched out to him with seven arms, shining brighter than gold, amidst clouds of myrrh and cinnamon; whereupon as he was spreading and stretching his soul towards the seven manifestations of Almighty God, whose invisible likeness was surrounded by many thousands of holy spirits and angels – swooping about a tower of the purest pearl wherein the immortal King did reside – then a sudden burst sounded above his head, as if the glass of the tower window had been punctured, and fell in pieces upon his hair and hands, and he was not looking at the face of the divine, but upon the hideous and screaming visage of his mortal pupil.

Thus did Edwyne understand his sorry wrongdoing, for by this feebleness he might have for ever denied his master a vision granted only to the purest and cleanest, even after death. And no blows were

---

[241] None of this sorry tale is surprising: the medieval court's ravenous procession through the country, in a swarm of camp followers, was dreaded by all. See also the famous letters of Peter of Blois (died 1200).

hard enough, he admitted. 'Good!' cried our master. 'Now you understand that my vow is for a purpose stronger than any mortal emergency.
Your father is a drunken brute,' he went on. 'This is granted you by
the Almighty Lord that you may choose a holier and a cleaner path
through the world's fighting, uncoupled from thy sorry relatives. Tarry
not, but seize the opportunity, that this blood upon your shirt is a
sign and a blessing upon withal, for my hands are yet shining full
marvellously.' And so saying, he showed us his hands, and I did see
them glowing like coals lightly blown upon by the breeze, and felt a
strange joy ripple through me, though the surf did crash beyond and
the gulls scream their sorrow out of this world full of sins.

Yet Edwyne's earthly ties proved too strong, and he and I returned
to see the court (for such I had never imagined to see) and bring away
his oath-fond mother, for he was very afraid that she too would be
arrested and be left at the mercy of the king's ministers.

On the way there he began to grumble in his sorrow, his head
cut about and bruised and his eyes swollen, and the devils that had
fled him during the beating began again to creep back through his
nostrils and ears and mouth, as they are ever eager to do, just as gnats
[*culices*] be, pricking him to speak ill of our holy master (than whom,
we knew, few had ever been holier). In this I saw my opportunity,
proud and jealous rival that I was, and fed his dismay.

'Yea,' I said, as we hastened upon the grassy track that was misty
still, 'the hermit forgets this world of suffering, that the Lord Jesus
never forgot.' 'The Lord Jesus would have struck the courtier dumb,'
said Edwine; 'nay, he would have sent a plague of toads upon the
whole fawning rabble, sparing only good King Henry himself!' I
laughed and said: 'Then you would be made the first minister, and I
the chief knight, with armour of worked gold and the thickest lance
ever seen, and we would fill our court's library with the most costly
and fabulous books.' Thus I fed his devils as if giving crumbs to flies,
that swell to hideous dragons within.

The mists were thinning as we approached the village, yet we
could not see it for the tents and waggons and the swarm of people,
while the stench of horses, oxen and men, and old fish and rotten

meat, mingled so thickly that it made its own vapour, that numerous camp fires added to yet further in a choking miasma. I said to Edwynn that this was very like the fog that awaiteth sinners in Satan's kingdom, and which afterwards moisters the fields of Hell and corrupts them, for nothing grows in that desolation.[242] Yet all he replied was, 'Ey, daf, keep thy peace!'

There in a sty for swine we perceived several pairs of feet, while a hovel used by shepherds was replete with fine cloths and straw beds such as armies use, numbering at least ten. The din was dreadful: men and women running about, and trumpets blowing, and buffoons play-acting beneath a tree to make courtiers laugh, for the young king himself was still a-bed, and none knew where they might be going next – not even Whittby [being certain], for they were tardy by more than a day. Never have I seen such loads piled upon waggons, nor poor sumpter-mules more weary, so that some had died in their harness, cruelly flayed. Great casks of sour wine were set upon carts, from which all drew liberally and grimaced as they swallowed; while nobles and knights, wrapped in cloaks brushing the torn and corrupted earth, did chew at a table on mouldy crusts dipped into a muddy broth, and all the time shouting orders that none obeyed: spitting all the while like the roughest serfs, they plunged their fingers into the cups as they drank, spattering much grease about.

Within the houses of the village (for the tents were for their servants), the highest ministers were billeted; yet even they looked dismayed and vexed when they emerged from under peasant thatch in their fine caps and cloaks, and some in glittering mail with their helmets under their arms, to practise [jousting or fighting] in the lists – for which horrid pastime many apple and pear trees were felled, for the orchard was the flattest place, and soft-grassed.

Of the original inhabitants, there was no sign, for cast out as they were, they had either stayed elsewhere bewailing their ruin (for the locusts were taking all), or vanished into the throng – especially that

[242] One of the greatest solaces on my return from our very real Hell-Front, was to find the clean fields and blooming meadows of England untainted by poison gas or chemicals, and torn only by the cutting plough and trampling hoof of quiet labour.

which convulsed [*agitavit*] about the church and the great barn, in which more long tables were set, heaving with people.

Hoping for droppings and leavings, or decent gains – selling their only skinny cow to the ravenous lords and their servants, or milk to the royal merchants by so much a pail – these [locals] were no doubt cheated in the pandemonium. Some were hired as washerwomen, slaving at giant tubs upon heat provided by their own long-stored fuel: one had her baby beside her, that she did coax her pap into when he screamed, inches from the bubbling water full of dirty cloths. Amongst these women Edwyn, alas, could not find his mother, but only his maiden aunt that was a simpleton with cropped hair like a sheep's, and spoke no more than twenty words in a loud voice.

The smithy was disembowelled, for the court had great need of repairs, and had loaded the anvil upon an oxen cart, and all the tools, that it might mend buckets or weapons or whatnot, wherever it stopped. For this, Edywin's father had received meagre compensation of £12, that he had refused, which led to the bitter quarrel for which he might hang – for the victim of his wrath lay between life and death, though the royal surgeons had bled him strongly and wiped and cleansed his wounds.

And likewise had the village been emptied of all its cart horses, oats, hay, halters and other apparel, and every beast in stye and byre and field, down to hens and several hundreds of eggs, for which coin makes no reparation when winter cometh, while certain ways and yards were ankle-deep in stinking dung and excrement from the press of the living creatures both human and animal, for none minded where they did their offices. I saw many lost women, alas, painted like harlots (for such they were) and loosely clad, showing bare arms and necks and worse, and some in carnal conjunction with men, scarce concealed! – for they served their clients with only a heap of straw as curtain, that anyone might peer round by chance, squinting through the choking vapours.

Many times have I seen Hell on this earth, dear reader!

All this awful sight was drawing me nearer to the pure way of the hermit, yet for one demon within me, that held out a sweet fruit.

I noted how idle and bored many of the courtiers were, despite the play-actors and buffoons and jugglers, who performed no doubt the same japes and mirths as many times before on the royal progress, judging by the hisses and boos; and e'en the court's [glove] puppets, that held me as in a trance, their squawking ribaldry in the canvas booth seeming more true than their human counterparts, failed to quicken any member of the dusty train of the king. And among the servants was an Ethiop,[243] that marvelled me much, for I bethought him at first to be the Devil who had slipped secretly in, though his features were as ours and with strong, white teeth.

Thereupon, watching Edywin pleading for his father at the feet of a noble with haughty nostrils like slits in a sleeve, who kicked him aside and then threw him a coin to further humiliate him, I left my fellow scholar under some pretext or other [*per causam alicujus rei*] and made hot-foot for the cliffs, ne'er stopping though my feet were bare upon the path.

My master being once again settled into meditation, I could borrow the harp from the cave without troubling him. Within two *milewey*[244] from leaving the hermitage, I was returned to the court and its clamour. The king (or mayhap his guardians) were not yet decided whither they would progress, if anywhere at all that day, for reasons no one knew: the mists had cleared to warm sunlight, and Witby was scarce a day away for a laden cart.[245]

Edwynn having disappeared, I sat upon a tussock by a fence, where it seemed to me there was a better type of young courtier – both men and women – perched on rugs and well-woven carpets in a quieter spot; and I began to play, singing also. Novelty rewarded me with coins, each one a marvel to me; for I did sing well under my master's tutelage, who maintained that nimbleness of fingers on strings is a

[243] A black man, probably captured in the Holy Land; medieval prejudice equated very dark skin with the Devil, though not of any specific hue. Such odious comparisons survive into our own day, alas.
[244] See earlier note: about forty minutes.
[245] This is an unclear indication of distance: a cart drawn by horses can haul for eight hours a day, that pulled by oxen can manage only five.

divine gift and that the songs of angels will make us seem as cackling hens and our nimbleness as that of a toad, but we must ever strive to imitate them: and my voice then was still that of a girl's. Soon a small crowd was gathered in a circle about me, and I did not stumble from nervousness but was lifted by the joy of so many people listening to naught but myself – my soul being full of wicked pride instead of humility. And thus I did win many pennies that day, growing as if by a charm into shillings! And the taste for greater glory was in my mouth, thanks to the Devil, who ever plants in us unwonted joy as well as pains, to further his treachery.

From the large but humble farmhouse that flew the pennants of the royal and legitimate sovereign upon its mossy thatch, the Prince of Princes himself emerged; sore pressed to glimpse him, there being many in front of me bustling to prepare for departure, and great carts and waggons, and whinnying horses and braying mules, I slipped between legs to the front, being yet small of stature. His own small-ness of youth caused him, anyway, to be half hid behind his favourites and the lords and guardians that ruled for him, though I could see the gilded hem of a blue silken robe brushing the carpet laid for the progress to his mount, and very beautiful pointed shoes of buttoned leather.

Then of a sudden his pale-hued, royal visage appeared, that was indeed one-eyed;[246] and spying the harp upon my back, he stopped. Thereupon a retainer approached me and bid me play. In the fore-front of that throng, and covered over in a sudden great heat, my limbs refused to move as though gripped by ague, and giddiness came over me as I had been assaulted with a cudgel.

And forthwith was the king hastened upon his way, seeming more anxious than angry, for he was too young to hold sway over his ministers, and I was left severed from all my hopes, and in pitiful shamefulness.

Soon the cries and trumpets faded over the hill, and the village was as an empty field of battle, much knocked, in which the only

[246] More precisely, the somewhat ineffectual Henry III had a drooping eyelid, inherited by his son – the much more confident and effective, if unpleasantly belligerent, Edward I.

sound was oaths against all who rule over others on this earth, and women weeping, and children running about in search of dropped trinkets and broken valuables and crockery, and the bleat of a single spared goat. The stream and the well that the inhabitants must drink from were full of garbage, entrails and other foul ordure, that mingled its vapours with the yet-smoky air. Even the little holy church was not spared, for she bore a drunken harlot within, left behind the altar and snoring, whose fate was to be dragged out and stripped, smeared in dung, and whipped black and blue until there was scarce a tooth growing in her face, that she couple no more with lewd men or husbands.

'Twas Edwin's father who beat her with the most zeal, using a carter's lash;[247] for the steel-dinting bull had been released by royal pardon, in consideration of the loss of his equipment, with a fine of £4, this sum removed from the recompense – the victim being recovered sufficiently to depart upon a litter with the rest of the court. And Edwynne's mother returning from a distant field, and cajoling her husband with many choice oaths as was her wont (for she blamed him, being a shrew), he bestrewed his anger upon the harlot.

Alas, I intended to consume a single precious page upon the tale of the court's procession, yet my pen was swept forward, as a tiny barque upon a wave of memories, and I have blotted no less than four! Mayhap the reader hath quite forgot where he was, and e'en now rebukes these pages for taking him upon another way, as though falsely signed. For this and more, the book begs his tolerance, remembering in turn how books themselves are tolerant of readers who scatter fragments of their fare, such as cheese and fruit, o'er their open pages, or mutilate lovely volumes with their knives, or scrawl unworthy comments in the margin, that it were better those scholars were unlettered and given o'er wholly to sloth.

For e'en the unlettered know this: that drowning men can yet survive by human intervention, yet when the waves be too high, the

---

[247] Usually with three leather lashes each ending in a lead weight.

depths too profound, and the stir of water be too strong, then only the Almighty can be called upon. When the victim be a blasphemous and cruel felon, intent on overthrowing all that be good in our land, then the Almighty is not only no resort, but maketh the waves higher, the stir stronger, the abyss deeper.

Naught could I do in the church at Notyngham, therefore, on hearing the gates close, but to watch helplessly as Robert Hod was seized, remembering the words he had spoken to me on the way, in that wild and desolate moorland place near Bakwele:[248] 'If I be took, Much, thou must not try to save me, but flee, that you may report to the others what hath become of me. For my bodily life, I count it not worth a nail, for once it hath been discarded, I will become my Creation, that shall itself dissolve into one boundless sea. Yet it is not time for that event to pass: the sacred marriage must take place before, as it hath been ordained from time immemorial, and only then can my spirit be truly freed, and with it the entire world of matter. I have been granted this message in my dreams, and the elect are about us even now, in angelic form. Hark to them!'

And truly, in that desolate place by the crags on the way [to Nottingham], I did feel their presence, e'en on the cool air that blustered between the peaks. Yet something within me (no doubt the last remaining morsel of my true faith) did dare to ask him, as a question issuing from the most favoured of all the outlaws: 'How dost thou know these things, master, and that they are not mere dreams – oft seen to be as frivolous as buffoons on a stage?' And he looked at me with great wretchedness, astonied that I should not perceive the answer, which he gave thus: 'The question must be, not how do I know these things, but how do others know them not? And not a speck, apart from a few of the chosen? For that ignorance is the chief mystery!'

---

[248] i.e. on their way down to Nottingham, as no doubt described in the relevant missing leaf. Evidently they descended via Bakewell and the moorland of the Derbyshire 'peaks' (which remains a somewhat desolate area to this day), well west of Sherwood Forest, and avoiding the main roads. It may be of interest to note that the area boasts a Robin Hood's Stride and an eponymous Cross.

O miserable wretch that I was! To be taken in by such deranged jabbering, oozing from his mouth as pulp from a poison fruit! How puffed up I felt, to be intimate with such a personage, as a counsellor is with a king, though that king be a mere wisp of straw on the winds of time – of the same brevity as the sparrow crossing the hall, as it was famously said long ago![249]

[249] Namely (as every schoolchild knows), by the Venerable Bede. History being regularly disturbed by the baleful presence of such types as Robert Hod (necessarily in positions of great power, as opposed to running a ramshackle band of cut-throats), we must be thankful that our modern era, in the wake of the War's terrible price, has brought a new, albeit shamefaced spirit of construction, hope and common sense, inimical to such 'poison fruits'. [*'B Company' scrawled in left margin of footnote in FB's hand, with 'ramshackle band' double underlined.*]

3

Yet I did obey him to the letter, on hearing the gates of the city close, by dint of my paralysis and not my will. For as the armed men [raised by the hue and cry] surged into the church, I remained pressed against the pillar under the tower, perched upon the high lip of the base that I might see the events unfold, with the golden boy He[n]ri beside me, my hand upon his shoulder.

How excited he was, as we clung to the fresh-hued stone! I pulled him closer to me as though his boon companion, for I was uncertain whether I had been descried with Hode by witnesses, and so entwined with his guilt. I was still bearing the felon's bow and quiver of arrows, indeed; they would be of small use to him now, methought – for he was thoroughly cramped by the press as the armed men[250] came forward, his blue coat and hood marking him out as openly as a torch in the night.

He, making no resistance, remained staring upon the damsel, who was being pulled away by her father and the short-statured baron,[251] yet twisting [*obtorsit*] her neck back to seek her former captor's face – for his hood had been pulled down and no doubt she did recognise him. Though hardly manly in my years, and many yards from her, I was nigh swooning, for I found her loveliness increased by the

[250] i.e. those raised by the hue and cry; although the law declared that 'all' local men should answer the call, certain hand-picked citizens must answer it 'swiftly and hastily'.
[251] The powerful, acquisitive and conservative Ranulph III, earl of Chester (*c.*1170–1232), was reputed to be short; he owned numerous estates and castles in the north, and would have been in his mid-fifties at this time. However, although ruthlessly ambitious in the Anglo-Norman manner, and probably pious, he was not particularly noted for cruelty in the fashion of his most important master, King John.

excitement upon her face (as I perceived it from afar), that mingled fear and astonishment and pleasure.

She was delivered into the north transept, out of my view, and my attention returned fully to Hod. He was already seized, for he moved as a branch on the stream, not of his own volition. There was more shouting, and a crash as of masonry, as the phalanx surrounding the prisoner thrust a way through the crowd of spectators and made for the south door.

Glimpsing blood upon Hod's forehead, I saw he had been struck by a club or staff; carried bodily like a drunken man, his feet dragging behind, he seemed in a reverie, with mouth agape. And all this while Henry did join in the tumult with piping cheers; yet nowhere did I spot brother Thomas, the Judas of the matter (as I thought of him then, poor doomed wretch that he was!). Then the south door closed upon them, and was guarded.

Thus was the Arch-fiend arrested, not as later he bid me describe it,[252] but as a dog is dragged on a rope to the dunghill.

I wished to descend from our perch and make my way out of the building by the north door, to see where they were taking my master; but the church of St Mary's was [now become] the market of Bagdad, the famed metropolis of the Muhametans: such a stir and bustle was there, and such a clamour, and such a turbulence of heads, fists, staves and swords, along with men's cries and women's shrieks that echoed greatly in the vast stone chamber of the place, with additional voice from the priests and sidesmen and so forth berating the mob from the chancel, that I wondered if any of us might emerge unscathed.

For word had got round already that an infamous felon had been taken in the holy place, during a divine service, and this itself caused such a consternation and excitement that those of the shyref's men not now accompanying the arrest did gain needful employment in breaking the heads of the common folk that were come into the church

---

[252] This is an undoubted reference to what was about to be the first form of the ballad, as we shall see. In that ballad (*Robin Hood and the Monk*), the malefactor leaves twelve men dead from the attentions of the '*too-hond sworde*', before the said sword breaks apart upon the sheriff's head.

to gape, and thus exciting them further; while another path was beaten out from the throng by dint of clubs and staves, for the express purpose of the damsel, who left along the north side upon the arm of the baron.

Much blood was spilt, therefore, and many folk were dishevelled, bruised and torn in that sacred place, yet not by Robert Hod.[253]

The vicar and his ministers were meanwhile shouting from the chancel that it was a violation, for the church was a sanctuary, and not even a murderer should be drawn out; and on coming down the side of the nave to the south door, where they attempted to egress, they fell into a scuffle that saw a glittering cope torn and trampled underfoot, and several holy men pushed to the floor, as the scherryf's guards grew wrathful themselves. And true it was that never before had such a violation been seen during mass! Though Almighty God knew better, for Hod cared no more for the divine service than the dog that was now barking at the affray, before relieving its bladder on our pillar.

When eventually Henrie and myself were able to leave, it was too late to learn by my own witness where Hode had been taken – but at second hand I knew immediately on emerging into the market, for the talk was of little else. Indeed, a parti-coloured buffoon with bells on his wrists was gaining pennies by miming the event in a ridiculous fashion, e'en to the shame of mincing like a woman in imitation of the grey-eyed Isabele, and thereby causing bursts of laughter. His reward was to have fists and feet laid upon him by a pair of the baron's oafs, whose rough jingling [*tinnitus*][254] put an end to the spectacle, for (being a stranger) he delighted not in the baron's influence, and knew not what gravity of insult he had committed. And again, Henry did watch the beating with a pleasure that sat ill upon his girlish

---

[253] Such affrays, not uncommon in the medieval period, might seem alarming from the perspective of modern standards. Preferring our violence to be thoroughly organised and in foreign parts (though of far more horrendous cost in lives and damage), we are able to retain the illusion that we are much more civilised than our pre-industrial forebears (see Peter N. Carter's essay on riots in *Medieval Lawbreaking*, London, 1909).

[254] Presumably from their coats of mail, though this may refer to their 'activation' of the buffoon's wrist-bells.

countenance; and even I, on seeing this harmless blasphemer of my lovelorn worship vanish under kicks and blows, was glad.

The gossips proclaimed that the dangerous outlaw had been took to a manor belonging to the baron many miles away, wherein a deep gaol awaited him, and the delights of the baron's many famed instruments of torture (such as the rack, or pressing by weights, or being filled by foul water) to be extracted of a confession. Others maintained that he had been dragged to a lightless cell within the thick stones of the castle, wherein the sheryff threw the worst malefactors, who oft perished in the stench of unclean straw or were gnawed alive by rats, there to await the justices.[255] And such glee did these common folk show, that it was only with great effort that I hid my anger from them and from Henri.

'Let us see which it is,' I said, 'for such a felon is not a daily dish.' And we joined those already drifting towards the castle, as we thought it probable that the high sherf would have taken him in under his own jurisdiction, as the law makes plain. Little Henry lost no opportunity to vaunt his own abilities, boasting of his favoured position in the eyes of father G[e]rald, let alone 'his courageous master, captor of felons'. The boy indeed looked the picture of saintliness in his oblate's cloak. Pshaw! [*phui*] did I wish to exclaim, and buffet those golden curls; but instead I played the amiable shepherd in the play, that his view of me remain innocent and opaque.

There was a small crowd already before the castle, straining to see through the iron gates into the courtyard, and jabbering together. Hod's repute had been inflated on the instant, by mere dint of his being arrested in the great church, yet few had heard of him this far south of his activities; whereas other outlaws, slain or seized likewise, had been swiftly forgot, though more local than he (being denizens of the forest of Scherwode, hard by Notyngham) – e'en when their corpses were dandled in iron chains at the gates or the crossways for the crows to peck and urchins to throw [stones?] against.

---

[255] The judicial powers of the sheriff were being increasingly replaced at this time by travelling courts (justices-in-eyre). The situation was complicated in Nottingham by dint of its two boroughs, Saxon English and Norman French, having quite separate administrations until *c.*1300.

'Hark,' cried Henri, 'I think I hear him screaming! That is very fine! He will have a second and much more unpleasant [*insuavem*] episode after he is hanged, which will continue for ever!' I was disgusted to hear him speak thus, in the mincing manner of my old master, for he was not yet ten and such phrases from a small, budding mouth sounded obscene. I wished to dash his brains out on the cobbles, for the devil's daughter of jealousy was dancing wildly in my chest again; instead, I told him in a calm voice that it was but the noise of the swifts, who nested in the castle's eaves high above our heads.

A baker's boy delivering bread to the castle (still covered in flour and stains of soot as if just emerged from the night's ovens) confirmed to us that he had witnessed the wicked felon, marked by rotten fruit and dung thrown at him in the lanes, being took into the passageway that led to the gaol; and he maintained that the cells were as horrible as the gaolers, with heavy iron neck-bonds so fashioned with spikes inside that if the wretches did not stand, but attempted to sit or lie, then they would be pierced, as in the sleeping time of anarchy.[256] Requesting a prayer in the abbey church for his sick mother, the boy gave Henry a honeyed loaf from his sack, in kind.

Thus Henrie and I broke sweet bread together by the castle, little thinking how fate would soon entwine our souls firmer than flour and water in a bakery, till Doom's trumpet! He laughed shrilly, pleased at his ruse, for the bread was free. When I said that it was not free, but paid for in the eternal coin of prayer (determined to be more than his equal in the imitation of brother Thomas's phrases), he laughed e'en louder, saying in his piping voice, 'I have no intention of praying for that simpleton's idiot mother, my friend! I care not an acorn for the poxy dame!' And then I saw that his goldenness and angelic countenance concealed a mean and vicious temperament, just as King John's[257] lewd and ugly ways did show as an infant, as plants or trees grow awry from the first day: the mildew [*mucor*] engendering with the seed.

---

[256] *turba*: presumably referring to the nineteen years of King Stephen's quite-recent reign (1135–54), when, according to the famous entry in the *Anglo-Saxon Chronicle* (R.S., vol. II, p. 231), 'Christ and his saints slept.'
[257] 'Bad King John' having been dead only some ten years.

Anon Henrie informed me that my former master had not glimpsed me in the church, being slow of eye. I asked: 'Doth he wish to meet with me?' [. . .] 'Indeed,' quoth the boy, 'though not here but in Lentonne priory, for the subprior [of Lenton] hath much expertness in the writings of St Iohannes Damascenus[258] and other ancient scholars, and [wishes to show us?] the priory's great herb garden, in which many diverse and useful plants grow, after the example of Macer.'[259] And the golden Henri was so excited by this, as much as by the arrest, that [I felt he was?] tormenting me, for of a sudden I was seized with a great grief, that I had cast all this fragrancy aside for the stinking life of a forest felon and cut-throat . . . [my new master?] now chained to the bare floor of a foul cell, from where many an innocent never emerges – or no longer of sound mind.

Gruffly, therefore, I [released?] my arm from his and said I must make my way swiftly to the butts upon the commons, where the wealthy merchant aforementioned would be waiting, no doubt impatient for his bow. In truth, I planned on running hotfoot to the stables where our horses were tethered, and returning by the main highway to the outlaw's camp, to summon help. Alas, Henry gave me a most winning and imploring look, [saying?] he did love the butts and archery, but his life as an oblate forbad him such pastimes, and that he was mortally sick of learning and of chafing his knees in endless prayer, and of the blows of the birch-rod. 'Mayhap you might bring me to the butts,' he pleaded.

And I, expressing horror that he should think of abandoning his master, heard the bells pealing noon, whereupon he said there was time enough – and that, were he to return a little late to the priory, he would say how the violent and dangerous press in the church delayed him – which was not a lie.

[258] Coincidentally (unless the passage is a confusion of memory), the prior of Lenton at this time was also called Damascenus. One presumes brother Thomas preferred to meet his page there, in safety, after betraying Hod. Lenton Priory was a Cluniac house; St Mary's was one of their endowments. Damage, from red-hot shrapnel during a shelling at the foot of Messines Ridge, soon after the document came into my possession, has rendered several lines of this leaf illegible. It is quite possible that my life was thereby saved.
[259] The eleventh-century author of a popular herbal.

How I did hate him then! – for his small hand was fast about my arm, delaying me. And I did understand how he was a curse in my life; had he not drawn my former master away from me with honeyed airs, as once Edwyne had with the hermit, I would never have embarked on my foolhardy adventure, and steeped myself in felony and sinfulness, living like a vagrant under the boughs![260]

Then suddenly the truth came to me, in my torment, how I was always in great need of worldly affection – that imperishable love of the Lord never being enough for miserable and weak sinners, though it be as freely granted as sunlight is.

And so greatly thirsting as I was, I would always find a fresh spring of affection: yet each time drawing too much from it, I caused it to dwindle or dry up; or I did poison it that it became clotted matter [*tabum*]:[261] as happened with the hermit, then brother Thomas, and must soon come to pass with Robert Hode, unless I were to save him from certain torture and execution. I cried secretly within: 'Alas, that I lost my proper father as an infant, leaving me only the offscourings of his love and influence, so I have to search for its manliness in diverse places: curses on that evil and lewd king!'[262]

My dagger was in my belt, and so incited was I by these dark, tormented thoughts, that I might have cut his [Henry's] throat then and there anigh the castle gates where the motley knot of citizens gawped: from tinker to baker to cripple to cook, alike thirsty for news, as much as the lean goldsmith or the fat merchant – or even the fair ladies gossiping and giggling (to the invisible demons' delight) so close to us we could smell their sweet violet [nosegays?] upon the air, and catch their nonsense – for they had already fashioned Robert Hod into the handsomest villain in the land. And Henry wondered what was the matter with me, for I was turned very pale under my dirty visage: and I all but broke into tears upon his little shoulder!

---

[260] As he himself seems to recognise, this is not fair in either case: concerning the hermit, he left voluntarily some time after Edwin had departed; of brother Thomas, he risked the outlaws' camp in order to retrieve his harp.

[261] My metonymic translation is more likely, I think, than 'plague' or 'pestilence'.

[262] King John, whose men were apparently responsible for the father's death.

It may be that the golden boy was replete with fiends, as a sweet apple can be full of writhing worms – fooling the hungry wayfarer under its shining skin, as it lies on the grass. Sometimes, even in my senescence (some eighty years later), I do think this of the boy; but only for comfort, to appease my horrible guilt.

My own present blotted and flaccid skin, that time alone has pocked and defouled, would make no one pause, however famished. Only the eternal fire might burn it and purify it, though each purification is swiftly followed on the morrow by the same former corrupting, as with an *antrax*.[263] for the punishment for murder is crackling flame without end, be it as hot as that which maketh glass, or melteth the hardest iron.

I knew the commons area was hard by the stables wherein we had tethered our horses, yet as we walked towards the city wall, I had no notion of where upon the commons the butts might be found, for all was feigning in my story. I was afraid the stables would already be guarded by the [sheriff's?] men, for immediate enquiries would have been made in such places, but just as worship was neglected in that time, so also was the capturing of malefactors. I believed Hod to be already pressed by a great weight of iron, or nipped by pincers, or hung by his thumbs and smoked at his feet, that he might give my presence away; or confess even to deeds he never committed, such as the stealing or murthering of children, or e'en the casting of spells upon the king. I felt the rope rub my neck, and was sore afraid.

My only thought was to flee the city, but we found the gates still locked fast, that not even a mouse might enter or leave until the sh[e]r[i]ff was ensured that none other of Hod's men be within Notyngham; though many said it was the baron's order that shut them. It is true that there was fear of insurrection at that time, for the king was very young, and many barons chafed at the power of his regents.[264] A rich Jew was arguing with the guards, that he might be let out by the [small] door in the great gates, and I saw coins pressed into the

[263] As in MS: Middle English for a malignant boil or growth, that those historians favouring an Old World origin for syphilis, see also as a syphilitic eruption or chancre.
[264] Henry came of age in 1227, two years after the date of our narrative.

sergeant's hand and, corrupted by this bribe, he let the door be opened, to the anger of the others held back by sharp-pointed lances from our forefathers' time.

Others were let in and out, that did not resemble felons, but each time money passed hands (as I understood it), to the increasing anger of the common folk who wished to pass also with their honest wares. And insalubrious stuff being thrown, such as rotten fruit, greasy pasties, putrid pigeons and even more unmentionable garbage, against the gates and the venerable walls of stout oak,[265] the guards before them were struck: and so the constable came out, with such a paunch before him that you would say he was holding a barrel under his hauberk, and a trumpet was blown. He threatened – as if in proclamation – that those throwing would suffer the hurdle or the pillory, as befits fraudulent traders (he said), for they were buying cheap and selling dear, and it was all corrupting for the belly (clapping a hand on his own); and this speech made many laugh – for by this he meant to turn all merry, and draw the anger out.

And no more stuffs were thrown, but the people waited patiently in the yard before the gates, trading and dealing and making sport among themselves; while all this time I also waited with Henry among the common folk, sore afraid, and saying he must return to his master forthwith. 'Pshaw!' he cried, each time: 'I am merrier with you.' We sat upon an old cask, and he jabbered of many silly matters (such as the theft of two geese from the abbey yard), as if he had not oped his mouth in a year.[266]

He glued himself to me so, that folk there might have thought he was my brother – unneth my own page, and not the monk's. I wished him dead, in truth, for he also awoke in me a strange longing for the monastic house I had left so many months before, that was my only home; and e'en the smell of the sea-cave years before that, in which my first master dwelt, rose about me as the fragrance of roses in a garden.

[265] The wooden walls, originally dating from the Conquest and extended thereafter on an earth rampart, were rebuilt in stone only in the late thirteenth century.
[266] Oblates being strictly limited in their daily allowance of speech.

I could not therefore prevent myself weeping behind my hands, for all seemed dark: which sight astonished Henrie. Placing his child's hand yet tenderly on my nape, he bid me not to fret over my merchant-master's archery, as all men would know that the city had been closed. I might have struck him – so hateful was it to be comforted by a mere piping imp, and so hardened was I by my outdoor felon life – if there had not been a great squeal of hinges at that moment, and the way made suddenly open.

I jumped down and darted between the many folk departing and entering, heedless of whether the golden boy was with me – indeed, I wished to shake him off, and thought I heard a high crying of my name behind me, that dwindled in the seething press of people I did thrust my path through, almost snapping the bow, until I burst there-out to freedom. The gates being shut two hours, the egress was like a deep ditch that is blocked and accumulates all sorts of annoyances and garbage and dung with a weight of water pressing upon it, and then is sudden released – wherein it flows much greater and more stinkingly than before, until the flood calms.

Upon the commons I made straight for the stables that lay anigh there, and took Hod's horse (that was a swift, small-headed palfrey, but not his customary steed) behind my own on a halter rope I purchased from the groom, telling him that my pious master was residing in the priory for a month, and giving the boy a penny [extra]. This took time, as the saddles had to be set and the horses bridled and girthed, whereat golden-haired Henry appeared before the stable yard, puce-faced from running, with a look as the angels must have when they cast us away into the arms of the fiends of Hell – so furious and sad it appeared at the same time, that it made me almost cower. I was already mounted, and without thought I spurred my horse past him, Hodd's palfrey following on the rope as best it might.

I near ran the angel-boy over in my haste – yet not once did I look back, despite his shrieking 'Ho!' at me. And soon I was upon the high road, going at a steady rack [*citatus gradu*].[267] Sleeping that night in a grassy ditch, I reached the outlaw's lair in the morning of the following day, as hungry as a lion; all the while seeing the wretched boy's face looking up at me in piteous astonishment, yet horribly mingled with that of the damsel of the bluish-grey eyes, called Isabelle, so his features nestled in hers under the wimple!

I was so gladdened to be again under the great boughs, with all the little leaves trembling and fulsome with the spring, that I even forgot for a moment my grief and burden. Then the men cried, looking up from their tasks (or more often their idleness) in the wood-ways: 'Here be the youth! What news, Muche?' Which made me proud again, for they were eager, as though I were a knight returned from the Holy Land; while not even Flawnnes called me a filthy name.

And stopping my horse in the clearing under the giant oak where the felons would gather,[268] I recounted to them what had happened, even before I had dismounted, my loins well chafed from the saddle.

Terrible were the wailings of the men, as I supped on venison broth and drank the seethed juice of birch,[269] that lay on my tongue like the sodden leaves of the very tree itself – until it shook its crown in my brain, and was worse [in its effects] than ale. The outlaws wished to ride to the cursed town[270] of Nottyngham immediately,

[267] The rack, between a trot and a canter, is the most likely pace when speed is required but a horse is being led behind, as I frequently witnessed myself in the late mass slaughter (which incidentally was as injurious to poor, long-suffering *equus* as any medieval battle, if in proportionately far greater numbers).

[268] The 'tristil-tree' or 'trusty-tree' (trysting- or meeting-tree) is a stock feature of the ballads – though this particular giant oak has been mentioned before, of course, and seems realistic. The ensuing scene with Little John is remarkably close to the corresponding moment in *Robin Hood and the Monk*, from which a missing leaf has deprived the reader of Robin's capture.

[269] Presumably fermented: the present translator, having voluntarily imbibed the unfermented variety for medicinal purposes, found its humble taste delightful – indeed, the closest one might get to drinking a summer wood.

[270] Suspicion of urban life and its mercantile properties, rapidly expanding then as now (though without the gobbling horrors of the suburban brick box), are a singular theme of the ballads.

but the hullabulloo brought out Littel John from Hod's hut, which sore surprised me, for I thought him in Sherwode. But nay, he had doused his anger in riding hard over the moor, and poaching a fine stag from the king's land (slaying it with a single shot): which beast's head, crowned by huge antlers, he had mounted upon a pole by the rocks to scare away all intruding evil spirits – a most unhallowed and heathen act, that was to those very spirits as a stinking offal to flies.

Seeing Litel John come out thus from Hod's hut, when no man was allowed in there save he be invited, I did wonder to myself how such a blasphemy could be tolerated: then I understood from Wil Scalelock, whispering in my ear, that Literl John was our captain from this moment, and all must obey him. 'How can this be?' I returned boldly (made reckless by the juice); for our new master was approaching the fire, and a veritable ogre he seemed to me in my weariness, having crowned himself with a chaplet of leaves that dandled about his ears.

'Such was it decided between them before,' said Will, 'if our holy master Robbert should be taken; and if he be killed, then no man will be master, for all the chosen [spirits] will be free in his divine essence. For our true leader Robert is greater than God, that even his dust and shavings of hair will be precious relics.' Yet God hath not hair, I should have said, for He is light eternal; but so deep was I in worthless heresy, that I merely assented with a nod.

Litel John commanded the men to cease their shouts and moans and mutterings, that made them like a rabble, or a gaggle of fish-wives, and after hearing from me [what had happened], he cursed the grey-eyed damsel and all womanhood, which was a blasphemy to the more devout of the heretics; for Hod had declared her to be his holy spouse, brought to him not by Fortune or even God but by the sea [of divine essence]. Yet none dared oppose Litel John, who was the strongest there, yet of no more brain (it was bruit among us) than a wine-tun.

Then he asked where was the monk from, who had so horribly betrayed our leader. And I trembled, for I did not want to tell him that I knew brother Thomas, nor that he was the monk they had robbed on the road when I was with him. This was a great error, for honesty might have allayed the suspicion that I was involved in the treachery by sleight.

Yet John was a vengeful man, and must have a tooth for a tooth; a devil crawled into my mouth and manipulated my tongue. I was a mere ignoble youth and full of pride, swelling e'en more when I saw the men all gape upon me for the answer, and my brain still moistered by the strong drink.

And so I said, 'He is of that hateful abbey that hath this very wood in lease.' And the men all cried out its name, and swore, for they cursed the holy house of St Edmund's of Dancaster, that wished to cut their trees for the making of their glass, as barley or oats are cut by the sickle to make bread. 'When does he return?' asked John; and I felt moistness in my mouth, which was bitter, for no doubt a demon was pricking my spleen with each hesitation. And this made me utter the truthful answer, which (as I had learned from Henrie) was upon this very day of Saturday: the journey to be made without a night's rest.[271]

'Then he will be returning there by the highway,' the felons cried, 'mayhap it's not too late!' Litl John hushed them with a roar, and said he must meet this tree-lopping Judas Iscariot alone, and prise from him what intelligence he could; before [avenging] our master Robrerrt [sic] in the right way, with a cut throat.

'You must accompany me, Moch the little minstrel,' he added, 'for only you might tell me how the villain appeareth, even in disguise.' I could not reply that he would recognise me, as his former pupil, for none present knew this. Instead I said: 'Happily will I do this, save he might know me from the church, as I talked well to his little page.' And John scoffed, saying, 'Didst thou tell the little page thou wast Robbert Hod's [page]?' 'Nay,' I answered, 'yet he is a crafty boy, and I left him too hastily on witnessing the capture.' 'Cease thy lambish fears,' said Litell John, 'for we too will be returning from that cursed

[271] According to a royal charter of 1155, the town's market was held on Friday and Saturday. The journey between Nottingham and Doncaster could be done (on horseback) in a day.

Notynggam, and you shall be disguised! And even I shall be dressed as a merchant, playing thy father, for our fame begins to spread.'[272]

I felt borne upon a strong current, too weary to resist, alas, like an otter [*lutra?*][273] that hath been winded by the hunt. And the others complained, saying why should they tarry in the wood, while their master was rotting in the stench of a cell, enduring tortures? And Flawnes of the thin face cried, standing upon a fallen bough and waving his horrible knife like a claw: 'Let us break down the door of the prison, all fifty of us well armed, having stolen into the city in disguise, and after laying hands upon the sheryf and his men, and striping them into ribbons, rescue our true master!' But Little John said he had received a vision in the master's hut, that place being called the *Schyninge Tempel*: for within it the obscure was revealed – namely, the future way – as if by a great light. Yet rather should it have been called (say I now) the Temple of the Nail [*clavis*], for no more than a nail was it worth.[274]

My disguise was that of a modest girl in a maidenly pelisse, with my face whitened by lye behind a fine veil, for I was feigning sickness of a mild ague and the air must not mingle with my breath. And the master forger, he whose fingertips had been shaved by glass to the bone, did practise his skills upon me as if I were a document, and the touch of him was cold and very horrible. And lest Litell John was known to the monk (which indeed he was, from the robbery), or e'en by repute, the forger crushed certain berries; drawing out the juice therefrom, he rubbed it into the skin of my companion, which made the skin swell and redden like a corpulent fellow's for many hours, as the juice of fresh walnuts make a man seem leprous. And Litel John was truly now the plump merchant, for a cushion was tied upon his stomach, under the shirt.

---

[272] It seems the outlaws have not recalled Much's original connection with the monastic house of St Edmund's, after many months. The situation is, in fact, rather more delicate than the narrative admits.

[273] The word is made unclear by a stain. Possibly '*lupa*' (a she-wolf; also a prostitute).

[274] A scholarly pun, *clari* being the Latin for 'shining', and *clavus* for 'a nail'. In the later ballad, John tells the outlaws to hunt deer.

Also, the forger gave false papers to Litl Johne, changing words and names on that which had been stolen; for verily the outlaws' camp had a great number of these [stolen documents]. This matchless villain could e'en forge a royal seal in wax! Thus nimbly does the Devil work, throwing all into disorder and turmoil.[275]

Then the felons laughed as I rode out, for I was truly like a maiden and of great beauty behind the veil, that rubbed out my boyishness like a strigil doth graze ink, yet keepeth the shadow of it. The loudest was Fawnes, calling me unnatural names – who, being struck with great force of fist by Li[t]erl John as he passed him, fell bleating upon the forest earth, his thin face seeming cracked like a dish.

We passed at a gallop over the wild heath to the road, and joined it at a good gait until we saw [the forest of] Sherwod some hours later, this forest being much coppiced and lopped; yet we had not crossed my old master, to my great relief. As we passed alongside the great fresh-leaved boughs and the motley darkness beyond them, Litl Johnn (being guised as a gold-hewn merchant, and I his gent daughter) feared being despoiled in turn, which caused us much mirth; at that time, however, Sherwode was not the most dangerous place for robbery, for many who hid within it, fleeing justice or others' vengeance, were not cut-throats.

The highway entered the forest, and lest men lose the track among the sturdy trunks and boughs, knots had been tied about the branches, and ribbons slung here and there as signs, as is the usual way; but when we came to a place where three ways met in a clearing, John laughed of a sudden and did not take the marked way, but turned left along a broad and grassy stretch that was more sunken. I pointed to the way of ribbons and knots, but he said that filthy robbers had changed them, that men might be lured into their trap, and deceived in the heart of the wild and leafy waste to the cost of their

---

[275] The terror of forgery is allied to the vital importance of knowing what is true and what is false, upon which knowledge an ordered society depends; much of the 'paranoia' of medieval society derives from this recognition, and the concomitant sense that the Devil is a master of deception. This naturally necessitated a similar ruse on the part of God: so He became man, in the unexpected guise of a Jewish carpenter's son.

goods and even life. I too laughed, and hoped privately that our quarry had been thus lured, so that we would not have to meet them.

A mile or two further on, where the desolate mass of trees were broken on one side by fields and pasture, we waited just as demons wait for folk to be tempted, and ransack their souls in this world of thronging [*pressus*].[276] And Moch, waiting in these ambushes [*in insidiis erat*], was therefore a fiend himself, ready with his hook.[277]

Nathless that very same fellow is now crouched at this awful writing work, with the autumn sea-blasts blowing through the cloister's open arches and flinging sprinkles of salt spume on his page; and lo, he doth tremble like any threadbare clerk that is paid tuppence for translating into Latin, and who, if he do not finish the piecework, be clapped in iron bonds in a filthy cell by his master, till the work be completed.

[276] A common term in Middle English, of which the Latin is a skilful echo, though hard to render successfully in modern English. Compare '*al this world of prees*' in Chaucer's 'The Monk's Tale' (Skeat, l. 3327).

[277] In the surviving ballad, which our narrative is now closely conjoined with, our two heroes wait in Much's uncle's house ('*Moch emrys hows*'), overlooking the highway. This curious, rather unlikely detail is nowhere present in our earlier account, but I venture boldly to suggest that '*emrys hows*' may be an oral distortion or smoothing, through repeated use in minstrel performance over some two hundred years, of '*embusshementz*', meaning 'ambushes'.

4

Yet the iron bonds are of my own making, and my master is the Lord God Himself.

Indeed, in these fallen days, clerks and scriveners form their letters better than my holy brothers, whose days are too full of idleness and vanity, save it be to brew intoxicating liquors – for they are mostly young, and soft as well-boiled fish in our fresh century. I am more wrinkled than any page in this fat volume,[278] and as scabbed o'er and blemished as many a fine book in our library, in which youths have done their worst.

Yet it is life itself that hath mutilated me, as if I have been too much read or fallen into greasy hands, as so many of our precious books are marked in their favoured places by toothpicks and straws; and worms breeding in their pages as they breed in my own cheek teeth, and paining me so with their gnawing and digging (which neither prayer nor myrrh, nor hot mutton-fat, did ever relieve), that scarce one tooth remains in my jaw's binding.

As we awaited brother Thomas and Henri upon the track, as wolves await their helpless prey, memories came unbidden of my earlier years, so that at times in my great weariness, and all but slumbering in the saddle, I pictured the hermit and Edwine approaching us, and not our true quarry. My greatest sin up to that time was the stealing of the harp, for the harp was my first master's; and in seizing it I cast

---

[278] The narrative is presumably being written into a 'book' of blank pages, no doubt as simply bound as its copy; the extended metaphor of this passage is already a familiar one at the beginning of the fourteenth century.

myself from him, to end in the thorny thickets of the fallen world wherein I was now caught fast.

Alas! that loved ones waxen dull and old, and felled are the favourite places, yet a man's sins remain as ripe as a new-picked apple! For with these sins come the memories as fresh as a fragrance of the fruit, and so did I remember then, waiting on that wood-way, how I first slipped upon the ladder, and plunged from the Lord to this mortal risk to my soul. Yet what recks me, so long after, that I was on the verge of such a calamity – but that these words glisten in my head and bid me set them down?

So it was under the wood-weft that I saw again in my mind how, after playing and singing to the courtiers that dreadful day, gaining in that act what to my miserable condition was a veritable treasure, I hid this windfall [*forte oblatum*], amounting to over 10s, in an old cracked pot in a secret place near my home, this being in a corner of an overgrown meadow.[279]

Lo, under Sherwode's tree-weft did I watch myself returning to the cliff that former evening with the harp, and the hermit (being long woken from his trance of prayer), gathering *glaswort* from the foot of the rocks.

I heard again my child's voice, telling him how I had sung holy songs to the royal throng, that they might mend their ways: 'And I secretly took the instrument from the cave, my master, for fear of disturbing you.' I heard again how urgently he bid me play to him, instead of berating me, explaining it thus: 'Baffled demons attacked me while I was at prayer, throwing gold that instantly turned to boils and blains on my flesh, martyred already with sores, for the sea air salts my skin as it does that of a fish.' Though no boils were visible, yet they hurt him like fire, and thus the Prince of Fiends sends us innumerable torments that bear no visible signs.

---

[279] At this time (the early thirteenth century), cash was a rarity in the peasant economy, most transactions using barter or payment in kind; a state some utopians would like to return to, understandably – regarding economics as responsible for the dubious entry of industrialism.

How glad I was in my child's heart, not to be scolded or beaten: yet far better would it have been for my Christian soul if I had been lashed like the harlot, even at nine or ten. The demon's worm settled comfortably within my brain, on that day, ready to burst forth like a moth in the darkness; and I did not see how the hermit's dream was a warning to me, for filthy lucre is Hell's gain in this our modern [*moderno*] age.

'In the bowels of Jesus Christ,' said then my first and holiest master, 'we long for home, that is the Kingdom of God. Arise, work, and pray: that is all we need to know upon this vile earth, that is scabbed o'er with suffering. Yet we must not hasten there too swiftly, but trust in the Lord to deliver us, and not through our own hands.'

By this he meant that the demons had tempted him to end his days: this being a heinous sin, but a common temptation to martyrs of the flesh. I saw how red and swollen were his eyes from weeping, and I began to sing again in my clearest voice, telling of the purest damsel that is loved by a knight, who serves her in battle and suffers pains, that only this devout maiden's presence can heal with her own warm hands, for she is none other than the spotless Virgin. And another I sang, of a devout lady betrothed to a dreadful and bloody baron; and yet she spoke secretly to her secret spouse every night in her bed-chamber, who shared her pillow and comforted her so that she felt a trembling ecstasy in her entire body, from head to toe; this spouse being (in reality) Jesus Christ, to whom she had sworn her eternal troth.

And the sun setting upon the sea (the darkness gathering its cloak about us), a light wind caressed our faces as we sat upon the sand and I plucked and sang. Between songs my master the hermit did say how the beauty spread before us was a temporal mirror of God's eternal beauty, just as the singing of such sweet lays (and not the profane howling of buffoons in taverns or suchlike) was an echo of the angelic harmonies of Heaven, and not at all worldly. And the song of the lady of the lovely shape, clean and fair and dainty – she that in maytime doth walk in the meadow with a coronet of flowers that she hath plucked in the company of another, though many times hath she visited the poet in a vision, bidding him sleep in his restlessness with a chaste kiss of her mouth upon his lips, for she is the most merciful and Holy Queen herself, the Mother of God – he did accompany with his deep voice, in a kind of murmuring moan, that was exceedingly sad and beautiful, and all the coin thrown was of the glitter of the last rays upon the sea.

All this I lived again in the thicket by the wood-way, waiting under that leafy vault for my final transgression. Yet it did not spur me to flee, bound as I was upon the wheel [of Fate].

How better would it have been if Edwynne had stayed as my rival scholar! Instead, perceiving a great need for weaponry,[280] there being at that time a general order from the king for 100,000 [crossbow] bolts, and their iron heads at so many pennyworth per thousand, Edwyne apprenticed himself to an armourer in Yorke.

'Nay,' he quoth, as answer to our protests, 'there is no finer profession, for I shall forge swarms of arrowheads and bolts with which the infidel shall be harassed, and beat out two-handed swords as sharp as cuttlefish, but of such tempered strength they might cleave a man in two to make him less than one – happy arithmetic! And I shall quench[281] chain-mail and closed helmets for the best knights [*optimos milites*] that the defenders of the one Faith be not harmed by the forces of Satan, whose skill with steel is not as advanced as our own.' And I remember he did boast that he would earn 10d a week straight away, which seemed to me a princely sum at that time: for to get and to win is all men's care, though Edwine was driven to it by his father's ruin. And our master said naught but wrote out upon the sand that passage from Ezekiel [xviii, 20] that beginneth: *Filius non portabit iniquitatem patris* [The son shall not bear the iniquity of the father].[282]

Secretly within myself I was glad my fellow scholar was departing, for my jealousy was swollen like a ripe weed; and my pride, pushing

---

[280] Likely to have been required for the campaigns in Aquitaine, led by Henry's powerful but unsatisfactory regent, Hubert de Burgh.

[281] i.e. cool the metal in a water-trough at very high temperature, thus hardening it. Plate armour was not yet in use at this time, though it was to prove much more effective against penetration.

[282] Which goes on: '. . . neither shall the father bear the iniquity of the son'.

upwards against its tendrils, had not light enough to grow. Ed[w]yn embraced the hermit his master, who wept that his favourite disciple was to leave the path of holiness, and sacrifice his letters to *pompa militaris gloriae*.[283] But Edwyn assured him, in all earnestness, that one day this humble pupil would be the chief armourer of the land, and that on each helmet would be engraved *gyf thou not stodyst thou art slogh yn Goddys servyse*, and on each sword, *fecit se liberum*,[284] these being the first sentences in English and Latin he ever wrote.

This made the hermit laugh for the first time in many weeks, and Edwinn seized the harp and delivered a song of the famished poet's desire for the downy flesh of a quince apple [*cotoneum malum*], which his love fever alone might soften to sweetness, with honey poured into the fruit's moist vale (for there is always such a cleft in that fruit's bare roundness), that its firm voluptuousness be all his fare, for there is no quince its equal in all of Cydonia.[285] And so well and passionately did he sing this, that the hermit watered at the mouth, and quite forgot that it was far from being sacred music, and wept again when his favourite pupil took his final leave, with many a passionate embrace.

Then was I alone once more with the hermit, and ever eager to learn and better myself – not for the sake of the Lord's service, but for mortal ambition (which is, in truth, constructed of dust). Yet that foul, blind moth did awaken from its lair forthwith: for that long-ago autumn brought gales, and shipwrecks, and this in turn caused me to abandon my first and best master in the most odious way.

---

[283] I leave the Latin untranslated. One of the most harmful and pernicious illusions of human history is the belief that there is something glorious in war – of whose sordid reality each generation must learn afresh at appalling cost, as if struck by an entirely preventable plague whose ghastly effects we forget within two or three decades.

[284] 'If you do not study you are slow in the service of God' and 'He made himself free'.

[285] This remarkable account puts me in mind of a certain 'French' postcard (scant solace either to the poor *poilu* or to 'Tommy'), that I acquired on active service in Flanders, picturing a banana and a pair of peaches under the heading '*Les fruits préférés du soldat pour les petites manoeuvres*', with the following couplet beneath the latter fruit: '*La pêche, ronde et duvetée / est gage de volupté.*' [***This footnote crossed out in pencil by FB, with a scribbled note in margin: 'Give us this day our daily CLAP.'***]

Here I shall recount it forthwith, for it must be revealed before an ever greater and more odious act be likewise confessed to, that the reader might witness the ordered nature of any descent towards eternal damnation, as down a flight of stairs or a ladder, though it start with a trivial step, and finally alight on the verge of a grassy forest way, beside a felon.

Such a sea-wind did come, one day, that it amazed all. I, being in my village, heard it first as a *swowing*[286] in the twisted pines along the track that led to the sea; taking cover from its wroth, I did not witness at first hand how, lifting the ocean to veritable mountains, it drove it against ships, that many were lost, and their men with them. Many believed that it was the beginning of the Last Day, for so dark did it become as if with a dragon's vapour, that lanterns were lit at midday, and horses and mules froze as if in ice, rolling their eyes in terror. Then a certain rarefaction of the air caused birds to drop from the sky, and dogs to groan like their masters, and many dwellings lost their thatch; and trees were unplucked, crushing the common folk in their houses wherein they had cowered in fright; while in certain places the fields not yet harvested were ruined by hail, that none had ever before seen fall so in the summer.

Thunderclaps sounded, and lightning flashed, as greatly as was witnessed in the thousandth year after the birth of Our Lord and Saviour, yet nowhere did rain drop more than a quart upon our heads, and it was as warm as ale. When a certain priest took a cross and holy water, and with a few others of his church paraded to a hill I know, said to be sacred in pagan times, to banish the devils amassed under it (that were abetting the storm), he was joined by many of the faithful. As all of them walked there, singing their litanies, an intolerable stench came on the wind, worse than the breath of a thousand Jews or infidels, and rotten fish dropped from the sky on their heads, e'en very large ones that crushed the priest and wounded three

---

[286] Soughing (in even moderate gusts, the Scots pine makes a sound very like the sea's surf).

others; yet where the holy water fell, a shrieking was heard under the grass and a pearl the bigness of a hazel-nut lay there, from whence the smell of a honeycomb rose up, that overpowered the stink (though some said that the perfume was of violets), whereupon the pearl vanished that none should quarrel over it, and soon after the wind calmed and the light returned.

I hurried down to my master before the storm had fully passed, the air still blustery but the sky's upper waters no longer churned black, and saw from the cliff how the sea was a strange blue-green colour, as of a bruise, and that it was flecked by white in many places, but not mountainous: rather, it was overdriven [*fatigatum est*] in its tussle with the wind, and its foam on the shore was yellow, as men's spittle be when they have fasted and are weary (and which is venomous to adders and other serpents). Many broken things were washed up on the shore, from ships and boats and the bottom of the deeps; yet I perceived, as I ran along the beach, no corpses therein.

Surprised to see my master praying in his [circle of] stones, as if naught had threatened us all with the End of Days, I almost cried out in my relief. E'en more astonished was I to hear that same cry in the mouth of another, coming from the sea; and turning my head I first saw nothing but the hilly brine, and felt sore afraid: for the cry seemed to be the sea itself, speaking through its noises, as oft a mill-stream will appear to shout. Yet neither sea nor mill-stream have minds, as trees and flowers do not.

Then, as I looked, I saw a head in the water, far off, and a hand – for a man was clinging fast to a great spar of wood, waving his arm. Yet he was too far off to touch, were I to enter the water to my neck, wherein I would drown, for only fishes know swimming (and a few foolhardy men, it is said). My master was deep in meditation, his eyes white that were rolled up to the sky, and his hands clasped tight before him.

I ventured into the sea up to my knees and was sore afraid, for the water and the yellow foam bit at my flesh, still angered after the storm, though with weariness in it. I hailed the fellow without reflecting that mayhap this was a demon sent to lure my master or his disciple into the briny deep. The fellow vanished then reappeared closer, clinging still to the plank, his cries now palpable above the sea-surge that clapped [*ferivit*[287]] against my legs; so near he was that I could see, when the swell permitted, the crooked nature of his nose and his rivelled skin, that was a sailor's, and the shirt torn about his neck.

Desperate I was to throw a rope at him, and I shouted back that I would fetch the rope, no longer afeared of disturbing my master, for a man's life was in peril. His shout returned over the surge, gladsome and eager, for he did see salvation nigh at hand, after what dreadful perils only the Lord knew, that had consumed his fellows. I fetched an old ship's rope from the cave's store, and threw it with much crying out towards the sailor, who had drifted sideways but not an inch nearer.

Still my master kept his eyes up to heaven, and I blurted out (for the thick rope fell short, my strength being only that of a child's), 'Master, prithee help us! There is a drowning man needs to be saved!'

I drew in the rope and cast it again, but the water having entered it somewhat, it was heavier still, and fell short once more. I cried again for help and this time, with the effort of a giant, after advancing up to my waist in the broiling [water], the rope came very near – but the man, in reaching out for it, lost hold of the board at a sudden shift of the waves, and slipped between them, and vanished from my sight. And then the waves, as if greedy for more provender, or like a lioness with her whelps, did boisterously sweep me from my feet and I fell and the water came over my head and methought I was drowned as boys oft drown in flooded pits and rivers and so forth, not finding air and stifling like any beast doth, unless the air gathered within the lungs be held in.[288] And there being no air held in, I stifled with a great and horrible seething in my brain, but the Lord throwing me up at that instant as if taking my neck in his holy mouth, and casting me onto the firm sand, I tasted air that set my lungs moving once more, for they were not too grieved; and being the bellows of the

---

[287] Although *percussit* is the past of *ferire*.
[288] Again, a virtual paraphrase of Bartholomew, VIJ, xxv.

heart, they must not cease moving or extinction cometh swiftly as to a fire not blown upon.

Throughout all these travails, my master did not stir from his prayers, yet he was very close. I was weeping, for I had tasted death, near stifled by the waters; and also I saw the sailor no more, and knew he had drowned. Afterwards by an hour or so, when I was sitting before the cave grieving inwardly, yet never ceasing to scan the ocean for the lost man – my ears still plugged by seawater, that had entered me even to the roots of my brain – my master stirred at last from his prayers, and stood and came towards me with an elated look upon his face. 'I took the vow,' he said, before I could utter a word, 'never to be disturbed or interrupted in my prayers, and though the Devil tempted me with the most skilful of temptations, I did not yield.'

I said to him, thinking he must have been tempted by devils dressed as shapely harlots, or such like luxuries: 'A man drowned, and I too was nearly stifled by the waves.' 'I prayed for thee,' he replied, 'and the Lord answered.' I asked, in a shaky voice: 'And didst thou pray for the man?' 'Nay, for I was hearing the song of the angels, and contemplating the great fountain of Paradise, that is full of enamelled fishes chanting night and day, that lull the listener to a sleep softer than goosedown, when your cries came from far below.'

And so disgusted was I, in my childish ignorance, that I burst again into tears, lamenting the worthy English sailor with the crooked nose, that I had nearly joined in death, and who might have been saved if the hermit my master had interrupted his prayers to cast the rope, he being of full-grown strength even in his thinness, with the two of us to haul it in.

My master seized me by the shoulders, and shook me until my teeth rattled, saying: 'Miserable boy! Dost thou honestly think that such a sacred and heavenly vision should be cast aside for such an earthly temptation? For e'en if it was no such thing, and not sent by the Devil to waylay me like a robber might a pilgrim, dost thou not consider that such a man might be full of sin, being a sailor, and lewd and licentious as sailors are, and ripe for Hell?' I broke away from his grip, and sat upon the rocks a few yards from him, trembling and nauseous.

My master continued, in a louder voice that I might hear above the surge and the gull-cries: 'Perchance he will be rewarded for his trouble, for God is ever merciful, and on seeing how I remained stead-fast in my truer pursuit, He will regard this miserable fellow as a holy martyr, and shower virtue upon his head, and lead him through the gates of Paradise to the succulent fruits and sweet fountains of eternal bliss!' And so saying, he walked away from me up the beach with a jug, as was his wont after prayer, to collect water from a spring that splashed from a cleft in a remoter part of the cliffs and made a winding channel to the sea.

The miserable fellow was no doubt sent by Satan; for by him and my own folly, I lost the holiest and best master any disciple could ever have, and much more besides, that I pray to have life enough left me in my great age, to recount in its proper place.

And by this means, I gained another who was kind, but weak and fleshly under his sacred tonsure; that being brother Thomas. And I left him also – unfaithful wretch that I was! – for yet another whose soul was an empty larder, without so much as a dry bone within; for the Devil had taken all and filled it with cockroaches. And that was the heretic Robert Hodd, whom I now think was feasted upon by that most fearsome, hooded accomplice of Satan, named Despair.

Alas, that I must recount such events in my life, with the demons jangling at their successes over my shoulder, like men and women at a puppet play! But all must be revealed in the hope that, by so doing, I may confess, and cancel my debts – not like a begging student imploring his father to pay the barber's, the baker's, the tavern-holder, but like a true penitent whose feet bleed with the effort, and has scarce strength enough to crawl up the holy steps to his conclusion, after such a pilgrimage.

For the harp that was the hermit's, and never mine, I stole.

That is to say, upon fleeing my first master's presence, I took what I believed he no longer needed, for all luxuries be a temptation. In truth, I scarce reflected as I took it; for so disgusted was I by his behaviour, and tormented by the sight of the drowned man's hope-sprinkled face in my brain, hanging there like a horrible mask upon the wall, that I seized the moment of my master's absence (he filling the jug past the rocky headland), to snatch the instrument and – horrible sin – the Holy Book, and then scrambled away without a backward glance.

Ah! but a mere child was I, dear reader: deprived of a true father, still grieving my poor dear mother, inflamed by my late success before the courtiers, shedding bitter tears for a drowned stranger and for my own near-stifling in the waters that only the Lord's mercy saved me from, I was but a sapling twisted by contrary winds, and the blows and buffets of a short life.

Did I not reflect that I was only saved myself from drowning by the power of my master's influence – that the Lord might not have answered the prayers of most other men with such promptitude? Nay, I did not.

It is my belief (with the wisdom and knowledge of years), that devils were swimming in the yellow foam: for they say that the lake of Purgatory is cold and very salty, and therefore must be supplied by the sea, and this makes an easy passage for the fiends in the shape of salmon, that leap great heights to the mortal world. And seizing their opportunity (for I was rendered weak), they entered by my ears and mouth and nose, along with the bitter waters, and took up residence within me; there to spawn to their heart's delight, until I finally turned from the sinful way and strove for purity within the shadow of this very cloister, that faceth the same waters I ne'er approach too close.

5

Here cometh my late master, brother Thomas, upon the wide wood-way, with his little page *clept* Henery, as you well know! Why do I see golden light behind them, as of a great brooch flashing, and goosedown wings pressed together above their shoulders, as though they angels be? O miserable worm that I am, even then I had some inkling of what terrible mortal sin I was about to commit; for upon hearing their gay chattering on the May breeze, and the soft bearing forth [*fetus*] of their lives northward on the broad and grassy way, I began to shake and quiver in my maidenly disguise, that if I had been carrying my bow – that is a fighting man's third arm, as must a sword be – it would have fallen from my shoulder.

We had been waiting no more than two hours, when they came.[289] Litle John was hid with our mounts behind a great bush further up, on the turn of a curve, and I whistled a warning. Slithen up to join him, I rode out behind [him] onto the green-hued road, that we might appear as if travelling northward also, but slowly, and not crouched in ambush (for the highway there did not expose much of its far length to the eye). And so we heard, as we walked our horses at a slow gait, the [harness] jingling behind us of the riders, coming around the corner at an amble, and swiftly they appeared alongside.

My old master was half hid by his wide hood with its edge of embroidery, as I was [hid] by my maiden's veil and capuchon, in which my skin could be glimpsed, white as a swan. And Littl John was

---

[289] In the ballad, the monk and his page are on their way to tell the king the good news; in this earlier and more down-to-earth account, they are merely returning home.

dressed as a merchant, with a woollen cap too small for him, and a green cotte likewise falling well above his calf, for they were fine clothes robbed and not made for such a giant: and I was sure, with my heart playing japes within me, that he would be seen as a felon, for his swollen face was yet rough, though his sorrel [courser] was very fine and handsomely girthed almost like a knight's, and upon it he had slung leather bags, as if fat with wool.[290]

Yet he did so bellow his greeting, and with such fawning friend-liness, that e'en I was astounded. 'Hail to thee, holy monk,' he cried, and my late master and Henry returned the greeting, the whiles I near swooned from fear. 'Hast thou come from afar?'[291] asked my feigning father, and brother Thomas told him, in that sparrow-voice of his, that was like a pecking at my heart, 'From Notyngham only.' Thus we rode our horses at a walk two by two, with Henr[y] beside me and our elders in front.

I, keeping my face lowered as if in modest mien, yet saw a leathern bag shaped like a harp behind the saddle [of Henry's pack pony]; and seeing this, the boy boasted of its beauty, that he promised to show me, and that it was made of sykamoure[292] and carved finely about the edge with the semblance of leaves and fruit.

No less horrible it was, to see how brother Thomas fawned upon Litl John, thinking him a rough and powerful merchant, while the golden boy simpered beside me, thinking me a sickly girl who coughed (to feign better, as Lazarus doth when dying in the play). I said naught, for my voice was like a cracked pot, manliness coming into it at that time, and I could not disguise it like a play-actor. 'My father was also a merchant,' said Henrie, 'but he drank what he was meant to sell, which is no great profit to aught but the belly; and now he resem-bles that scarecrow,' he added, pointing to the field, and brother

[290] Presumably meant to be samples: merchants were already growing rich on England's wool trade.
[291] The question in the later ballad is, '*Ffro whens come ye?*' [**Pencilled double tick against this footnote, with 'That is the question!' in FB's hand.**]
[292] As in MS: the sycamore not being a native tree (introduced only in the fifteenth century), either the harp was made on the Continent, or the wood was imported.

Thomas laughed in delight at his simple merriment, while Llitul John feigned the same delight.

And there being a field of rye all about [the scarecrow], the crop already grown to above the knee and blowing most prettily with wild flowers and rue and fennel, the golden boy prattled of the delights of spring; and broke thereupon into song, a song that I once sang of cuckoos, seed and green leaf,[293] yet with such sweetness to his voice that even Litel John was drawn, listening. For no man can resist the honey of music, when it be well delivered, for it soothes the foremost cell of the brain, even unto bringing the infection of madness out of it. But so deep in me were the servants of the Arch-fiend, after the months I had spent in proximity of his breath and influence, that this song of Henery's merely maddened my jealousy, and swelled my sinews [*nervos*],[294] so that I near bit my veil.

Brother Thomas looked upon the golden boy with such loving fondness, that tears started to my eyes: would I had never left the monastery, scarce seven months before! 'What ails thy daughter?' he then asked, turned in the saddle and frowning at me. And as we rode forward gently, with the thick forest at our shoulder, the only sounds being the creak of our saddles and the press of our hoofs in the marl (for the way was badly drained on that stretch, and much injured, with brambles tearing at the fetlocks of our mounts), Litul John said: 'Not only hath she the ague, holy brother, but we were robbed last week of thirty marks by a filthy felon, by the name of Robert Hode, on this very road. And my dear daughter hath since been sore afraid of travelling, though I hear the villain hath been taken, that some men call The Robbing Hodde.'

Brother Thomas sighed and said, 'So likewise were we [robbed] in the autumn rains, on Boenysdale Moor, and he stole of me a hundred pounds! And true it is that the villain hath been ta'en, and now languishes in Notinghm gaol, with many foul oaths – and be

---

[293] Compare the well-known lyric preserved in the Harley MS, beginning 'Sumer is icumen in'.
[294] Medieval 'sinews' are the same as modern 'nerves'.

The Robbing Hodd no more, but only The Empte Hotte.[295] And I know this because it was I, brother Thomas of the holy house of St Edmund's, who caused this happy event.' 'What, holy brother, did ye arrest him?' exclaimed Litull John, as if astonied. 'Aye,' said my former master, 'I fell upon him with my own hand, chastising that Hob the Robbour.[296] That is to say, I laid it upon him, and Almighty God made my palm as heavy as lead on his shoulder, so that he dropped to his knees in the church and was took like a lamb.'[297]

Litull John was amazed, as I was, by this lie, but thanked my old master heartily; adding that Robert Hodd had many men with him in felony, who would be knowing of such a famous deed, and keen to avenge their leader for the great hurt done to him. And it was indeed a great risk to journey with this brave monk, he continued: 'But now I know that the Lord Himself is at our side – no doubt because you are a true man of God, His holy servant, having walked an undefiled path from your mother's womb, unspotted by the lewd temptation of the lesser creatures, those simpering Eves; and will do so till the day of your death. Therefore there is naught to be feared from felons or murtherers or *roberdesmen*!'[298] And here he turned to me as if feigning reassurance for his beloved daughter, albeit lesser than a man. 'Mayhap my dear daughter will follow such a chaste path, that if ever a unicorn appear from this forest, it will lay its head in her lap, and catching it I might make my fortune.'[299]

Ne'er had I heard Litull John – as slow to learn as he was strong in body – so eloquent and crafty, for he was the spit of a swollen, grasping merchant: and now I think it clear as day, that such types of heretics (all God's enemies as much as the heathen or infidel) are so lusted after by the Devil, that he rides them as he will, even as he

[295] As in MS: 'hotte' means basket (from which the type for carrying bricks derives). The medieval mind delighted in even feeble puns, as readers of Chaucer will know.
[296] See my Preface.
[297] Compare the succinctness of the ballad's version: '*I layde furst hande hym apon.*'
[298] As in MS.
[299] A traditional belief: the Virgin Mary herself was often symbolised as a tamer of unicorns, and her Son as entering like a unicorn into her womb.

rode Adam and Eve with his serpent's wiles, until they fell beneath the load and took us all with them.

Brother Thomas darted looks about him of great nervousness, for he had but little succour from the Almighty, and cared not an oyster for chastity, being most fond of the contents of the bath-house! And there being none other on the grassy way as far as the eye could see, save for one lean and famished-looking tinker trudging beneath his load towards us, with his tame dog likewise all boniness (too weary even to bark or snap at our hooves as we passed by), then in my old master's eyes there must have appeared a whole swarm of robbers and murtherers emerging from the thicket: for he was ignorant, alas, of the true proximity of the felons, whose well-whetted swords were yet sheathed (mine hid beneath my womanly gown). He asked us, then, to accompany him, pulling forward his great hood and disguising his fear by saying what a pleasure it was to ride in such company, all the while casting glances at Litul John, as if to comfort himself with the false merchant's great size and breadth of chest.

I rode forward with them as if in a dream, let me tell you; all the while seeing the hideous falsity of the monk, that echoed Hod's great hatred of all brethren in Christ, that he called (as he did all those of true faith, along with the heathen or infidel) the 'unbelieving'. For it smarted like a rod, that my old master had not mentioned my harp and my horse, stolen at the same time [as his hundred pounds], nor talked of my vanishing many months before, nor of my reappearance that morning unto Henry in the church, as if I was of no more importance than a flea. Hideous pride, that launches us first of all upon our downward journey!

Then, as the others talked, Henri turned to me and said that his harp was very fine, yet if he played near hens, the poultry ran away in terror, for the strings are of fox-gut, this being sweeter and more insinuating than sheep or wolf. And thus he prattled, received by me in silence. Then he stared at my face, and said, 'Why, my lady, your face is sudden striped.'

True it was, that the air being warm for May, and my turmoil of humours bringing sweat to my skin, the white paint of lye had begun to run so that this could e'en be seen through the fine material.

For what is a lady's veil, but something that doth not hide temptation, but increases it by cunning concealment, that shows more than it covers, and pricks the eye of lust yet further? And the light cloth (blown by the breeze) stuck to my cheeks, and was already tainted by the ashes.

I could not answer, but turned to the side and coughed, all the while seizing a fold of my gown with the hand that held the reins, that I might lift [my gown] swiftly when the moment came [to reach for my sword]: and I prayed that moment might come now, though so dreadful did I think it that my bowels turned. Then I heard Henry say, in a loud voice as high as a piglet's: 'Master, I hope we are not riding with a leper, that hides her condition behind a veil and a thick coat of lye, as many do.' And brother Thomas ceased prattling to Litl John and turned to us in his saddle, asking further what his 'angel' meant. 'I am sure she is blemished,' piped Henri, pointing at me, 'for I perceive pustules unbecoming to a fair damsel. If it be leprosy, master, we are riding too close and must leave them in all haste.'

Brother Thomas looked agape upon me, and my actions only encouraged this hideous speculation, for in my distress I hid the revealing veil behind my hand, yet shaking my head as if in furious denial. Litel John said, scarce concealing his anger, 'I counsel thee not to spoil thy virtue with such horrible insults, little page, or by your master's permission I will fain answer it in bold stripes upon thy buttocks. What sayest thou? That my fair daughter is unclean?'

Yet no stronger action could he take, for a group of serfs were approaching, as many as a dozen, wearily plodding in tattered shoes of felt; and they were holding hoes and forks and other tools of the field and were blear with their slavish [*servilibus*][300] toil. They stood aside to let us pass, ogling me and muttering filthy words, and loudly letting off wind like young boys; then they whistled afterwards in their simpleton's arrogance, ending in a distant peal of laughter of the type that Satan's kingdom resounds with over the agonised cries.

[300] Both literally and figuratively, serfs being landless slaves; as the distinction between serf and unfree villein became less and less, we find in them the direct descendant of the modern agricultural labourer.

And thus also, more and more, do swarms of young boys (even on their way to school) jangle and jape at their superiors, and on their egress do whoop and halloo as if there is no order nor custom left in the world, nor the sting of birch, nor pricks and prods, nor the cracking of juvenile heads upon each other, as in my time there always was.[301] And Henrie would have been among them, if he had not been shut up as an oblate, for he was very forward in his speech; ne'er gabbling and jangling and japing like other boys who run about out of doors in play and game, yet of equal impudence.

Brother Thomas was sore aggrieved, and rebuked his angel-page, that high voice saying, 'Thou must curb thy tongue, and seek pardon of the fair maiden. This is e'en worse than swearing, my boy!' To which Henry turned to me and said, with a cunning gleam, 'A woman is certainly cleaner than a man, for she be made of Adam's rib, which was flesh and bone, whereas man is made from clay. Wash a clod of clay and the water will be very foul; wash a rib and the water will certainly be foul, but less so. Shame upon me to think otherwise.'

And even Litell John gave a roar of laughter at his wit, which relieved the monk, who chuckled mightily; all of which served only to irk me further: for I saw how precocious the imp was, and yet how all his brilliance was borrowed, like lustrous silks too large for his small frame.

Again we re-entered the new-leaved forest, that shielded the sunlight as a cloth might over a players' stage, and taking a false path known to Litel John, went far out of sight of the serfs, or of any other wayfarer; and though the track did creep about more than a true one, my old master was too busy casting glances at Litul John (and at me behind) to notice. He simpered foolishly after Henerie's false apology: while the boy's eyes were sharp with victory, and not suspicion. Meanwhile, I tried to conjure the angelic forms that had hovered about myself and Hodd on the desolate wastes near Bakwel: but none came, of course, and instead it seemed there was a cackling of hobgoblins from one side, and the dim coughing of wolves from the other.

[301] This is quite untrue, of course: only in our own milder times has the habit of persuading youth through thrashing or belting seen an eclipse in favour of Montessori and other educational fashions.

As we passed by some brushwood bound in faggots, Litul John asked cunningly if St Edmund's Abbey held the forest on Bornsdale Moor, and my former master said, 'Ay, we hold much land thereabouts on that wild heath, even the wood where that cut-throat felon and blasphemous heretic lurks, that I dragged to gaol with the Lord God's aid.' He then laughed merrily, so that his face seemed to divide like an apple; and he added, 'Having much glass to make for the new chancel, we must cut this wood down and burn it all to the last branch; which will be a great service to the world, for much wickedness lurks therein.'

Then Litull John's falsely swollen, reddened face did of a sudden redden even more, and he grasped the bridle of my former master, who all but toppled as his mount was stopped. Then likewise did I hold the golden boy's horse by the straps. In so doing, alas, my veil caught on a high bramble and twisted from its place, and Henry was much astonished to see me revealed – the white lye so spotted or streaked, or fallen away from the skin, that I must have resembled a harlot.

Yet though he pointed (if scarce able to stammer out my name), I was again paralysed like a rabbit, and could do no more than hold fast the bridle of his horse. Litul John, meanwhile, was occupied in pulling on the gullet of [brother Thomas's] great hood, so that the poor fat monk I once loved, and who saved me from a miserable death on the wayside, fell from his saddle with a cry – just as formerly into the mire of autumn, so now into the green of maytime.

Immediately I woke as from a trance, and struck the angel boy a wild blow with my arm to silence him; he did not topple, for he was too light and clung to his horse's girth. Such an error, suitable to a milksop, might cost a man his life, but not when the other is [a lad of] nine or ten. Instead, he gave out a moan, and looked at me in terror – yet with such loathing mingled in, it was as if the hatred of Christ Himself was shining upon me as a sapphire might quencheth venom, flashing upon it from the finger of the King of Kings as He lifts his righteous sword.

The angelic face before me heated my choler as a burning stone doth heat water, and I drew my own sharp sword most lustily. Meanwhile, Litel John had sprung from his saddle and stood over my old master, who knelt upon the track and clasped his head, that bled from the fall. 'Why dost thou treat me so sore, merchant?' the wounded man cried; 'art thou a felon, in truth?' And Litul John said, 'Nay, no felon but the loyal captain to one who is no heretic, wretched monk, but a free spirit and master of creation, greater than God, a true believer as thee be unbelieving; and who dwells in the wood that thou wouldst have cut, and whom thou took yesterday in Notyngham, as you did boast of just now.'

Comprehending then of whom Litl John spoke, my poor old master went white as ash, and raised his arms and cried out in his shrill voice, 'Quick, sound thy sweet voice, my boy, I beseech thee!'

'Twas just so that very first time we were robbed on the road, for life is a wheel that returns and returns: and so without reflection my mind stirred itself as if I should sing. Strange how time itself then changed from quicksilver to clay, for it seems to me now that [what was but] a fraction was truly daylong, so oft and slowly doth it rise before me in every horrid detail! My former master's gaze was not upon me, but upon the usurper, as I did straightway realise. The boy's mouth opened and out of it came not the song, but the revelation of who I truly was, in the form of my name – in such a harsh manner, that it was no less forceful than a clattering jay's alarum in the woods. Then, pointing his finger at me, he called me a traitor [*proditorem*]. My girlish disguise of lye had been rubbed away entire by now, and the sweaty veil so ripped by the thorn, that I was returned to mine own self.

My only thought was to stop up the hole from which such a dangerous witness poured forth: for suspicion ran among the outlaw band like poison, and accusations grew fat and thick upon it, and the punishment was instant death, or (e'en worse) a slow dying in the Dark Pit. Yet was I paralysed in my confusion, for in truth all of this was [happening] in a few breaths.

Then it was that brother Thomas, looking upon me with open mouth, did also receive my true self on the white page behind his eyes, as though it had been writ there. *Omnia autem aperta et nuda sunt eius oculis.*[302]

Alas, reader, thus will we be called for at the Last of Days, each and every one of us, one by one over the rolls of thunder and the wailing of the wind! That great wide mouth released my name upon the air in a single stark stroke that ended on a hiss, as of a red-hot brand plunged into the [blacksmith's] trough.[303] Seeing the holy man then struggle to his feet, and lunge towards me as though I were a knight to be unseated, or mayhap his salvation, groaning and crying out as if I were his own lost soul, Litel Johnn without thought brought down with both hands that sharp and weighty sword upon the plump neck beneath the cloth, that all of it was cleaved through quite, flesh and weave together.

Stilled on an instant was the monk's piteous revelation, and there shot up such gouts of blood from the shattered veins of the trunk as it toppled like a hewn tree to the ground, that it steamed upon the dappled flanks of Henrie's pony, and made the animal half crazy (not being a war-horse trained to it), thus throwing the golden boy onto the grass of the way.

Being not harmed, but merely shaken, he scrambled to his feet and stood there staring down at the cloven corpse, as if stunned with a cudgel, his mouth wide open as though he might swallow the sense of what he could not comprehend by his eyes. And in this he was as a mirror to myself, for it was indeed a very strange thing to see my former master beheaded. 'It appears,' laughed Litel John in his cruellest manner, gazing fiercely upon mine own face, 'ye have never before seen a man lose his head, let alone one known to thee!'

And in truth, such is the violence of our times, few of the common folk have not witnessed such a sight, whether crowded about a

---

[302] Marginalia from the Scriptures, in red ink, possibly eighteenth century. 'All things are naked and open unto the eyes of Him with Whom we have to do.'
[303] This suggests that the author's name finishes on a sibilant, like the monk's own name of Thomas. Other common possibilities are Giles and Nicholas, though the latter is hardly 'a single . . . stroke'.

scaffold, or at the end of a hue and cry,[304] or anigh some skirmish between puffed-up nobles and their retainers; and though I had been present at many a robbery, the victims had only been pierced or cut about. By God's grace we have all passed many a gibbet or spike on bridge or at crossways with its ghastly lesson, but this is usually a dried-up thing, as if made from wax, and e'en the longest and fullest locks be crusted and lank, and the stink soon blown away, or superseded by the fouler odours of the town. The criminals[305] put thus are seldom known to us, and scarce resemble human beings, in their boniness. But to see a familiar face stiffen of a sudden, and pale, with mouth open as though to utter words above the place where the neck unnaturally ends, is surely the most terrible sight of all: for the victim guards a semblance of life in his open eyes, e'en more so than if a man be pierced through lungs and liver, or hewn at the heart, though I know not why.[306]

And when that face be known to you . . . [*hiatus in the* MS] . . . [or] a golden boy's, resembling an angel's perfect prettiness, is it not worse still? And if the hands that swung the blade be thine own, what then?

'Nay, Johne, I knew him not,' I insisted, thus sinking deeper downward towards the pit of slime. Little Henre raised his face, that bore a most ghastly expression in its sorrow, and cried up to me, 'Thou liest!' 'Thou liest!'

So help me God, he was the very waxen image of all that appalls us most, for there is nothing more terrible than knowing one's own guilt in the face of an accuser, who is so struck with fear and horror

---

[304] There are many recorded instances throughout the Middle Ages of constables beheading murderers, traitors or robbers on the spot immediately after arrest – see, for instance, the fate of four among Sir Robert de Rideware's band of ruffians, who had robbed some merchants of Lichfield in 1342 and were met by the bailiff and his men. The result then, however, was that the merchants lived in terror of the knights' revenge (the interesting text of their legal petition is printed in *Archaeological Journal*, vol. iv, p. 69).

[305] This seems an exaggerated term, given that during the thirteenth century a man (or indeed woman) could be hung for the theft of the value of fourpence.

[306] This is true, as I can vouchsafe from my own late experience in the war. Pinned down for a full two nights behind a shattered embankment, cut off from help, with the severed head of my late comrade gazing upon me from a position it would have been suicidal to reach, my nerves suffered a blow from which they have yet fully to recover. [*The last four words in proof double-underlined by FB, with 'Adventure!' scrawled in margin.*]

that he be as a spectre or a corpse. And in his madness he shrieked and tore his hair, saying I was a most heinous traitor, a Judas, a most foul beast that hath returned to its sty; for our master had ever named me urchin, that he found in the filthy ditch – and said that I was ever naught but a *servant corores*![307] I commanded him to cease this blabber, stiffening above him in my saddle and hefting my sword in both hands; for I could not bear these words, so shrilly ringing out and pressing into the ears of Litel Johnn like wasps into a fruit.

Yet he did not cease, but began to strike my horse and my leg with his small fists, and sobbing between his hateful cries, called me a demon that had lain in the gutter for my poor dear master to find, beguiling him with its voice.

'Nay, if thou wouldst not be pierced, keep thy peace!' cried I, though to no avail, for he went on regardless: 'Yet my holy master did always say to me how thou wert a sparrow to my nightingale!' His face became blotched and blinded with tears that poured like wine from the spigots of his eyes, and yet his hysterical shrieks continued to trumpet forth most [clearly?] . . .[308] 'And now,' [continued Henry] 'my dear master's unconfessed, unanointed and unaneled soul be deaf to all but the moans of Purgatory, far from the chorus of the angels, thanks to thy heinous treachery! Thou horrible clump of clay! Thou ass-brained demon! Thou daf, thou boor, thou liar! Thou pagan pick-purse! Thou slothful son of a serf!'[309]

Though I am now at my leisure to proceed tranquilly with my

---

[307] As in MS: an Anglo-Norman legal term for a 'runaway', or 'rover'. It specifically refers to serfs or unfree villeins who have left their lord or master without special licence, and might be recaptured at any time. It is doubtful, to my mind, that a young boy having just seen his foster-father beheaded would be articulate enough for such a calculated insult or the ensuing additions, but the narrator must needs put himself in the best light possible, and memory is ever a skilful fabricator. The later ballad is far more matter-of-fact and pitiless.

[308] A tear in the parchment renders two lines illegible. This entire episode, covering three leaves in the original, suffers from wear and stains as if much read, like a favourite page in a child's storybook – but remains unmarked by any later pen.

[309] Although there is something faintly ridiculous, even comic, in this litany of insults, the final 'son of a serf' is a suitable trigger for the fatal attack, given the narrator's sensitivity to his family's perilous position just above that bottom, most servile class.

history, stopping to comment upon this and that – or e'en to put my pen down and smooth out the folds of my garments, or walk my old limbs about the cloister in profound thought, or take a bucket to feed our abbey's pigs with scraps (for pigs swallow aught that be given them), before returning wearily to my writing labours – in truth this is an impudence, as there was scarce the hair's width of a moment between Henry's last words above, that uttered the miserable name of the Lord's betrayer, and my pursuant action.

Nay, I cannot hold it off any longer!

Just as I was taught in the wood (and without waiting for any command), I did howl mightily in the manner of a wolf, raising my heavy sword on high; and bending down [from the saddle], swept the two-handed blade low across to smite the screeching boy above the shoulders with no more than a small jolt to my grip, that the nightingale might sing no longer, nor utter words of betrayal, nor insult, nor admonition, nor even kindnesses, nor ever see the Maytime flowers again.

Sometimes I think I was indeed a real felon: the type of person for whom this action bears the same kind of wrath as is required to break a man's nose, and who thinks no more of it afterwards. And it was not as in the kind of play loved by lewd folk, where the slain man is resurrected, and dances foolishly, healthy in every part: nay, the boy's two parts lay divided for ever, his single soul fled – and warm, fresh and pure was the blood that spattered all my face, turning it to crimson, and blinding my eyen with its child's ferventness.[310]

And so the piping voice was stilled, and the soul deprived of its small house that was clove in two, and I know not whether the boy hath joined the numberless sinners in Hell, as an unbaptised infant might, wandering disconsolate on its plump little legs (though ne'er singed in my view) – or mayhap hath received the eternal grace of Our Lord: but nothing will wash his stain from mine own soul, for

[310] Numerous were the ancient mock-rituals and folk plays (often performed in May), that involved a beheading and a resurrection – symbolic of the death of winter and the entry of summer.

his blood crept deeper than my flesh, and beyond e'en the grasp of confession and repentance – were I to crawl in stinking rags on ten thousand stony pilgrimages, under hail, storm or burning sun, with a hundred lashes for every mile passed, though the distance be eternal.

6

See how the ivy's shadows fall upon the page, their shapes carven and fretted by the sunlight! Though by God's bidding I have seen more years than any man I know, yet I do still delight in such simple sights, more precious to me than any number of gawdy palaces. And though my entire body aches as I write, yet but three fingers serve. And though all our books be held in an iron-girded oaken chest, there are but two locks between all their treasures and a thief, and naught between them and fire. And so likewise between this life and the next, there is naught but a breath, that the lungs press out and then cease, which ceasing they have never done once in an entire lifetime.

And whither the soul is bound, dependeth on the simplest action in a life; for all worthiness may be shredded on an instant by a single fault, as the stealing of a carpet from a hedge might cause a woman to hang, who is otherwise blameless, if the judge be as severe as He is severe in His hatred of sin; just as wicked actions may be pardoned by true regret and heartfelt confession, from the infinite well of His compassion and forgiveness. Yet in that confession, if there be the slightest tread of fraudulence, then the confessor may hope for as much of Heaven as the most haggard and shaggy demon.

There is no fraudulence in my confession.

It is not as those false books be, full of images of the Virgin Mary Our Holy Mother, that are yet inspired by a devilish and notorious art, and must be burned as heresies.[311] Clear proofs of my fidelity to

---

[311] No doubt a reference to *ars notoria*, whereby books of spells and illicit learning are made.

the truth are manifold, and e'en to be found in the nonsense that is sung of Robert Hodd, now appearing under the false coin of *Robyn Hoode*, and of his rabble of felons: for in them I hear my very own words as clipped coin[312] – yet some remain true, just as some leeches be not false murtherers.

And if you take these several true words one by one, you might see their actual lineage in all that I have been setting down in plain witness here on these pages, over the last twelvemonth or more, in order to drown these direful ballads and so forth, that have all the merit of the ghastful and rueful noise two cats make when proffering to fight one another.

Thus if one jingling rhyme says that Muche and Litel John went forth to the king, and another that we hastened straight to No[t]yngham to free our master,[313] then neither is true. And that infant scrap that declares Moche did smear himself in henbane to make the grey-eyed damsel called Isabel love him, is of no more verity than the gabble of a hen, or of a rimpled woman, toothless, with frenzy in the head.[314] For durst I own that these crippled and disgusting ballads are my distant progeny, against which I pit my bitterest gall [*galla*].[315]

Instead, we buried the four parts of the cloven cadavers in the soft ground of the forest by the false way, far from anyone's sight save that of a curious *ruddock*;[316] then covering the turned earth with rent moss, that it look not grave-like, I could not help a prayer escape my lips (in a whisper), but Lityl John thought it an oath. We little spoke, for fear we should be heard by human or spirit or owlish ear, for it is well known that owls bear murtherers' secrets to others, repeating

---

[312] i.e. false coin: coin-clippers were punished by savage mutilation or death.

[313] It seems that, as both these incidents occur in *Robin Hood and the Monk*, the latter was an amalgam of two pre-existing ballads.

[314] Alas, this choice verse or song does not survive; henbane, part of the nightshade family, was known for its power to attract women.

[315] Possibly a reference to his ink, which in the Middle Ages was drawn from gall-apples (caused by wasps) on the bark of oaks, the acidic liquid being mixed with soot or iron salts to give it darkness, and with nut oil for body. 'Gall' (as in plain 'bile') is Latin *fel*.

[316] As in MS: the robin – a delightful detail that spans the centuries.

the name of the guilty. And I knew that Litel Johnn had heard my name spoke by my former master, and my face recognised, for he did glance at me in suspicious wise as we toiled, using our swords to make a shallow grave.

Having seized all the papers that brother Thomas was carrying on his person, including a letter from the clerk of the shyref declaring what had occurred (with the shyreff's seal upon it), we set out for our camp. I bore Henry's harp, that was indeed of beautiful workmanship and of the sweetest tone, e'en sweeter than mine own that had been broke to pieces by my present companion, and which I still grieved for secretly.

Look louringly upon that last inked page, for on it I wrote 'mine own' – when that [harp] had in truth been wickedly thieved from the hermit: I rebuke my own temerity, for I must ever strive to be purer in myself, e'en at my great age, as the sea sets itself to smite the sand each moment, ceaselessly, though its waves be more than five thousand years old.

As we washed ourselves free of blood in a [flooded] marl-pit on the highway, my companion seized my head by the hair and asked me most grimly if I had aught to confess: for now he knew that brother Thomas, the betrayer of our master, who didst boast of his filthy triumph, was that same fat monk they had robbed last year: and whose loyal page was none other than myself.

I replied, trembling, that brother Thomas was indeed my former master. 'He being indeed that very same monk you robbed in the rain a year ago,' I asseverated, 'when I was with him on the road. Yet I was afraid to say this before the others, and most particularly Flawnes.' It is nigh eighty long years since this came to pass, but I feel afresh the pricking at my throat of his dagger, and the pain of my gripped hair, for the burly felon believed he now knew who it was had informed the monk, as to the whereabouts of our great master! And for that minstrels and other sly wretches, merry-andrews and buffoons and tumblers, oft pass secrets and inform, under the guise of merriment and solace, he was right to be suspicious.

I denied this fervently, asking would I have committed murther if this were true? – nay, one does not slay one's friends. And Litel John laughed, for he cared not a straw for killing, friend or enemy, as he had swallowed entire the foul heresy of Hodde's: that for a free spirit there was no sinning in the world, only the act that is fully desired and chosen by your self; and that the one sin possible is to be fearful of sinning and of the utter freedom of self-desire, were that desire to bring down all Creation and cover the lands with the seas, as in the Flood.

Then he released me, or rather threw me to one side, saying he would sunder the bones of my thighs by stamping upon them, if I were lying. For despite his belief in freedom from sin, he did hate any act that was against himself or his master – though oft he took grievously against the latter, as thieves must quarrel between themselves. (And now no doubt they gore each other with their horns in the burning fiery torment of Hell, in perpetuity.) *I do not the good thing that I will, but the very evil thing I hate.*[317]

And this injury to me I believed he would indeed carry out, for he was built like a bull and of a bull's sour-tempered visage: and I trembled mightily, saying that if I were lying, may he sunder my arms also, for I would be like a traitor fit only to be broken on the wheel. And I bid him look at the seized papers; and so doing, Litel Johyn found nothing to prove me guilty.

In truth, I was in a kind of palsy that taketh men after battle or some great shock; for all seemed like in dream, and my limbs grew heavy and then light, and my mind was so full of evil spirits it was as a raised stage of boards, with a hollow treading of boots and a ringing in my ears as of trumpets, horns, tabours and pipes, mixed with coarse shouting and the mocking fooleries of players braying like donkeys, that my brain became as a churchyard full of wrestlings and lewd pastimes.[318] Thus, instead of regretting my hideous act of murther,

[317] Marginalia in Hand A: a quote from St Paul's Epistle to the Romans (c. vii, v. 15). I have again adapted the Wycliffite translation.

[318] Such amusements were not always secular: the Feast of Fools, which took place (mostly in France and Flanders) at the Festival of the Circumcision on 1 January, involved drunken clerics riding donkeys into church, dressing up as women, wearing monstrous masks, using obscene gestures and language, and generally running amok.

I was lifted [*levatus*] from it, and delivered entire to Satan like a mouse be to a cat or a weasel, there to be played with for sport.

Yet God in His mercy is ever on the look-out for repentant sinners, even the worst. After youth, or after virtuous old age,[319] the cold earth will have us each one, whate'er we do; and He will pluck us therefrom like turnips.

We rode back to the outlaw camp, and there Litell John related what had happened, not naming brother Thomas as my former master, and thus keeping me safe from their violence. He told [the felons] that the monk's head had been cut like a buck's;[320] and his prattling page had fared likewise at the hands of brave Moche, and a great cheer sounded that might have been heard across the moor to the very horizon.

The ram's horn was blown with its mournful sound, and a meeting was held under the great oak, to plan the release of our leader from his dungeon. One outlaw there was, named Roger Wylde, who had been kept in the same prison in Notyngham by the baron for unlawful reasons, and whose foot had rotted away there after a month, and so he walked with a crutch. Yet he was fiercer than any, and a fine rider and bowman, despite being crippled. He made a drawing upon the ground, telling us how a way might be made into the prison, from a postern door in the castle. If we persuade the sentry there, by imposture and false papers, we might enter and turn left by the kitchens, then descend by a low and modest door into the dungeons below, and hide in a certain place indicated [upon his drawing], that is a blind recess. The porter passing that spot with his keys, as he does at a certain hour every night, we might overpower him and unlock the dungeon.[321]

This same gaoler having two fierce hounds that biteth sore, being closed in a dark place by day and then released by night for the prison

---

[319] The text has *post modestam senectutem nos habebit humus*, etc.; but perhaps we should read *molestam*, and translate, 'irksome old age, etc.' – as in the popular thirteenth-century song, 'Gaudeamus igitur'.

[320] Probably meaning (as a sinister joke) that it had been 'cut off close behind the ears', as in the later heraldic term 'caboshed'.

[321] Although this shares elements with the plan in the later ballad – namely, the false use of papers, disguise and the overpowering of the porter – the outcome is quite different (and perhaps more realistic) in the present narrative.

watch, we must take marrow-bones in our pockets, for they are ill-fed and covetous, as all hounds be; and hating the rod their master uses freely upon them, they fear anything that smelleth of him, and so Whyld said that we must wear their master's cloak or other article.

Will Scathelocke said we must be numerous enough and well-armed, that we might enter hidden in a cart of rushes, for they have much need thereof; and all present roared their affirmation. But Littel John with great firmness said, 'Nay, we must be two only, and slip in and out like mice through subterfuge, and not fight a battle we would be sure to lose, trapped in that cursed castle. Again I will take Moche, for he is a mere boy, and no suspicion will fall on us then. And one other only will I take, to guard the horses beyond the walls.' And he chose a young felon that called himself Merciles Greenleas,[322] who had long and lanky hair like a wench's.

There was much protest from the outlaws, and I feared I would faint from the clamour, and my heart-grieving, and from the swarm of tiny fiends in my head; yet Litel John so smote the tree with his great fist that its leaves shook, for he was a veritable Herod[323] in his wrath. He said, 'The boy will bring his harp, for while none of you handsome ass-heads will ever be admitted while the scerf[324] fears aught, few ever refuse a minstrel; most of all a blind one!' And by this I knew he meant me to be as a fraudulent beggar or fiddler, that only pretendeth to be sightless – which state is the most wretched of evils.[325]

---

[322] Little John disguises himself as Reynolde Grenelefe in the fifteenth-century *A Gest of Robyn Hode*.

[323] Herod's exaggerated anger was a popular element in the mystery plays (e.g. the thirteenth-century *Ordo Rachelis* in the Fleury Play-Book, where Herod, furious at the Magi's escape, attempts suicide).

[324] As in MS: presumably 'sheriff', usually better spelt as 'sheryff' or 'sceryf'.

[325] It is not clear from the Latin whether (like Bartholomew), he feels blindness itself is the most wretched state, or the evil of faking it. Minstrelsy, of course, was the one possible occupation for the sightless, aided by their powers of memory and sensitivity of hearing: as Mr Cecil Sharp notes (*English Folk Song: Some Conclusions*, 1907, p. 22): 'A blind man, one Mr Henry Larcombe . . . from Haselbury Plucknett, sang me a Robin Hood ballad. The words consisted of eleven verses. These proved to be almost word for word the same as the corresponding stanzas of a much longer black-letter broadside preserved in the Bodleian Library.'

And I was afraid that, so numerous are those who pretend to such states for false gain, I might be tested with a flame before my eyes.

Our forger prised the seal from the monk's papers and pressed it with great skill onto another paper finely writ by him, to persuade the serjeant that we had the sheryf's seal, if he were (at the first) to refuse us entry. This being a desperate and bold plan, with little chance of success to my mind, I retired to my hut in great perturbation of thought, while Litl John raided the Nonerye, that held but two women caught on the road – one being a cross-eyed tumbler who stood on her hands for the felons' merriment, the other a serving-wench with scars of pock upon her face.[326]

Having placed Henry's harp on my lap, it was in vain I tried to make sweet music from it over several hours, for my fingers trembled so, and great was my sorrow and shame. I perceived how the ends of my fingers were blistered, as though the strings of fox-gut were of brimstone. And then I considered how all my body would be so blistered, and continually, by the flames of Hell; and that it was five thousand, one hundred and nine years since Cain first suffered there, for some say he lived seventy years after slaying Abel in the year 3875 [before Christ], yet this is a mere morsel of time to what remains.

When I slept, the dead boy's angelic head danced in my dreams like a bitter gall: at first it was covered by all manner of workmanship in gold and silver and precious stones, like the choicest relic, and grinned at me as it dripped blood; the head then shrank and attached itself to that cold worm of slime, the houseless snail,[327] to crawl upon my cheek and into my nose that I could not breathe, the obstruction prattling all the while over the cackling of the night-crows [*nycticorax*],[328] and shouting the name 'Jubal', son of Adah – Jubal being the father of all those who play the harp, as it says in Genesis [iv, 21].

---

[326] It is significant that he describes them, but makes no mention of visiting himself. The 'Nunnery' now resembles even more the kind of miserable Flanders bawdy-house familiar to participants in the late catastrophe.

[327] Only in later times distinguished as a 'slug'.

[328] Medieval Latin, possibly a type of owl: we find the same curious term in Walter Map's *De Nugis Curialium* (1180s–90s).

Such was my terror and shame that I might have died, yet the Lord brought me out of this horrible vision into life, that I might be living proof of His mercy.

And now I think that the boy's fate was being certified to me, as being one of purgation or even damnation, either because he was unaneled and unconfessed, or that he had committed sins I knew not of; and was indeed a liar and e'en worse in that holy house of St Edmund's, that was a soft bed for the catamite [*cinaedo*].[329] Yet e'en out of my dreams I could not wash my hands of his red blood, for I had more blood upon me (to my mind) than a butcher, or a barber, or a soldier, or e'en an executioner.

And when I rose that morning at dawn, I was as one who has been in the stocks: so benumbed that I could scarce stand, let alone walk.[330] Yet once in the saddle, I grew hardier, and many of the felons wishing me courage in the way desperate men do oft show generosity to their kind, I felt an unfeigned and boyish excitement, swelling again with pride as if bound like a knight for the Holy Land. Yet was I as far from that inspired office as any person can truly be: mistily and fresh though the woodland air lay about us in that dawn, bitter as wormwood was the air in my mouth, for my entire body was corrupted. Though a gallon of honey were to have been poured over my head,[331] to the intoning of innumerable paternosters, nothing could have sweetened me, save the intervention of the Divine Will.

The hill-tops were gilded by the early sun, when the three of us rode out side by side to rescue our master from the lightless dungeon. How lovely was that May morning, with white blossoms upon every hand, and the tender leaves of the boughs trembling! Among the

[329] This revealing outburst shows again the increased intolerance towards 'unnatural' lust (whether in monasteries or without) during the thirteenth century, when it became linked to heretical activities.

[330] My own grandfather remembered, as a small boy, being much impressed by a drunkard who, after two days in the stocks and entirely sobered, could only crawl out of the village. Flares on the salient would reveal to me humped sentries in forward positions who, after two nights of cold and hunger, crawled back similarly benumbed; yet these were guilty of no crime.

[331] Honey was associated with God's mercy.

countless birds and their melodies, there sang a ruddock on a high branch, which promised fine weather,[332] and much solace was there in the wayside blooms as we continued dry-shod on our horses, whistling and disputing when men passed us, as honest minstrels might, and humming like the bees upon the bramble-flower.

And I thought, being still seethed in heresy and unbelief, that Hodde must yet be living, or the Creation would have dissolved around us into the illimitable sea of essence, in which I would take angelic form with all the elect, and know true bliss. And this foul incredulity – or rather, over-credulous nonsense – had so taken hold of my brain, that I truly believed that all living things and all human souls must depend for their existence upon a single felon, which is worse even than [the beliefs of] Jews or infidels.

Litell John was costumed in black, that he might pass the better unperceived in the dungeons, with a false beard of goat's hair stuck on like a player's, though with his brute face unswollen by the tincture of berries; while I was nearer my true self, knowing no one in [N]otynggam, with naught but an oil upon my eyelids that made them darken as if bruised, and a black cloak too large for my fourteen or fifteen years. I recall nothing more of our journey but a sudden feverishness that gripped me in Scherwode and made me alight, to spout foul liquids among the trees (to my false father's great impatience); as a pilgrim recalls nothing of his sea-voyage but sickness and the taunts of sailors – if they do not toss him overboard as some do, with all his companions, after taking their payment.

Very soon on the following day were the two of us before the postern gate, that lies well within the ditch [and rampart] of Nottyngam – walled meanly in wood in those far-off days, with over-gilt upon the names where . . . [*sentence unfinished*]. The city gates not being long unbarred, we had passed through them as smoothly as grease, the whiles a pustulent leper was being driven off with stones, as none would whip him for fear of contagion.

---

[332] That the robin is a fairweather bird remains a popular belief among country folk in our parts.

The postern gate, flanked by two towers with many arrow slits pierced (these even cut in the merlon[333] of the battlements above), was set into the south side of the castle, whose stone is very stout. The serjeant on this gate believed us, by our papers and appearance, that we were hired for the [sheriff's] entertainment over supper,[334] yet said we must return in the afternoon, for there were too many idlers within already.

Thus we waited instead in the town, and lest any from the castle should be there, I played the harp in the market place, while Littl John sat by me to take the offerings of coin or bread, and to guard me from the taunts and japes of other boys, and malicious folk.

It was indeed difficult to keep my eyes closed as though blind, and most frightening: for (unconjoined to vision) the sounds of the city seemed very loud and hellish; being all a confusion of cries and creakings and the clamour of ambling hooves, and occasional clashings of irons, and the moans of oxen, and many an iron-shod wheel on stone, and the ringing of great bells, and dogs barking and sheep bleating and pigs [snorting] and birds warbling,[335] upon which was laid much incessant chattering of passers-by, yet all so incoherent [*sibi non constans*], that I did think I was going mad.

And yet my harp was piercing this tumult, as was my high and melodious voice, I know not how; and though my fingers began to bleed, I continued to pluck the strings, forcing sweet songs out of the murthered boy's instrument. Guilt raged so horribly in my heart, that it was turned into hate by the demons within, as oft occurs. I began to despise the boy I had slain, that he had made me suffer so; I told myself he was truly the favourite of a Judas (that being my former

---

[333] The part of an embattled wall between the embrasures.

[334] This being served at five o'clock; dinner was at nine or ten in the morning.

[335] The last mentioned shows how, compared to our own industrial age of steam and omnibus and motor car, the medieval period did not suffer from high levels of noise, unless one was a blacksmith or similar, or caught in a thunderstorm. Warfare in the age of armour would have seemed startlingly loud to our forefathers' ears, however (especially after the introduction of gunpowder), but as nothing compared to the unimaginable, fantastical din of its present-day counterpart – which has left this participant, for one, with a perpetual thin shrilling in the ears.

master): and as I sang I recalled all the slights suffered by me at my master's hands in the monastery, and how his affection had cooled, and what he had said of me to Henrie, and that I was only a lowly servant to him after all.

Thus even the best milk curdles. Worse still – though it pains me to the bone to utter such a truth thereof – I felt a pride and even a strange thriving in the violation of the most precious vow and commandment;[336] for the devils within were puffing upon my sinfulness and making its stink rise thicker, turning its smoke to that of incense with their trickery, and filling my brain with satisfaction. All this [did I feel] as I mimicked a blind harper near the great church, nodding solemnly at the pity and compassion shown to me in the words of those passing by – especially the young and tender-hearted women, whose dulcet voices were a vehement temptation to open my eyes and regard their beauty, for their speaking was so delectable that I could not imagine their faces being otherwise than lovely.

And thus even carnal love was added to the brew, as I sang sweetly of brave knights and their damsels – as I once did likewise in street and market place several years before, when a small and lonely and foolish runaway of but nine or ten.

Meanwhile, my brute companion in evil invented the reason for my blindness – when folk asked him thereof – that was so piteous to relate, I marvelled at his wit; for he told how robbers attacked and strangled his beloved wife when I (their dear and only child) was yet six or seven; and that too much weeping while praying for her soul, lost me mine eyes.

How easy is it to lie and invent, and fool others for gain in this dismal world! Better be the man or woman, who keeps their soul shut up straitly in a holy house of thick walls, and their lips likewise but for chanting the scriptures, that no shrewd, adulterine words weave their loathsome patterns in others' ears . . .

[336] 'Thou shalt not kill.'

This spasm of righteous polemic lasting a full two leaves, with many scriptural citations and a digression in which heretics, Israelites and the followers of Mahomet are equally hotly pursued, I have omitted most of it and taken the opportunity to make a natural pause; what is more, the author then takes a characteristic jump backwards to the time of the hermitage, before resuming the narrative proper.

Part Four

I

I once knew an honest, poor and worthy woman in my childhood village, who in old age was severely bent, and her left arm so crooked that it no longer had feeling: which was surely a sign of true virtue, that she could do no wrong, for the Devil loves the left side. Similarly, those struck dumb are removed from one great source of sin, while the deaf are free from blandishments and evil persuasions of others. The wretched blind, however, deem white as black, and black as white; west as east, and silver as copper, and ayenward the same.[337]

Thus groping and grasping, he may be led astray or fooled, and so his situation is the most wretched. And what if we are all inwardly blind, whether our eyes are sighted or no? Then we can only wait (perchance it never comes!) for the scales to fall away, and be lit up from within by a certain knowledge of truth and falsehood; thereby the Devil can no longer play with us as our boy or hound, leading us sightless to the fatal bridge and leaving us there upon the brink.

Those who confuse light with colour – the one being pure, the other (though desired in its natural form, or in the sacred adornment of our churches) prey to all manner of deceit, as foulness be hidden by lurid raiments, or blemishes and malignant boils by tinctures and paste – confuse also God and His ministers; for even the holiest among the latter may be the Arch-fiend in disguise, whereas God can be no other. Think then, how shrewd a man must be to distinguish good from evil in these cheating times, save he be aided by prayer, worship,

---

[337] This seems again heavily indebted to Bartholomew or one of his sources.

or divine intervention. How much less skilled was I in those days, being merely an orphan youth, of a boyish levity! Look at me there, acting the sightless harper in the market place, wringing false pity out of good hearts (that pity, honestly minted, being clipped by my forgery of blindness). See my fingers, seethed in a boy's blood, yet plucking the fox-gut melodiously! Do I not seem the very picture of solemn fortitude and patient virtue?

Had I not refused, many years before, the holiest man I have ever known? Had I not cheated him, and stolen from him, in the vain belief that not only had he let a man perish in a storm, but also myself (his own pupil) to be half stifled e'en to a similar fate among those salty, liquid hills: this belief lending a justice to my actions?

God vouchsafe me His mercy! For while the blotless man was replenishing his jug with water, I seized his precious harp and fled with it, not once looking back e'en from the top of the cliff.

And so I tore myself mercilessly from the hermit my first master, to become a vagabond, full of false dreams of the minstrel life, and of great palaces and courts in which I might play and make all merry.

There was I certainly and most powerfully blinded, against which my semblance of blindness be naught! And now upon the threshold of the eternal judgement, on the very sill of doom, I see how at that moment of rash theft and escape, I was torn from the bowels of my faith and of God's grace, and am now utterly resigned to His infinite compassion, as likewise to His awful wrath that may gush uncontrollably[338] from His hatred of my youth's dreadful sins. Though it be as horribly fearful to anticipate the blistering flame and eternally boiling pitch in the dark place ringing with shrieks and wailings and screams, as it is sweetly gladsome to be touched (in prayer, or sometime on a spring morning along the garden paths) by the balm of Heaven and of spiritual joy, I do not attempt to peer beyond death, and descry my fate, however imminent: for I am no sorcerer or necromancer gripped by unbelief.

[338] A typically medieval humanisation of God, of whom the very least we expect these days is to control His temper; more likely, judging from recent events, He seems unable to control mankind, who periodically ceases his mischief only through exhaustion.

See how swiftly I flee upon the path – as though chased by an angelic host, grieving for that divine instrument – to my foster-mother in the village! Those hairy arms of hers I had come to detest, for she had used them to chide me with blows in recent months, and I left her with no more than a lie: that I must work in the lord's field, to salvage the corn. Well I remember the look she gave me, of maternal solicitude, for she was a good and loving woman behind her crooked back and hairiness, and wanted only the best for her foster-son, being therefore glad I was already doing labour services [*opem*][339] at such a tender age (I was, as I have said, no more than nine or ten), and not wasting my limbs upon words.

Having concealed the hermit's harp in a thicket near my buried coins, I retrieved both, carrying the former upon my back in its own leathern sack shaped like a wing, and the latter under my leathern belt. Foul was it on the ways, the storm having been a fierce one, and it had done much damage to the crops. And those country folk I passed for the first [few] miles did know me and some did care for me as an orphan boy, however simple their faith and their lives bare of all graces, and oft untrue one to another in their envy and poverty, and as heedless of their incontinence as beasts; yet I threw them only deceit, as scraps to dogs.

And now was I all deceit, from my toes up, even to myself: for I had in mind to find a manor house, where I would be adopted as the lord's minstrel, and from thence be delivered to the king, and live in his palaces, and one day to accompany him under the royal standard to the Holy Land, and other fabulations that seethed in my mind as I trudged upon the muddy ways; for I had been thoroughly perverted by the royal progress, and most especially its pale, mincing courtiers in their extravagant sleeves and coats and shoes, who listened to me with such praise in their haughty, yet softly-smiling faces.

Alack, what bliss coursed through my brain as I painted my future! And what despair soon followed (like the foulness in the sewers left

[339] These being in lieu of money rent, a tenurial obligation of these feudal times that was much resented – as was the payment of various duties and taxes such as merchet, heriot, or the annual tallage.

by a feast), when hunger and poverty were joined by bruises laid upon me by drunken rascals upon the way, or the blows of those finding me sleeping in their barn or outhouse, however fierce the rain: for there is little compassion in the world, and less even now than then. Sometimes my music pleased, inflaming simple country folk to dance (instead of listen), which dances are believed by many great teachers to be a vanity invented by Satan, who always leads [the dancers] according to those holy enough to descry him.

I thereby received bread and scraps of meat, but so full of trickery is the world, that most took me for a thief's accomplice, selling music as a lure to make them distracted, while robbery took place. Just as butchers sell sodden meat, or quacks mislead us with worthless herbs, or bakers fold sawdust in their oaten flour, so did I seem. For I was too young, folk thought, to be all alone and not a beggar or a vagabond.

The keenness of winter can be felt in autumn winds, and e'en more so when thy flesh is scarce upon the bone: for swiftly, swifter than I could have imagined, did hunger and cold weaken me, and my poor clothing grow ragged and soiled, and the rain beat down upon my houseless head. Fallen Nature's frivolous cruelty and indecency [*turpitudo*], covered o'er in the summer-season with pretty flourishings, is so great that 'tis no wonder she appears to take the Devil's party, kindled by pagan sorcerers and lechers in their secret rituals, and by lewd and ignorant peasant dances in the open fields.[340]

One question began to trouble me, in my wanderer's feverishness: if the sky's blue be that of a girdling sea, then why is rain not salty to the taste when it falls on the tongue, when it drives against the mouth? I asked my holy master this question in turn, for I saw him in my madness of dreams, and he told me without moving his lips, as a dead man might speak in our minds, that at some point in its curving up into sky at the edge of the world (which men call the Antipodes), where mist obscures from the ascending mariners their upward movement into an element that remains air, but is lighter

---

[340] The original has the incorrect *in cantio aperti*, where *cantio* [enchantment] is probably *campi*. This is a familiar diatribe against paganism on the part of Christianity, which has never resolved its relationship to the natural world's fecundity and moral heedlessness.

than the air we know down below, the water loses its saltiness. 'For salt is swiftly dried into crystals,' I heard him say (as though the sea-cave had become my own skull), 'and is therefore heavier than the liquid it floats in, and must perforce drop away, unable to ascend as swiftly, leaving only fresh water around the boat as it sails above or alongside the towering cliffs of fog, that we call clouds.'

Many times since have I considered such things, even through the mutter of my reading, marking my place in the book with a straw and furrowing my brow in the sudden [silence]. Crouched half-frozen on the outer seats of the cloister winter after winter, I have oft put my goosefeather down to stamp a meagre warmth back into my limbs, letting my thoughts circle around and about as I pace the familiar flagstones. And e'en now, past my ninetieth year (truly, it seems I am condemned to this mortal life for eternity), my body shuffles in its servitude, in poor imitation of its former habit.

Yet it never suffices, for the holy man's voice no longer sounds in my head. I am gnawed by lack of knowledge, as my fingers are scabbed by this very scratching pen. I am no nearer knowing why tears are salty, of the same taste as the sea, or why rain is not. All I do know is that God made such things that we may live to praise His works, for if rain were salty it would render streams and rivers and lakes unpalatable, and mankind would die of thirst. For no man can survive by drinking his own tears, however craving of water he be, or sorrowful; though through that wandering time I oft was forced to, for my suffering made them fall very thick and fast.

Few helped me, though I was but a child of nine or ten. Meeting with wayfaring ruffians and dubious idlers – of the type that go forth on false pilgrimages and exact alms, or don a false hermit's garb at bridges and fords (and sit all day, so forslothen are they) – I knew not whom to trust. One villain, blinded by a red-hot brand for thieving boots, wished me to be his guide, and robbed an inn of its linen while I sung there (for he was no more blind than myself). And when the robbery was discovered, I was seized and almost hanged on the spot, with only my honest tears and bewilderment saving me from death.

Many were the times I thought my harp would be taken from

me, and I retreated to the blear wastes at night, rather than sleep among habitations, e'en when my playing had earned me shelter. Only when I passed a holy house of brothers, or a nunnery, was I certain of a roof – but even then there were vagabonds and vicious types that I was fearful to sleep among, however soft the rushes upon the floor.

A troupe of jougleurs [*joculatores*] and masked players, admiring such skill in one so young (for all the weakness of my piping voice), at first proffered me to accompany them on their travels; and glad of company, I did so: and our minstrelsy of music and jesting was heartily loved by both common folk and nobles. But these play-actors, being utterly forsworn to their ways of drunkenness and lechery, so disgusted my childish soul (despite their kindness and wit), that I finally fled them.

This came about as follows: we entertained at a lord's feast, in a rich manor near Chesster, and the ladies smiled at me, rustling about me in their brocaded silks e'en as the actors shrieked and tumbled. Afterwards we slept in the hall among the scraps, and a dog bit me on the ear, and I saw of what baseness were these lords and ladies, for they snored drunkenly in their beds as loudly as the minstrels sprawled on the floor;[341] and the next morning those same beauteous ladies had turned to ill-tempered ogresses, their hearts no better than the stinking manure of the courtyard, wherein all the filth of that fine house did drain.

I still had the hermit's goodness within me, that railed against these loose practices of adulthood – which transgressions are less hidden from a masterless and orphaned child without a home. In Yorke, where the glorious minster was being made even vaster, and all was scaffolding of a giddying height that groaned and bent with so many men upon it, I found piecemeal work with the stone-layers and wallers and rammers; handing them their gear and tools, or guarding the windlass, and busying myself on my small legs – cheered to it and also cursed sometimes by these labouring artisans. Yet was

---

[341] The great hall was often, in the more old-fashioned manor-houses at this time, the only sleeping place (while the courtyard was that of a farm).

I cheated of my payment, for I had no licence, and left that place indignant and chastened, my throat sore with white dust.

Once also in Du[r]ham, shrine of holy St Cuthbert, where the abbey church sheltering his sacred tomb was already old[342] (and of such colourful immensity within that no eye had ever seen the like), I joined a company of malefactors disguised as tumblers. Two mighty and wondrous towers were being added to the church, upon whose amplitude of sandstone [*tofus*] the workmen were like chattering ants; and we enacted the story of holy St Cuthbert in mime and antics, to the crowds come to gaze upon this mighty labour, while others of us cut their purses. I played the archangel Mikhel, with a silvered face and my harp plucked by my silvered hands, whom the other buffoons pretended they could not look upon without foolish yelps and cries, so blinding was my divine light: no greater hypocrisy is possible, alas, and I blush to think of it e'en now, feeling the sword of the true St Myhel pierce my bowels with cramp.

Forbidden, under threat of mutilation, to play this knavish buffoonery before that holy wonder, we roamed through many a market or fair, fifteen or twenty strong, thieving and rifling, and none dared oppose us – for we had surety [*sponsionem*] of a powerful lord[343] nearby. I did this only because I was nigh starving, yet follows well the punishment after; a mad, foaming dog being loosed upon us as we slept, many were bit before I fled that sanguinary place for good, without a scratch.

After months of this savage life, I grew too weak to sing, and soon I was truly begging. But at that time as now there were many beggars, for the [civil] war[344] had been very fierce, and many crippled or masterless men roamed the ways. And one morning, seeing the poor coming from the woods under baskets laden with moss, yet talking to one

---

[342] Most of Durham Cathedral was built between 1093 and 1133; the western towers between 1217 and 1226.

[343] Such seigneurial gangs were a surprising feature of the thirteenth and fourteenth centuries.

[344] The so-called Baron's War during the reign of King John, a turbulence that had barely ended at this time.

another or whistling, I wished fervently to return to my village home, where I was known and cared for. But I was fearful to, for the harp's value was very great and, thieved, would cause the culprit to be hanged for certain, unless the jury took pity upon a child. Even were I to bring back the instrument to its former blessed owner, falling on my knees in contrition, I feared the punishment would be harsh.

There came a day when I saw a lord's stone manor on a hill, and plodded up to it and knocked weakly on the great door; I was chased from there forthwith, most uncharitably, with only a stump of dry loaf given to me by the servant, for there were swarms of children begging in that area – there being much want among the peasants, scarce recovered as they were from the wars, after the great storms. And on the path down, these meagre young creatures, with sores on their faces and unshod feet, took me in as one of their own.

Though they were urchins and rascals, and always hungry and filthy, these children were full of mirth and games, oft kicking any round thing to hand, and loving to climb trees and other perilous japes and exploits: and when stealing apples and pears from orchards, they took only those that were bruised and fallen, for the beating or whipping would be otherwise very severe. Yet I stayed not with them more than a few days, for when I played and sang, they wished me to teach them, and this I could not do without their soiled, greasy hands touching the strings, and much damage being risked thereby. Although the spirit of music entered them by the ears as it might a brute beast, soothing them and lifting them in wonder, their ragged state made me fearful of mine own; for whereas they would always be bridled by their servile condition,[345] and bowed under till death, I considered myself released from peasanthood, and mercifully erect.

I felt sure by now I was nearing Lundene, though still [gone] only southward as far as the neighbourhood of Dancaster, which then I knew

[345] They are not necessarily the offspring of serfs, however; the unfree tenant was equally trapped, as I have noted earlier: paying his lord in both labour services and 'produce rent', unable to sell his land, and devastated alike in time of failure. However, although lacking freedom and open to abuse, the feudal system's self-supporting villages offered the security, stability and sense of 'community' that we have mostly lost under capital enterprise.

not from the See of Grece or Babyloine.[346] Several times I had been misguided in my direction by evil-hearted wayfarers and sly smilers and half-crazy wastrels, and almost run over by many a cart as I lay strengthless upon the grassy verge. And once in blear light an old woman at her cot's door took me for a demon, thinking my harp to be my leathern wings, and raised a hue and cry – that I only escaped by plunging into a wood, and was much torn thereby.

Thereupon, on crossing a field in great terror of pursuit from that wood, I stumbled upon a piece of cork ballast, as was oft washed up on the hermit's beach: yet this field was very far from the boundless sea. I looked up, thinking of what my good master had told me of the upper sea and its ships, but saw no proper oaken keel far overhead, but only a small dark cloud in the shape of a ship, that might have been mere fumosity of water. I burst into tears, full of grief and regret and hunger.

For, being hungry as a lion, I yet had no meat, and whatever abode I stopped at to beg, there was not even paste in the kneading-trough, so poor it was thereabouts; and the peasants crushed nuts instead and mixed them with ashes, and many were sick or dying in their cots. The nights were colder, though not yet so keen as to freeze the puddles upon the roads. And when some burly villeins found me sleeping in a barn, and took the filth and encrustations upon my face and limbs for leprosy, I was near pierced with a hay fork and most terrorised, and my harp thrown after me so that it struck the ground with a crack.

I wandered about I knew not where for another day or more, half-fainting as I trod, my harp's wood split and my spirits in despair, until I lay in a dry ditch on the wayside, waiting for the comfort of sleep, that owing to my weakened state, would have been eternal – and e'en that I much wished for!

And then it was that brother Thomas found me, and took me in, for he said I was like a sleeping angel, and that his heart swelled with sorrow at my state. Though the road was not unpopulous, it was as

[346] The Mediterranean or Babylon.

a river that passes, and out of all who passed me and saw me, none stopped to see if I were still alive, nor if I required a Christian burial, for it was spitting sleet that day and they would not tarry.

Yet the good monk tarried, reining in his mount and alighting, to find me still breathing and not a cadaver for the dogs or wolves to gnaw at. And giving my harp to the carpenter of the abbey, he made it as new, as he made myself as new in both health and appearance.

2

And what was his reward, this Good Samaritan? To be cloven like an apple.

Though he was no strict follower of the Rule, and e'en gave the demons many a handle to lift him by, neither was he more wicked than most mortal sinners, whose weakness is their chief burden. Nay, what evil was there in his act of so-called betrayal? 'Twas not he in person who attacked Hodde in the holy sanctuary of the church, breaking sacred law: he but pointed the finger. And should so great a heretic and murtherer and robber as Roibert Hodd be granted sanctuary at all, who wished for all churches and holy places to be razed, along with those he named unbelieving – these unbelievers of his being not only every good Christian, but heathens and infidels alike? For Hodde cared for woods and other desolate places more than places of worship – and even the former he descried, believing them to be material clots in the sea of essence, like the greatest cliffs or rocks also were, that would dissolve on his death with all created things and flow eternally as from his bowels.

Strange it was, to feel the old and better influences revive in me from years before, as I played in the market place [of Nottingham], fraudulently blind yet singing my former songs of both courtly and sacred bent, so that the noise dulled into a roar as of the sea by the good hermit's cave. Thus confusion already seethed in my heart and brain, when I heard a voice I knew, of most dulcet and maidenly tones, praising my playing: and opening my eyelids a fraction, as the blind can do, I perceived through the mist of my lashes, just as a painted buffoon peeks through a curtain at the audience, the grey-eyed damsel on the arm of her nurse, gazing upon me but a few feet away, in a dress brocaded with gold and silver.[347] That she did not recognise me was no miracle, for I had never entered the Nonnery when she was lecherously imprisoned within, and she had never descried me skulking among the felons, though I was smitten by her at first sight.

I was so took by surprise that I stopped plucking my instrument, and oped my eyes wide for an instant, that some were startled by this; and thereupon I received the sharp dart of influence from that virginal gaze, so sorely that it lies here still in my liver, and troubles me even in my ninetieth year and more.

Then a simpering servant of hers did squeal, and thus the attendant throng were relieved into laughter and jeering: for I was staring straight at the lovely maiden Isabele, with both mine eyen crystal clear. She had plucked her eyebrows and her fair brow seemed like a hill of snow, and now she drew her wimple's cloth over her mouth, as damsels do when grinning overmuch in merriment.

Litell Johne, whose false beard did make him look e'en more like Herod, struck me with his elbow, bidding me continue; but on seeing our deceit unmasked, he raised his hands and brought up from the well of lies yet another pail of foul water: 'Aye, a wonderful thing it is,' he cried, 'when my son's sight returns under the influence of a noble and fair presence; though 'tis always but a passing spasm, alas, as men do sometimes recover from ills for a day.'

And he secretly pinched me as the spectators paused in their laughter, ever gullible: and rolling my eyes, I shut them again and began to sing a famous song of love and knightly dalliance: yet my voice cracked like a pot, and shame covered my features in a red hue, and opening my eyes I saw the grey-eyed Isabele exposing her red mouth again, to cry out, 'Methinks the poor boy not only cured of his blindness, but also become a lusty man!' True it was, that my voice was uncertain at this time, yet I could pitch it very high and thus

---

[347] Such patterns being 'woven with the design of the fabric, and not added afterwards as embroidery' (*A History of Everyday Things in England*, M. & C. H. B. Quennel, 1918, p. 70).

avoid perturbation. But her presence robbed me of all composure, as if she had broke my voice over her knee. Yet in that moment of great embarrassment, her thoughts entire were upon me, and me alone, as men terrorised by a thunderbolt know e'en in their wickedness that God deems them worthy His attention; or (as happened here last month) a negligent monk, cajoled by the Holy Mother in a fever'd dream, yet knoweth in his misery that he has been picked out by the Virgin from innumerable holy brothers.

The throng laughed heartily, and clapped, and grew greater in number, for simple-minded folk are drawn to cruel laughter as wolves to carrion – as in the time of [King] Stephyn, when mirth and torture were as one. Litl John buffeted some in the front, who were pushing too close, and in the melee we escaped, he dragging me by my elbow while some ruffians threw dung and stones and butcher's entrails after us, as all cheats merit in their eyes.

Hastily looking back as we fled, I perceived the damsel and her retinue had moved away from the common herd to the shadow of a shop, but her face was still alight with merriment under the fine linen cap, and the nurse nodding gaily. Was this the creature whom Hodd revered as his holy bride, the heretical Virgin to his false Pope of Heaven? Nay, what snares these women are, that lure us by their come-liness and red mouths and fine stitchings and outward adornings of gold and silver thread! Who pluck out our livers and roll them in their lily-white hands, till we swoon with their dalliance, and swear ourselves bound to them and to serve them all our days!

Litl John was much displeased, and gave me a good clout upon the head with his palm, for we had drawn attention to ourselves; yet when we came to the postern gate, my head bowed as if sightless, the aged serjeant had not heard of the disgrace, and bid us enter after telling us of a lewd song he had heard long ago in the Holy Land, where they cry like wolves to peculiar instruments – for he had taken the cross[348] and earned a hideous scar on his face, that passed like a piece of rope over one eye, rendering it as useless as a walnut shell,

---

[348] i.e. embarked on a Crusade: possibly that of Richard the Lionheart in the 1190s.

and made him have pity on me for my worse affliction; yet he was not one whit the better for it in his soul, for he reeked of countless visits to the tavern.

Swiftly we followed the instructions of the lame felon Roger, turning left instead of right, and though we passed servants hurrying hither and thither with meats and jugs in the corridors (for the feast approached), none stopped us. Down narrow, turning stairs we hastened, after opening a low door: well set into the stone and slippery with dankness, the way was unlit, and we had no tapers, so that we must feel our progress with hands and feet. And verily I knew blindness then, and it was indeed wretched. By these stairs we showed ourselves[349] in a dungeon passage lit here and there by torches, that exuded a bitter smell, and it was indeed as Hell must smell from afar off: for e'en less than a hundred miles across the plain of desolation, Satan's kingdom would stifle a living man with its smoke and stench.

There were small monkish cells on either side, those occupied having their heavy doors well locked, each entrance little taller than my own boyish height; the groined ceiling of the passage being low enough to cut my companion's head, he had to bend like a cripple. Our feet splashed through puddles [bleeding?] from the stone, and the slabs were slippery with filth. From within the cells there were groans and cries and shouts, made indistinct by the thickness of stone and oak; one prisoner sang, yet so bawdy was the song that it outmastered those of the felons, being the type one hears only on ships or in the lowest sort of tavern, full of harlots and cut-throats. There being no gaoler nor even guard [permanently?] in the dungeons (each door having two locked bolts of great heft), it was safe to smite the oak for an answer, that this might betray the occupant and reveal Hodde to us without raising [the alarm].

After curses and groans from within each door that we struck, and once a mad burst of laughter, as though we were disturbing fiends instead of wretches, Hodde's voice did answer the blow with a

[349] *Volito*, though *volo* is possibly meant: 'to fly' in the sense of 'move rapidly'. The parchment has shrapnel damage on the borders of the leaves at this point, touching some of the words nearer the margin.

blasphemous oath that seemed afar off and strange, saying we did come from a sow's womb [*volva*].³⁵⁰ Wherefore we knew the door, and though almost lightless there (for the torches were sparsely ranged, and the passage twisted crookedly like a burrow), Litl John marked it discreetly with his dagger.

Then we found the hiding-place Roger Wylde had told us of: like a close-fitting closet or a garderobe, it was set into the wall further up and black with shadow, yet doorless. It was no wider than the holy cell of the Blessed Christina, that virgin of great repute, the tireless disciple of Roger of St Albans,³⁵¹ who crouched on cold stone for four years, and endured such fasting and discomforts that no prisoner even in the dungeons of Nottyngam might have known the like, to attain her incredible heights of grace: yet she was hidden from all but her saintly master, who instructed her and tended her, uttering counsel through the thick planks that shut her in so that she could scarce move about. How different was our purpose!

Feeling a hook on the back wall, and a thick chain, we conjectured in whispers that it was a chamber for hanging a man upside-down, from the cruel times of the Normans, when these barbarous practices were common;³⁵² although such tortures might still be used hiddenly by villainous lords.

I was much afraid, yet forced myself not to show it, for my trembling might be felt by Litel John, so close were we pressed together in this recess, as two peas in a pod. The noises of the dungeon echoed horribly, and moisture dripped; so foul was the air, as though this place was truly a garderobe, that I almost retched – and knowing that, if we were caught, then this prison would be our final destiny (were

³⁵⁰ Although *volva* means the unqualified 'womb', it is usually a sow's (to a knowledgeable Latinist); this being a favourite delicacy among the Romans. Otherwise the insult makes no sense.

³⁵¹ Christina's remarkable life of self-imposed hardship and miracle-working is found in the *Gesta Abbatum S. Albani*; she lived in the first half of the twelfth century.

³⁵² Unlike the rest of Europe, torture was strictly prohibited in England except in cases of alleged treason; later in the century, in cases where the defendant refused to go before the jury, pressing with weights (*peine forte et dure*) was allowed as a subtle method of persuasion.

we not to hang), I felt a stifling as of one still breathing in a coffin, buried by error.

Horrid it was! Wriggling and slithering forms betokened rats, that squeaked with joy to find us, and several were crushed by my companion's great tread. No living being can understand what it is to be in such a place, who hath not suffered a spell in a dungeon or similar hell-hole. And in the enchantments of sleep, that close-bound closet in the bowels of the castle of Notynggam still claspeth me about, with the breathing through his nose of the huge felon in my ear, so that I think again I am like to perish, and that this might be my eternal prospect after death. Terrible fate!

Quick we were to keep still as cadavers, when the foosteps rang out through the passages, with a clattering that betokened two men in mail. These not being the gaoler, but the sentries on their round, who had no keys but only a flaring torch that threw hideous shadows about, we pressed almost into the stones until they had passed. They were talking to each other most obscenely, and reeked of ale, or they would have perceived the glitter of our eyes.

So stiff and cold were we, by the time the big-bellied gaoler came with several guards, we had lost all awareness of time passing, for no bells sounded deeply enough, and no windows showed the changes of light. Yet it was little more than two hours! Imagine what it must be, to suffer years or a lifetime of this type of place; 'tis scarce a wonder, then, that men lose their minds and gnaw their own limbs – or dash their heads out upon the stones, rather than suffer such an existence.

We heard [the gaoler and his men] open the steel bolts of each door in turn, and hand in victuals, to curses and shouts and some-times blows that stifled hideous screams; yet it was not now that we must intervene, but later, when the gaoler passed on his own before sleep, as was the rule, to tell the wretches that it was night, and douse the torches behind him before emerging by another stairway anigh the recess. So clasped by cold and dampness was I, that I might have been immersed in a well, and hardly cared whether we were discovered or no, if it meant being brought to daylight and soup. The men passed us carelessly, and quiet fell again upon that dread place; save the odd moaning and curse and the squealing of the rats, that troubled our ears with visions.

Finally then the gaoler came on his own, announcing nightfall, and bidding the wretches pray for their souls – though he said this with a great and mocking carelessness in his wheezy [*anhelus*] voice. And pausing no doubt before Hodd's door, he asked in a womanly manner: 'How is the tender clerk?' – as though the infamous felon were an uncouth beanus![353] We heard not the answer, but only the gaoler's mocking laugh and his foul oath, for he seemed drunken.

As he passed us with his torch, having doused each wall-light behind him, Litl John leapt upon him and took him by the throat, while I snatched away the flaming torch before it expired in a puddle. And the poor fellow was pierced in his great belly so thoroughly that the sword's point rang against the wall on the far side of his entrails, and he expired with a snort.

Littel John took the keys in his hand from the dead man's belt, and there being many, he hastened to try each one in the marked door [of Hod's cell], until the bolt slipped and the oaken bar lifted, and we could enter. Yet we did not see a room in the light of the torch, but rather a great void and emptiness, at the base of which was a floor of sodden rushes and pools, walled with stones the size of great cushions, and heaving with vermin. The stench was so sour that it almost overpowered us (as where a sewer flows into a stream or a ditch or a cess-pit, outside a well-populated town), and we searched for a way down. Indeed, there was naught but a half-rotted ladder, for this was the deepest dungeon, in which only desperate criminals were sometimes kept. And in a corner, well chained, squatted our master alone, seeming fearful of the flaring torch, as if it was too bright.

How haggard he looked, even after a few days! In his eyes was not the gleam of conviction and assured victory, but that of madness;

---

[353] A freshman (also *bejaunus*) at a medieval university (from the French 'bec-jaune' or 'greenhorn').

hast thou not heard how Satan's huge round eyes mirror his own kingdom of fire and torment? A rat tugged at his sleeve, as doth a fiend's claw tug at a sinner's by the bath-house or the tavern; yet he did not shake it off, letting Litle John shatter the creature against the flinty stones. Our leader's mouth was open like a simpleton's between new-sprouted whiskers, as matted as those of a beggar's; his hands lay idle beside him, and no more blasphemous oaths issued from him. He was fastened to the wall by a chain soldered to iron rings about each of his ankles, which rings bore sharp spikes upon the outside, and were pressed so tight they had rubbed his flesh raw.

There was not a stick of furniture in this dungeon, nor a dry patch of rushes to sleep on, but all was rotted and infested, and so thick with fleas that already they were biting us and drawing blood, for their carrion was meagre. Were my torch to have been extinguished, absolute lightlessness would have descended upon us, for there was no window or even slit for air.[354] Little wonder, then, that Hodd was half crazed already, raising only his arm to greet us as we searched to unlock his chains!

Under cover of the night, we bore him out of that dread place to the outside wall by the *jaylers steyres*, as Roger Wylde had named them, pausing only for Litl John to don the dead gaoler's cloak. Indeed, as we were warned, the two watchhounds barked upon hearing our steps, and hurried towards us with slavering jaws and bared teeth; but on smelling their master the gaoler's cloak, and being thrown the marrow-bones, they softened sufficiently that we could pierce their shaggy throats with our daggers, and they expired with no more than a whimper.

[354] It is sometimes a convenient conceit to depict the Middle Ages as barbaric, but this description suggests that at least in Europe, certain areas have indeed grown more civilised; prisoners in the late and intensely horrible conflict were relatively well treated, aside from plagues of cholera or individual punishments, and civilians, though suffering untold miseries and mass death, were mostly spared that direct cruelty of individual soldiers that has always marked an army's passage. In what is now promisingly termed our 'hundred years of peace', it is possible to regard history as a story of progress, with intermittent spasms of violence that serve (perceptible only in hindsight) as creative spurs, however terrible their effects at the time. [*'This is nonsense! Nothing will bring back Alec!' Scrawled comment in pencil by FB against this circled footnote.*]

The wall being lowest in one place because of a loathsome and stinking dung-heap that rose against it like a hill, we scaled it forth-with; Hod being half carried by the big-shouldered felon to the parapet, mumbling much nonsense. Our leap was softened by the mud that met us, yet still I was winded, and we could see little: the moon being veiled in cloud. The castle wall here being also the outer wall of the city, with no need of the rampart, we had only the muddy ditch to pass: but on climbing down it, I slipped, and injured my knee so that it was torn. Yet I could not tarry, for there were many huts of paupers there, amongst which would no doubt be men and women eager to please the sceryf, and earn a few pennies by raising a hue and cry and arresting us, if we were to wake them in their kennels.[355]

Though I was lamed, our horses (having been left with Mercilesse Greenlese in the woods close by the road) were just as fleet[356] when we sped away before dawn, with our chief sitting with Litell John upon the same saddle, as though no discord had ever occurred between them. And none being crouched in the brushwood, ditch or coppice to rob us (as oft robbers are robbed themselves), therefore we returned to our own malefactors' camp safely by dusk of that same day.

We were greeted like the victors of a great battle, under the leafy trees. Hodd was carried to his hut, where various potions of crushed beetles, herbs and common oil were applied on his skin, as he had begun to rave like a mad beggar, running a fever that threatened to carry him off. So potent had been the foul fumosity of the dungeon, that I too fell sick with diarrhoea [*alvi profluvium*], although I now think it the effect of my great and mortal sin.[357]

*　　*　　*

[355] We know next to nothing about the medieval poor, as the records rarely mention them, though they made up a third of the population. This is a rare glimpse of an extra-mural 'shanty' town, that must at the time have been a commonplace.

[356] This episode of the freeing of Hod is interestingly paralleled by the ballad in certain details: the gaoler stabbed right through 'to the wall'; Little John taking 'the keyes in honde'; and the final scaling of the fortification from the easier side ('ther as the wallis were lowyst / Anon down can thei lepe'). Otherwise much is omitted.

[357] More likely to have been due to his torn knee, infection being as dangerous then as it is now.

A full fortnight later, we were recovered enough that a celebratory feast was held under the principal oak, during which revelry I first recited the adventure to the strains of the stolen harp, while the felons listened in their drunken manner to one also reeking, yet able to rhyme; after which they resumed their jests and merriment. Some took their archery gear to the rock-bluff, while others (stripped to the waist) wrestled each other for pleasance through many a pull, so that their flesh was glossy with sweat – then slaking their thirst the more, like eager swains at a tournament.

Seldom had I felt such contentment and pride, and verily thought myself a great figure in the world, incontinent with drink and wanton cheer; so that e'en my murder of a fellow-Christian vanished in mirth, yet was no more gone than a deer in the dapple-grey of a copse, that fooleth the sight by resting still.

Yet all I was doing was raking hot coals about myself: for being carried about beside John on many a shoulder, both marvellously clad in stolen robes and green-leafed crowns, like knights in glittering helms after victory in battle, I touched the very roof-beams of pride.

Hodde watched, yet he was not comfortable, even when toasted many times by the company; and when he stood upon the hewn log in his tight-fitting mantle the colour of dried blood, his speech was rambling and full of fantastic words that none there understood. His great hood that fell down his back, seemed limp and like the flayed integument of some monstrous organ.

He was not as before, indeed, and horribly resembled the poor quack's skull, hid high above the leafage. The light that once gleamed in his prominent eyeballs was doused, and his voice was weaker and somewhat cracked: and his teeth – that his lips moved over in that aforesaid curious way (as if sucking upon a plum) – showed more distinctly in their crookedness, between a neglectfulness of beard that gave him the false air of a desert prophet.

I felt a restlessness among the men, for Litell John had command of them and had not the same power over their minds, but only over their baser natures that sought pillage and profit. And I saw how certain of the younger felons nearest me were e'en giggling during the speech! Yet when one among us, a rascal called *Coillon*[358] (from his extreme ugliness of nose, that had been rivelled and pecked by disease), was found to have wronged one of the women in the Nunerie, by breaking in drunkenly that same night, Hode banished him, with a fresh disfigurement that was a veritable improvement, for the aforesaid protuberance no longer shadowed his face; while those who had giggled were guests for several days of the dragon's pit, and the revelries were thus ended.

We soon heard from others, how the sheryf had raged after the escape, and punished the guards with a beating on their bare shoulders, and how the one-eyed, aged serjeant on the postern gate had been rewarded with a spell in the very same cell, that would no doubt be fatal to him; although this news, being imparted by travellers waylaid by the felons on the road, might have little resembled the truth.

Well before the feast – namely on the ninth day after the exploit – having been called as usual into Hod's fraudulent temple for heretical instruction, I was asked to recount all that had happened, for he was confused (it seemed) by the visions he had seen in the utter and stinking blackness of his days in the dungeon. He was so thin, now, that he might have outfaced a skeleton for gauntness, and his hair was lank, and the whiskers were already thickening into beard, yet his wicked brow-mark shone like precious fat. Other men have spent months or even years in such places, and survived better! To my mind, Hodd had devils in him that had delighted to be in that underground place, that was so like their true home, and they had issued forth from his mouth and nose and buttocks to taunt him: and these being of such number and so plumped up on his wickedness and heresy, he was as a horse – or, rather, a sow – driven mad by flies.

When I came to the reckoning of Henrie, I broke down at the finish, for the illness had weakened me sufficiently that I could not hide my feelings as before, and wept until my entire face was moist.

Instead of being sore displeased, he put his arm about my shoulders and said, 'Verily, thou hast done a great service, for this angelic

[358] Testicle.

247

boy was destined to become a great and powerful bishop, burner of heretics and oppressor of the free spirit, remembered by posterity as St Henry of Lincoln – for that city is where he was destined to serve his Lord Pope. And he was to live to a great age, writing many brilliant treatises of huge renown, e'en rivalling those of Augustine. And on his death the Spirit within him, which is called *anima*, would have become the *otherwe* as with all beings, in many floating veils; save that his was so glutted on so-called heretics, that it would have overcharged its vaporous vessel as certain clouds do, with a dreadful breaking noise, and rained a kind of running flux, causing corruption of beasts like a cattle-plague, and grievous illness and famine.'

Amazed, I asked him through my tears, 'How do you know this? For you did not meet Henriy, and he was but nine or ten, though indeed he was exceeding proud.'

Hodde then laughed, and his eyes kindled again with something of his former spirit, his dark line of single eyebrow creasing above them, and his gaunt nose moving, that he did very much resemble that bird which finds a savoury goodness in excrement and carrion, and dieth of hunger.[359] 'I know all things, and it is a wonder that men know them not,' he said. 'But search in your heart, and you will know them too, for you are of the elect. Indeed, you will be placed even higher than myself!'

And I was so much stupefied that I could only stammer forth: 'Higher, master? How can that be?'

Following a pause for thought, he said: 'After the sea of divine essence hath covered all that we know, and extinguished humankind, but for the few angelic forms who have had the truth revealed to them, you will be placed so, extraordinary as it might sound. I saw this in the dungeon: you flitted far above me, like a lark.'

He paused, and went to the corner of his birch-lined hut, that resembled a pagan temple full of idolatry: there he took out a hidden flask of wine and drank a long draught, like any tavern-haunter. Indeed,

---

[359] Presumably the vulture, familiar from the Crusades; according to Bartholomew, 'when he ageth, his over bill waxeth long and crooked . . . and [he] dieth at the last for hunger'.

he had a sweet scent about him of the incontinent drinker, a common plain fault that I was blind to. Then he wiped his whiskers and turned to me and said: 'Aye, you were far above me, a light in the darkness, I swear. This is because you have done a most powerful deed, in ending the life of that future oppressor, that might e'en have prevented the sea of divine essence from outbreaking these earthly limits and flowing, so dangerous and venomous was he. That was the purpose of my suffering in that hellish room those three days, that you might release us from the bonds of the future.'

Then, after coughing moistly as with a rheum, he came up to me again and whispered close: 'So must you do the same once more with your blade or your bow, but to another far closer and better known to us.'

His warm lips touched my ear, as the Devil's do in tempting us, or as a harlot does in lechery; and immediately I fathomed his meaning, with such a chill about my battered heart that it well nigh stopped. Seeing that I did not ask him of whom he might mean, he murmured the name, and laughed (for I now believe he was intoxicated). 'But I cannot,' I stammered, 'for he hath done no evil, and is one of our company, and indeed hath just saved your own life, dear master.'

As men doubt whether there be a God and yet be displeased by this very temptation of the Devil, so was I heartily displeased by Hode's words, though just before I had been puffed up like a toad by his praise. But e'en more displeased was Hodde by my recoiling, and he pinched me about the neck, and shouted, 'How canst thou doubt my words, when I was right about the one you have slain? Dost thou pick and choose my words like cherries?'

I denied this, but did not know what more to say, for no soldier must doubt a single one of his general's words, or all collapses: for every stone in a great cathedral partakes of the whole, and so it was with the heretic Hode. If this stone be hollow, then why not that one also? Mayhap, then, none can be trusted, and the whole edifice is but a playing company's pasteboard castle.

Yet I nodded as if in agreement, for I was eager to be free of his grip, and of his coughing, and of his foul, wine-tinctured breath on my ear. 'Watch him closely,' he added, in a soft hiss, 'for he doth mean to finish us, before we finish him! Thus you must choose the moment soon, e'en within days. This our little forest kingdom is torn by deceit and fraud and corruption, like Ingelond[360] itself. Perverse is the world, and it is best to be rid of it: and by tipping over the cup of wickedness when it is full, to the very brim, we shall know the boundlessness of endless bliss.'

Thus like a serpent did he beguile, and I was much torn, and full of fear; for part of my brain did keep the memory of him when he was prostrate in the dungeon: and like an ordinary and most miserable vagabond was he then, sprawled on those befouled rushes!

[360] As in the MS.

3

To slay Litle John was so far beyond [my] ability and will, that I could not see how I might obey my master, beguiled though I was by his flattery. Yet I began to comprehend how the big-shouldered felon was taking advantage of his master's state to presume command; for when Hode had hobbled from his hut during the second week of his sickness, with that new beard upon him from neglect, saying that they must move the camp to a wilder place upon the coast, after the advice of a vision, Litel John had refused, and our leader was too sick to complain. Yet I now believe he did complain, by bidding me after to slay his lieutenant.

In the days following the feast, Hode ordered the men to erect more poles all about the edges of the wood, where the low line of defence ran (its timbers much in need of repair). They stuck heads of poached deer and boars and suchlike upon the tops and decorated them with feathers to make hideous masks, as those blaspheming pagans do, that are not yet rooted out from certain wild places, nor from our very towns and villages.

Some of the fire was in him still, for when a haughty, blond-haired retainer of the cruel baron's was caught on the road, and perforce dragged before our leader, the poor wretch was hanged on the instant from the great oak in his fine blue mantle, and then his head like-wise stuck on a pole at the marge of the trees: its face receiving cuts [*cultro vulneratum*] from Hodde's sharp knife, so that the victim's own mother would not have recognised him.[361]

---

[361] This unpleasantly violent incident of deliberate disfigurement (indeed, the second in the narrative) is remarkably echoed in the ballad of *Robin Hood and Guy of Gisborne* [Child, 1888, III. 91–4]. Appearing in print for the first time in the eighteenth century, the text cannot be dated yet preserves certain archaic features that suggest at least a late-medieval provenance.

'Now,' said Hodd, in his address to the assembled company, 'we have no need of guards or sentries, nor even a wall, for the divine essence flows about us in a ring, and is harder than steel to our enemies!'

Litl Johnn thought this all folly, and said so there and then. 'Amazed am I,' he cried, 'that we are trusting to this ruse of sticks, as solid as a happy dream, when our enemies are eager for revenge. E'en now they may be encircling us, and yet no alarum will shrill, until they leap on our very throats.' To which sensible observation, born of much soldiering in his case, some of us were in timid agreement; others were troubled by this disloyalty, for they still believed Hodd to be one of the elect and that this horrible pagan vice might protect them, as earthworks protect a town; and the remainder like myself did not know which way to blow, but looked about anxiously for the enemy slinking up to us through the trees.

Alas, what evils we are prepared to believe; in the same way dames – even a baron's lady – are happy to believe in ten sorts of delicious wines, when the huckster draws them all from one miserable and tainted barrel!

At this, Hodde told him that he [Little John] was an unbelieving knave, and not worth expending an arrow upon, and would be less than ashes when the day came of the overbreaking of the spirit. 'Indeed thou shalt be a spot of grease on the great ocean flowing from my bowels, that is broad and without a bottom [*largitio non habet fundum*].' At this we all laughed greatly; but Hode, wickedly smiling, bid us be silent with a raised arm, and added: 'Thou art not pure, John, because there is a morsel of your spirit that is tainted with doubt, that believes sinfulness be possible, like a speck of dung in the sweetest honey. Therefore you sin in every action, and even raising your little finger, you are defiled, a mere servant of that cursed horned creature, the Church.'[362]

---

[362] Such anarchic, mystical beliefs, recurrent throughout the Middle Ages, survived remarkably intact among such groups as the seventeenth-century Ranters in England, and are even perceptible in our own day among certain eccentrics and charlatans. Such wild dreaming has as its core, however, an interesting rejection of the principle that God has delegated His decisions regarding sin to an earthly authority, the Church, along with the appropriate penalties; it also refuses to accept that earthly unhappiness is a means to happiness in the after-life – which equation does indeed come close to an acceptance of poverty and political injustice.

Litl John looked about him then, and seeing us all grinning like fools, turned to Hod and said, 'The only sin I committed was to free your miserable cadaver from the gaol, wherein we saw what the blessed one had come to, fevered and stinking.' Hod scoffed, though he was troubled by this: clothing it in merry words and speckled with oaths I cannot repeat, he said: 'Then were I to cut thy throat, knave, you would esteem it not a sin, for verily it would be a just reward for your bad judgement. Though I would deem this act of murther a very wise act, and even blessed, for I desire it most strongly, and all that the pure in spirit desire, is blessed.'

I gasped, astonished that he should be declaring his bloody wishes so openly; yet I now see it as his skilful way of deceit, for no man would normally declare himself openly to the victim, if he meant it in earnest. And thus he put on the cloak of dissembling, as all devils do, by his plain-spoken honesty;[363] and so the assembled company cheered and clapped, thinking Hode to be sending soft missiles of ribaldry, and not deadly poison as they were, while I sat silent and morose in my own darkness.

And likewise John did not reply with his mouth, but pulling down his breeches in an indecent manner, turned his posterior towards our leader and let out a great wind, with a noise as loud as players and buffoons make by strongly blowing into a bladder and violently breaking it. Yet this was performed with his own anatomy. And then he cried, after the manner of our leader's blasphemous declarations: 'And that, too, is most sweet, for nothing is foul that is made by the divine essence!'

Hode asked me the next day about the grey-eyed damsel, searching my eyes as he did so, so that I stammered in my speech. 'I feel the end drawing nigh,' he said, bowing his head in the hut, 'when we shall be united, the virgin and myself, and all shall be liquified in bliss. But first my chief rival must be effaced [*delendum est*], and the task is yours; for last night a vision came to me, wherein I saw you triumphant, trampling his huge cadaver.'

[363] We have here an intimation of Iago's bluff, perplexing character in *Othello*, three centuries later.

And I did feel fear and pride mingling; for he looked upon me as a father doth his son, that would beat him more sorely the more he loveth him – the father loving better the son that is most like to him.

Then he took me from the hut to stand under the great oak. There were few felons in the clearing, for some were crouched in the shrubs miles away by the highway, others still guarding the camp, and most engaged on sundry tasks here and there. Looking up, he bid me watch the myriad little leaves so blithe and bright in the summer sunlight, and moving in gusts of a full breeze with birds warbling among them. 'Every leaf is honouring me,' he said; 'each one, numbering thousands upon thousands, is acknowledging and honouring my presence, for they are part of my inmost being, and they praise me as their father.'

Indeed it seemed to be as he said, as I looked up into the giddy heights of the bough-laden tree: that were like the heights of a great abbey church springing from the roots of the pillars. Each leaf was moving in obeisance and fealty and honouring, as handkerchiefs flutter at a famous knight in a tournament. His eyes were shining as he stared upwards with his gaunt face, his lips moving over words I could not hear at first. 'We must build higher,' he murmured. 'Higher and yet higher. Thou must perform thy deadly task tomorrow, as it is writ. Do not extort from me instruction, let there be no delay, only remain fierce and merciless, and remember that you are the purest in heart; and whatever the pure in heart desire, pure are the waters thereof.'

Then there was a bray of the Jew's horn from the margin of the wood, for Litle John had returned with Will Scathelock and others from the road. No booty had been taken; each time the wayfarers had been too poor, or were moving in armed parties of twenty or more. This was so increasingly since Hod's escape; no one now dared venture on the highway alone, if he were worth robbing. And when Litl John came up and told us this, Hode said, 'Nothing hath his being of naught,' which is a phrase of Boethius, and was sarcastic in his mouth, for Hodd smiled when he uttered it, as if nothingness was indeed something in his mind: and whatever he said did oft seem as doth a solid substance, e'en when it was a contradiction [*quod contra dictum est*] unto itself, or grievous heresy. And we all know that the one true God is incapable of contradicting Himself.

At that point the breeze grew in the trees, and the great oak swayed its boughs with a creaking noise, that it seemed to be obedient to its master. I saw Hode lift his bearded face and look upwards at it again, with shining eyes like an ascetic, and lips moving silently once more; in that moment I understood how he was inviolate in his purity, and that we were corrupted, for none other among us would so resemble a saint. My unbelief was such that I saw in him the effigy of Christ: compared to the other felons in the clearing, whose glances were mostly sidelong and whose brows oft scowled – so steeped in vice were they – he had writhed to be unharnessed from both good and evil, evil and good, as though these were the same, no different than are two numbers in dice! And seeing naught but righteousness and purity in all his own thoughts and actions, he therefore had a hideous piety about him.

Yet was he more dangerous than any man there, or any man I have ever met since, and worse e'en than Judas, by whose treason at least our Christian salvation ensued: for having no consciousness of goodness, as a gold coin hath not (though it be golden), then neither the milk of loving-kindness nor the meat of virtue was necessary to him; and therefore he could not be touched by spiritual hunger or need, nor be influenced by the comfort therein of a kind or generous action – nor recognise the shadow of sin, that makes such actions the brighter. What other man – lest he was demented, or deprived of all reason – could wish to slay the friend who had saved his life?

This was one who, to test his mettle, would be prepared to dash infants against the wall, or raze a town through fire, as Nature doth when roused. Just as a tree hath not a care for humanity, but may topple upon our heads without a thought for sinfulness, or a wolf devour an infant without shedding a tear, or an owl or a crow blind a dying man after battle without pity, so Hode was of this kind: his heart a wilderness, his head a temple to the 'holy Earth', as quacks and witches call her.[364] And these same fools give this so-called fallen goddess titles such as 'guardian of heaven and sea' – thus denying entirely the after-life, and our Saviour, as well as God Himself. So was Hodde a pagan and a heretic combined, of a pitiless purity of evil, entirely consumed by Satan – like a wooden idol consumed within by worm, yet still complete upon the outside, as Ezechiel[365] saith of the pot of brass, full of filth and scum that must be burned away.

If, in so many areas, the lewd will of man hath replaced the sacred will of God, then Hodde's will was distinguished only by its presumption [*arrogantia*]. As felons flocked about him, even the roughest and most villainous types, then so also did those whom unkind fate had thrown into lordlessness, who were not naturally cut-throats but merely outlaws; and even some were peasants like myself, fleeing correction and labour, yet whose pauperism had not opened them to Christ, but only to uncleanly living and drunkenness – that Hodd told them was blessed and no sinfulness, for they desired it, and desire is as natural as thirst, whether for gold or for women or for spilling Christian blood. 'And as naught that flows from the divine essence can sin, as a tree cannot sin,' he would say, 'therefore the Church is a painted board to make us fearful and blind.'

Yet despite the allure of such words to those under the yoke of poverty and unending labour, his kingdom did not spread beyond the margins of that wood upon its hill, for all his vainglory; unless we count the wasteland of moor that spread about it on every side, useful to no man, and the company of informers and helpers planted here and there in the towns without, eager for the End of Days, and those vile persons who traded with him in stolen coin, furs, papers, salt and other such precious goods – of which false merchants there were innumerable examples.

---

[364] Two such incantations survive in a twelfth-century medical MS of the British Museum (MS Harl., 1585, fol. 12a ff.), where 'Earth' is variously addressed as 'Queen of the gods', 'Mother Earth', 'the Great Mother', and 'Holy Goddess Earth, parent of Nature, who dost generate all things, and regenerate the planet . . .' These rare survivals are an indication that pockets of paganism were possibly far more widespread in the Middle Ages than is assumed – alas, dwindled these days (in England) to a belief in gossamer-winged fairies.
[365] Ezekiel, xxiv, 3–11.

Indeed, he would have been forgot entirely, like many another criminal, but for my influence, alas!

If I had not ta'en the spark of his evasion [from gaol] and blown upon it, it would have died forthwith in the darkness. But whatsoever I sang to the harp [*ad citharam cecini*], all men sang it gladly after me:[366] other minstrels (and e'en parti-coloured players and buffoons) followed my songs and words, and so it spread beyond my ken, like the touch of leprosy passeth from one to another.

I sang even then, on that same evening of the day when he had gazed up into his arboreal servant, our meeting oak – that I placed myself beneath to be better heard, for its roots had heaved up the earth to make a natural stage. 'Sing a song of Robbert Hode, king of the outlaws and of the realm of the *othar*,' he cried, in his usual manner, 'and of his glorious escape from Notyngam.' So I did, for I was prepared: and so near to the truth was it, that gasps came from every side, and cheers and hulloos, and my fingers seemed enchanted as they touched the fox-gut of Henry's harp; my voice was ne'er so high and melodic, though cracking here and there (to the felons' amusement): and sweet and inspired was my rhyming.

I had a youthful gift of memory at that time, that enabled me full well to compose and place the words (or their likeness) in the den of memory, in which chamber of the brain they were as though inked upon a roll of parchment, the which my vital spirit could read in the light that he carried from the den of wit. Thus if the rhyme were not too long, I could sing it without impairment on the very same day it was conjured by my virtue imaginative,[367] plucking and

[366] It is likely, we now think, that the earliest medieval 'balades' or 'rimes' were not so much sung as musically recited or chanted over the harp's accompaniment, in the manner of a bard (such as in earlier times would have recited Homer's poem). The Latin terms do not help us (*cantus*, etc.).

[367] This passage, typically indebted to Bartholomew (Libra iii., Cap. xxij), reminds us of something known to the traditional reciters and singers of rhymes and ballads in our own times: that certain stylistic features make them easier to memorise. Additionally – at least in our local public house – the words are rarely identical with each performance, as Mr Cecil Sharp points out (*English Folk Song*, 1907, pp. 28–9), while admitting the exception of blind singers who have learned the words parrot-fashion.

pressing the strings as I saw fit, that I seemed as in an amazing trance.

As dusk fell after my singing, and we all ate and drank about the cooking fire, I noticed Littl John regarding me and smiling, his heavy brow lifted, for he was covetous of his own glory; and he came up to me and bid me compose a ballad that spoke only of his own exploits, of which (having been a soldier, he claimed, at many a battle and long siege) he had a full quiver. 'Then my name shall be very famous all over Inglonde,' he said.

So fearful was I of the murderous thoughts implanted in me by our leader, that I nodded, and stammered some feigning agreement, and after a while I walked away from that spot. Spending much time with Hodd, at his command, since his escape from the dungeon, while he was sick and I swiftly recovered (oft keeping my silence while his words wriggled like serpents in my brain, from den to den, infecting all with their poison), my reasonable spirit was hindered in its proper workings in the body: just as Eve was impaired, and she in turn impairing Adam with her allure.

For he would tell me that I could do everything as I wished and desired, and not divide the world into angels and devils, which is something born only in the contriving brain: for the truth is oneness, from which all flows. And once, taking a leaf from a creeper that had penetrated his hut between the planks, he called it Christ, and God, and then chewed the leaf and swallowed it: 'My spirit is in all, and all is in my spirit,' he proclaimed, blaspheming thus horribly through his crooked teeth.

Troubled, as I said, by Litl John's request, I walked away as if to do my offices unto the place wherein they were generally done: this being a stinking pit past the horses, near the marge of the woods, as it is in any town. Then taking the path beyond that spot, I came out through a gap in the low timber wall (that was no more defence than a straw wicket), into the slender young birch-trees on the very edge of the camp. Yet shamefast at my secrecy, I craftily kept out of sight of the sentry who still (despite Hod's will) watched the heath from a high bough some fifty feet away, and would have pierced me through with his arrow if he thought I was escaping – for the felons feared betrayal most of all.

There, alas, I had at first a most horrible vision among the young birch, for it was now the confusing light that followeth a bright sun's setting. I found myself beside one of the poles on which a boar's head had been affixed, full evilly as in pagan lands, and bestuck about with feathers, and malodorous. And in the gloam I bestrewed it wrongly, and saw it as brother Thomas's great head, with his broad mouth hung open. Further away in the gloaming [I saw] another the like – but this being the pole of the aforementioned baron's retainer, whose face Hode had nicked with his knife, it was yet more horrible; and the torn features made very like Henry's by my impaired wits,[368] that receiveth all through the eyes onto a blank whiteness in the brain, and fashion new and impossible sights thereby, I almost fell into a swoon: for the heads did sing in plainchant most sweetly to my ears as I gazed upon them: *Gloria in excelsis deo. Et in terra pax hominibus bone voluntatis. Laudamus te. Benedicimus te. Adoramus te. Glorificamus te.*

Such is the power of God's influence in even the most spotted of souls, that at the heart of that hideous pagan place, surrounded by bewitching, heathenish idols of the cruellest sort, this heavenly confirmation did ring in my ears very joyfully; and I softly and quietly sang also, as though in the very heart of the holy abbey, far from the forest of unbelief. And seeing this abbey lit by myriad panes of coloured glass, that had been moulded by God's grace out of the ebbing light through the glade (the sky by a trick seeming still bright against the foliate darkness, though the sun was sinking beyond the hills of the moor without), I understood by the lovely, sacred singing that the wood entire had been transfigured into glass: aye, all the greenwood into brittle glass, as the seas become the sky in which the blessed cannot drown, for they have no breath but are beyond breath, yet they live eternally.

[368] Although he chooses not to remind us, both Henry and the retainer were 'blond-haired'.

And my soul rose up in joy at the thought, for how base is Nature compared to the eternal light of the Lord!

Then, being taken out of this revelation by a distant tumult, I understood that something was amiss in the clearing, and wondering sore what it might be, I tore myself from the transformed place among the birches (that had passed by God's mercy from pagan to Catholic), and sped with a sinking heart to the centre of the wood. There I found Litl John in altercation with Hode, who was brandishing his sword, for without such a blade he would have been crushed by his rival – his strong sinews having shrivelled greatly during his fever.

The other outlaws, in a state of drunkenness as was their wont on many evenings, and e'en into the night,[369] had made a circle about these two: either shouting for calm, or cheering on the fight – so low had Hode sunk in many of their fickle estimations, that the fraudulent Pope of their heretic church had no longer full authority over them. And some of these last were wrestling or sharing blows with those loyal to Hodd, so that a melee had ensued about the cooking fire, as in a knightly tournament (or more like a tavern brawl), with the great drum being beaten by Flawnes in merriment, and another piping most poorly on a wooden flute.

Then I saw how Litel John, though unarmed, was taunting his master, for he was large and lithe and sure-footed, whereas Hod had been laden with ill-health, and was now in the harness of drunkenness, resembling a hopping, broken-winged crow with swollen eyes and straggling beard. And Ives of the cloven lip being next to me, I asked what the quarrel was about. ''Tis all your doing,' he laughed, 'for you promised John a song of his brave exploits.' 'Nay,' I replied, much dismayed; 'he asked me, and I could not disagree.' 'Without doubt,' said Ives, 'but our true master forbids this, for if John were to get a greater name than he, then the bliss promised us would not be forthcoming.'

Indeed, Robert Hode was shouting vociferously at Litel John,

[369] Nocturnal activities (beyond the emptying of latrines and so forth) were very few in the medieval period, and to be frowned upon or suspected as potentially criminal: most taverns closed at dusk.

calling him the agent raised from Hell by that Devil the Church, and no natural man of freedom and wildness, and that he was sent in order to impair the end of days and the overbreaking of the [sea of] divine essence, and clip the wings of the elect, that all the land be turned to brambles from which none will tear themselves. Meanwhile, fights were breaking out among the men increasingly here and there, as bubbles appear in heated water that is close to boiling: the clamour was very great. I saw even the sentries arrive from their posts, drawn by the noise, for it was a clear, moonlit night on which an attack was little to be feared; among these was Will Scathelock from the rocks, his melancholic face lit by eagerness to batter a few heads.

Then of a sudden Hod leapt at Litel John, who surprised by this and no doubt himself worse for drink, was slow to spring away; and receiving a seeming hurt on the thigh, he drew his own sword and would have rent Hode's flesh in turn, but others ran up behind and wrestled with the big felon to drop the sword – for these melees among the outlaws rarely involved blades, but ended in cuts and bruises only, as hawks that are mewed up too long yet tear at each other lightly.

It was at this moment that I decided to flee. The holy revelation was still flowing from chamber to chamber in my brain; and its sacred spirit affecting my animal spirit, as fresh water flowing into salt, this last passed the marrow of the ridge-bone and touched the sinews of moving, engendering a great fervency in all the parts of my nether body.

I slipped away from the battle, with only a last glance at Hodde, who had himself been disarmed by Philyp and the lame John Cardinall, while all about a veritable carnage of fists and sticks did rage, with such a violence of hands laid upon each other's gullets that it would have been amazing if none were slain, though many still laughed as if it were all in jest, yet bore bursten skin in many places, as pilgrims bear badges. Mayhap one or two shouted after me, but I kept my pace soft and slow, as if returning to my hut in weariness, yet once in the trees I crouched low and was utterly consumed in darkness as I fled.

With the harp on my back, but without my bow or any other of my meagre possessions in case a felon crossed me, I came swiftly to the rocks. Though a torch burned there for the look-out to spy any long shadows it cast upon the moor, signifying a human presence, I ran further on into the desert of heath: for I trusted the look-out had been tempted away by the fight. My own shadow dancing before me like a long-legged fiend of the woods, my courage nearly failed me, for all in front was dimness (as though belonging not to this world nor to no man), as the future is for all of us – save we make magic enquiries after the pagan fashion, and pollute our unknowing.

And behold, thus I escaped the palace of the Arch-fiend, Prince of All Error!

Swaddled in night, I made for the glassworks I had left but the year before, on that fateful day; being the last place the felons (I believed) would ever think to find me – until I was ready to travel further north, and to my long-departed home.

One way only was there to restore my life's crooked limb: and that was to go on a pilgrimage to the holiest place I knew, this being the hermit's cave. I knew not whether he was still alive, and doubted it, but natheless I had to return what was not mine before I could make full amends. Nay, it was not the same instrument, yet Henry's harp was e'en finer than the hermit's, and this appeased me – being a simple young fool at that time.

I deserved to be burned by the breath of God's nostrils, as all heretics and murtherers deserve; instead His mercy blew upon me, I know not why – except it be to communicate my story, or such of it as is sufficient to display His workings in this fallen world full of lures and pitfalls.

As I hurried as best I could over the darkling heath, startled by night cries very like a peacock's (though they were of owls or other creatures), and fearful of wolves and night demons, I saw again Hode's face in my head, as I last glimpsed it in the light of the fire: red and inflamed were his eyes, like a veritable fiend, as he struggled to fight. Yet a cunning tenderness slipped into my heart on the back of a tiny devil, and I wept for Hodde then like a lost father, feeling a sickness and dizziness of brain. *This also was the fiends' doing, ever amorous after sinners.*[370]

For inside this meagre vessel [the brain], there was raging a battle as fierce as the one under the trees: my inward devils struggling and thrashing against the inpouring of the spirit of Christ's mercy, and my spirit rankling like an infected wound doth, under the clear skin.

And at any moment I expected to be pierced by an arrow, and the point to be soaked in my blood to the very root, long after I had placed fifteen-score [yards] between my back and the hill,[371] on that awful glimmering waste.

[370] Marginalia in the familiar and rather crude sixteenth-century Hand A, invading the left-hand column. 'Amorous' is meant in the bad sense [*libidinosi*].

[371] *i.e.* 300 yards, the accepted maximum range of a longbow (though a crossbow might reach 500 yards) – as we know from records in its later heyday, matching present archery contests. I have myself witnessed such long flights in Regent's Park before the war, in the strip belonging to the Royal Toxophilite Society, in the company of my late friend Alec Hoxforth, a most talented bowman.

4

Something else Hode told me at that time, when he was ill, that much astonished me.

On informing him what such-and-such a felon was doing, and what was being said about the fire (as he had bid me be his ears and eyes for that period), he suddenly murmured a curious phrase, that yet I thought I recognised. And on asking him to repeat it, he said it again, but in the Latin version, as is its proper place, yet thrice repeating the last word like a charm, '*obriguerunt*'. And I was puzzled, for it was a line from the song of Moses, hailing the vast power of the Lord: 'Then were disturbed the princes of Edom; trembling withheld the strong men of Moab; all the dwellers of Canaan dreaded Him, or were overwhelmed.'[372]

He, confessing then that he had once been a priest – which hardly surprised me – admitted also that he had been most obedient to the Church, and eager not to sin, and more devout than any he knew; for he had wished to be a vicar of the Lord ever since he was a boy. He wore a hair-shirt in those days, to battle the better his temptations, that would come to him in swarms and prick him with desire to drink or be lecherous or swear or blaspheme; and lewd thoughts snatched him from his inner prayers, e'en in the middle of a service. Horrible faces leered and grinned as he spoke the sermon, and these devils pulled away their breeches and did such things with the Holy Word as cannot be repeated: all this went on in his thoughts, most

---

[372] Exodus 15.15: I have again adapted the translation from the Wycliffite Bible (Bod. 959) from *c.* 1382, as the least anachronistic: in using the vernacular, Hode appears to be anticipating Wycliffe and the Lollards, and their call for an English Bible, by well over a century and a half.

vividly, despite fasting, and lashing himself with whips tipped with sharp flints, and going about barefoot on the cold earth of the church[373] when snow lay upon the ground without.

Then it began to come to him, insidiously like a worm, that such weeping and gnashing of teeth was fruitless, for it did not keep off the devils: and one day when talking alone with an honourable lady of the congregation in the back of the church, he placed a hand upon her, and instead of casting him away, she relented, and took off all her costly vestments and stood naked and white as Eve. Such joy he had of this, and such an overwhelming of relief, that he lay with her secretly many times in his house, and e'en in the church behind the altar: she was clearly the devil in disguise, and his young man's gluttony could not resist her comely flesh-meat. And then did he keep, after mass, the host in his mouth, that he might pass the Body of the Lord into hers when he thus kissed her, and both enjoy further exultation.

Thus he fell into diabolical disgrace, and was cast from the body of the Church; pursued by the lady's relatives and husband-to-be, he was fortunate to escape with his life – though so soundly beaten with clubs, that his head was cracked, and scarce an inch of his body was not painted blue, and he feared his brains might flow over his face.

He fled abroad, and there fell in with certain men and women in northern Francia, who were of the same mind, that to sin is impossible, for God (though they gave Him not that name, being blasphemers, but sundry others) is in all things – and how can He Himself sin? There they roamed (as they do now, alas!), gaining many followers in their absolute denial of Hell: and indulging in drunkenness, whoring and the sins of Sodom, they thieved and blasphemed until some were seized and burned, and others hanged, and yet others recanted after torture.[374]

Hode escaped all this by his usual cunning, fleeing upon a stolen

---

[373] Most parish churches would not have been paved at this time.

[374] This could well refer either to the suppression of the scholarly Amaurians in Paris early in the thirteenth century, or the burning in Strasbourg of adepts of the Free Spirit in about 1215. This particular heresy (noted previously) was singularly active again at the time of the writing of this account, at the beginning of the next century; thus our narrative was appropriately timed as an anti-heretical tract, if nothing else.

horse. 'I was saved then,' he said, 'not by what others call God's mercy, but by a damsel of such gentle beauty and simple honesty that I did believe her to be an angel. I happened upon her fetching water at a well in a village near Boloigne,[375] and then and there, as we were talking, I vowed that all I had thought and experienced should be cast upon the dung-heap, and I was born afresh. For truly I have never loved a creature before or since, as I loved this maid. And being no more than a cowman's daughter of sixteen years, she was glad to be courted by a man of refinement, for despite my vices and crimes (as they are termed), I had kept my graceful appearance and scholarly ways.

'She bore a simple devoutness, as many such do, and I made no headway with my heretical thoughts, wooing her instead with flattery. Yet I loved her so, that this was not falsity, but truth, and of my true beliefs I said not a word. I laboured well upon the farm, so that the time came when we should be married. I was happy as a lark, agreeing to be married in the church, with a mass, for the whole family was devout – and so impressed was I by her goodness, that I e'en began to think once more that there was a God in Heaven, and such a thing as love, and that I should please Him, for He seemed willing to deliver fruits to the greatest sinners, that they should be saved.

'Alas, if sins exist (which they do not), that decision [to be married in church] was a most heinous one, and I was punished for it. Within a year she was dead, of a most horrible carbuncle in the brain, and God to me was either a savage and ungrateful torturer of the human race, or He did not exist.'

Here Hod began to weep silently, which was vexing to me – for I knew him as one who never spilt a single tear. So I asked, in a most hard-hearted manner: 'Pray, did this cowman's daughter have bluish-grey eyes, master?' And he looked up and nodded, and such a meekness did I see in his face, that tears came to my own eyes.

After this most grievous loss – for which he did squarely blame

---

[375] Boulogne.

his weakness, in being thus married in church with a full mass – he returned to England as a half-crazed penny-preacher, wishing to spread the heresy through the countryside: a most dangerous pursuit. But he soon fell into outlawry, murther and robbery. In truth, I felt less certain of him then, because it seemed to me he had become what he was through love's sickness, and not through a message of truth from the *othair*.

Thus did he recount his earlier years, saying I must turn it to song; and I confess that I felt encompassed in the warmth of his false flattery, being further intoxicated by the sorcerer's soup [of mushrooms], that once more turned the white birch bark upon the walls to mysterious hues and forms.

All this I recalled on my fleeing the camp, and vowed never to sing of him – but you, patient reader, shall see what became of that vow!

The only routes I knew were two in number: one which led to the road by many a circuitous turn, and the other to the glassworks by way of the hill of bracken, from which I had first espied the outlaws' wood. Thinking how I might be pursued by the felons on the first, and they swifter than me on their mounts, I made for the bracken hill, stumbling oft into holes and ditches, or torn by gorse and brambles under a thick-starred sky. Soon, as the easterly welkin paled to dawn, I arrived upon the hill very weary, and there I slept upon the green fern – for though Riched had cut most of the brown leaves for the ovens, new growth had flourished the more, and it was very like a shallow sea, reaching over my knees when I entered there.

I had a great wish to find a familiar face from my former life, but could not ever return to St Edmund's, and prayed fervently that Ricchet would be present at the works: howsoever brief had been our acquaintance, I had clothed him in the raiments of a gallant elder brother, and such brotherly . . . [*sentence unfinished*].

I awoke, and seeing it was well after dawn and very fine, with a lark trilling so high above in the sky, that it must nigh have been touching the waters of the upper sea, I climbed cautiously to the very crest of the field of bracken: from whence I could descry, on the rolling horizon, the pale blue hill, more than a league distant, capped by the outlaws' thick-boughed lair, from which smoke rose: and though 'twas the very contrary to the hill of Moses, yet I felt an inward dread![376]

It being a clear day, methought suddenly I espied a flashing from the wood, that chilled my joy and made me crouch deeper in the fern. Though I had learned the secret of that glass-flashing (for it was indeed simple, like a huckster's code at dicing, or as prisoners tap through walls),[377] I knew not whither it was sent, nor from what secret places it was answered: never had I considered that one of those places was this very field!

I felt horror pinch me all over, for it was flashing *S E K*[378] many times; which meaning 'to seek', was always flashed upon the half-hour on suitable days, that the signaller without might know there was a message. Yet there was no one else on that hill, lest they be crouched in the shallow fern.

Mayhap the felons knew I was here, and sought to terrify me – Hode watching where I hid, in a way that lay beyond all human sense! 'Ey,' I moaned to myself, 'what if that lark has been rapt by him into being his eye, or he hath become the lark itself in high contemplation?' – as Hodde was indeed (to the credulous part of my youthfulness) the vast soul of all things, absorbed into the divine essence of Creation; that to believers is named the Godhead?

Again I expected a barbed point to pain me at any moment, as I waded through the bright-green ferns, in the direction of the glass-works. Yet there was no movement around me but the searching bees, butterflies, mice, and other creatures of the Lord's Creation that in summer, as we know, doth laugh in the merry sunshine.

[376] 'Forsothe al the puple herde voices, and siy . . . the hil smokynge; and thei weren afeerd, and shakun with inward drede . . .' (Wycliffite Bible, Exodus, 20.18).

[377] A well-known 'telegraphic' method based on the ancient Greek system of a five-by-five grid: 1-1 indicating A, 1-2 for B, 2-3 for M, 5-5 for Z, and so forth, with I and J combined. Our signallers used the same system on the Front, by means of the heliograph (an apparatus using mirrors and the sun), or the powerful Lucas lamp, particularly effective from pill-boxes in the Ypres area; or the exclamation mark of Very lights and rockets in emergencies.

[378] Abbreviated from the Middle English word, 'seken' or 'sechen'.

Rare are those places without the common people, so crowded is Yngelond,[379] yet lonely were those low hills to me, and most barren of fruit or corn. Of all the four-footed creatures therein, I saw only a roe deer fawn at the edge of a thicket, quite immobile, and some fleeing rabbits and a hare bounding before me. Reaching the sunken track we had taken from the works but a year before, and being now a mile from that fiery place, I was overjoyed to see a human figure advance upon me; and e'en more joyful was I to see that it was Richerd!

In my unhappy year as an outlaw and felon, I had seen him always as that angelic vision upon the ladder, his face effulgent in the sunlight from the unglassed lancets, far above the heaviness and stink of the fallen world. Yet he himself seemed discomfited to see me, though I embraced him as a lost brother. Much out of breath from hurrying, he had to be thrice reassured that I was not returned from the dead, but escaped from the heretic outlaw, Robert Hodd, and was indeed making for the glassworks.

'Hast thou escaped from those wolfheads,' he cried, 'and fearest not they will pursue thee?' 'Nay,' I answered, 'yet a little fear did I feel just now, for I saw them signalling after their fashion, with glass and sunlight, as others use fire or trumpets.'

At this, Richet looked past me, from whence I had come, as though the flashing was there upon the track; and as my eyes dwelt upon him, I wondered why he seemed so disturbed, moving his mouth as though chewing food. Mayhap it was because I had grown sudden taller, as boys do at fifteen or sixteen, and had sprouted soft hairs upon my upper lip, my voice discordant and uncertain. 'I pray thee,' he said, gripping my shoulders of a sudden, 'go not to the glassworks, but further on, further on; and talk to no one until you are ten leagues distant! Tarry not at Pont[e]fract, for Hode has many an informer there, nor even in Yorke, but after that you may be safe.'

I nodded, much amazed at his knowledge, and said I knew that in Yorke (and other cities and towns) there were merchants and traders

[379] A common complaint from the thirteenth century on: the population stabilised at 6 million in 1300, remaining thus (with a dip after the 1349 Black Death) until the Industrial Age, when it rose sharply once more.

doing business with Hode, to their own profit, and important officials who were in league with him – for several of the outlaws were from the noblest families, guilty of crimes none could hide or forgive them for, and thus they had fled to the woods.

And then he clapped me upon the shoulders and laughed: 'Weylaway, did he make a true felon of thee?' I told him that I had sinned in the most horrible ways, and felt tears starting in my eyes – and a shuddering gripped me.

Then Richet said: 'There is naught in the world that is sinning, but for one thing: to call any action sinful.' And I saw only gravity and no jesting upon his handsome face.

As a cliff might crash into the sea under the waves' repeated blows, I then understood what he was: I gaped, but my tongue clove to my mouth, and I might have swooned but that Ricchet held my arms.

'Nay, little brother,' he said, 'do not forgive me, for as there is no evil but the false name of the priests' God, like a chain about our spirits, so there is no need for forgiveness. What I did, in sending you into the lion's den, was a righteous act, because I felt it in my heart, and our hearts are made by the divine essence. Our master wished to have a brother in the glassworks, for the trees must not be cut [for glass], that greenwood being his temple.' Then reaching into his pouch, he pulled out a portion of glass, smoothed at the edges and very clear, and of fantastic lustre in the sunlight. 'I will tell them you are nowhere northward, but how report doth tell of a nut-brown swain, with a harp upon his back, on the southward road to Nottynggam. This also I feel in my heart, and thus it is good.'

He embraced me then, and I relented, though I was angry indeed within, and bewildered. For no doubt on that very day we had cut bracken, he had signalled to them from the crest that I was coming that night; and thus I was so swiftly and mysteriously spotted and taken. 'I will call thee *Trich Richerd*,'[380] I said, 'for you are the best of dissemblers.' In my heart, however, was more sorrow than I could

---

[380] As in MS: this spelling of 'Trick' reminds us of Chaucer's 'tricherous' ('treacherous') and 'trechour' ('traitor').

express, for mayhap without his encouragement I would not have sought my harp, but stayed on in the holy house – and remained undefiled by heresy.

We parted swiftly, and I knew we would never meet again. Then the whole world did seem as issuing from Hod's bowels – every person in it, and every tree, and every grass-blade and every creature, down to the littlest [*de minimis*], for he seemed the author of all. Yet I hurried forth into it, passing the glassworks at a distance yet close enough to smell the smoke of that foul and burning oven, that yields such perfection of coloured light.

Entering upon a deep road going north, I skirted Berny[s]dale and Pon[te]fract by a westerly ford [of the river], for it was the dry month – though the false hermit there demanded alms for the favour of praying for my safe passage across, when he was but a sluggard and shirker with a long beard. For I was seeking a true hermit, whom I last left six or more years earlier, in the foulest and most treacherous manner possible, betraying his infinite trust and love.

Dear reader, who hath been faithful to my words for so long, that no doubt your eyes ache by the light of a candle or the glare of a window, as my hand and every feeble part doth (for so taxing be this writing business, when it be in your own hand, as none can believe who have never studied) – do not inflict bodily harm upon this manuscript, in disgust with the author. For I am not now as I was then, flitting from branch to branch, ever uncertain; or as that wild and vagabond musician, the grasshopper, that doth always leap and fritter, and sings from morn till night. I have remained within this holy house for near eighty years, scarce leaving it for a single night; for by the door that, with Adam, we were cast out of, so by the second Adam[381] we might enter into Paradise, that we once knew and have ever a distant remembrance of – though this Eden be e'en sweeter than the earthly garden, for it hath the name of Heaven enscrolled above its narrow wicket gate.

Thus I fled northwards, while unknown to me the archangels

---

[381] i.e. Christ.

towered above as over an ant, ready on an instant to crush me with their thumbs, for I was too small for their burning swords. Although I deserved no more, God the Ever-Merciful stayed their hand, and Christ and His Sacred Mother, the Steadfast Virgin, were privy to His conspiracy, for they in Heaven's clearness and brightness of light, made dazzling by the high walls of crystal that surround that sacred realm, smiled down upon me in pity rather than ire.

The common folk (as much as the nobler), much loving of music and e'en making it with their own disaccording voices in taverns and so forth,[382] bid me sing and play at each stage whereat I paused from pressing forward upon the way, thinking me only a minstrel of youthful years. Earning my food and humble shelter by this means, how could I refuse? For otherwise I had not a penny on me, and this music was my spending-silver.

Alas, the English delighting not only in song but in drink, and oft draining full goblets, whether of wine or ale, in a single draught – and bidding you do likewise in those unrulier times, I witnessed scenes of great debauchery in tavern and inn and also in great halls. Thus is the life of a minstrel speedful to sin, and all manner of pollutions, however pure and honourable his singing matter; and may open the door to the enemy of mankind as much as doth the buffoonery of a play.

Yet here is the strangest thing, that was like an enchantment: whene'er my fingers began to pluck the fox-gut of that fine harp, its fox's wiles entered by the tips, and travelling through my arteries to the ventricles and chambers of my brain, then down again to my mouth, it made me sing of the betrayal and capture of Robert Hodde, and his release from that foul dungeon through our pluck and wiles; so that each time I was forced to make my confession openly – though no one knew it who gaped upon me, listening to my chant.

[382] A happily unbroken tradition in most of our rural public houses, which still boast their local songsters – often declaiming ancient ballads of inordinate length while being politely, if not reverently, listened to for the umpteenth time by the assembled drinkers: and long may this continue, for it is an essential link with the dim and unchronicled past of the English commoner.

And the shower of pennies cast at my feet, and the roaring and clapping of tables and benches after, did show the power of God's ways: for although I thought then it was the Devil's spell, so cruelly strangling my infant salvation, it was in truth the Lord's way of merciful punishment, that I should confess (and not deny or secrete) my great and mortal sin. For was it not Henrie's harp I played, and his own wretched spirit that each time hovered over me – weeping with its ghostly fingers in prayer-weft, dropping hot blood from its hideously gaping neck upon my hands (a thing that only I could see) when I sang the verse of his slaying: thereby scorching upon them greasy marks that turned in years to come to these dark blots [*maculas*] upon the withered back of each hand lying before me now?

Again and again they bid me sing the rhyme, never tiring of its tale – and not suspecting that Moche the minstrel was there before them in the flesh, murtherer and thief that he was. When I turned to other songs, such as *Ey! ey! What the night is long! And ich, with well mochel wrong, sorwe and mone and caste,*[383] and so forth, they did laugh to see me so distressed, my eyes red with tears – as though I uttered what was true. And so wearied was I by this playing, that I would oft swoon after: which instead of making them desist, enticed them to urge me, with water upon my face, to recover and play more songs – e'en the very same!

So my progress to the coast was hampered, and weeks fled by; for by this means I earned, not only bread and sustenance, but sufficient pennies to turn into shillings and ensure my keep for further weeks or months, such is the attraction of lucre. And in this, I was but as most men are; for things have grown worse since: who careth for aught now but to fill his bags, and heap up false treasures, e'en as the

---

[383] As in MS. This is a remarkably close variation on the final lines of 'Mirie it is, while sumer ilast' (Bodleian MS, Rawlinson G. 22(14755), f. 11b), preserved by accident on a parchment used in the binding for another work. '*Alas! How long is the night, and I, by very great wrong, sorrow and moan and vomit* [or possibly '*conjecture*'].' The last word, torn away in the flyleaf parchment, has usually been guessed at as 'fast'; this extract suggests another possibility, rather more secular in tone: and also that the verses continue. It seems the song is already a familiar one at this date (1226).

innocent die of hunger and poor folk go a-begging? Yet always (though I had already reached many leagues north) was I fearful of seeing one of the outlaws among the folk in the taverns or markets where I played. And e'en when a minx, daughter of an alehouse-keeper – and of exceeding comeliness – stroked my face with her long fingers and lasciviously confessed to loving me, I grew afraid, thinking it a trap to lure me to my doom, and wrestled free.

Imagine my horror, then, when but five weeks or so after I fled the wood, travelling north of Yorke and scarce two easy days from the hermit's cave, I passed an inn at the dinner-hour, with a long table set before it for the cooler air, crowded with traders and so forth (chattering like jackdaws about a great fleshpot), and heard of a sudden my own rhyme being declaimed in a mangled fashion, to the horrible accompaniment of a fiddle betwixt the verses, and foolish gestures – turning even that table quiet!

Seeing servants fetching more meats from the kitchen, I enquired after them of the hired minstrel, and they said, 'What? Wouldst thou play instead of master Alan de Auleige?' And even these rascals seemed to suffer from incontinence, for they laughed in a ghastful manner. Never having heard of master Alan de Aulleige, I feigned indifference, and would have waited nearby until the end of the meal; but the fat and irascible inn-keeper coming out of the door, kicked me off as a vagabond, calling me a dog waiting for scraps – to which I vociferated that master Alan de Auleige had stolen my song, and I would have redress.

Then master Allan de Auleig hearing this amazing insult, and on the instant recognising me, generously bid the inn-keeper to leave off breaking my ribs; thereupon telling the assembled that I was a minstrel sent from Heaven, and that it was from none other than this green-looking youth that he had learned the ballad of the outlaw Robbert Hod! He was dressed in a threadbare parti-coloured coat with a red belt buckled by lustrous brass, and had long grey hair about a digni-fied face, marred only in the middle by a nose somewhat red-veined and pocked: his graceful appearance went ill with the manner of his playing. The people demanding I play myself, I did so, and so great was the delight after the aghast silence, that I was carried about on their shoulders, and must sing it ten more times, with Alan de Auleigge playing alongside, until e'en my hardened finger-tips bled.

Later that evening he told me, having partaken of many a full goblet of wine, that he formerly played to the king and to the nobles of the kingdom, but that scandal had cast him forth from such wealth and elegance, to this pitiful state, wherein he was to be found, stirring vulgar laughter with lewdness, for that was what men and women preferred. 'No more can I return to my former position,' he confessed, 'than tares and thistles and weeds might grow back again to corn. Yet beware, good minstrel youth, for corn can swiftly decline to tares and thistles and weeds, yet not the other way round.'

I told him (well intoxicated myself) that I was a thistle of the sorriest sort; but he denied this fiercely, weeping and clasping me on the table-bench, and saying that on the contrary I was a golden sheaf of corn, a reminder of what he had once been: a celestial musician, a veritable darling [*deliciae*] of the highest in the land.

Not sobered after this encounter, but prideful the more, I thought to end my course towards the hermitage, thinking again of the golden pastures of the royal court, and its worthy ladies furred with ermine, red-lipped, combing my ripe ears [*spicas*][384] with their tender fingers.

Happily the talk in the morning was of a robbery on the road I had earlier taken, and fresh blood upon the wayside, that made me fearful of turning south to perchance fall into Hode's clutches. Watching the hounds quarrel over the platters[385] dropped from yesterday's groaning table, I saw how such delights are fleeting, and love of them but feigning devotions.

Bidding goodbye to master Alan de Aulege in his bed, where he was confined with a grievous discomfiture of the stomach (for the wine was more crabapple juice than Rhenish), I continued northwards, each step bringing me closer to my salvation. And so eager was I for this, that I went barefoot like a pilgrim, cutting my feet on the sharp

[384] i.e. of corn, continuing the traditional metaphor in an original way.
[385] Food at this period was still eaten off platters of bread rather than plates, the meal taken with fingers from a shared bowl – 'to common' was to share one's food with others and ayenward. The crust of bread was generally left for the animals.

flint-stones: which was no hurt at all compared to the hurt of the truly zealous, for I have seen (with mine own eyes) crippled children crawling on their ribs through the dust for many a mile, to be cured by the holy relic of this or that saint! And there are lepers pained with grievous sores, snorting rather than speaking, who labour up flinty hillsides in the foullest garments and with a ravening hunger, to reach certain chapels and saintly sites, in fitting penance for their parents' sins.

A few miles from the village wherein God and Fortune[386] decreed I should be born and reared to the age of nine or ten (at which whelpish age I tore myself away like a limb from its body), I first saw familiar sights in the land roundabouts, and felt afraid. I had fled as a thief and made myself outcast; the common folk would know me, and raise the hue and cry, and I would hang, or suffer torment in the stocks or the dungeon.

Though time doth not linger, six winters is not sufficient for memory to pass away like a shadow. I should have gone disguised, I thought; yet then I reflected that my disguise was the mask of years, for I had so much changed from boyhood, that e'en neighbours would not recognise me.

Still, I was fearful to pass by way of the village, and so I took a more difficult path by a thick wood, untended since the time of King Stephne, that lay to the west of the cliffs; I heard the far sough of the sea within its tangled boughs, yet could not draw nearer the coast easily, for there was scarce a path through the briars and greve of fallen branches – being a wood that in former days the common folk had always avoided, as it held within it pits of immemorial antiquity, called *wolfpittes*.

Glad I am, that I had not more courage to avoid it, though it was darker still on a day burdened by grey clouds! For soon I came to a small clearing, wherein was the aforesaid pit, that was in truth a great trench softened by time. And part of it being covered over with branches, grass and suchlike, to form a thatch much as a bird

---

[386] The two have a complex and awkward relationship in the medieval mind.

weaves its nest, I thought it an animal trap. Lo, to my amazement and great fright, out of it crept a man of most filthy appearance, in naught but nakedness, though at first I thought he wore a green kirtle of silk: for every part of his naked skin was of that hue, tinted e'en to the finger-tips.[387]

I would have fled, but that no green men are said to be dangerous – only red ones (sent in this fiery hue by the Devil), of a deeper red than heavenly cherubim, and hideous: the former are born in a Christian land where no sun riseth but only twilight, because this land is in the contrarious part of the world to our known, and separated from it by a great stream, yet taketh what is left of our light. And it happens that from this land under the earth, that the more learned name Antipodas, a man or woman may sometimes fall into our own world by passages in their fields, much like rabbit-holes. And bells ring there continually, as Petrus Comestor describes in his history of the world.[388]

Therefore I did not flee, but only took out the knife from my belt. The green man stood there trembling a little, and snuffling [*vocum naribus protulit*] like a pig, as certain idiots and simpletons do who are thus called 'swine's heads' by those lacking Christian compassion. He had a smooth skin unblemished by hair, like a woman's, yet so dark and filthy was he about the mouth, that leaves and branches did seem to be spewing forth from the lips, as in [the carvings of] our churches; this filth being the juice from summer berries – as such wild fruits, with nuts and certain leaves, are all that the green people

[387] For similar sightings of green folk, see, for example, Giraldus Cambrensis, *Itin. Cambriae*, or William of Newburgh's twelfth-century chronicle.

[388] I have nowhere found any mention of antipodean bells in Comestor's book, *La Mer des Histoires* – a favourite of the Middle Ages. This whole passage is muddled, in comparison with the account of the green man himself, which will put some readers in mind of Poor Tom in *King Lear*, and yet others of young men known to them as having always borne a decent intelligence or wit (and even scholarship), who have lately returned mentally broken from the war, and are now hidden away where their spasticity, tremblings and meaningless prattle cannot disturb our 'hundred years of peace' wrought by those same worthy and pacific politicians recently so heralded for their bellicosity and belligerence. [**Marginal emphasis by FB against last three lines, with 'All is hogswash!' scrawled in pencil.**]

consume. The hair on his head was not green, but brown, and fell to his shoulders in a matted foulness. He was no bigger than myself, yet of broad shoulders and sturdy limbs, and seemed afraid of me, putting his hand to his face as though I were stinking.

I took a step forward, eager to converse with such a being, and ask him questions of the Antipodas: for my long sojourn in the outlaw's lair had made me bold with such phenomena, as many were the times I would perceive bearded faces and suchlike in the underwood. He opened his mouth, that was twinkling with juices, and gave forth such a howl of distress that I retreated; thereupon he shivered and trembled, clutching himself, and swept up the moist leaves and moss of the floor and rubbed his smooth body with them, leaving it greener. This no doubt being his way of protection (whether efficacious or no), he grinned and seemed defiant.

Thereupon he crouched down and performed his offices in front of me, as oft do half-crazy vagabonds or men taken by the delectation of over mickle drinking, who lose the stableness of virtuous shame e'en in the churchyard.[389] Not cleansing himself of his defilement, but standing and laughing at me in my puzzlement, he looked about him the while with a darting movement of the head, and I saw it was to profit of the merry sweetness of the birds, that were many in that wild wood. Truly he was a Christian example of innocence, so unblemished that e'en the horrible necessities of our earthly existence troubled him not with shame. And so pure was he, that the flies coming to his dung were few in number, and small and slender in shape: for so also were his *tordes*[390] formed, more like a badger's than a man's.

Of a sudden he approached me and stood close by me, not touching but only making noises to himself, in a manner of grunting, and seeing his mouth a-drivel, I wondered if he was famished. I felt not afraid, but more wondering in this wise, that such a being could stand

---

[389] I might say that at least in my rustic English village, which has as yet no mains drainage, piped water or gas, or electrical and telephone lines, this countryman's practice is still widespread; the less charitable claim that you can smell our settlement from two valleys away, as no doubt you could have done seven centuries ago.
[390] Pieces of dung.

close to a stranger, his superior, and not cast glances upon him, but only upon the ground thereabouts. Now and again he chuckled, as if to a merry jest, and sighed sweetly with satisfaction. Though the air was not hot, he seemed to feel no cold in his nakedness. Some will claim he was mad or a simpleton, as many men and women are, both in vagabondage and in beggary; but I say to them that he was of a most perfect sweetness of innocence, as of the first Adam, while the wood-dweller Hode was full of the most grievous errors, as of Adam's son Cain, and e'en much worse.

Putting my hand out to touch him, I erred in my impatience, that was a thing of the fallen world: he darted away, and vanished into the trees, leaping over briars almost like a deer. I tarried awhile, filled with a virtuous humility that came not from me, but from the green man; then (eager to press on), I advanced to the edge of the wood, that I reached in another hour, feeling most pilgrim-like with my chafed feet and empty stomach. For to my mind the green folk are better Christians than we be, and to meet them is to be blessed.

And there before me, yet still a mile away over bleakness, was the majesty of the one Ocean, striking the foot of our kingdom not three or four miles southward of the hermit's dwelling. The day being grey and misty, though not cold (for it was still summertime), I felt the air grieving for all that I had lost, and it was with heavy heart that I scrambled down the rocks onto the beach, to turn my face towards the north and trudge slowly nearer along the wet marge; not expecting to see my first and most holiest master alive, but only his grave, yet I did seek to find words of grace and greeting and contrition.

My heart was in no great ease, with the harp heavier and heavier on my back, its gut making a ringing sound within the leather – as though hating that I must make an offering of it, to be moistered away by the loud sea air till it crumble to naught, and with it my appalling mortal sin.

5

s I hove closer, my heart laboured, and my lungs were thick like that of a swine's. I prayed aloud, shedding my heresy as easily as it was donned – for that is the way of youth. It is ever pliant and fickle. When the sweep of familiar cliff came into view, it was as if I had never been there but in a dream. All seemed smaller, for I was truly half the size when I had left. Here a rock that was a vast boulder bigger than a whale in memory, was now shrunk to a barrel; there a hole in the cliff that had been greater than a dragon's maw, was like the opening of a cellar – for e'en the opening of a cellar had been huger to me, at nine or ten. I saw from afar the black shape of the hermitage that was really a cavernous hole in the rock, but at that distance was as a small blot of coal-tar, and I stopped in nervousness.

All the while the sea made piteous lamentations beside me, though it was not rough, for the buffeting wind had not e'en the power to shatter the grey vapours of the mist that shielded the far edge of the illimitable Ocean (where its waters drop many fathoms before rising upward in a curve to make the upper sky). Yet I took my courage in my hands and revived it, as it were, by speaking unto it soft words. I remembered what my very first and holiest master said was the best thing and the worst among men. He asked me this one day, and I could not say, for sin is never good, and neither is fasting ever bad except for the evil breath it causeth, and so I could not answer; and he laughed and said, 'Word is best and worst.'

Now I knew that in giving me word – that is, the skill and learning to form letters into words, and thereby discover all the true knowledge that lies in books, even unto names and measurements and things mysterious – he had given me both best and worst. For it planted ambition in me, and a taste for the world beyond our humble place, that envenoms the innocent soul, and makes it forget its true and righteous home. Yet word is also an indubitable miracle, given by God to Adam that he might name the creatures – though that only in his mouth, for Adam could not write but only speak words (which is also a danger, for a man can lie and blaspheme with his tongue alone).

With these thoughts seething in my brain, I advanced towards the cave, more than ever determined to lay the harp as an offering upon the altar of this holy place (imagining the grave itself to be there), and to pray and fast for such time as I felt my sins washed sufficiently from me. Afterwards, I planned to set out for the abbey [at Whitby], before I was too weak with hunger, and offer myself as a brother: thus had I conceived my future over the last weeks, amidst the brawl and din of lowly places.

Astonied was I, therefore, to find no trace of holy cross or round altar stones, nor even the planks we used as our table and bench, nor the ash of the fire at the cave's mouth, but only stinking sea-wrack and many rocks tumbled before it, as if no man had ever trod in that place. It seemed that a great storm or e'en a whale had vomited the rocks against the cave, that it was well nigh stopped up.

Some of these rocks being three feet high, the cave-mouth was well nigh blocked,[391] [and] I had to climb these rocks, and press myself through the narrow mouth, pushing my harp before me. Scrambling over them to enter the blackness of the cave by its narrow mouth [*hiatus in the MS*] . . . wherein I stood, blinking and peering, for there was little light in the hermitage on that gloomy day.

All was moist and dank within, and the wind made a moaning sound as it doth in a shell, though the air seemed not to move. My unshod feet, cut by the journey and pained in their wounds by the saltiness from the beach, felt a strange vegetation, here cool and slippery

---

[391] The copyist appears to have slipped and repeated a line, and again with 'narrow mouth'.

and there encrusted – yet the pain was gladsome to me. I had no taper, and there being but stale and foul air, the dimness of forms perceived could not stretch their lines to me easily through the thickness, and I was almost as if blind.

Hard it was to imagine those former scenes of learning and labouring at words, and all that passed between us – including moments of merriment – in that dark and dank chamber, wherein formerly all was wisdom and virtue visible, lit by a holy grace! Then my eyen received more lines, and the blackness thinned to greyness, as it doth in such places; and I perceived at my bare feet a hunk of crust that was like manna from heaven, for I was exceeding hungry. And picking up the bread, I was amazed to find it soft, as though placed there that morning or mayhap the day before. Taking a bite, I saw it was as sustaining as the Host; for verily I had not eaten in two days, since the inn wherein Alan de [A]uleige had called me a miracle.

Looking about me then, I saw many more morsels of bread, most rotting quite away and others hard as wood, and e'en a few cooked fish entire. I came to realise that the food was many inches deep, like rushes that are never replaced, but only renewed, and that the floor of the cave was hid quite by this mixen. Naturally, there was a rustling within it of rats or crabs or other vermin. So horribly famished was I, that I seized another hunk of bread, its staleness made supple by the moistness, and chewed it there and then.[392]

Of a sudden, hearing voices over the wind and sea-surge outside, as if approaching over the beach, I crouched down that the scarce light not pick me out. And looking up at the cave's opening, that was shaped like a shear in cloth, I saw two faces, belonging to a couple of most ugly and boil-marked appearance, set brightly there in comparison with my darkness. 'Lo, master,' the man and woman called, in the vulgarest of tongues, 'in the presence of thee we recall our sins and give thee thy daily bread, that we might go to rest and joy for evermore, amen.'

---

[392] A recent theory assigns the medieval tendency for vivid, waking visions to an intoxicating substance found in bread left too long in damp conditions.

With these ridiculous words, said with little feeling but in a serf's uncouth coarseness, the faces disappeared – yet not before something was thrown in, that was another hunk of bread to add to the hundreds staled or rotted underfoot. Imagine then my horror, when in the single shaft of dim light that penetrated that abode, a claw did seem to stretch out into it, and grope about beside my foot, until it seized my ankle so fiercely that I could not release it!

I was so struck by terror that I could not move, perceiving only the claw of a monster or a fiend, human-like but with nails as long as the bony fingers and twisted about in their length most horribly, and belonging to a pale shape I could not discern but imagined too foul for human eyes. Pulling my leg away, I brought the claw with me, and also its owner; for the shape was dragged thus to the foot of the rocks, gripping me with an unhuman strength as I tried to climb.

It was indeed not a fiend or monster, but a poor man ready to expire, quite naked but for a stinking rag about his loins, and more bone than flesh, as one sees oft among beggars or lepers or at the gates of towns: those near-corpses scarcely decent in their rags, whose mouths are unflinching portals for flies and other worms, and that none know what to do with until they are truly dead.

So bony was he, that his hips stuck out like plough-shares, and even in that dimness I might have counted every rib, for his stomach was a hollow and his skin mere beaten leather stretched upon the frame: yet it was not a leper's, for in leprosy the hide be all over wet and fatty. I perceived a strangeness about his feet, and peering closer, I saw that his ankles and feet were swollen out of all measure, as though they belonged to an ogre, and had a shiningness.

As for his face, as it stared upon me, it was more eyen than nose or mouth, for his vital spirits in withdrawing had remained in each eye as tides are left in pools where depressions in the rock or sand permit it; and so it was with him.

'Master,' I said, for I knew immediately it was the hermit. He was as hairless as formerly, though not from shaving but from the sparseness and bleachness of the long hairs remaining about his mouth and over his ears, so that it seemed he had none at all, like certain old men.

I bent down to touch him, for my revulsion had gone, and had been replaced by a great love and sorrow; and thus I wept upon his form, that was cold like a corpse's, its wasted brawn tettered all over with sores and encrustations that were not the botches and whelks of leprosy – though e'en then I would have embraced him, as St Hugh of Lincoln kissed many a leper for the good of his own spirit![393]

Spilling my salt tears upon his shrunken body caused no pain to him, for he was already salted like a herring. I marvelled that he had come to such a state, and that death had not taken him, for when I lifted him back upon the bare ship-boards that served as his pallet, he was light as thistledown. 'Master,' I quoth many times, 'I have returned to care for thee – I, your first pupil!' And to my amazement, his ravelled lips moved among their sores, and he whispered, 'Edwyne,' with a clutching of my neck.

'Nay,' I answered, saying my name, with a great soreness in my heart: not conceiving how he might not recognise me, bleared as he was with dying in the dim light of the hermitage. And on that instant of saying my true name, I felt my neck released, and he turned his face to the wall of rock at his side.

What more should I have sought, or expected? As a hound who bites a child, and is called back by his master, does not trot to him gaily but slinks thereto, knowing he doth deserve rebuke, so should I have done: yet I expected forgiveness and redemption, for I was stupider than a hound.

I carried the harp to his side, and said, 'Lo, my spiritual master, I have brought back what I stole from thee in my pitiable ignorance;' though this was an untruth, for the harp was Henrie's. And removing it from its leather [case], I tuned the instrument and began to play, with a softness that the cave rendered louder, for its roof was high as naves be high for the better rendering of voice to the Lord Our God. The hermit's face turned back towards me, and his large eyen grew rounder, drawing in all the lines of light possible: and he said something,

---

[393] The actual infectiousness of leprosy was exaggerated by the medieval mind, in contrast to its lax or ignorant attitude to far more virulent maladies. The remarkable St Hugh of Lincoln was canonised mainly as a result of freely kissing leper victims.

but very hoarsely, and his throat-ball moved up and down as big as an apple.

I stopped plucking, and bent to hear him: his breath being foul, as with many who fast, and none of those bread-givers having entered in to wash the filth that defiled his bed as it defiles an unnursed infant's bed, there was a great fumosity of stench: yet I felt in the presence of sweetness, as though walking in an orchard where a multitude of apples putrefy upon the grass. 'Pray, give me water,' was all I heard. And perceiving a bowl of wood upon a rocky shelf, I held it beneath a meagre trickle [of water] that bled at the back of the cave, as it always had done e'en in the driest month, and brought it to his mouth. How eagerly did he drink! I wondered then why no one was with him as a nurse, who might want succour to their soul, and earn blessings thereby; and an answer swiftly came, and other answers too.

He drank his fill, and laid his head back, seeming comforted as he gazed upon my face – for that is the greatest medicine of music. I told him that I had returned, not for his forgiveness – for I had not expected him to be still in this miserable world – but that I might begin to make amends, by returning what I had thieved, e'en though it was too late; then to hasten me to the holy house at Whitby, to deny all pleasures of the flesh within a stony cell, and pray steadfastedly for my one true spiritual master's soul, that the Devil had lured me from into the worst vice and crime imaginable – e'en to believing that Jesus was not the Son of God! 'For how could He be, when there was no God, to the vicious heretics I fell among? Instead, I find thee still living, and all I wish is to comfort thee, and to keep vigil by thee, master, and to keep you tenderly, until such time as God wills to welcome you into His bosom.'

Then after a long silence, in which the hermit seemed to sleep, he oped his ravelled eyelids again and spoke so soft as he held my hand in his, that his words were near drowned by the sea-surge without, rock-dimmed though it was. 'You call me spiritual master, that am near spirit, and wish to be pure spirit: yet I cannot shake off this filthy body, for the Lord keeps me in this state of pain and suffering, that I might purge myself of my great wrong.' One by one these words were squeezed from his lips like pebbles, and I was astonied to hear of this great wrong, for he was a true ascetic and the holiest I have ever known.

Indeed, I wished him to speak of mine own wrong, not any of his, if the truth be told: for so little advanced was I in humility, that I was as a prince that plays at being a beggar. My wretched and shameless deeds, starting with the theft of the harp, and the ungrateful abandoning of this holy man,[394] elbowed each other to be first at the door of my thoughts.

Then a face appeared again at the opening, of a woman honest and comely-looking; and with similar words babbled, more bread was thrown, with a piece of fish that smelt stale. No answer made the hermit, but merely a sighing, and the woman's face disappeared. I said how foolish the common folk were, to cast food like coins into a pond, and not take proper care of him: but he waved his hand, dismissing my derision. 'I will not have them nearer,' he declared, in so small a voice that I must crouch to hear: 'not even monks or priests, for all is decayed and nothing pure and whole. It was writ in Heaven that my pupil must return. Now I might depart in peace, for you must be my confessor, Edwyn.'

A flame of jealousy fretted through all my veins then, and I stood, ready to depart. All his mind was on my rival, and it seemed he had quite forgot me – this idea worse than if he had berated me and cursed me! Thus our chief humour haunts us always, by use and long custom made to be our companion – as some like ale, and others wine, and so forth. I said to him: 'I am not Edwyn,' and once more said my true name. 'Thou art Edwine,' he replied, 'for I had no other pupil, and thou must confess me.'

Then I saw that he had confounded, in his delirium, Edwine and myself, as we might be two almonds [crushed] in a caudle of milk: for the chamber of his memory was no doubt shrunk or infected. I was wretchedly pricked to the heart as with a barbed point, and wept

[394] The original motive of his misdeed was in fact the drowning incident. [**Scrawled in FB's hand halfway down the right-hand margin against the main body of the proofs' text: 'end of the bloody Fatigue – back to the bloody line hey ho'.**]

silently beside him, hiding my face. Ne'er was there more miserable creature in the world! He groaned and held a hand to his chest, as there were sore beatings there, and I was affrighted, thinking him to be breathing his last.

He fixed his eyes upon me, as the dying do, very roundly: and this brought me to a confusion; for the force of that look had entered my eyes and already put the demons within me to strong flight, some creeping into my nether parts as toads creep away from the light into dim and moist corners. Feeling pain from these fiends' tiny bristles and claws, I knelt at his side, and held his hand, struggling with my grief and sorrow. He whispered to me: 'What say ye, Edwynne?' And I replied that as one who had committed a great and mortal sin, and had not yet done penance withal, how could I confess him, in my iniquity?

'As best thou mayest,' he said. So comforted was I by this, that the pain of the demons' horns in my toes and fingers ebbed, as if milk and honey had entered there, and I nodded and said, 'So be it, master. I shall confess thee, though I am no priest, but a miserable wretch who hath neglected virtue, denied God, believed that the soul hath no existence proper to itself, conjectured that both Hell and Heaven are cozening inventions, and likewise all that is writ in the divine Scriptures, and also sinfulness itself.'

'Then art thou worthy to hear me,' he said; 'for what priest is not full of crimes?' And true it is, that too many priests are unworthy, for some are unlettered, or haunt taverns and are drunken, or wear jackets instead of cassocks; and most hasten through the offices as if they mean naught.

So he confessed, and I must set it down here, that you may see how merciful are the ways of God, that even the greatest sinner may return to Him after sufficient penance, as it was revealed through Christ Jesus for all time.

He said to me, ever hoarsely and painfully: 'You know already that at the age of eighteen I went to Oxenforde and studied law, and lived with three other clerks near the river, in a noisome alleyway, and how my heart was stirred by a certain young woman, married to a goldsmith of mature years. And how, goaded by lust, I came to her in the guise of an intimate lady friend, dressed in a lady's gown, to allay suspicion. I had pressed her red mouth as a man and now as a woman, and the pleasure of her flesh was mine. Many the song I sang to her with my harp, of birds and garlands and flushed cheeks the colour of plucked roses, and suchlike foolery.

'Alas, one day after enticing me thus with her comeliness, she held up my woman's dress and laughed at my nakedness, saying I was no more to her than a basket of pears, being prettier as a woman than as a man; and that my privy parts were ever drooping and forwelked, like a buckthorn berry above two grape pips, and other such poisonous untruths, that such women ever interlace in their remarks. For it was just as rumour had it, that she was steeped in carnal lust, and had no scruples, and had early plucked every petal of the flower of virginity and satiated herself on the worst debauchery: and now she was weary of my attentions in the midst of other like and e'en handsomer youths.

'I protested violently, smiting her upon the face. Then whetting her tongue well upon her teeth, she threatened to pour out my corruption openly before her husband, and to tell him how I had lured her through enchantment, and violently forced her to deceive him.

'Returning to my lodgings in tears, there I conferred with my three companions; and we went to a low tavern near our hostel and drank much ale and became merry, the three others laughing and saying that I must consult a sorcerer – meaning it in jangling jest, for they were without malice and drunken. Foolishly I did so, there being at that time in Oxenford a sorcerer famed among the clerks for his powers; and so excited was I by the love of her, that one would call it anyway by the name of sorcery, for I was bewitched.

'Of such horrible degree was the witchcraft he soon performed, that my lady died in her bed the same night, strangled as by a ghostly hand, and with scratches maiming her face so that it was more ribbons [than flesh]: these scratches being neither human nor a fiend's, but those of a cat – for the sorcerer had taken a living cat and flayed its black hide and stretched it out, eating the warm meat at a lonely cross-ways one dark night, and muttered evil invocations as I lay carnally upon the skin in the open space nearby, that the spirit of the cat might carry my smell to the woman as she slept, binding her in hot desire to my flesh for ever. Instead, the cat's spirit stifled her, as cats stifle infants in their cradles: for the feline spirit had met with Satan upon the way, and was filled with wrath and guile from his pricks, and was fatted by man's enemy to an enormous size.

'Learning about her death, I fled the town straightway; but my three companions were arrested the following day, along with the sorcerer. And there being no doubt of the latter's guilt, the wicked man confessed; and those in the tavern who had witnessed our foolish words, gave testimony against my companions, who were quite innocent of any guilty deed or action. Nevertheless, they were taken outside the town walls and hanged, while the sorcerer was burned to ashes near them, with the skin of the cat tied about his head.[395]

'So it was not as I had told you before, that I left Oxenfford after a vision of the Virgin Mary! I did indeed, however, become a ragged minstrel, and then a brother at the holy house near Saxmund[ham], before falling into a wandering life that led to this sea-battered place, where I came *forwandred.*'[396]

This was indeed a grievous crime, I said, for it had killed three young men innocent of it, and even the lady might not have deserved such a terrible turn, as to be strangled and mutilated by the Devil, for all her lechery. He wept tears, then, that burned their salt upon his wizened face. Indeed, I felt that he had revealed to me a foul ulcer within him that I could not cut out, the confession being too great a burden even for an angel's broad shoulders to carry away.

---

[395] This incident tallies closely with the well-known story told by the chronicler Roger of Wendover, that took place in 1209 and was the starting point of Cambridge as a proper university: following the execution of their three fellows, all the clerks left the city in protest, 'leaving Oxford entirely empty', to the benefit of Cambridge. However, there is no mention of any witchcraft in the original story, the murdered woman being killed 'by chance'. Also, if 1209 is an accurate date, then the hermit must have arrived almost immediately in the village, as a fugitive clerk rather than a wandering minstrel-monk. It is possible that our author has confused the two stories, or deliberately 'borrowed' from the more familiar one, in a way that is typical of medieval practice.

[396] Spent with wandering.

Then with painful gesticulation, he bid me fetch a heavy black stone that was in a niche behind his head, and after carrying it to the light and examining it (at his insistence), I saw it was a snake stone: that is, a fossil[397] carved with a spiral shape that some say is a figure of the sun, and others a snake curled like an adder sleeping in sunlight. No finer or larger of these carved fossils had I ever seen, though as a boy I would sometimes find them broke upon the beach or the cliffs. They are said to be the remains of a great temple of the giants, that was covered all over with such carvings, and scattered by God's wrath upon the strand, for he hateth all idols and false temples.

And the hermit said, so soft that I must again put my ear near his lips: 'Look ye, how our lives fall away as into a whirlpool, beginning pliant and full, then diminishing day by day until we reach the centre, wherein we disappear. Now I have made my confession, I may pass into the Lord's arms. For this, thou must carry me in the night to the sea's marge, with this snake stone tied about my chest so that it cannot fall, and leave me there.' I protested that the boundless waters would rise and stifle him, the tide being pulled high by the moon at that season: but to no avail. 'I have need no longer of life and breath,' he said, 'for by fasting and prayers I have earned His favour; and if not, then I must meet my punishment. My soul is restless as a horse that smells battle!'

A plump woman's red face appearing at the opening, and more bread being thrown, I would have bid the pilgrim go away, but was stayed by the hermit's hand. 'Wilt thou do this?' he asked, in a hoarse whisper. 'For I have endured too many winters, Edwyn, waiting for thee.' And knowing how many hermits, in their vow of absolute poverty, do reject also any funeral rites, and leave themselves to die in the open air in remote places, like beasts, I might have agreed – but for this fact: that he believed me to be Edwynne, my rival in his affections. I could not bring him succour in this wise, for jealousy was ever my companion.

---

[397] L. *fossilia*: originally, a 'fossil' was anything non-metal dug out of the earth. Clearly, this one is an ammonite, in which the area abounds, and they are still sold as 'snake stones', to holidaymakers, in honour of a later 'popular' tradition maintaining them to have been a plague of snakes petrified by St Hilda of Whitby (c. 614–680).

'Nay,' I declared, 'for I tell thee, master, in God's name I am not Edwyne, and never have been, for Edwine is far away; and whether living or dead, I know not, and care little!' He stared at me much troubled and distressed, before saying: 'Who art thou, then, for I think I know thee?' 'O master,' I cried, so that my voice echoed in the cave, and came again to my ears like a report of one's own misdeeds: 'I am the son of that humble house to which you first came and were succoured by, for my mother and father gave thee food and drink; and when my father was slain by the king's men, you saved my mother from violation. And in thanks ever after we brought you bread, and you tutored me as your first pupil. Wherefore should you forget this, and my name? I owe you all my first learning, without which I would have remained a simple peasant. I am not Edwyne, master, and cannot feign him as a player might, for if indeed I must aid God in pulling the holy soul from your mouth, as though I am a midwife to its newborn innocence, I must do it in my own guise!'

So fervently did I speak, that he frowned and began to tremble as if a thunder-clap had sounded in his ear; and to my amazement, he covered his face with his filthy rag as gossips oft cover their faces with their aprons in jesting shame – revealing thereby his soiled loins. 'Thou art the fruit of my other great sin,' he wailed, 'that burns me now as the white-hot iron of the ordeal.' I fell upon my knees, dreading what I should hear. 'What dost thou mean, master?'

'Not master, not master, but another e'en closer,' said he, with many groans and silences between his words: 'I broke the sacred vows of your mother's fresh widowhood, tempting her (weakened as she was by her sorrow) into infidelity, and refusing to wed her after. Shame was visited upon her at your birth, for you were born a full year after her husband's death; yet none knew the culprit.' I would have spoken, but so great was my astonishment that I choked upon the first syllable, and my mouth was as though filled with lime.

He went on: 'The cunning fiend had led me to her humble door as my first temptation, yet was I not truly pricked until the king's men slew her husband but weeks later; then she came to visit me, eager to be my devoted disciple. But instead of behaving with discretion, and shutting her in a cell hidden from my sight, as the Blessed Christina was shut from the sight of the good Roger of St Alban's, I failed to resist the temptations of the flesh, and enjoyed the pleasures of it incontinently. Thou art indeed my ill-gotten son, and now you are returned to torment me, for e'er from the beginning were you thrust upon me as penance by your mother – threatening me always in the way women do – when I would have had you cast for ever from my sight, though of my own substance!'

6

No words might describe my feelings at this moment; but hearing a scuffle at the rocks, I looked up, and saw the plump dame's hideous face leering at us for an instant, before it withdrew, having heard [everything]. All natural affection, of father and son, was withered between us at birth, for that relation lay unsanctified by the proper office of matrimony: indeed, I now understood why the hermit had always seemed circumspect [*cautus*] with me, and in a great heaviness at times – no doubt in his heart wishing me drowned in the sea, yet never able to refuse me as a master might refuse his pupil.

No tears came to my face, but rather, a great heat that flowed over it and made me swoon. Finding myself upon the floor of the cave, with stale bread and fish at my nose, I rose and staggered to my feet, his words rushing into the ventricles of my memory with a horrible force. Astonied was I to find him crawling upon the piled rocks, towards the light, yet unable to climb further in his profound feebleness, so that he sprawled upon them quite naked, groaning the whiles. 'I beseech thee,' I cried, 'if thou art my true father, let me show thee a son's loving-kindness, that God pardon us both for our misdeeds!'

And so saying, I took the wretched man in my arms, and covered him into decency with my cloak, and sat with him there in the cave upon the rocks, as the Virgin held her dead Son across her knees, for he was as light as a leaf in his dying.

We might have remained thus, full peacefully, weeping and murmuring prayers and blessings upon each other (though he could but barely speak, having exhausted his spirits), till the hour I might have left my father to God's mercy in the waves, at his request; but for the woman who overheard us. For soon over the sea-surge I heard another clamour, which was of many men and women, come to crowd at the cave-mouth; and soon they were tearing away the rocks to see better, though none dared enter.

Fearfully I retreated with my father to the very depths of the cave, wherein we lay upon the cold stone, in the darkness. And the voices grew with the light as the rocks were pulled away, just as the stone was pulled from Our Lord's sepulchre: yet neither angels nor disciples were they, but common and vulgar folk, knowing not right from wrong but only feasting on their own curiosity, their cries rebounding all about us as I held my father tight.

I knew not whether they were come to punish us for the scandal, or worship us as a miracle, for they only cried over and over as gulls screech together above a shoal or a fisherman's boat: 'Lo, show us, show yourselves to us, pray show us!' And they were so many at the greater opening, several of whose faces were familiar to me in my memory, that they thickened the darkness within by shielding the sky's light. Yet so great a respect had they for the hermit's powers, that none ventured over the threshold: for as I learned later, they had been told that any person entering who was not of a similar holiness to the dweller within, would be shrivelled up by God's bolt.

Then seeing how great was the press upon the first row, and all the rocks now torn away that the broad cleft was fully as it was before, I stepped forward into view with my father in my arms, and walked towards them over the cave floor at the pace of a funeral.

This striking them into silence, that the only noise was of the waves and the sea birds without, I cried to them, 'Behold, the holiest man thou wilt ever see, ready to greet his Lord. Go home and pray for his soul, for he wishes to be left in peace.'

Then one lean and mis-shapen fellow at the front cried, 'He is not holy, for he engendered thee out of wedlock with Widow Margery!' And this being my mother's name, it was as if he had struck me in the face, and I knew not what to say. Then another, a woman with a spiteous face like a hog, cried also that he was not holy, but a lecher and a fraud; and her bearded sister next to her took up the shout and complained that she had given half her bread and meats to the hermit, who was no true hermit; and an old brute with a filthy wisp of straw for his hair shouted, 'So are all hermits fraudulent, for they are idle and take our pittance, like the priests and the monks, while we labour in the ditch!'

So fearful was I of their grimacing and cries, that I took a step back; and then one burly offspring of an ogre [*montrum quoddam teterrimum*] came forward fully into the cave, and seeing he was not struck down, laughed and turned to the others: 'See, how very holy be-est I, fully equal to this blessed hermit's cell!' And another meagre fellow, limping like a *hamelled dogge*,[398] stepped in and pointed at the mixen of bread, stale fish and other scraps and morsels, saying, ''Tis no surprise our bellies moan, half our victuals lie here! This be a thieves' den!' 'Nay,' another shouted: 'it is the Devil's! For dragons and monsters come here to sup with him, and why else were we forbidden to enter?'

'Ay,' screamed a scraggy woman, whose blotched face seemed known to me from when I was a boy; 'and why else is our village so afflicted, that our children die, and our sons are snatched away, and our boats are lost, and half our beasts also from the murrain, and that the wind is ever blowing away our thatch and grows fiercer and more freezing by the year?'

And all let out a huzzah of agreement, shouting that we were the very Devil and his son in disguise, living in such darkness as was found in Hell and thus agreeable to us – forever willing are the common folk to pin their troubles upon others, so buffeted are they in their sufferings by infirmity of faith. The scraggy woman, seeing the snake-stone in my father's clutch, pointed to it and screeched: 'He might turn us all into wolves or toads, so powerful is their malefice!' Then with a start I recognised her, as being the mother of Edwynne: of foul-mouthed fame and a wicked gossip, ever the conduit for the cloven-hoofed enemy of mankind.

Shouting at them all to go away, dismayed by this turn of events, I felt a shudder in my arms and saw it was my father: his eyes were

---

[398] As in MS: dogs found to be pursuing game secretly were mutilated by cutting off a foot. From Anglo-Saxon *hamelian*, to mutilate.

open and staring, yet no longer piercing in their look, and his tongue lolled from his mouth. I clutched his body to mine and wailed, not believing the witness of my eyes, that can oft see a mountebank's death and believe it, before the player springs to life again with a cackle, and a filthy story on his painted lips.

Meanwhile, the bolder among them pressed in also, trampling their former offerings and making a great din within the cave. Having now retreated to its back wall, wherein no further escape was possible, I placed my father the hermit behind me and shielding him thus with my body, implored them to have mercy upon us both. But such force has a rabble when moved to anger and spite, it is not resistable by either pleas or reward, but moves willy-nilly as a tide between rocks, that is stronger e'en than those rocks. And the twisted, grimacing visages, very like those carved upon the water spouts of our churches and other places within them, that Satan himself be a-feared to approach the holy edifices, came closer towards us, yet hesitant still.

Nimbly I snatched up the harp beside us and began to pluck, chanting the ballad of Robert Hodd in such a wise that all ceased clamouring and stopped, as if enchanted. Again the words unrolled in my mind as if writ on parchment, and again my suffering and guilt gave such colour to the song that all were struck dumb and grew open-mouthed, as had happened in the inns and halls and so forth.

No man or woman can resist the charm of music, we know, if it be not discordant; but let me tell you, that song was scarce of my doing – my fingers barely my own as they pressed and plucked: it was as though my hands had been cut off and golden ones put in their stead, the same as have angels. Little did I know that this playing would be the last of its kind they would ever accomplish [*confecerunt*]!

The cave made my voice and instrument greater still in sound, that some of the peasants turned their heads all about, thinking others were singing and playing, when it was but an echoing of the rock; then as I finished, many demanded another song of this outlaw, Robert Hod, for he pleased them greatly, being despisers of monk, baron and sherf alike. And they called him 'Robben' in their thick tongues, as though in their minds they knew him familiarly already and were clapping him on the back and saying, 'Ho, Robbyn, my good fellow!'

But then the misshapen, lean rascal – no doubt of the Devil's service, from his forliven looks – stepped forward and addressed them, saying, 'Do ye not know, fools, how Satan beguileth through music, and how the filth spewed forth by minstrels enchants us like any sorcery, preparing us for Lucifer's feast, at which our souls shall be the mutton, boiled and seethed and chewed, and that pain we cannot imagine renewed each day – for the fiends are ever famished, and gluttony rules them?'

He pointed at me as I protested, and cried in a most horrible and harsh voice, 'Beware this Devil and most especially his son, that he hath hid all this while in the shadows, only as a trap to lure you in, singing of felons and outlaws and their wicked murthers – for the Arch-fiend grows weary of stale morsels of bread, and craves thy flesh to slobber on, and thine eternal souls to swallow limb by limb!' And an oaf cried from the crowd, 'He slew a woman through sorcery, that her body was cut in ribbons by a black lion!'

So terrified then did the rabble become, that some scrambled out of the cave's opening, while all pressed together, backing away. Then this vicious fellow was joined by Edwyne's mother, that oath-fond gossip, who declared that she had known me when I was a boy (which was true, though a fact despised by me), and that I had ever had something strange about me. 'Pray, where did this rascal vanish to? For he brought his foster-mother to an early death from grief, by leaving his home without so much as a farewell – and she having replaced his own poor mother, good Widow Margery, that perished of a cancre, growing on the very spot his infant lips would suckle upon! Ay, he hath been hid here all along, for he is the filthy, unlawful offspring of this false hermit and sorcerer, and 'tis said that he can slip in and out of Hell by the cleft there, like a rat doth!'

And so saying, she pointed to the back of the cave where I had lain my poor father, there being in that rock a cleft too narrow for a body, but of infinite depth and blackness within. 'What doth he bring, but the shadow of Death where'er he passes? And this I did ever believe, but none heeded me, by God's blood! For my dear son Edwine was snatched by them both from his mother's bosom, and puffed up with learning, that he left his proper hearth and perished in the city, where plague and ruin await all!' She burst into tears, whereupon the fellow with the limp cried: ''Tis never too late to make amends!'

Much confused by the news of my foster-mother's death, and of Edwyne's perishing, I had no words to say in my defence, but felt the harridan's words like blows upon my face; for it is easy to succumb to such accusations, when your life is spotted and filled with fault in word and deed. While a clamour again arose among the invaders, I saw Henri's face, and brother Thomas's, and Edwyinn's, and even the fat gaoler's, among many others that included the one-eyed serjeant's, swirling before me like phantasms; and then my father the hermit's face joined them, though its bodily twin was but a few feet away – and I knew at that moment that he was indeed expired.

Bewildered by this, and nigh swooning, I crawled to my progenitor's side and fell prostrate upon him, not knowing whether he was alive or dead, for he still had warmth. Thereupon there was more screeching, and shouting, and I felt blows flying into my face, and my father being torn from my grasp, so that I was certain my last hour had come as well as his: and more afflictions would I have suffered, but that I fell unconscious under the kicks and blows and tramplings, as if the waters themselves were stifling me.

The Lord spared me, and I woke from the dead in a pale light, smarting from my bruises and with blood dried upon my face. I had dreamed I was being scourged and lashed by priests at the very gate of Jerusalem, which holy city was regained and lost twice in my lifetime, and remains still to be won from the hands of the infidel.[399] 'Spare not the stripes,' I was crying in my dream, while the priests (among them the long-fingered minx from the tavern, in the ridiculous garb of a nun)[400] shed tears as they beat, just as they do when striping the tender limbs

---

[399] The First Crusade founded the Christian kingdom at Jerusalem in 1099, lost it to Saladin in 1187, and after two brief spells of Christian rule, lost it for good in 1244, from which date it remained in Mohammedan hands until four years ago (1917).
[400] Presumably ridiculous only because of its wearer.

of child pilgrims, for the good of the sick and the afflicted. And in the sky I saw a banner unfurling, that said *Hod* instead of *God.* Wishing to tear it down, I could not, for Hodd himself was lashing me the fiercest, standing of great size among the priests and saying, 'Wretch! Dost thou belch forth words for flattery's sake?' And I was [shrieking], 'Bring me water in a bowl, dear God!' – yet substituting 'Hod' for 'God' each time, against my own volition.

When I awoke, however, I saw merely the desecration of my hopes; for my new-found father the hermit was gone, taken by the rabble, of which the only sign was a threadbare shoe. And lo, I saw the harp smashed and trampled into pieces in a corner: for nothing abates the fury of the mob. Yet why had they not returned to burn me also? Mayhap they thought me dead, or were afraid of the Devil's vengeance in that cavern, that oped to his smoky kingdom in their foolish minds: thus the Lord protected me, saving me for further penance.

Alas, when I tottered from the cave, it was into a blear dawn of mist and obscure shapes, in which e'en the sea-surge was muffled. The air being so full of moisture, it was resolved into a rain that besprinkled my clothes and my hair, as though the air itself was sorrowing. I called out, lest his final migration had been a false vision: 'Father! My father!' – but no answer came, and my own voice was stinted by the moistness and thickness of the clime.

Perceiving then a dark shape by the edge of the waters, like a [beached] boat with a furled mast, I advanced cautiously towards it: and there I found a martyr's end! My hermit father, fastened by the wrists to a ship's timber, hung perished, with his body half burned from below, upon a pyre that the moistness had no doubt extinguished: and the mob departing before the fall of night (of which darkness they are always terrified), and happy with their task, they had left the execution half complete.

How wretched was my grief, as I raised my father's head, that was miraculously unblemished by the flames that had destroyed his nether regions! I had believed him to be expired in the cave, yet terrible it was, despite his pure faith and trust in the eternal physician, to see (by his open mouth and tormented brow) an expression of agony, and the same pain in his hands by which the rabble affixed him on the pyre (as Our Lord was affixed upon Golgotha hill): for though blackened and blistered, his hands were as an old beggar's are in palsy, most twisted in the fingers.[401]

Seized by choler, I purposed to slay every man and woman in the farms and thorpes about – lumping them all into one, innocent and guilty alike, that I should not waste time in scattering their brains upon the earth. 'Twas in my mind just as Abbot Arnold said of the people of Biders, who had Albigensians mingled among them: 'Slay the good and the evil alike, for God shall well know if one of the two wishes [? *si uter volet*].'[402]

O wretch that I was! What had the hermit my father taught me, when speaking of his childish part in that ill-fated Crusade? That he had not slain a single Jew, for 'they knew not what they did'. Similarly, the rabble of serfs and cobblers and ploughmen and carters and so forth knew not what they did, for extremely fearful and ignorant are these people, turned like a weather-vane by the slightest wind. So horrible (I reflected) would now be their pain-to-come in the after-life, as the flames consumed them for ever and ever – watched from Heaven by the very saint they had burned in like manner – that I might have wept for them, too: though I was not yet merciful enough for such a selfless pity, and my head and body ached from their blows, and e'en I had lost a tooth.

---

[401] This may have been the effect of heat, or simple rigor mortis, rather than pain: I have had personal experience of such startling changes in the faces and members of dead comrades, due to the passing of time (even mere hours) or abrupt shifts in temperature from, say, cosy dug-out to frozen trench.

[402] A muddled reference to the storming of the Cathar-held city of Béziers, where much of the captured population claimed to be Catholic; according to Caesarius of Heisterbach in his *Dialogus Miraculorum* (*c.*1220–35), what Arnold actually said was: 'Slay them, for God knoweth His own.' Whereupon some 20,000 inhabitants of all ages, whether orthodox or heretic, were put to the sword. Pope Innocent III heartily congratulated him on this ecumenical and time-saving 'extermination'. [*Marginal note in FB's hand: 'And so the padre congratulated B Company.'*]

I buried my father in the hollowed-out cleft in the cave floor (wherein he had always requested to be so consigned), leaving the remains of the harp upon his poor breast, then pulling the slab across, that he be quite hid, all the time praying fervently. I remained there until the evening, scarce knowing what day it was, or how long I had remained without consciousness in the cave – my poor brain beleaguered by an armed host of thoughts, all striving as one to press in to its narrow gate: meanwhile my liver swelled to no avail, for by this member we love, and loss of the loved one heats it and pricks the liver sorely: and so I spouted much foul matter outside, from my bowels, and nigh succumbed to wanhope.

Recovering with a youth's pliancy, I climbed the cliff as in years past, to view through the mistiness what had become of the little oratory of stones and reeds; and there I saw a modest heap of offerings beside it, under a shelter as for farm beasts, that the rabble had evidently plundered – for much was scattered, and the oratory itself blackened by flame and roofless, the stones still warm to the touch. And lest more ignorant pilgrims come, not knowing the holy hermit was now a sinner and heretic, and that a gratuitous sanctity had been placed upon him, they had thrown briars and brambles all about and also on the track in a great thicket, as though upon a path to perdition.

For this murderous crime, I did not think punishment would be forthcoming, were I to report it; for that part of the coast was wild, and the local priests were drunken and incontinent, and ever hateful of hermits and holy men who berated them for falling from the true way; indeed, the rabble might well be congratulated for their action, as the pharisees were in the time of Our Lord.

Then did I regret once more my return to the hermitage, for it had brought disaster in its wake – and oft 'tis better to be ignorant! A small voice said to me in mine ear, as I wept: 'Nay, he hath burned away the last morsel of his mortal sin, suffering upon a martyr's pyre; and is now in Heaven as pure as a naked babe. What are a few mortal moments of awful agony, compared to an eternity of bliss?' And I was much comforted by this, though my heart was yearning for extinction – as doth a duck yearn for flight, caught fast in an iced pond.

The mist slowly clearing as the day ebbed, methought to walk to the abbey by the strand, for the sea ever gives a glimmer of light, if there is any moon (which there was, and near waxed full): the waters' foam being of such a similar whiteness, that it attracts the light. With many a prayer on my lips, I left my father's remains in their simple bed (though wishing to return soon, to erect a great tomb of stones fastened by proper cement), and trod my weary way to Wittby, commending myself to God and the saints' protection.

Determined was I to abandon all worldly ways, and to love filthy lucre as little as personal ambition – lies and deceit and greed and fraud being each the hook [*uncus*[403]] that together drag the whole human race to primaeval chaos, even more so now than before. I thought also to recover my father's bones, and carry them about in a shrine, in a full procession of monks, that poor cripples with their feet twisted up under their thighs, and the most miserable and sore-sewn of beggars, and all of any station who wished to be healed, such as soldiers without an arm, might crawl up to it and be made whole.

Very soon, not halfway along that darkling strand, was I trapped by the high tide upon a rock, with naught behind me but a sheer cliff! Why was this, when I had prayed so fervently to God and all the saints? Alas, I had fashioned in my teeming brain such glorious pictures of that aforesaid procession, with the wooden shrine covered in gold leaf, and its [carrying] poles hung with blue satin, and such chantings and sighings and bewailings and utterings of holy words, and all covered in clouds of incense from the swung censer carried before, that e'en kings bowed down, and queens knelt in their snow-white garments, and warrior-knights of hugest renown lowered their swords in homage.

Miserable worm! Now what wouldst thou picture, hugging the

---

[403] This being a large iron hook, rather than a fisherman's.

naked rock, drenched to the skin by the salt waves eager to suck thee into their black maw, with naught but the inconstant moon as thine eyes' guide? Do the ocean's seethings about thy knees speak any holy words, other than Death's importunate chatter and moan? What garden of delights dost thou see now, in this savage place, wherein a glimpse might be had of the end of the human race and of this earth, that shall be purged even to her inmost bowels, as land moveth and becometh water, and all be swallowed up to the greatest and highest of our human works in stone,[404] and down to the tiniest, fleetest louse?

Yet I lived, as thou must have already perceived, to sit here upon this cold bench in an autumn of some eighty years later, writing out my early life in faltering confession. After entering the holy house of Whittbey, wherein I was received with kindness, as coming directly from that most holy hermit (though I told not a soul there of my true connection to him), I was several times pierced by the sweet pain of love in the years that followed, but always I vanquished its wound in prayer and fasting, as I have vanquished all temptations, both of the mind and of the flesh.

The greatest sin is pride, with envy on its heels; both these horrible afflictions of the Devil I have wrestled to the ground, and covetousness likewise, which is a form of lust. Yet they are never lifeless, quickening into breath when my guard is dropped: thus each day is a never-ending vigilance.

The grossness [*crassitudo*] of the world outside, adrift in greed and lechery and bloodthirsty wrath, and growing worse with every year that passes, as the winters grow icier likewise and the summers e'en cooler, harries our walls: yet all within is peace and contemplation, or upraised

---

[404] The twelfth and thirteenth centuries saw the greatest period of cathedral-expansion, the colossal buildings' towers being the highest man-made constructions on the known earth at that time. This passage, despite its religious zeal, has a certain queasy resonance for those born into the age of Messrs Darwin, Nietzsche, Marx et al. – and especially for those who had a chance recently to experience primaeval slime at first hand in present-day France and Belgium, into which ooze a living man could vanish within seconds.

voices of exultation, e'en when the sea rages at our easterly stones, and the wind buffets our hoods upon the parapet or in the cloister.

Of Robert Hodd, I saw nor heard no sign more, save from the wayfarers travelling north; these, when questioned by me, would sometimes say that his outlaw band had thinned from internal strife; that Littl John had left for Sherwode with half of the felons, never to return; and that Hodd himself was thought to be dead from poison, raving to the end in his temple-hut, seized by the utmost agony as his devilish vices clawed him within. Others claimed a corrupted branch from the great meeting oak had fallen upon his head, cracking it wide ope just where the heretic's mark was burned in, for he had dangled many innocents upon that tree; and here I confess to thinking of the poor leech, who was also a tregetour, and the powers he no doubt had of devilish enchantment and subtle revenge.

Some of these wayfarers were minstrels or players of the roughest kind, who played (with greasy fingers and mouths dripping with sop, as they all do) various ballads, among which was ever a mangled version of mine own on Hode, as well as others proliferated from this single seed, their foolish noise emanating from the windows of our guest-house, despite our prohibition.[405] Yet none knew that it was my hand had planted that hideous seed, for not only had I never again touched the strings of a harp, but I would say ne'er a word as I listened by the window: to pass on with my head bowed as if in holy contemplation.

Only a few days ago, within this very autumn season, did this happen again; for while I was hobblingly [*claudo pede*] aiding a young brother feed the pigs in our yard before Vespers, a high voice sounded that I thought mine own in my head, for it sang of Robben Hode and Lytyl John and e'en Moche himself! Perceiving it to be from the tillage without, that is our oldest domain, and approaching the sound as did the brother of the prodigal son, who was in the field and heard

---

[405] This is all the more interesting because, in the opinion of some folk historians, it was the very popularity of the Robin Hood ballads in the following (fifteenth and sixteenth) centuries that ensured the survival of the ballad form into our own day, however debased it has now become.

the singing of the feast,[406] I saw our workers gathered on our acres hard by the wall, paused from their digging labours, while a young woman among them gladded them boldly with her piercing notes as though within her own home: for it seems as if all the world is singing of Robert Hodd, that in their mouths is ever Robyn, Robbyn, Robyn Hode! And so my dreadful sin is in every ear, like the deathly hoot of an owl, and I might never forget it until Death deafens me from this world for ever and ever.

One time after forty or more years, and already old, I ventured to visit [the holy house of] St Edmund's in Dancaster, wherein few, if any, were left who might have remembered me as brother Thomas's page. Father Gerald having long departed this life, our meal included venison from the chase and plump fish caught by the brothers' nets and baskets in the part of the river that flowed within the walls,[407] boiled and fried and daintily prepared with pepper and spice. Likewise were the liquors as generous as in those former days before father Gerald, for the present abbot followed Isaac in believing wine to be restorative to health; yet I did not rebuke mine hosts for their indulgence, saying merely that porridge of salt and oatmeal heated in old beef-broth customarily sufficed me, as it sufficed the poor.

The coloured windows in the completed chancel were so fine, and the decorations everywhere so costly and precious, with glorious images swarming on every hand (e'en beneath our feet), that I could not help gasping in wonderment. Then did I sudden notice, in the glass of one of the lancets, the figure of a hunter winding his horn, his apparel (pierced by the sunlight) of a most startling green.

'Ay,' the brother monk said, 'that is Robben Hod, that they sing of in the ballads.' 'Why,' I asked, most astonished and dismayed, 'is

---

[406] 'For his eldere son was in the feeld; and whanne he cam, and neiyede to the hows, he herde a symfonye and a croude [fiddle].' (Wycliffite Bible, Luke 15.25).

[407] Hopefully up-river of the kitchen and the monks' latrine or *reredorter*, though this is by no means certain: sanitary considerations being as little regarded then, through ignorance, as in the late glistening slime of Flanders, through circumstance.

such a wicked felon – and notorious heretic – here within the body of your holy church? Pray, tell me!' 'I know not if he were a heretic, or e'en a wicked felon,' said the young monk, 'but they say he was placed there out of fear, his greenwood lair being the very forest we felled to the last tree.' I felt a darkness rise within me; and seizing my troubled voice, as it were, to calm it, I said scoffingly: 'Out of fear, brother? What canst thou mean by such a word?'

'Fear was indeed the word they used, who remembered,' he continued, chuckling merrily (being a jolly youth), 'though all of those be passed away by now, may the Lord rest their souls. For the tale goeth, that he cursed our house most horribly and wrathfully as the trees fell about him, and said he would ne'er set foot under our sacred roof, unless it were to burn it to ashes and charred wood, and that none could stop him but his own shadow. Therefore, as precaution, it were thought wise to include him in the very glass formed by the burning of his forest, that he might cast his own shadow on the abbey floor. Just as we include diverse monsters with beastly [heads?] or goat's legs, or women with fish's tails, or green men spewing out roots and leaves, that such freaks and fiends be weighed under by the burden of the presence of the Lord – as He does certainly seem burdensome to them, from their expressions!'

Most troubled was I anon, when I saw the sun alighting suddenly on the glass, that made the figure sail unto the floor, where it glimmered greenly by my feet like a snake: and I heard the mournful wail of a Jew's horn travelling to my ears, as if from mine own past, that I have here set down in clear letters for our ultimate and divine Master and Holy Father to read, that I might be [forgiven?] and aneled.

The young monk frowned upon me anxiously, and held my arm, for I had begun to turn very pale, and sway from side to side. 'What ails thee, dear brother?' he asked.

But I could not say the truth, for none would have believed it, so [discreet?] have I always been in my bearing and my spoken thoughts, until I put my pen to this paper. So likewise must I end now by lifting my sharp-nibbed goosefeather for the last time, as one day soon my lungs will putteth off air for the last time: and since I write this by candle-light, scarce seeing my own words, I will retire gratefully bed-ward till the bells of Matins ring.[408]

[408] Which will be at 2 a.m. The parchment here is damaged by white-hot shrapnel burning it upon the verso side, some of the burns being severe enough to have pene-trated the leaf, obscuring a few words on the recto. The photogravure opposite, showing a lady with exaggerated eyes peeping at the viewer over a cloth that covers her mouth, is of the somewhat crude but delightful drawing that appears in the MS, a few inches below its last line. Resembling English work of the late thirteenth or early fourteenth century, we can assume it was copied from the original by the conscientious scrivener – to whom our general gratitude, of course, must be wholesale and never-ending. [*This footnote crossed out by FB, with a pencilled scrawl in the margin: 'withdraw to safety, Alec – bolt – for Godssake – leg it –'*]

Acknowledgements

With grateful thanks to Jas Elsner and Zoë Swenson-Wright for their invaluable help, to Niek Miedema, my editor Robin Robertson and my agent Lucy Luck for their support, and to my wife Jo and my children Joshua, Sacha and Anastasia for their encouragement, humour and love.